FLIGHT TO ANYWHERE

A Selection of Recent Titles by Elizabeth Darrell

AND IN THE MORNING
AT THE GOING DOWN OF THE SUN
WE WILL REMEMBER

THE RICE DRAGON*
SCARLET SHADOWS*
UNSUNG HEROES*
A VICTORIOUS PASSION*

* available from Severn House

FLIGHT TO ANYWHERE

Elizabeth Darrell

severn
House

This first world edition published in Great Britain 2001 by
SEVERN HOUSE PUBLISHERS LTD of
9–15 High Street, Sutton, Surrey SM1 1DF.
This first world edition published in the USA 2002 by
SEVERN HOUSE PUBLISHERS INC of
595 Madison Avenue, New York, N.Y. 10022.

British Library Cataloguing in Publication Data

Darrell, Elizabeth, 1931–
    Flight to anywhere
    1. Helicopter pilots – Fiction
    2. Love stories
    I. Title
    823.9'14 [F]

ISBN 0-7278-5766-5

Typeset by Palimpsest Book Production Ltd.,
Polmont, Stirlingshire, Scotland.
Printed and bound in Great Britain by
MPG Books Ltd., Bodmin, Cornwall.

ACKNOWLEDGEMENTS

As with *Unsung Heroes* I am indebted to aircrew of 7, 18 and 27 Squadrons based at RAF Odiham for their generous and friendly co-operation during my research for this novel.

I owe special thanks to Squadron Leader Bob Parratt MBE and Flight Lieutenant Paul Smyth for so patiently answering my many questions.

One

S quadron Leader Randal Ivan Price, known from his
schooldays as Rip, made a final tour of the country
house he had bought in a bid to save his marriage. He
rescued several personal items including a long-lost shaver
he had forgotten about, but everything else would remain.
He had sold the place fully furnished to a Swedish banker.
The furniture, fittings, carpets and curtains had been new
when he and Fiona moved in with their children. She had
taken Neil and Lydia to live with her parents just five months
later, so the house had stood pristine and unoccupied until
now. From tomorrow young voices would once more echo
through the ultra-modern rooms; a united family would again
cavort in the indoor pool and chase each other through the
extensive garden.

Coming to the house was probably a mistake, but Randal
had obeyed a perverse urge to see it before the Swedes
exorcised the ghosts. He had put himself through so much
during the past year he thought he knew how to deal with
pain, both physical and mental, yet his throat was tight with
emotion as he went from room to room.

Neil's bedroom, fitted with highly expensive furniture said
to be designed to adapt to the needs of a child as he grew.
A serious little boy with Randal's dark, lively eyes and
enquiring mind, who had in this house finally formed the
bond of trust every father wants with his son – even fathers
who spend a lot of time out of the country. Randal recalled

1

Neil at teatime proudly modelling his brand new uniform for his father who would have to leave in the morning too early to see him off to school for the very first time. The boy had looked absurdly small to be wearing long trousers and a blazer. That was the last time Randal had seen his son.

On to Lydia's room papered with a nursery print, the ceiling painted pale blue and dotted with stars that twinkled in the low light at bedtime. Blonde, blue-eyed, destined to be as gorgeous as her mother, the child had known how to charm almost from birth. Randal had been putty in her hands whenever she teased or cajoled. He had adored her.

Reaching the master bedroom he was swamped by memories that touched him more deeply than expected. Fifteen months ago he had stormed from this room, from his wife, from her calculated sexual baiting, knowing they had reached the point of no return in their fiery marriage. At the end of an exercise in Poland ten days later he had decided to offer a compromise for the sake of the children but, as he drove towards home, four pre-teen boys had dropped an old anchor from a motorway bridge on to his car.

He had been pulled from the tangled wreck to lie in a coma on life-support machines until medical skill and his own tough physique pulled him through the critical stage. It was then that Randal wished they had let him die. The damage to his upper spine left him paralysed from the chest down. His marriage and his flying career had simultaneously come to an end.

Gazing now around the room in which he and Fiona had so passionately celebrated their fresh start together after the separation she had enforced, Randal momentarily relived the exultation he had known when everything had been right between them. Only it had never lasted. Turning away he walked through to the large entrance hall, lost in recollection of Fiona's expression when she had seen him lying helpless in the hospital bed. He had made it easy for them both by being deliberately cruel: he would be a millstone round her neck and of no use as a father, a cripple in a wheelchair unable to control his bodily functions. Better for her and the children to make a clean break there and then. She had made no protest; offered no denial of his forecast of their future. Her tearful, rapid departure had been more potent than words.

Dropping his keys on the hall table Randal took one last look at the house he had bought with such high hopes, then went out closing the door on that episode of his life. He drove away without a backward glance. Time to face the future he had striven for over the past year.

After several operations on his spine the doctors had given their despairing patient a sixty per cent chance of getting around with the aid of crutches. Snatching at that slender hope Randal vowed if he walked he would fly again. The specialists had shaken their heads, then discovered that a born pilot who faced confinement to a wheelchair was a law unto himself.

Randal had aimed to be back in a cockpit within nine months. It had taken a year and proved to be a worse ordeal than he had guessed. A naturally vigorous, extrovert man, he had nevertheless wept with frustration and despair after exhausting therapy sessions. Yet, three weeks ago, he had persuaded a medical board that he was fully capable of resuming flying duties. His bull-in-a-china-shop determination failed to get him what he really wanted, however. They would not approve a return to his old squadron, saying the stresses of being operational would prove too much for him. So it was that he was on his way to take a flight refresher course, after which he would train to be an instructor. Not what he truly wanted, but he would be up there where the clouds scudded, engaged in the great love of his life. God, how he had yearned for this day!

He stopped for a pie and pint just after noon, his car

causing envious glances through the pub windows. It was his single extravagance, paid for with the interest on his shares in the family frozen food empire. An avid Formula One fan, Randal loved fast cars. The fact that he had almost lost his life in a scarlet Porsche had not stopped him from buying another. He had had hairy moments in helicopters but continued to fly them, and the chances of something being dropped on him by delinquent boys a second time were well beyond the bounds of probability.

The beer, the sheer pleasure of *walking* in to a pub, the elation of again being a man with a future in the skies drove to the recesses of his mind the bittersweet memories revived by the house he had just relinquished, so he covered the last few miles relishing his return to a familiar routine. He had always been a good mixer, had thrown himself into the raffish life led by aircrew, had enjoyed to the full every new experience. He intended to do so again. Rip Price, Mark Two, was about to hit the heavens!

The guard at the gate studied the Porsche with envy as Randal drew up and held out his service identification. Interest was then transferred from the car to its driver as the man bent to the window.

'I was told to watch out for you, sir, and direct you to Squadron Leader Newman's office. Seems there's a flap on.'

Randal frowned. 'Can't be anything to do with me. I'm just checking in as a new boy. You've got the wrong man.'

'No, sir, yours was the name I was given.' He handed back the identity document and gave instructions how to reach the main office block. 'Squadron Leader Newman'll be glad to see you. Seems urgent.'

Randal was puzzled. There was no way he could be involved in an emergency. The guard had got it wrong. Being the man he was Randal nevertheless sought out Newman, to put things straight, but the third-floor office was empty. He poked his head round an open door on the other side of the corridor to ask the absentee's whereabouts.

A flight lieutenant glanced up from her notes and smiled. 'There's a flap on. Perry's been firing on all cylinders since lunch. You don't happen to be Randal Price, by any chance?'

'I am, yes.'

'Great! You'll find our wandering boy with Wing Commander Beavis. Down one floor, second on the left.'

More puzzled than ever, Randal descended and walked towards the sound of two raised voices. The senior of the arguing men was tall and pale, with bags under his eyes. He glared at the intruder in civilian clothes.

'What do you want?'

'I'm Price, sir.'

'At last! We've been waiting for you to put in an appearance,' he said testily, as if Randal were unforgivably late in reporting for duty on the morrow. 'Now we can get shot of them! They've been here since the crack of dawn and have buggered up the whole day.' He indicated his companion. 'Perry's got it all organised. Go and do your stuff, then we can run 'em off the station and get some bloody work done.'

Newman headed for the corridor. 'Come on, we'll get you kitted out double quick.'

Randal followed and seized the man's arm. 'Hang on, hang on! Kitted out for what? There's a mistake here somewhere. I haven't flown for over a year.'

'Yeah, don't we know it!' Newman was a few years older than Randal and at least ten inches shorter. His piercing blue eyes were hostile as he clarified the situation. 'At a time when we're snowed under with the MoD's latest lunatic ideas on filling in forms as thick as bloody books with details of personnel down to the state of their underpants, the last thing we want is a poncy photographer accompanied by a titless feminist under our feet while they wait for Wonderboy to arrive.'

Annoyed by his attitude, Randal said, 'Just what the hell are you on about?'

'PR want pictures of the Gulf hero who was almost taken out by four kids on a motorway bridge and has returned to the defence of Queen and country. One theme they're pursuing is that the Air Force looks after its own. The other is that we're all courageous, dedicated chaps who prefer to die wearing a flying suit.' He gave a sour smile. 'You'll be in all the dailies soon.'

Randal's temper erupted as a glimmer of light appeared. 'No, I sodding won't! There's no way I'll dress up and put myself on show for the Press. There were dozens like me who drove themselves to the limit to get back on their feet.'

'But their fathers aren't business tycoons. The reading public won't give a toss about unknowns. The heir to Price's Frozen Foods is big news. They buy and eat your stuff every day.'

There was such disparagement in his voice, Randal challenged him. 'What's your problem, Newman?'

'I've had to set this all up because I'm the guy who'll have the honour of giving you your flight check after the course,' he said. 'Beavis has been on my back since lunch and I've had a Squirrel sitting on the deck all day doing nothing. Some guys have been hanging around ready to pose with you for some of the pictures, so I've had you up to here.' He made a savage gesture at his throat. 'Get kitted up and out there ready to act the hero. The order came from high up, so if you want me to pass you on the flight check you'd better bloody carry it out.'

Tempted to tell the man what to do with his flight check, Randal bit back the words. He had struggled too hard to risk surrendering his pilot status over him. Seething with resentment against Newman and those in high places who had burdened him with this, he pulled on flying gear then walked out to join the small group beside the helicopter.

The photographer made as much fuss over getting the right shots as one would when filming fashion models, and Perry's 'titless feminist' wanted an appealing story to go with them. She added fuel to the fire within Randal with her questions. Dressed in dungarees, with a straggly fake-fur wrap-around which intermingled with her piebald hair, she was the type of woman he heartily disliked.

He told her acidly that he was just one of many servicemen and women who successfully overcame injury with the help of medical experts, and suggested she visit Headley Court to write a feature on the patients and staff instead of making an issue of a single case.

She gave a superior, mocking smile. 'I've always found aircrew to be totally lacking in imagination. All they really understand is beer and cockpit histrionics, and it's my job to make them appear more accessible to the civilian population. Successful PR isn't achieved by quoting generalities, you know. Tell people about a thousand stray dogs in an RSPCA shelter and it goes over their heads. Give the heart-rending story of just one, and offers to give it a home roll in by the barrowful. In this instance I have to home in on the pathos and glamour elements.'

There was a concerted guffaw from the group clustering around the helicopter, and this intensified Randal's anger over her snide remark about aircrew's interest in beer and flying. Add sex to the list and she could have been Fiona speaking to him. He said in biting tones, 'My cockpit histrionics aren't due to start until tomorrow, but I'm well overdue for some beer. Goodbye, Mizz Francombe.'

'I haven't concluded my interview,' she snapped as he turned away.

'I have.'

She followed as he crossed the tarmac. 'Are you always this rude?'

'Are you?'

'I'm merely frank.'

He halted. 'Okay, let me be frank. All you've done is ask inane questions like: "How do you feel towards the boys who dropped that anchor on you?"'

'And you answered: "How would *you* bloody well feel?"'

'But you won't put that out to the national press. It hasn't the necessary pathos and glamour. You'll write something like: "When asked how he felt about the boys who caused the crash that almost ended his life, Randal Price said they were just four lively lads whose youthful prank went wrong. He was sure they had learned a hard lesson over the outcome." That, Mizz Francombe, will bring the aah factor you're after, rather than the truth that I'd like to wring their bloody necks and drop *them* from a motorway bridge. You don't need to interview me. You'll write whatever you want.'

Her plucked eyebrows rose over shrewd, pale eyes. 'Do you really want me to publish the fact that you'd like to murder those kids? It would have the country up in arms, and you'd be shunted into some backwater for the rest of your career.'

Randal sighed. 'Look, you've picked the wrong man. I hope to God I've never inspired pathos, and there's no flaming glamour about me. I'm just a nondescript-looking working pilot.'

'Who earned an AFC during the Gulf War, who drives a flashy, expensive car, and who is married to the beautiful socialite daughter of celebrated racehorse breeders,' she added crisply. 'How much more glamour do you want? Incidentally, are you and the stunning Fiona now going to get back together?'

'Go to hell,' he said savagely, leaving her standing. She would write a smarty-pants piece to go with the photographs, and there was nothing he could do to stop it appearing in the national newspapers. When her concoction of pathos and glamour hit the news-stands he would be marked down here at Shawbury as a wealthy poseur indulging in histrionics both in and out of the cockpit. God, what a start to his comeback to the remaining love of his life!

Dirk Marshall stopped on the hard shoulder and turned off the ignition with a shaking hand. His heart was pumping crazily and his brow was clammy. His thoughts had been elsewhere when he pulled out into the fast lane to overtake a car. Next minute, a roaring yellow missile had rocketed past no more than a hairsbreadth from his rear bumper and from the bonnet of the third vehicle. The driver of the Maserati had avoided a pile-up with a superbly judged swerve through that marginal gap, then had hurtled back to the outside lane to become a dot in the distance. Nerves of steel, apparently.

While Dirk struggled to gain his composure, the road ahead slowly faded to be replaced by a vision of a Balkan valley lying beneath summer heat. A valley where military paraphernalia stood in irregular piles around the perimeter of a tented camp.

They had delivered supplies on their last run of the day and, after mugs of tea and doorstep sandwiches apiece, the four-man crew had prepared to head back to Base, from where they would depart in the morning for home and seven days' leave. As he and Mike walked together to the Chinook, Dirk tried once more to break through the barrier his close friend had inexplicably erected around himself throughout this stint in Bosnia.

'What say we all spend next week on the Isle of Wight? Speed racing in my boat, high jinks on the beach, barbies while the sun goes down. Sam'll certainly love it, and my parents enjoy having him around.' He made a wry face. 'I think they wish he was *my* son.'

9

'You're welcome to him,' Mike snapped. 'And to Paula. You've always lusted after her, so now's your chance. I'm getting shot of them both as soon as I get home.'

Shocked and deeply uneasy, Dirk grabbed Mike's arm, forcing him to a halt. 'For God's sake, why? You can't walk away from something as good as you've got.'

Mike's face beneath the flying helmet was pale and set. 'If you think it's good you're as big a fool as I was.'

'Of course it's good,' Dirk insisted. 'I've watched from the sidelines all the way through.'

His friend's mouth twisted. 'Yeah, she made sure you were always there. Safety in numbers.'

Dirk stiffened. 'Just what're you getting at, Mike?'

'Forget it!'

'No, let's get this straight,' he demanded loudly, holding him back as their crewmen passed to board the aircraft. 'Are you claiming you never wanted me around? It was *you* who bloody invited me every time.'

'Okay, so I let you share my marriage,' Mike agreed in raised tones, 'but I'll put an end to it without your help. I don't need your sodding advice, and I don't want you sniffing around until I've moved out and got a solicitor on it. *Then* you can take over . . . if you still have the stomach for it.' Turning away to climb through the forward door, he added aggressively, 'Let's fly this bastard back so I can get pissed beyond thought or feeling tonight.'

Worried over Mike's emotional state Dirk offered to take the return leg, only to be told, 'I'm not getting pissed until we touch down.' So he eased his long frame into the left-hand seat and they began the start-up routine. Once they were off the ground and heading for home an unusual silence fell as Mike stared doggedly through the windows and Dirk grappled with the worrying situation that had developed.

When a light appeared on the warning panel as they gained height to cross the mountain range, Dirk reported it in an impersonal manner. Mike cursed under his breath. As the non-handling pilot Dirk took appropriate action to deal with a malfunction that was not severe enough to demand an immediate landing. Yet, a few minutes later, the Chinook plunged like a stone to the craggy heights.

Still seeing nothing of the motorway, Dirk recalled lying shocked and bleeding while rescuers extricated Mike's body from the wreckage as darkness fell. The paramedics said he must have been killed on impact, along with one of the crewmen. The other survivor had broken both legs and ruptured his spine.

As Dirk saw again the alien heights, the pile of wreckage looming in the snow-filled darkness, and Mike's crushed and lifeless body being zipped into a black bag, a stentorian voice broke through the visual nightmare. He turned in a daze to find a furious, white-faced young woman standing beside him.

'If you want to commit suicide, jump off a cliff! Don't involve others. You're not fit to drive a milk float, much less an MG, you bloody maniac!'

Unable to relate to her outburst, Dirk stared blankly.

'If you're drunk, I'll—'

'I'm not,' he murmured.

'You damn well look it.'

'Just . . . shaken.'

'That makes two of us.'

He struggled from his confusion. 'I didn't see him. Just . . . didn't see him. Not until . . . God, what a sensational piece of driving.'

'I hope I'm never forced to witness another,' she stormed. 'You'd better get your eyes tested and put up L plates.' She held up a mobile phone. 'I want fifteen minutes' start to reach junction six before you get on your dozy way. If I spot you coming up behind me I'll call the police. I mean it!'

She walked away to a blue Fiesta and resumed her journey.

Dirk was also leaving by junction 6, but he was happy to give her all the time she wanted. That brush with death had revived something he thought was well out of his system. When he felt ready he drove at geriatric pace, his eyes out on stalks until he gained the quieter road leading west.

He soon stopped at a pub to down two steadying whiskies, but they failed to banish the demons because Mike had been his boozing partner from the day they had drunk their first under-age pint. They had had some memorable binges in their time! All over the world, in plush hotels or in backstreets where the girls came as cheaply as the hooch. Sowing their wild oats! Then Paula burst on the scene. Their friendship had survived. Just!

Ordering a third whisky, Dirk took it to a nook away from the bonhomie and football arguments around the bar, and stared from the window at empty flower beds and pedestal planters beside bench tables for open-air drinking and eating. There was no need to take Paula's letter from his pocket. He knew it word for word; they had been running through his head when he had almost caused a fatal accident.

Dear Dirk,

I was hugely grateful for your help and support over the past year. I don't know how I'd have got through it without you. But you seem to have mistaken my gratitude for something deeper. I've always valued your friendship – we both did – but everything's changed, hasn't it?

I think it would be best if you stopped coming here and got on with your life. I'm now ready to get on with mine. That's what Mike would want.

Take care when you fly,
Paula.

For three days the shock of her rejection had dominated

Dirk's waking hours. He could not accept it. She had been eager enough to cheat on Mike with him while the poor devil was alive. He had waited for a decent interval to elapse before suggesting they get married but, now she was free, Paula apparently aimed to play the field and present young Sam with a series of 'uncles'. Was that really what Mike would want?

Gazing at fields beyond the pub garden, Dirk remembered seeing Paula for the first time. He and Mike were at the wedding reception of a fellow pilot, drinking and sizing up the talent in the hotel grounds.

'I'm going to have a crack at *that*,' Mike told him, waving his glass in the direction of a girl poured into a blue dress that revealed she had a sensational body.

'I'm having first crack.' Dirk had moved swiftly to vault a wrought-iron seat and reach the group she was in. Closer inspection showed she had the green eyes that usually go with tawny hair, generous breasts and a very smackable bottom. Mike was soon beside him to notice all that, too.

Their initial light-hearted vying for dates with Paula soon turned serious, but she had married Mike within five months. Five months after the wedding, Sam had entered the world and Dirk was asked to be his godfather. At first, a series of fun-loving girls had made a foursome whenever squadron duties gave the men time at home. As Sam became more demanding the casual dates petered out and left a close, happy threesome: Mummy, Daddy and Uncle Dirk. Then, on Sam's third birthday when Daddy was on emergency relief in Northern Ireland, Mummy and Uncle Dirk had drunk too much and done the unforgivable. Six weeks later Mike was dead.

Getting to his feet, Dirk tossed back the whisky and pushed his way through the door and out to his dark green MG. Starting the engine, he surged from the car park on to the road in his usual fashion, alcohol having ended his bout of caution.

13

Damn Paula! She was depriving him of the chance to put things right and instead condemning him to the continuing guilt of feeling that he should have died that day, not Mike.

As he raced towards Dorchester Dirk told himself it was as well he was joining another squadron. Everyone on the other station expected him and Paula to get together, so his sense of humiliation would have been greater. No one at Hampton would know of the relationship, even if they were aware of the tragic deaths of Mike and Jake. He would bloody well show her he could get on with his life without her help. Outside Dorchester he stopped at another pub for a few beers, just to prove to himself he could manage without a boozing partner.

It was early evening and growing frosty when he drove rather erratically up an unlit twisting lane to reach a plateau that stretched as far as the coast. Somewhere along it lay the village of Hampton Heyhoe, and three miles beyond that 646 Squadron was based. A narrow road ran across the top of the cliffs and several times the MG left it to rattle over rough ground before swerving back to the tarmac. Dirk told himself it was not that he was under the influence; it was merely impossibly dark along this stretch.

Hampton Heyhoe proved to be the kind of picturesque village beloved by American tourists: village green with war memorial, colour-washed thatched cottages, post office cum general store, a solicitor, estate agent and tiny Lloyds Bank, a café with Pickwickian overtones. And a two-hundred-year-old inn! Dirk turned in to the small forecourt of the Bird in Hand like a homing pigeon returning to roost. Those last beers had made him thirsty and he had another three miles to go before he reached the Officers' Mess bar.

Bidding a fond farewell to the landlord, who had become a close friend during the past forty-five minutes, Dirk made his way to his car brimful of confidence. The future was now enticingly rosy. A new squadron, a new set of friends. Everything he needed to get on with his life.

He dropped the car keys twice before they somehow found the lock on the door. He scrambled in behind the wheel and dropped the keys again before successfully starting the engine. He shot out to the road and followed signposts indicating the direction of the Station. He wildly negotiated a number of S-bends before finding himself on a long, straight stretch and gunned the accelerator. The powerful beams of his headlamps caught the white line of surf ahead where the cliff edge had crumbled in places bringing it closer to the road. For a brief moment he wondered what it would be like to spin the wheel and race out into space. Would he discover how Mike had felt in those last few moments of his life?

The road suddenly branched into a Y junction. To the left lay a coastguard station, beach and café. Not that way! Dirk hauled the wheel hard right. The MG almost hit the hedge, then it careered from side to side for a hundred yards before upending in a ditch well within sight of the main gate.

'Bugger it! That's busted the lights,' he mumbled unsteadily as he lay across the wheel and slowly switched off the ignition. 'Pity it didn't bust me.'

Maggie Spencer was glad to see the lights of the Bird in Hand ahead. It was a long drive from York, especially with no one to talk to. She had stopped at Dorchester for tea and some essential shopping, but this last stretch had seemed more than usually long. It was good to be getting back to work. Her leave had been a disaster from the first day, when Peter McGrath had asked her to marry him. He had known from the start that Mark Hascham, the Harrier pilot she had briefly loved, had been killed as she watched his aerial display turn to tragedy. She was not ready for any kind of commitment; she had told him enough times. They had been meeting for the past year, but her duties as an operational pilot and his

15

as an army doctor had spaced their dates widely. They had always kissed hello and goodbye, held hands as they walked, but any attempt by him to take things further had been firmly diverted by Maggie. His proposal had now forced an end to an enjoyable friendship.

Cutting short her planned week in Peter's company, she had visited her twin brother, his wife and their twin boys. Maggie wondered whether she was cut out for motherhood; she did not share Phil and Fay's rapture over every grunt, gurgle and grin the babies produced. Already unsettled over the scene with Peter, the besotted parenting got on her nerves within two days.

Then a call had come from her father to say Mum had collapsed and been rushed to hospital. Maggie and Phil had driven separately to York. Their GP brother, Rob, could not leave his practice and solicitor Charles was abroad. Phil, who ran a small company building luxury yachts, returned to his wife and children the following day, but Maggie stayed on. Mrs Spencer was the type of woman who enjoyed languishing in bed to be constantly fussed over after what had proved to be no more than a severe attack of vertigo. Despite these demands for pampering, Maggie did enjoy some quiet times with her father. He did not share his wife's belief that their only daughter among four children was forsaking her true role and attempting to be a man by flying a military helicopter. Dad understood her love of what she did. He also understood that she could not wait to get back among people with whom she felt most at ease.

All in all, her much needed leave had been a series of stressful interludes rather than a period of relaxation after five gruelling weeks in the Middle East during the latest escalation of hostilities. To cap it all, some moron had put her a millisecond from death on the motorway. She had seen it about to happen and instinctively braked. If she had not, the other moron in the yellow rocket would never have made it through the gap. When the green MG pulled over to the hard shoulder she had stopped and given the driver the kind of bawling-out she would give any aircrew who put her life in danger. He had sworn he was not drunk, but he certainly looked to be in some other world. On drugs? Or maybe the shock had rendered him incapable of thought. He should try flying a Chinook. That soon accustomed a person to danger and the unexpected.

At the junction, Maggie bore right but was soon brought to a halt by a truck from the Station. It was dragging from the ditch a dark green MG. She stared in disbelief. She had noted the motorway maniac's number in case he tried a repeat performance before junction 6. This was the same car! There was no sign of the driver but he surely must have been on his way to visit the Station. The lane led nowhere else.

One of the gate guards watching the operation walked up to Maggie's car and bent to the window she wound down. 'Oh, it's you, ma'am,' he said cheerfully. 'Sorry to hold you up. Won't take 'em long to get it back on the road. Good thing he was so near when he ditched.'

'Who was it?' she asked tautly.

'Dunno. New face to me. A flight lieutenant, wouldn't you know it?' he added under his breath. 'He won't be driving it for a bit. Stove in the radiator and broke both headlamps.'

'Was he hurt?'

'Not so's you'd notice. Just pissed as a newt!'

As he walked away Maggie's temper rose alarmingly. That bastard *had* been drinking! B Flight was expecting a pilot replacement for Simon, who was now ferrying for a construction company. If this dolt was the newcomer, team accord was sure to be disturbed. This could be the final straw after her seven days of irritations and reverses. They had better not ask her to share a cockpit with a man who held life so cheaply.

By the time she had unpacked, showered and dressed for

her evening meal, Maggie had channelled her anger into a plan of action. If this man could be so irresponsible in a car, what was he like in a Chinook? Andy Forbes, B Flight's commander, was usually wise enough to avoid personality clashes within his crews, so she would tell him at the outset why she had such a low opinion of their new pilot.

As she left her room she saw the unmistakable lanky form and flop of dark hair of Jeff Norton a short way ahead along the corridor. This man with whom she enjoyed a warm friendship was very smartly dressed, and a waft of expensive aftershave reached Maggie as she caught up with him.

'So who is she, Jeff? As I've been away for a full week I'm sure you've had time to find a replacement for Sonya, who was growing too interested in brochures of wedding gowns. Couldn't let that continue, could you?'

B Flight's Romeo grinned. 'You really understand a guy's need to avoid that fate worse than death.'

'For the girl, you mean.'

'Oh, very ho ho!' They walked to the stairs and began to descend. 'I need to discover what life's all about before I sweep some lucky creature off in my manly arms.'

'What you haven't already discovered about life isn't worth looking for. Is this a hot date tonight?'

'Are you talking Fahrenheit or Celsius?'

'Okay, play it close to your chest, but for you to tart yourself up it must have some significance.'

They reached the impressive oak-panelled hall that had survived several generations of boisterous young men and women. There, Maggie detained Jeff as he made to leave and related the facts of her narrow escape on the motorway.

'And would you believe it, when I got here his car was being hauled from the ditch a hundred yards from the gate. Corporal Beamish said the driver was totally pissed. A flight lieutenant.' She took a deep breath. 'I have this terrible sinking feeling he might be Simon's replacement. Have you heard anything?' Before he could answer, she added, 'If he is, there's no way I'll fly with him. I'll tell Andy that before briefing in the morning.'

'You'll have a job. Andy had a call from the hospital. Teresa went into labour yesterday, six weeks too soon. He hightailed it a very worried man.'

'Any news?'

'Jean and Vince heard there are complications. Don't ask me what. Anything to do with giving birth turns me off. *Very* off.'

'So you're never going to make a woman pregnant?'

He grinned. 'That side of it turns me very *on*. And speaking of that, I have to go. She'll be getting anxious.'

Grabbing his arm as he made to leave, Maggie returned to the urgent matter in hand. 'Do you know anything about the moron driving the green MG?'

He removed her hand from the sleeve of his soft leather jacket. 'Name's Dirk Marshall. He *is* Simon's replacement. He *did* arrive pretty well pissed, but not enough to stop him organising a truck and a gang of guys to pull his car from the ditch and deposit it in the Mess car park. Has a very persuasive tongue, I gather. In Andy's absence I did the honours and fixed him up with a room. He's in the one next to yours.'

With a knowing grin Jeff dashed for the door, leaving Maggie uncertain whether or not this was true. However, she had no worries over flying with Marshall. *Dirk*. What a posey name! With Andy away Jeff would take his place, and he knew better than to cross her on this.

In the bar Maggie found her girl friends, and she crossed to them rather than join a noisy group of aircrew well tanked-up and radiating a 'boys only' exclusion zone.

'Hi, Maggie, sit down and give us the dirt on your wild seven days away from here,' said Lisa Compton who was in Personnel. Her stunning complexion, blonde hair and catwalk figure lured a constant trail of men who discovered they had problems only she could advise them on. Highly intelligent men suddenly found they could not understand simple deductions from their pay, or why their extra allowances had been increased or reduced. The devious male mind could invent all manner of excuses in pursuit of the female, and the women members of the Officers' Mess found their behaviour hilarious.

'Your last seven days would have been more interesting than mine,' Maggie replied, sitting at the small corner table. She glanced at the slim redhead beside Lisa. 'Or yours, Pam. I guess there's also been a long queue outside your surgery every morning.'

Pam gave a faint smile. 'Health at Hampton has improved so greatly I've decided we have a station full of supermen.'

'And women,' added Lisa. 'Don't be sexist, Doc.'

Pam's smile broadened. 'I'm not. The women are all happy enough to see me. The men won't come in case I tell them to drop their pants.'

Maggie grunted. 'Isn't it marvellous! Give most of 'em the least bit of encouragement and they're unzipping their flies with gusto, yet they go all coy with you.'

Lisa laughed. 'I promise you, if *I* suddenly told them to do it during an interview they'd be out the door like a shot. They come for a bit of feminine attention and a furtive peek at my legs. The number of times they manage to drop something on the floor as they hand me the relevant papers! When they get back to their mates they lie their heads off about how they scored with me. It's macho bravado, that's all.'

A steward brought Maggie her usual gin and tonic as Pam said, 'There's an added fear in my case. You'd be surprised how many supposed tough guys turn pale at the sight of a hypodermic. They'd sooner pass out in front of another man than with me.'

'Poor dears! Women have been consulting male doctors for yonks and managed all right,' Lisa observed.

'We're made of sterner stuff, that's why,' Maggie murmured, her attention caught by the appearance of a powerfully built man she had not seen in the Mess before. 'Who's that?'

Her companions glanced round. 'No idea. Someone's guest,' mused Lisa. 'He's pretty impressive. Got the "wow" factor, and I can't see *him* dropping his pants for a woman medic.'

'Unless he was in her bedroom.'

Pam's wistful tone caused Maggie to study her expression. Squadron Leader Pamela Miles had been at Hampton only four weeks and found it difficult to integrate. Lisa had a whole team in Personnel, and Maggie was one of a large number of aircrew. Pam worked with three other-rank male orderlies, so she found life in the Mess somewhat exclusive. As she had recently divorced an army officer who left her for a girl of eighteen he met in Cyprus, life was lonely for Pam among people mostly linked with flying.

'So what *did* you do on leave, Maggie?' prompted Lisa.

As Maggie described Phil and Fay's preoccupation with their twin babies, and her mother's self-imposed invalid status, her spirits dropped again. 'I was glad to be back until I discovered we have a bonehead replacing Simon. Why do all the nice guys decide to leave?'

'Why's he a bonehead?' asked Pam.

Before Maggie could reply they were joined by a vivacious girl wearing her overcoat. Jill Landis was an Air Traffic Controller. 'I was hoping you'd be back, Maggie,' she said brightly. 'Got to dash – time for walkies. Just called in to ask you girls over to our place on Saturday afternoon. It's Arnie's birthday. He'll be one year old, and he's missing Pete so much I thought I'd give him a party to cheer him up.'

Pam stared. 'You're giving your *dog* a birthday party?'

'You will all come, won't you?' Jill begged, ignoring the incredulous question from the new arrival unaware that the Great Dane was treated as if he were their child by Jill and her navigator husband, presently in Bosnia. 'I've made a cake.'

'From crushed Bonios?' asked Lisa with a giggle.

Jill's frown was quelling. 'Come about four. I won't tell Arnie so it'll be a lovely surprise when you turn up. Must go. Be good . . . if you can possibly manage it!'

Maggie watched her friend hurry away and murmured, 'What is it that makes normal, intelligent people go ga-ga over babies and animals?'

'You'll find out when you get one or the other.'

'Not me, Pam; I'm the hard-hearted type.' Maggie got to her feet. 'Are we going to eat, or wait here until some other besotted idiot invites us to a parrot's engagement party?'

The other two stood and joined her. 'Your leave did you no good. You've come back a real grouch,' Lisa asserted.

They walked past the bar towards the dining room. 'You mentioned something about a bonehead joining B Flight,' said Pam, picking up on the earlier remark. 'What's that all about?'

'A maniac who can't steer a car in a straight line. God knows what he does in an aircraft. Answers to *Dirk*,' she added disparagingly.

'After Dirk Bogarde,' put in a slurred voice from the bar. 'You see, girls, my mother was an ad— admirer of his. In fact, I was conshi— consheived in the back row of the Odeon, Lesh— Leshter Shquare.'

Maggie turned swiftly. She had last seen him sitting in a low sports car, staring at her in a vacant manner with a face drained of colour. He seemed much bigger now, and he was leering at them, face flushed by alcohol. He gave an exaggerated wink.

'Don't you think you've already had more than enough?' she snapped. 'You almost killed us both on the motorway, then you had another go at suicide in the lane by the gate. For God's sake go to bed before you *drown* in a sea of beer.'

Lisa and Pam followed Maggie to the dining room, noisily agog.

'Did he really almost get you killed?'

'Is *he* Simon's replacement?'

'What was that about suicide in the lane?'

'You gave it to him pretty straight!'

'Come on, Maggie, *tell*!'

Although she sat at a table Maggie realised her appetite had vanished. She had no wish to go through the story again. It had been a pig of a day and she suddenly felt like going to bed with a paperback thriller to help her forget it.

'Look, I think I'll skip dinner,' she said, getting to her feet again. 'I had a long drive from York, and I'll probably be flying tomorrow.'

Lisa was disappointed. 'You're not going to leave us in suspense?'

'You look rather tired,' said Pam. 'An early night is probably a good idea. Have some cocoa or hot chocolate.'

'Yes. See you.'

At the top of the stairs Maggie turned into the corridor and anger bubbled up again at the sight of someone attempting to unlock her bedroom door. She marched up and snatched the key from his wavering hand. 'Can't you even read numerals? This is *eighty*-four, not ninety-four.'

He was swaying as he studied her through bleary eyes. 'I took your advish. Din . . . din break my neck on the shtairs.' Grabbing at the door jamb to steady himself, he treated her to a drunken grin. 'Can't we go in and get . . . coshy? Got to . . . got to get on with my life. Yesh, got to.' He nodded too vigorously and groaned with pain.

'Then get on with it well away from me.'

She unlocked her door and turned as he made to follow her in, giving him a hefty shove in the chest. He staggered back a pace or two, then his knees buckled and he dropped heavily. Maggie slammed her door. The men could put him to bed when they turned in. She just hoped they would not leave the mess there all night if he threw up outside her room.

While she undressed and made herself a mug of hot chocolate, Maggie told herself her mood was simply a reaction to the baby-dominated period with her twin who appeared to have moved another stage away from their former special relationship. Marriage to Fay had been the start; the twin sons further distanced Phil. This did not distress Maggie as much as once it would have, but she knew faint sadness over the loss of that unity they had once known.

She also felt mild regret over the ending of her friendship with Peter McGrath. He was fun, good company and not aircrew. She had enjoyed his medical anecdotes and, she had to admit, his devotion. He had not got as much in return, poor man, but she was going to miss him.

Then, of course, regardless of what she had said to 'Dirk Bogarde' that close shave with death had really shaken her up. Small wonder she was so wrought up; why she needed a paperback to help her forget twin babies, a melodramatic mother, a lovesick army doctor and a new pilot with a death wish. His mother should have given the Odeon a miss that night!

Carrying the mug of chocolate to the bedside table Maggie sank on to the bed in her dressing gown and slippers, staring at the carpet. The hot drink remained untouched as she finally admitted the true reason why her return today was so lacklustre. She took up the newspaper she had bought in Dorchester, still folded at the page on which there was a photograph of B Flight's former boss. Apart from a haunted look in his eyes, no one would guess from the picture how ill he had been following the horrendous car crash. Dear God, she could have suffered similarly but for the skill and daring of the driver of a Maserati.

FROZEN FOOD HEIR CLEARED TO FLY AGAIN

The headline was an example of the angle of this particular tabloid, but a column alongside the photograph was in public relations-speak.

Squadron Leader Randal Price, AFC, the helicopter pilot on whose car boys accidentally dropped an anchor fourteen months ago, resumed his flying career yesterday. No one at RAF Shawbury believes he will pass a flight refresher course with anything less than the same skill and panache that gained him an award for courage under fire during the Gulf War.

He will then begin instructing others in the complications of flying helicopters. The car crash left him initially paralysed but with the skill of civilian and military specialists, and the strong determination for which he is well known, Squadron Leader Price fought overwhelming odds to win through. When asked if he had ever given up hope the pilot said he might have done without the unflagging support of doctors and colleagues. He added that when a person signed up in the armed forces he or she joined a team that backs its members through thick and thin. It's the way they operate.

Mrs Fiona Price and the couple's two children stayed with her parents, renowned racehorse breeders Gerald and Mary Holland, during her husband's long fight back to health. Yesterday she spoke of his passionate love of flying. 'It's a miracle that he overcame such horrific injuries,' she added with great emotion.

At their luxury home near Harrogate, Hartley Price, the frozen foods giant, said he and his wife were overflowing with pride at their son's strength of will against adversity. Personnel at Shawbury turned out

25

in force to welcome Squadron Leader Price back to 'the team'.

Maggie read the piece again with the same mixed emotions it had aroused the first time. Randal's aggressive attitude to the media was well known in 646 Squadron. He was more likely to tell any probing journalist to go to hell than cooperate on a nauseatingly sentimental column like this about himself. All that mush about personal courage and determination! Oh yes, he had those qualities in abundance, but he had used them in this instance simply as a means of getting back what had been taken from him. He would never have made that comment about joining a team that backs you through thick and thin. Some did and others did not. Every service person knew that.

As for his parents, Maggie knew they were virtual strangers who, aside from one visit to his bedside as he lay in a coma, had concentrated on their business lives thereafter and dutifully sent flowers or baskets of fruit each week. It had not bothered Randal. He had been a boarding scholar from an early age until he joined the RAF, so there was no real bond between parents and son. Mention of their 'overflowing pride' was sickening in its hypocrisy.

Finally, Maggie came to the crux of the cause of her depression: she did not know what to make of Fiona's 'deep emotion'. The reason why she and the children were living with her rich, successful parents was because she had severed contact with Randal after the crash and had been nowhere near him since then. Sexy, stunningly lovely and ten years younger than her husband, she had led him a tortured dance throughout their marriage, and the prospect of a partner confined to a wheelchair had not been her idea of a pampered future. So far as Maggie knew, Randal's eyes had been opened and divorce was definitely on the cards. Now she was unsure. Badly unsure.

When her lover had plunged to his death in a ball of fire, Randal had helped Maggie through the trauma of witnessing it. She had then helped him through his tragedy, visiting him in hospital whenever her heavy duties allowed her enough time to drive to the military rehabilitation unit, Headley Court. She had more often telephoned encouragement to a man battling to achieve what many said was impossible. With this complex man she had begun to enjoy an understanding very similar to the one she had had with her twin until recently. Now she was confused and deeply hurt.

On returning from a stint in the Middle East Maggie had rung the number of the flat Randal had latterly taken on a short lease near Headley Court, but a woman said he had left without a forwarding address. Maggie fully expected him to make contact. He had not, and she had no idea why.

This news report told her where he was and that he had won through, but why had she to learn of it this way? After all her encouragement and support surely he would have seen her as the prime recipient of his great news of success with the medical board. Surely, *surely* he had not returned to pursuing his demanding, self-absorbed wife! It seemed preposterous to consider that he would lay himself open to further humiliation at Fiona's hands, yet what other explanation could there be? One thing appeared certain: now he was fully back on the ball the universally popular Rip Price had no further need of Flight Lieutenant Margaret Spencer.

Two

W hen he awoke, Dirk Marshall had no idea where he was. His head thudded dully, his mouth was rough and dry. He must have been on a bender of formidable proportions last night, but where and with whom? He wished whoever had put him to bed had left a note giving some clue as to his whereabouts.

Heaving himself upright with his usual morning-after groan he saw his bags in the open wardrobe and some of his clothes draped over the back of a chair. He was in standard Officers' Mess accommodation, that much was clear, but he had never seen this room before. Through the rice pudding that was his brain came a faint recollection. He had joined a new squadron. He vaguely recalled driving along cliffs to a village called . . . er . . . Hampton Heehaw? Well, it would all come back to him after a quart of breakfast coffee.

Shrugging on his robe, he grabbed his sponge bag and went in search of the bathrooms. A short way along the corridor, deep in thought, he cannoned into someone coming swiftly from one of the rooms. He put his hands on uniformed shoulders to steady himself and . . . *her*? He had a brief impression of hostile green eyes and short blonde hair before she thrust him away with a hearty, 'Oh, for God's sake!' and hurried to the stairs.

Tepid water and energetic lathering brought a partial return of energy as Dirk puzzled over where he had seen the girl before. Concentrating on her features, it was a while before the fact that she had been wearing a flying-suit sank in. A navigator? A pilot? He had only ever encountered two female pilots (a term they deplored, saying no one ever referred to *male* pilots) and that girl was not one of them. Yet she had looked familiar. Angrily familiar!

Back in his room Dirk began to shave, then caught sight of his bedside clock and groaned. He must present himself to the Squadron Commander at nine and the Station Commander at ten thirty, but he had yet to dress and he badly needed black coffee and breakfast before facing them. He was cutting things fine, not the best way to start getting on with his life. Paula had told him to do that. He now remembered her letter and the pain of rejection. Recollections suddenly raced back: the near pile-up on the motorway, proving to himself he could get drunk without Mike beside him, skidding into a ditch. He hoped these morning interviews would be with reasonable, relaxed men.

Wing Commander Gerard Jeffries, commander of 646 Squadron, was clearly a rule-book aficionado. He made a heavy point of Dirk's arrival before expressing his hope that his new pilot would concentrate more on his sporting ability than on lifting a tankard.

'It's every man's duty to maintain a healthy body with physical exercise. You're an Olympic athlete. Keep that standard.'

Dirk added silently that every man had to maintain a *happy* body with regular intakes of beer.

Martin Ashe, the Station Commander, was more laid-back with a good sense of humour. He knew Brad Farrow, who had been in the Olympic four-man bob team with Dirk, and he had been at university with his former boss. They chatted genially on these topics after the official welcome and general appraisal of Dirk's career. Only when he was leaving did the senior man say dryly, 'Move that pile of junk from the Mess car park p.d.q. It's bad for aircrew morale when they see evidence of a pilot's deplorable sense of direction.'

Moving the pile of junk involved a telephone call, the advent of a tow truck bearing a hired car from the nearest large garage, and a hefty shock over the estimate for repair of the MG. Dirk had heard it all before. 'Yeah, but we gotta send away for the parts. It all takes time and costs mount up. Specialist work, this is. Can't put just anyone on it. Don't want a botched job, do yer?'

An early night set Dirk up for a much better start to his second day at Hampton. Unfortunately, things did not continue that way for long. He ate breakfast with a fair-haired navigator named Chris Foley, who repeated the story of Andy Forbes' absence due to the problems over the birth of his second child, and aired his fears that Gerard 'Judge' Jeffries would overrule Jeff Norton at the briefing.

'Great promotion hunter is the Judge,' he confided. 'Won a medal in the Falklands campaign, good pilot and all that, but he won't bend a rule or look the other way when it would make things a damn sight easier – as our former boss, Rip Price, often did. Mrs Jeffries is the same. The wives can't stand her. You married?'

'No.' Even to his own ears it sounded bleak.

'Stay that way,' Chris advised bitterly. 'You at least keep all you earn. I'm paying maintenance to my ex for an eighteen-month-old baby I'm not really certain's mine.'

Dirk grunted sympathetically. 'Got someone else lined up?'

'Not likely. Once bitten.'

'The cure for that is to go hunting and be the one who bites,' he said, as much to himself as to Chris. 'Works every time. D'you fancy going out on the town one night?'

'What town? There's the Bird in Hand along at Heyhoe, or the Master of Hounds at Framworth in the opposite direction. Course, there's the beach caff in the summer. Real swinging place, that is,' he added with a roll of his eyes. 'Hey, look at the time. Better get across to briefing. If Jeffries decides to interfere he'll be marking the second hand on the clock.'

As they crossed to the car park they were hooted at by a girl in a blue Fiesta who wanted a clear path. Something about her face and that car immediately added up to a fact Dirk could barely believe.

'Who's she?'

'B Flight's only woman pilot. Maggie's one of the boys, game for anything except getting thoroughly pissed. She's a great guy.'

'Really?'

His companion picked up on the caustic tone and glanced at Dirk. 'Had a brush with her already?'

'You could call it that,' he murmured, still grappling with a premise that was surely beyond the realms of acceptable coincidence.

Chris chuckled. 'She can get uppity and snap a bloke's head off, but that's just girly self-preservation. With odds of twenty-seven to one it's understandable.'

'Is she any good in the cockpit?'

'Don't ever ask that in her hearing if you want to survive. Did you hear about two Chinooks last year going in under fire to pull out a detachment of our troops acting as peacekeepers sandwiched between advancing Serb and Albanian rebels? Our Maggie was on that job with Jeff. Those two are close. Not in any sexual way; a genuine platonic friendship. If you tangle with her you'll maybe get Jeff on your back.'

Driving across to the squadron offices Dirk accepted that if Maggie really was the girl on the motorway, he had made an enemy before his first flight with 646. If she had told her friend about it, he would have made two. The way to deal with it was to charm the girl. It should not prove too difficult.

There was no time for flattery when they gathered because Jeffries was there watching the clock on the wall. Seven aircrew were present and, as the black second hand jerked inexorably towards the twelve and eight-thirty exactly, Dirk did not envy the absentee.

Jeffries began. 'It seems that Andy will be away for at least another week, so I've been juggling with aircraft availablity and the tasks we're faced with.' He made no reference to why Jeff, as senior pilot present, could not do the job just as well. 'Ned and Frank will return from Split on Thursday with their crews. The rest of the Flight are away until the end of the month. I've done my best to ensure that you all get an equal crack at the rough and the smooth, but it's a damn difficult business and I don't want any whingeing.'

This attempt to clothe with stressful overtones what every flight commander coped with day in, day out was interrupted by the entrance of a thickset sergeant with bright red hair, who seemed surprised that the briefing had begun. He looked pointedly at the clock, then at his watch.

'Sorry, sir, I'd no idea the station clocks were five minutes fast,' he said in a thick Glaswegian accent, then sat beside Dirk with apparent unconcern at his lateness.

'I suggest you take your time from them like the rest of us,' Jeffries told him sharply. 'Synchronisation can mean the difference between life and death, as we discovered in the Falklands conflict.' Encompassing them all in a fierce glance to ensure they had absorbed the inference in that comment, he continued. 'Jeff, you'll take Chris, Sandy and Ray out to Salisbury Plain to move tracked vehicles for the Army.'

'Why can't the Army drive them where they have to go?' Jeff asked swiftly.

'Because they're running an all-units exercise over the

next three days and can't drive the things smack through the middle of it. I said no whingeing.'

'How long a job will it be?' asked Chris.

'As long as it takes,' was the testy reply. 'There are eight of the damn things to move during the hours of daylight but you should do it by early afternoon tomorrow. I want you back here ready to replace one of the crews returning from Bosnia on Thursday.' He transferred his attention to Dirk and the brawny sergeant beside him. 'Our two new boys will team up with Maggie and Dave for a pleasant trip to Shawbury.' His smile was intended to emphasise how pleasant it would be. 'They want a Chinook fitted up to take troops and casualties in a hostile situation. There's some kind of foreign deputation visiting with NATO top brass. You'll stand by to show them over the aircraft and answer questions. I expect you to impress them with details of what you and the Chinook are capable of.'

Maggie said, 'I'd rather not do that one, Boss. Can Jeff or Chris take it on?'

Dirk was surprised by her urgent tone and the pallor of her cheeks. He was further intrigued when both Jeff and Chris offered to take it.

Jeffries' smile vanished. 'You're moving vehicles. It's an exacting business and I want you both on it. The Army'll be out to find any fault, as usual. No, I need Maggie at Shawbury to show the unisex nature of this squadron. Dirk is a highly experienced pilot whose previous service with the Special Forces Flight will please NATO visitors. He'll handle them with ease. He's been an Olympic competitor for the Air Force and that's a bonus when demonstrating to foreigners the quality of our servicemen. Sergeant Ted Griffin, who wishes to be known as Griff, will find this an excellent initiation to squadron routine, and Dave is a fellow Scot who'll answer any queries he may have.'

Maggie said again, 'Boss, I really don't want to do this.'

Jeffries sighed audibly. 'This is not an air show. No flying displays, just you on your best behaviour smiling nicely at the overseas visitors and pleasing the top brass. There'll be lunch laid on. It's the kind of day we'd all like to have.'

'Then why the hell don't you go?' muttered Chris softly, mystifying Dirk further. What was behind the curious tussle?

'Jeff has the nav details and Met report. He's programmed to take off at ten and Dirk at ten thirty.' He took up his clipboard. 'Right, go to it!'

The moment he stepped from the dais Griff was on his feet, saying in an undertone, 'Sir, I've no stomach for flying with a woman in the cockpit.'

'What?' said Jeffries, taken unawares.

'I was no' told you had a female pilot or I'd have asked to be posted elsewhere. There's no way I can work with her. My family have been seamen for several generations and we all have the superstition about having a female aboard. They bring disaster.'

'*What?*' said Jeffries again, thoroughly thrown. 'You're not going to sea, man.'

Griff spoke even more confidentially, but Dirk could still hear what was said. 'Sir, she's already nervy and upset. Just look at her! I'd no' be confident of my safety in any aircraft with her.'

To his great discredit and Dirk's disgust Jeffries glanced at Maggie, then murmured disloyally, 'No need to worry about safety. Dirk will be doing the flying. She'll be his co-pilot.'

The born troublemaker persisted. 'Superstition is a powerful force. It takes a man's mind off his work and he can make bad errors of judgement. I'll be fine with the other crew.'

To Dirk's further disgust, instead of nipping Griff's attitude in the bud, the Squadron Commander caved in. He called across the room, 'Jeff, one small change. I think, after all, that Griff will gain more valuable experience working with you. Sandy can go to Shawbury.'

When Jeffries left, Maggie turned on her friend. 'Why didn't you back me, you bastard?'

'I offered to swop with you, so did Chris,' Jeff countered hotly. 'You heard him. He wouldn't budge.'

'He soon budged for that carrot-headed idiot,' she raged, revealing that she had also overheard that conversation. 'He's superstitious about flying with a woman. Well, I feel the same about that bonehead who's just been made captain of my aircraft on his first day here, but no one pays any heed to what *I* say.'

'Mebbe because you behave like a hysterical housewife,' Griff said bluntly. 'Now ye know why I refused to take to the air with you.'

'That's out of line,' snapped Chris. 'Maggie's an experienced pilot who's encountered several dangerously hostile situations. We're all happy to be in her crew.'

'That's your choice,' came the aggressive reply from a man taking the habitual familiarity between aircrew sergeants and officers to the very limit. 'It's no' mine . . . sir.'

'Leave it, Chris,' said Maggie. 'The Boss did the right thing. With that attitude, Sergeant Griffin would be a danger in our crew.'

Jeff looked deeply unhappy. 'I'll have a word with him, Maggie. The obvious solution is to send you in my place with Chris, and leave Griff in Dirk's crew. That'd get you out of Shawbury. The stupid bastard knows . . . he should have more sense. If he'd left me to get on with it, I'd have—'

'Oh, drop it, drop it,' she said wearily. 'Maybe it's time I applied for a transfer.'

Dirk watched her walk to stare from the window, then he murmured to Chris, 'Why's she so het up over this Shawbury trip?' He already knew why she was angry about being teamed with him.

Chris frowned. 'You're bound to learn about it sooner or later. A year or so ago she was manning a Chinook ground display at an air show when she saw her boyfriend crash in a ball of flame during his aerobatics in a Harrier. You must remember the media speculation over the fact that he was South African by birth. They tried to make some racist political issue of his death. It was very traumatic for Maggie. Maybe the thought of being parked on the ground answering questions is too much like that terrible day. Even so,' he paused to glance at the silent girl, 'she seems rather OTT about it. There must be an additional reason why she doesn't want the job.'

'An old flame she'd rather not meet?'

'She could cope with that. I've never seen her like this before.' He glanced back at Dirk. 'Why's she got it in for you? A *bonehead*?'

He turned that off easily enough. 'She probably heard about my aborted arrival; saw the wreck of my MG in the car park.' He gave a faint smile. 'Hardly a recommendation for steadiness at the controls, is it?'

Chris smiled back. 'My maternal grandmother was an actress who says one should always make a grand entrance. She'd approve of yours.'

'I can't say I approve of the crewman who's just wished himself on you. I think I've come out of the deal the winner.' He studied the new sergeant now talking to Ray. 'Is the Boss always so spineless?'

'He just happens secretly to share our Glaswegian chum's attitude towards women, except that it's no secret to B Flight, however hard he tries to pretend.'

They all got down to discussing routes and wind directions, so it was not until they were walking to the aircraft side by side that Dirk had an opportunity to speak quietly to Maggie.

'I don't blame you for thinking me a bonehead. It *was*

you on the motorway, wasn't it?' When she did not answer, he said, 'You took a hell of a risk laying into me like that. Haven't you heard of road rage?'

'Yes, I was experiencing it.' She glanced coldly up at him. 'I'm not afraid of men. I've a karate black belt. Any one of you who tries it on finds himself on the ground before he knows it.'

Filing away that information for the future, he spoke again. 'As you saw, I was in no state to retaliate. I was in shock. That madman in the Maserati came up so fast there was no time to see him approaching.'

He had never known a woman who could look as fierce as this one. 'Are you offering the same excuse for the ditch outside the main gate?'

'Are you always as hard as this on your fellow men?' he asked.

'Only when they treat life as cheaply as you do. I wish I had phoned the police with your reg number. They'd have found you well over the limit and put you out of danger's way.'

'Maggie, I hadn't been drinking. I told you that at the time. My attention wandered at a vital moment.'

She halted on the tarmac, the breeze ruffling her short hair and pale sunshine filtering through cloud gilding the fine threads. 'The same way it wandered when you hit the ditch, and when you tried to open the door of my room with your key? Let's get things straight right away, Dirk Bogarde. I'm flying with you today only because our esteemed boss has a skull as thick as yours. Tomorrow I'll apply for a posting away from here. B Flight used to be a good team. I no longer want to be in this new one.'

Dirk climbed aboard after her and settled in his seat. He had no recollection of trying to enter her room . . . or of anything else he might have done that night. Surely he had not trotted out to her that hoary old line about the back row of the Odeon and, if he had, surely she had not believed it! She could not be thinking of leaving Hampton for such a tame reason. Male intuition told him there was more troubling his reluctant co-pilot than his advent, and he guessed the answer might be found at Shawbury.

During the short flight Maggie's notion of transferring to another squadron strengthened. It had been a sudden urge, prompted by the morning's events, yet even her return to Hampton two days ago had lacked the usual pleasure of getting back to work with people she knew and liked. The sparkle had gone from her professional life. Maybe she needed a change of scene. Too much had happened while she had been with 646.

There were three reasons why she had asked not to be on this task; one of them was sitting beside her in the cockpit. Jeff knew her feelings about flying with this irresponsible man, and she would have explained privately to Andy. Team loyalty had kept her from making a point of it with Jeffries. Flight members did not rat on each other to their squadron commander, especially if he was one of the type they had. Their new crewman apparently had no such scruples.

Jeff and Chris had jumped to the conclusion that she wanted to avoid reminders of the day Mark had crashed, and to some extent they were right. Showing civilians over a static Chinook display was what she had been doing on that terrible day, but it was eighteen months ago and today would be slightly different. All the same, that was her second reason for preferring to shift vehicles on Salisbury Plain.

Her third was something she would not even tell Jeff. Randal was at Shawbury. The hurt he had inflicted by cutting all contact with her had been doubled by reading the newspaper report. If he had been lured into another destructive relationship with his wife, or whatever else had caused him to behave as he had, Maggie did not want to see him. In her present mood she was liable to explode.

Exchanging only the necessary flight conversation, she continued to boil with anger over Judge Jeffries' appalling lack of loyalty towards her this morning. Not only had he undermined her professional skill by reassuring Griff that she would not be the handling pilot, he had finally brought into the open his badly-disguised attitude to women in aircrew by suggesting her role today was simply to demonstrate lack of sexism in the Air Force and smile nicely at the male visitors. She had served with 646 for two years and had successfully undertaken everything any pilot could be expected to do, even under hostile fire. Yet Dirk had been held up as the highly experienced pilot who would handle with ease those questions put by foreign visitors. With him and the pugnacious Griff in B Flight, even the support of her colleagues would not compensate. Definitely time to make a new start and restore her self-confidence, which had taken a beating recently.

When Shawbury hove into view, and the familiar soft Scots accent of Dave Ashmore and the cheery baritone of his friend Sandy talked them safely past obstacles and power lines down to the tarmac, Maggie's anger was still barely containable. She had worked hard to be accepted as the Flight's only woman pilot. The old team had soon welcomed her aboard, but there had been too many changes and even the man who once had commanded that team had turned his back on her. If all 646 wanted was a woman to smile nicely at important visitors, she would provide a vacancy for them to get her. This girl was not the one they needed.

They completed the shutdown after parking, then Dirk smiled across at her. 'Not bad handling for a bonehead, eh?'

'An *Olympic* bonehead. Don't play down your sporting

fame. You're here to impress everyone today.' She climbed from the cockpit to see a car pulling up nearby. A short, slight squadron leader got out and gave a parody of an American-type salute as he approached, grinning broadly.

'Dirk, good to see you! Thought you'd have done for yourself before now, you reckless bastard.' He seized Dirk's hand with obvious pleasure. 'Must be at least four years since we had that close-run encounter with the *Polizei* at Laarbruch.'

Dirk laughed. 'I hope you've grown older and wiser, Perry.'

'Time for that when I retire.' He glanced with interest at Maggie. 'Hello, what have we here, you old dog?' He gave her an optical once-over. 'Dirk and I are old boozing pals, but I know *we've* never met. I'd have remembered.'

'I'm afraid I wouldn't.' She offered her hand. 'Maggie Spencer.'

'Perry Newman.' He had a strong grip. Deliberately strong? If he did but know it she could have him on his back with one swift movement during this handshake. She was sorely tempted.

'Don't judge me by this reprobate, Maggie,' he said smoothly. 'We men aren't all the same.'

'Aren't you?' She introduced Dave and Sandy, then asked, 'What time are we expected to do our stuff?'

'Fourteen hundred. That's if they've got through lunch by then. You know how these things drag behind schedule.'

'Our boss told us we'd get a good lunch,' said Dirk.

'Not with the guests. They'll be in the dining room. The rest of us'll have to make do in the breakfast bar. Spartan fare, but time for a drink first.' He walked to the car. 'Hop in! I'll stop at the Sergeants' Mess along the way.'

Maggie dived in the back where Dave and Sandy squeezed in with her, leaving Dirk to exchange raised-eyebrow looks with Perry over Maggie's choice of seat.

'Bit of an old banger, I'm afraid,' Perry said as the car rattled around the perimeter. 'We can't all afford a Porsche like your former boss. I suppose you know he's doing a flight refresher here.'

'Any chance of meeting up with him, sir?' asked Dave eagerly.

'Doubt it. He's on show today. Good PR when civilians are around.' He drew up outside the Sergeant's Mess. 'Here you are, guys. I'll collect you, sober and with flies correctly done up, at thirteen thirty.'

Left alone on the back seat, Maggie asked, 'What did you mean about being on show?'

The car shot off suddenly as Perry said over his shoulder, 'Wonderboy has been detailed with several others to have lunch with the VIPs. Not only is he little short of a walking medical miracle, he happens to speak several European languages, which will additionally amaze them. Of course, frozen fish fingers don't cut much ice with Continentals, but being heir to a business empire gives him a gloss they recognise only too well. If all else fails, he can always mention his marital connection with racing bloodstock. The sport of kings neutralises the whiff of trade associated with his own family.'

Maggie rose to that. 'Sour grapes are favourite here, are they?'

'More so than women with a chip on their shoulders,' was Perry's cool response.

In the Mess Maggie went to tidy up before seeking a cold drink. Perry's sneering comments had cemented her dislike. She knew Randal would hate lunching with VIPs; it was not his scene. He was happiest with aircrew around a bar, or taking part in other off-duty pastimes with them. He threw himself into everything with energy and, quite often, outrageous disregard of the rules. He had never used his family's wealth and influence to impress people; he had deliberately distanced himself from it. The same with his parents-in-law's renown in the world of horse racing. He had regarded himself as just another working pilot.

In the act of combing her hair into shape, Maggie's hand stilled. She was thinking of the person Randal had been before the crash. She had seen a different aspect throughout his fight back from severe injury, of course, but could she be certain he would now hate being selected to mingle with today's distinguished guests? How could she tell what he was like back in harness? He had severed contact with her. Maybe Perry's attitude was justified. She sighed. Was it merely her unsettled mood that made everyone appear cynical and obstructive lately?

Once in the crowded bar with a mineral water in her hand, Maggie spotted someone she knew. Jake Tring had been on her course at Cranwell. They met up with enthusiasm, eager to hear about each other's progress. Some of Maggie's usual warmth returned as she laughed with Jake over anecdotes of their early errors during pilot training, then passed on news of others on their course. Jake introduced her to several Shawbury instructors, so she was soon one of a relaxed, friendly group.

During the telling of an exaggerated story by an instructor with a way-out sense of humour, Maggie's interest was lost as the movement of those around her gave her a clear view across the room of the man she had parted from last November on the closest of terms. Randal looked badly thrown by the sight of her, yet he would surely have heard that an aircraft from 646 was flying in. Hot on the heels of that came the thought that he had not expected *her*. Would he imagine she had eagerly volunteered to get here to see him?

A shout of laughter greeted the end of the yarn, and jostling officers blocked visual contact with the man sup-posedly on show to the VIPs. Maggie was thankful the overcrowded bar prevented direct confrontation, but she had foolishly discounted Randal's personality. There was a tap on her shoulder and she turned to find him behind her, beer glass in hand, looking very formal in full uniform.

'Hi!'

Play it cool, she told herself. 'If there's a bar anywhere in the vicinity it's odds on you'll be in it.'

'You know me too well.'

'I thought I did.'

He let that pass. 'You've cut your hair.'

The team had all commented on her new style in typical fashion when she returned after Christmas. 'Your dad's electric shaver run amok?' 'Which of your nephews was given a Swiss Army knife?' 'Who's been practising with a pudding basin?' 'Get caught up in the Moulinex, Maggie?' 'Won't have to wait half an hour while you put on your bone dome now!'

Randal had just given the subject personal overtones which, together with the warmth in his eyes, made nonsense of his silence over the past two months. Maggie was lost for words.

He indicated her glass. 'Can I get you another?'

'No. No, thanks. Aren't you supposed to be elsewhere, in more exalted company?'

He frowned. 'Who told you that?'

'An obnoxious pipsqueak named Newman. Well, aren't you?'

'Someone'll fetch me when they reach the Mess.'

'We're doing our stuff when you finish with them.'

He gave a faint smile. 'I'll do my best to get them tanked up enough to believe anything you tell them.'

'You've always hated that brand of duty.'

Barged by someone trying to reach the bar he put a hand on her arm to steady himself. 'It's not usually as hectic as this. VIPs attract attention-seekers.'

43

'Newman claims you're one.'

'Yes.' He broke contact. 'Who's in your crew?'

'Dave and Sandy. They were hoping for a word with you. We knew you were here. Read it in the paper,' she added pointedly.

'Sorry I'll miss them. Who's your co-pilot?'

'Simon's replacement. Name's Dirk Marshall. Know him?'

'Know *of* him. Spent two years with the Special Forces Flight. Olympic bobsleigh team; takes part in powerboat racing. Sporting type well out of my league.'

'Everyone's out of your league when it comes to sport,' she said, unable to smother a grin. 'You invent rules to cover how hopeless you are.'

Amusement lit his eyes. 'You guys never know all the rules. I have to educate you.' He hesitated momentarily. 'Maggie, it's good to see you.'

She struggled to keep things light. 'You almost didn't. I wanted to move armoured cars on Salisbury Plain.'

'Christ, what's the sudden attraction in that?'

They're a better proposition than Marshall. He drinks.'

'Don't we all?'

'This fool has a death wish. I'd sooner keep well clear of him.'

Randal frowned. 'He walked away from that crash outside Banja Luca about a year ago. Two were killed. The pilot was his close friend. You must remember it.'

'Air crashes weren't my favourite topic at the time.'

He sighed. 'Sorry. I suppose I was then at the stage of sitting in a wheelchair reading the gory details and wishing I was as dead as them. God, I must have been a pain in the arse.'

'You were,' she murmured, then forced a change of subject. 'But not as much as our other new boy: a crewman who thinks women mean disaster.'

'We all think that, but we've learned to live with you.'

'He refused to fly with me – doubts his safety if I'm at the controls – and Jeffries more or less went along with him.'

'*What?* He should support his pilots, not undermine them. Give them a bollocking in private if they deserve it, but *never* show open lack of faith. Didn't Andy intervene?'

'Andy's not there. Teresa's having a difficult birth.'

'God, I'd make Jeffries squirm if he ever did that to one of my team. He might once have been a hotshot pilot, but he's bloody hopeless at command. You know how many ding-dongs I had with him when he tried to overrule my decisions. He's so bloody eager for promotion why the hell don't they give it to him and get him out of our hair?'

Warmed by his championship Maggie said quietly, 'He's not in yours any longer. Make the most of it.'

He frowned, then said harshly, 'I'd give anything to be back with the team, despite Jeffries. I've little interest in being an instructor. You know me; I'm an impatient bugger at the best of times. I'll turn student pilots into nervous wrecks within three lessons.'

'No, you won't. In the air you're the calmest, steadiest pilot I know. It's on the ground you're an impatient bugger. And a lot of other things besides . . . as the therapists at Headley Court know too well.'

'You too, I guess.' He hesitated, then began quietly, 'Maggie, I—'

'Found you at last, you bastard,' exclaimed an impatient squadron leader pushing through the crowd. 'You're supposed to be on tap, not chatting up the birds. The CO wants you as of ten minutes ago. Come on!'

Randal had no option but to leave. He gave her a forced smile. 'Take care and give 'em hell . . . like you gave me sometimes.'

'Watch those students during the third lesson,' she replied, badly undermined by those last words and wishing their talk had not been interrupted.

Dirk appeared at her side. 'Perry suggests we grab some lunch before this lot surge in to commandeer the tables. He's set to drive us over at thirteen thirty to pick up the others, then get us in place well before the VIPs are due to turn up.'

While she ate a mediocre light meal with two men she found boring and unlikeable, Maggie left them to reminisce together and enthuse over past macho exploits while she thought about her brief encounter with Randal. Why had she not asked him point-blank what had got into him lately, instead of pussyfooting around the subject? She would let no other friend treat her the way he had. She should have let fly at him the moment he walked up and calmly said, 'Hi!' as if nothing had changed. They had had many a set-to during which they had spoken plainly enough to each other. Why had they both been unable to do so today?

Her thoughts drifted back to a return flight from Bosnia almost two years ago, when she had been assailed by a sensation of such distress she could not hide it from her crew. When told about it Randal wanted her to have a medical check and meant to ground her until he knew the result. She had been forced to reveal to him that she and her twin shared a sixth sense that enabled them to feel each other's elation or pain, however far apart they might be. On that flight she had experienced Phil's deep distress over the miscarriage that had endangered Fay's life. Randal had remained cynical and wary. Only when Phil had responded in the same way on the day she had watched Mark plunge to his death, had he been driven to believe in something beyond his own experience. He teasingly called these strong impulses 'magic messages', which showed he continued to find the twin link hard to comprehend.

Curiously, it was that same sixth sense which had sent

Maggie to the hospital on the morning Randal had been told there was a possibility of his walking again. It was the only time she had experienced it with anyone but Phil. Since the birth of his baby boys their bond had weakened – there had been no more magic messages – so Maggie was surprised by her reaction today. There was certainly something she did not understand about Randal's behaviour, yet she knew without doubt he was as unhappy over it as she. Not exactly a magic message, maybe merely feminine instinct, but she knew.

The visitors were brought to the Chinook almost thirty minutes late. It was no surprise; official lunches invariably overran optimistic schedules. Answering questions and explaining the many functions of the aircraft to these polite civilian VIPs was not too reminiscent of that air show, Maggie discovered to her relief. The Chinook had been fitted with seats for troop-carrying and with several stretchers, as it might be during wartime. Dave was fully trained in the treatment of casualties, so he was at ease with queries on that subject. Sandy explained how they fixed slung loads when transporting supplies and vehicles to men on the ground, so most of the interest was centred on the cabin. Perfunctory glances in the cockpit prompted comments or half-hearted questions put to Dirk. Maggie was treated to polite, slightly embarrassed smiles, that was all. Within twenty minutes they had departed.

'What a bloody waste of time!' exclaimed Sandy, watching the cavalcade of vehicles crossing the tarmac. 'Most of them were so pissed we could've told 'em anything and they'd have nodded.'

'You've our old boss to thank for that,' Maggie told him with a faint smile. 'He promised to do what he could on that score.'

Dave closed up the first aid box and wandered forward. 'I carefully explained the nature of any temporary relief we're able to give casualties, and how we have a medic aboard if the aircraft is fully fitted out as an ambulance, then I discovered the two guys I was talking to didn't speak English.'

'Neither do you, Dave,' joked Sandy. 'All that "och aye" and "hoots mon" stuff ain't English like wot we speak.'

'I think we'll get going,' put in Dirk brusquely. 'Maggie, will you fly the return?' It was a surprise and her expression must have shown it, for he added, 'I've developed a head-ache.'

She put on her helmet and moved to the right-hand seat without a word. Getting permission from the tower for take-off in twenty minutes, they set about checking their route south to Hampton then started up. Maggie was concentrating on the checks and getting underway, so it was only when they were halfway into the flight that she really began to notice how oddly Dirk was responding. His words were sometimes so indistinct she had to ask him to repeat his navigation instructions, and he kept putting his hand up to his helmet as if the weight was too much for his neck to support.

'You all right?' she asked.

His head turned sluggishly. 'Uh?'

'What's wrong?'

'Bloody headache. Getting worse.'

Maggie spoke over the intercom. 'Dave, you can do your stuff for real. Anything in the first aid box for a bad headache?'

No sooner had she spoken than a terrible suspicion entered her mind. She had not been with him and Perry in the bar before lunch to witness what and how much Dirk had downed in that half-hour. A headache, slurred speech; surely he would not be so professionally irresponsible! She looked across at him again. He was pale and his eyes were closed.

'Here's a couple of aspirin,' said Dave, pushing through to the cockpit with a plastic cup of water. 'From my personal first aid supply. Best I can do.'

'Thanks.' Dirk took the cup, but dropped the tablets as he tried to swallow them. 'Oh, *hell!*'

'I've more in my bag.' Dave vanished then returned with them.

'You'd better shove them down his throat,' Maggie advised with a grimness not lost on the Scot.

'Okay by you?' Dave asked Dirk.

'Yeah . . . sure,' he replied sleepily, and opened his mouth.

Dave cast a frowning glance at Maggie before dropping the tablets in. Dirk drank, but much of the water ran down his chin, so Dave took the cup and glanced at Maggie once more.

She said, 'Lend a hand with the nav, will you? It'll be dark before too long and NVGs are hell with a headache.'

'We might make it before dark. With a clear sky like this visibility should be good.'

'I'd still like a hand with the nav.'

'Aye, of course. It'll be better than listening to Sandy's everlasting accounts of what they're doing at the model railway club.'

Maggie did not follow up on this popular ribbing of the hobby enthusiast. She was stiff with anger. She knew several pilots who regularly drank themselves into a stupor at night, but none who broke the rules when flying. Dirk would be finished when they got back to Hampton; she would make certain of that. Her reluctance to fly with him had been based on a sense of his pretentious disregard for anyone but himself, but she truly had not imagined he would go this far. If he had flown with a navigator as co-pilot today they could not have left Shawbury.

With Dave checking the vital navigation, and the man

beside her growing more and more disturbed by the pain in his head, Maggie thought feverishly of how best to deal with the situation and eventually came up with a solution that would spare her an interview with Jeffries. After his appalling lack of support this morning, Maggie had no confidence that he would take her seriously about anything. This way, the decision would have to be taken by others.

It was necessary to use night vision goggles for the final fifteen minutes, and everything then turned black and green which always took a moment or two to adjust to. Dirk mumbled something about not being able to see a bloody thing now, which heightened Maggie's fury. It was then she decided to contact Control and ask for an ambulance to be standing by when they landed. She told Dave her intention.

'For a . . . *headache?*'

'I won't mention any symptoms, just say he's very obviously unwell and needing attention.'

'Oh, aye,' said Dave with swift understanding.

The ambulance was there. Two paramedics came on board and were sworn at in a slurred voice by Dirk who told them they were overreacting. When he clambered from his seat his legs buckled, but he still insisted all he had was a monumental pain in his head. When asked for details, Maggie merely said that during the return flight it became evident that Flight Lieutenant Marshall was distinctly unwell. She thought the Medical Officer should check him over.

When the ambulance drove off, Dave asked, 'What d'you reckon is wrong?'

Maggie gave him a candid look. 'I'm sure you have as clear an idea as I have.'

His mouth twisted. 'I guess we won't be seeing him for a while.'

'That depends on what the MO reports to our revered boss.'

Dave grinned. 'You're a very canny woman.'

'Let's hope Pam Miles is, too.'

He fell in beside her as they walked from the aircraft. 'About that stupid claptrap concerning Griff's family all being seamen with superstitious natures . . . his brother is in the Army. I wish I'd reminded him of it in front of Jeffries.'

She smiled at the man who had become a friend after early personality clashes. 'I think it's time I moved on, Dave.'

'Don't let a bastard like him drive you away,' he said in protest.

'It's not him, it's . . . Things have changed. The team's not like it used to be.'

'No, I agree, but some of us are still together. Pity to break it up further.'

'My leaving won't make much difference. You'd get a guy in my place, and then you'd be all boys together. Much more enjoyable.'

Dave's dark eyes gleamed. 'If you're angling for a compliment, you'll not get one.'

She grinned. 'If I did you'd lose me, anyway. I'd drop dead from shock.'

In her room preparing for dinner, Maggie's anger returned. It had been a beast of a day, one way or another. Griff should have been smothered at birth; *she* should have bawled Randal out. The only good outcome would be that when Pam Miles contacted Jeffries with her findings, Dirk would not know what had hit him. She dressed swiftly, intending to opt for bed and a book after dinner.

In the corridor outside she met Pam, heading for the showers.

'Ah, Maggie! Glad I caught you before I go to my meeting. I'm sure you'd like to know news of your least favourite pilot. Good thing you recognised the signs and got him to the Medical Centre pronto.'

'Couldn't mistake them,' Maggie said sourly.

'Headache, blurred vision, loss of concentration – all pretty obvious,' Pam agreed, 'but not so easily diagnosed after a delay of forty-eight hours.'

Maggie stared. 'Sorry?'

'He must have thumped his head badly when he drove his car into the ditch. If he'd come to me right away I'd have grounded him until I was sure there was no concussion. He'll be kept under observation until I'm satisfied he's recovered from it. The poor lad couldn't have known what overtook him so suddenly today. You were marvellous to cope with it all and get him home.' She pushed open the bathroom door. 'Must dash: a get-together with the local doctors for a discussion on possible sea pollution levels this coming season. Can't have our personnel going down with sickness and fever, can I?' Before closing the door she added lightly, 'Your bonehead may get under your skin, but he's surprisingly biddable when he's not entirely *compos mentis*. Good-looking, isn't he? Like Tom Cruise, only bigger.'

Three

It caused Randal great satisfaction when Perry Newman had no choice but to pass him on the final check of his refresher. He now knew the causes of the man's problems. Through station gossip he learned that Perry was being bled financially dry by a vengeful ex-wife with three children under the age of eight; that he was one of those people who, through bad luck or unfavourable postings, had never been in a war or otherwise hostile situation offering a chance to earn distinction to attract those in high command. Lastly, Newman's young stepbrother had applied to fly helicopters and been told the RAF presently had their quota – the 'walking medical miracle' being one of them, of course. Randal was not surprised by the man's attitude but it annoyed him, because it had spread to Newman's cronies who lost no chance to make snide remarks.

If Perry was struggling with problems, so was Randal. Recovery in hospital wards had taken him from the service world he knew to another. He was finding it surprisingly difficult to put aside those long, desperate months in company with some patients whose lives had been irrevocably shattered, and ease himself back to the midst of healthy, active men and women who knew little of agony and despair. He felt something of a fish out of water; certainly no longer part of a team, as he had been with 646 Squadron.

Sex was the hot topic around the bar at the end of the day. There were a number of women in the Mess. As

53

Shawbury was the helicopter training centre for all three services there were also Army and Navy students to bring strong inter-service rivalry. If any man scored with a girl from another service there was a deal of bragging, and an exchange of insults on the macho superiority of the victor and the uniform he wore. In the past, Randal would have joined in with gusto. Not now.

His private life was a mess. His marriage was over, but his injuries had put it on hold. Now he was back on his feet he supposed he should instruct a solicitor to get divorce proceedings under way. Then there was Maggie. Seeing her last week had unsettled him badly. When she had every justification for bawling him out she had not, yet he was sure she had not yet recognised the true nature of their relationship, as he had a year ago. Memories of Mark Hascham must still be preventing her from seeing him as anything other than her former boss.

Therein lay the root of Randal's restlessness. Talking to her had intensified his yearning to be back with an operational squadron. After his accident he had made the usual bargains with God. *If you let me walk I'll never ask for anything again.* He walked. Then it was: *If you let me fly I'll lead a blameless life.* He was flying. Now he wanted more, but he had the decency not to ask for bargains. He had not kept his side of them. A week later, however, it appeared that the Almighty had been working overtime on his behalf.

An encounter in the bar with a navigator he had met on a night-flying exercise, who was just passing through, gave him great food for thought.

'You heard about Andy Forbes, I suppose.'

'What about him?'

'His new baby's got some rare condition that means it'll never be normal; needs constant attention. Teresa took a bit of a beating giving birth and has to stay in hospital for a while. Her mother's looking after their three-year-old, but she can't stay on much longer. Andy's asked for a transfer. Wants to stay in one place, have regular hours. So Six Four Six is looking for a flight commander again. Not sure anyone'll be keen to apply. Seems to invite bad luck. First you, then him.'

An hour later Randal put through a call to Group Captain Mark Grainger, who he had flown, badly hurt, to safety during the Gulf War. Randal had earned an AFC and Mark's eternal gratitude. They were also friends, and what were friends for when they happened to be in a position to give you a helping hand? Mark was happy to give it. So, instead of learning to be an instructor, Randal began a Chinook refresher course prior to taking up his old job as commander of B Flight, 646 Squadron. Perry Newman was hopping mad, with justification. Randal Price was over the moon, with the double satisfaction of knowing he had for once done what Perry accused him of.

It was just past noon when Randal drove through Hampton Heyhoe and on to the long straight stretch beyond, with low cliffs running parallel to the road and the sea stretching smoothly to the horizon. He pulled up and walked to look down on the beach, suddenly choked. He would soon be thirty-six. He had met Fiona just after 646 Squadron came to Hampton from Germany. Crazy for her, he had married her within six months. He had fathered two wonderful children and loved them dearly. He and Fiona had quarrelled and made up; quarrelled and made up. She had lived here for a while, then left him to return to her indulgent parents. Randal had bought her back with a luxury home and a promise not to involve her in RAF activities. They had quarrelled and not made up. He had been driving home after an exercise in Poland, knowing his love for his wife had been more of an obsession blind to her selfishness but planning to compromise for the sakes of Lydia and Neil, when a rusty anchor had dropped on his car.

All that had been while he was based here. Seven years of his life! Turbulent years. He had discounted the memories it would invoke when he applied to return. He had also discounted the fact that Maggie, whom he had grown to love, was here. The reality of this familiar area brought home to him the truth that he could not turn back the clock. Gazing across the sea over which he had flown so many times he knew a sharp sense of loss. Then he remembered his fellow patients who had no hope of recovery, and those few with head injuries who had lost all knowledge of themselves and needed everything done for them. Poor devils! He made a fresh bargain, this time with his own body. *If you can take the strain I'll make the next seven years more rewarding than the last seven. I'm dependent on you.* He went back to the car and drove on.

Randal did not know Martin Ashe, the Station Commander, but the man knew all about him and gave him a warm welcome. 'You wouldn't be here if there were any doubts about your ability,' he replied to Randal's swift assurance that he was fully fit. 'I've been warned that your determination amounts to obstinacy in certain instances, and I guess you used it to good account at Headley Court. Those of your old team who are still with Six Four Six are doubtless familiar with your other vices. I shall have to discover them, although I've heard dark rumours.'

Randal grinned. 'From Group Captain Grainger?'

'And others. Your career hasn't exactly been a copybook one.' He smiled. 'Thank God. I can't abide men with such neat and tidy minds they can never see the wood amongst the trees. I'm sorry to be losing Andy Forbes, but you'll fill his shoes and demand a larger size, if what I hear about you is true.'

After this pleasant interview Randal went to see Gerard Jeffries. He did not think of it as an interview; they had worked together before and crossed swords on many occasions. The Squadron Commander's office was as stuffy as always, his desk laden with files, reports and memos to demonstrate how overworked he was.

'Hello again, Boss,' said Randal, offering his hand.

Jeffries struggled to his feet to clasp it. 'The bad penny, eh? How are you, man?'

He had always refused to call his flight commander Rip like everyone else on the station, in case it suggested he shared the general liking for him. Nothing has changed, thought Randal, studying Jeffries' thin features and crisp black hair, but 'man' was better than Perry's 'wonderboy'.

'It's great to be back, although I'm sorry for Andy and Teresa – tragic about the baby. Being an instructor will suit his situation better. He'll be on hand to give her the support she'll need.'

'Yes.' Jeffries sat and waved a hand towards another chair. 'Look . . . er . . . man, I'm well aware of *your* situation and I'm prepared to shoulder some of the burden. The admin side can be left to me; you'll have enough to do to cope with the flying.' His black eyes narrowed. 'Are you quite sure you're up to it?'

Fighting to control his rising anger, Randal said crisply, 'I wasn't brain damaged, you know; just couldn't move my legs for a while. Now I can, and my brain's working as well as it ever did. That's why a medical board passed me fit to take up where I was forced to leave off.' He pressed on as Jeffries made to speak. 'Maggie said there are some recent changes in the old team.'

The other man picked up on that. 'Oh, you've been seeing her, have you?'

'You sent her to Shawbury last month with one of the new boys.'

'Ah, yes.' He sighed. 'A disastrous day. Dirk Marshall succumbed to delayed concussion on the flight back. He

57

was out of action for three days. I've had to deliver another lecture about keeping fit. There's too much time lost through careless behaviour.'

'A man can't wilfully give himself concussion, surely.'

'He can by getting so drunk he drives into a ditch. I trust you've improved on that score since your accident.'

'I wasn't drunk; an anchor was dropped on me. Perhaps no one gave you the details at the time.'

Jeffries' mouth tightened. 'I was merely commenting on your past habit of spending a lot of time at the bar at the end of the day rather than toning up on the squash courts.'

'Oh, *that.* No, I haven't improved on that score,' Randal said with a happy smile. 'Got a lot of drinking time to catch up on.'

'Maggie's applied for a transfer.'

It jolted him, as intended. Jeffries had always hinted at a more than professional interest from Randal in the Flight's only woman pilot. He tried to sound casual. 'Oh, when was this?'

'After you met her at Shawbury.'

He acknowledged a point to Jeffries. 'Has she got it?'

'Not yet. She hasn't the influential friends you have. I approved it, though.'

You bloody would, thought Randal. You've never been happy having her in the team, no matter that she's as good as any of the men. He changed the subject. 'Who else is new since I left?'

They talked for a while about six replacements to the original team, the initial skirmishing over. Jeffries appeared happy enough with them, while continuing to ride his old hobby horse about hands holding rackets rather than pint glasses during off-duty time. Randal longed to remind him that he had twice broken his wrist playing squash, but the rest of them had never done it lifting a beer glass. He resisted the urge. It would go over Jeffries' head, anyway.

They parted after thirty minutes, with the honours more or less even and Jeffries lying in his teeth as he said, 'It's good to have you back, man.'

'Thanks. I never thought I'd manage it,' Randal replied, adding mentally, *I bet you prayed I wouldn't, chum.* As he left the office, he said brightly, 'I'll be on the job in the morning tackling the admin and the flying, as before. You have enough to do coping with all that on your desk.'

He was thoughtful as he drove around the perimeter. Jeffries had made much of Dirk Marshall's sporting success and his impressive tally of hours in Chinooks, yet Randal had heard gossip about the man during his refresher course at Marshall's former squadron, and it was not all good. He had apparently made errors of judgement and hit the bottle quite seriously after the crash that had killed his friend and a crewman. He had been grounded for a while, then cleared by the MO to fly again. There were hints that his relationship with the dead pilot's widow had been rather too friendly before the crash. There was no proof, but a close threesome like theirs soon became a close twosome when one man was out of the country. It happened all the time. Marshall had been wonderfully supportive to the widow and her small boy, and it had been widely expected that they would eventually marry. He had applied for a transfer to get her away from unhappy memories, but the widow had had other ideas. She took a job with a travel agent in her home town of Bristol and moved there two days after Marshall joined 646. According to several of the station wives, the volatile Paula wanted no more of RAF life . . . or the man who had lost out when she had married his friend.

Add to all that the news that Marshall had driven into a ditch while totally plastered, then collapsed with concussion while flying with Maggie, and it seemed to Randal he had inherited a problem. He had also been lumbered with the sergeant who refused to fly with a woman. Jeffries had said nothing of it, of course, but Randal knew how to deal with that. It was Marshall he was more concerned about. Maggie had wanted to move vehicles for the Army to avoid the man, and he could well understand why, now he was more informed. Had she asked for a transfer because of Marshall?

Maggie herself was an altogether different problem, one he was unable to solve because it was beyond his previous experience and out of his hands. He had severed contact with her because, with masculine lack of subtlety, it had seemed the only thing to do. Maybe it was all to the good that she would not be staying at Hampton. Out of sight, out of mind . . . perhaps!

Parking outside the Medical Centre, Randal went in for the regulation chat with the MO. He was taken aback to discover that Squadron Leader Miles was a woman; a redhead, very easy on the eye with a soft Cornish burr in her voice. He hesitated in the doorway. Still, he was not there for an examination.

She glanced up and smiled. 'Hello. Welcome back to Hampton. Come in and shut the door. When you were here before, Jim Prior would have been the MO. Nice man. I hope you'll regard me in the same light.'

'That'll be impossible,' he said with an appreciative grin.

'Please keep comments like that for the Mess. In this surgery I'm the doctor and you're the patient.' Her equable tone robbed her words of any suggestion of ma'amishness. 'Take a seat. I'd like to run through a few points with you.' She consulted his medical notes. 'You're a fascinating change from the usual run of men I get in here.'

'Shouldn't you keep that comment for the Mess?'

Her head came up quickly, and she gave a rueful smile. 'Your reputation came ahead of you, so I should have been prepared for that. I suppose you've had a lot of practice in dealing with bossy female practitioners.'

'I wouldn't call you particularly bossy. Just a normal woman.'

She tried unsuccessfully to smother the smile, and instead studied the wad of medical data in his file as she questioned him on the report from the medical board. 'They concluded that the stresses of an operational squadron might be too much for you, so what are you doing here?'

'I'm going to prove them wrong. They gave me a sixty per cent chance of walking. It became a hundred per cent. They said it was unlikely I'd be fit enough to fly. I've been doing it since January. They make mistakes.'

Her amber-coloured eyes studied him frankly. 'You've a very high opinion of your capabilities.'

'If I didn't have, I should keep out of a cockpit. You can't shilly-shally around when you're flying more than twenty tons of aeroplane. If you're not absolutely sure of yourself, stay on the ground.'

'Well, I hope you'll be sensible enough to admit it if you do find things too stressful.'

Randal was starting to grow irritated. He had been cleared by a five-member medical board, but she was turning this introductory chat into an in-depth consultation on his fitness. 'What I found impossible to bear was being paralysed from the chest down and having my bodily functions regulated by machines,' he told her harshly. 'How can returning to normal prove too stressful?'

She treated his outburst with continuing calmness. 'I take your point. So everything's back to normal now, is it?'

'Yes, I'm your all-singing, all-dancing working pilot again.'

'And no longer impotent?'

'*What?*' he choked.

'Mmm, I see! It's usually the longest-lasting problem in cases like yours,' she said soothingly. 'I'm sure they warned you it could be permanent. One can never tell, I'm afraid, but there are drugs to alleviate the condition and I'll be happy to prescribe them for you. You're a young man, and—'

He got to his feet, silencing her. 'You're here to keep personnel fit enough to do their job, and I've told you I can do mine. My sex life is my own bloody affair. Keep out of it!'

He slammed her door behind him, got in the Porsche and gave it maximum acceleration to relieve his sense of humiliation over the one bargain God had failed to fulfil.

When he entered the Briefing Room next morning Randal was greeted with a cheer from five of the men present, which made him momentarily emotional with its suggestion that he had, after all, turned back the clock. He covered it by saying, 'You won't cheer when you hear what I've got lined up for you.' Then he added with sincerity, 'Thanks, guys, it's great to be back.' He could not possibly express fully to them how it felt to take up the life he loved after a year of battling desperately against his own body. Instead, he took a few minutes to reacquaint himself with those of his old team who were present.

'Pete, how are Jill and Arnie?'

The navigator whose unexpected marriage to the flighty traffic controller had been brought about by mutual ador-ation of a Great Dane puppy, said, 'Both doing fine. Jill gave him a party on his birthday. I missed it, but she saved some cake for me.'

Randal shook his head, laughing. 'I worry about you two.' He turned to the other navigator. 'How's your glamorous grannie, Chris? Any free tickets for West End first nights being offered?'

'Nah, only for strip joints in Soho,' joked Pete.

'The Larry Olivier awards are coming up soon. I might wheedle some out of her for that. All those starlets with their boobs falling out, eager to do anything for any man who promises to mention her to a producer he knows! Still, as Gran insists that I only invite "nice young men" that rules out everyone in this room.'

After the predictable jeer Randal continued. 'Jimmy, congrats on the baby last summer. Heard the news on the grapevine. Are you planning to round off the half-dozen this summer?'

The father of five merely grinned through comments such as: 'Don't know how he finds the time' . . . 'Or the energy' . . . 'Ought to be past it at his age' . . . 'I've been told half of them resemble the guy who delivers pizzas.'

Randal smiled at Dave and Sandy sitting together. 'Has the model railway club finished that mock-up of the ancient Tibetan line yet?'

There was another jeer as Sandy admitted they had had some setbacks because of dicey modelling clay, then Randal asked Dave if he had yet got his leg over anything but the saddle of his Harley Davidson. The imaginative responses to that proved the lads were still on top form, and Dave took it all with his usual Highland aplomb.

Randal then met the two newest members of the team, but he did not immediately warm to either of them. Ted Griffin was tough-visaged and built the same way. He had bright red hair, hard green eyes and an uncompromising manner. Not a type one would care to encounter in a dark alley when he had been drinking. Yet his record showed that he had done very well on the Air Loadmasters' course, so he could apparently adapt to discipline. His response to Randal was nevertheless wary.

Dirk Marshall was almost Griff's opposite. Well-built, certainly, but with an elegance more suited to a dancer than an Olympic athlete. He was well-spoken and assured, and that corny description 'tall, dark and handsome' was tailor-made for him. So what had the man done to make his friend's widow run from him?

'I was charged to give you umpteen messages from your old squadron,' Randal told him, 'but they're far too vulgar for this lot's sensitive ears so I'll see you later.'

Against yet another vocal expression of team solidarity, he told them all to calm down and get to work. 'We've had two bids for our services today, rivalling each other for total lack of appeal. I believe the Flight moved some vehicles for the Army last month. They now want half of them back where they were.'

This was met with a groan, and spirited cries from Chris and Griff that they had done it last time. 'Why can't the Army move the bloody things?' moaned Chris.

'They're running an exercise.'

'*Again?*'

'What would they do with themselves otherwise?' muttered Sandy.

'Okay,' said Randal. 'Dirk, Pete, Sandy and Jimmy can take that on. Chris, you, Dave and Griff will help me collect and place on site three empty metal drums at an MoD establishment near Weymouth.'

'I don't believe it,' wailed Chris. 'I volunteer for the other after all.'

'I warned you it was one of those days. The drums can't be dealt with any other way because the space between existing buildings is too narrow to admit them. After scratching their heads for several days the boffins thought of us.'

Jimmy snorted. 'Why does everyone think of us only when they've got themselves in an unholy mess?'

'Because no one but us can get them out of it,' said Randal, the grumbles and moans sounding sweetly familiar to him. 'Dirk, you're programmed for ten hundred. We go half an hour later.'

Preparations for the two tasks got under way. The discussion on routing, weather conditions, wind patterns, and how they would best lift three circular slung loads increased

Randal's sensation of being eighteen months back in time. Adrenalin flowed joyously through him.

The first Chinook took off on schedule, but as Randal and his crew were preparing to walk out to theirs Gerard Jeffries burst in looking deeply worried.

Randal frowned. 'Something wrong, Boss?'

When it came to emergencies Jeffries was very much on the ball. Not for nothing had he been decorated during the Falklands War. 'I have clearance to divert an aircraft to assist at an incident near Coventry involving two trains.'

Chris, Dave and Griff moved up to join their pilot, despondency over the MoD drums changing to eager alertness. Randal asked how much detail they had been given, and Jeffries smoothed out the chart to circle with his finger the relevant area.

'The trains were heading in the same direction when they ran into each other where both tracks merge at this junction *here*.' He jabbed the spot hard as his dark eyes bored up into Randal's slightly lighter ones. 'It's one of those impossible catastrophes that somehow happen.'

Randal turned cold. He still had occasional nightmares about waking up and finding he was attached to machines, unable to move. 'When did it happen?'

'About an hour ago.' Jeffries straightened. 'The trains are jammed in a cutting surrounded by fields. One carriage has ploughed into a small bridge, cutting off access by road from either direction. But it's only a minor road and, in any case, two fields away from the railway. The only way to reach it at the moment is from the air. That's why we've been called on.'

'It sounds like one hell of a situation. Many on the trains, did they say?'

'Didn't have to. One was a crowded commuter service, the other a football special crammed to the hilt with fans going up for the big match this afternoon.'

'Christ!' breathed Randal, thinking of the casualty rate.

'You'll only get full appreciation of the problems when you're there, man. We've been asked to evacuate the uninjured and maybe some walking wounded. Police and rescue services are desperate to get survivors away so they can reach those trapped in the wreckage. I guess it's utter chaos there right now.' He sighed heavily. 'Pity this didn't come in before Dirk took off. I thought about getting him re-routed, but it's too tricky for mid-air briefing. The only other alternative is to send the standby crew from A Flight, but they're on call for purely military emergencies so a swap-over would present you with the same problem.'

'Which is?' asked Randal, unwilling to believe what he was hearing.

'You could be faced with something equally demanding and more politically vital. My hands are tied. You'll *have* to take this on, I'm afraid.'

Randal was uncharacteristically silenced as he watched Jeffries leave. The man had just indicated to the crew that he did not think their pilot and flight commander was capable of doing his job. It was the basest act of personal and professional dislike Jeffries had ever committed during their relationship, and it left an embarrassed hiatus in its wake. For once, Randal's quick temper did not flare. The show of disloyalty cut too deep for a mere burst of anger. He took a few moments to recover before turning to his stony-faced crew.

'Dave, round up a couple of extras to help in the cabin for this.'

After reworking their flight plan they took off and headed north-east, exchanging only necessary navigation and hazard warning comments over the intercom, while taking in the information coming in over various radio frequencies. The morning had started out fine with weak sunshine, but cloud built as they crossed Wiltshire. The Met report forecast rain over the Coventry area by thirteen hundred, which would further hamper rescuers trying to pull people from the wreckage.

Randal remembered driving beneath a bridge on a glorious October late afternoon when stars were faintly visible in the darkening sky, then hurtling into the fiery red sunset before it was suddenly extinguished. His rescuers would not have been hampered by rain as they pulled him free of his mangled car.

'. . . church steeple!'

He came from his reverie as Chris's urgent voice sounded in his ears, and he automatically veered away from a country church on rising ground dead ahead.

'Sorry, Chris, my intercom lead must be on the blink.'

'Along with your forward vision?' Chris darted a glance across the cockpit. 'Everything okay?'

Randal's temper did flare now. 'I don't need a bloody nursemaid.'

'Fine. Fine.'

He began to wonder if they were all watching him, doubting his ability. Did they share Jeffries' opinion? Or Perry Newman's? That cocksure, red-headed MO believed operational flying would prove too stressful. The medical board report had put that same belief into words. A little gentle instructing would instead be within his capability. Had that warm welcome from his former colleagues been forced? Did no one but himself believe he was fit for the job he had twisted Mark Grainger's arm to get? All right, so his thoughts had wandered for a moment. It happened to everyone now and again, and there were three others to warn of obstacles . . . not that he would have flown into the church steeple. Chris had overreacted. Did that mean he was nervous about this flight?

Randal shook himself mentally. He must regard this as

just another task and shut his mind to the human element. He had let himself identify with people who had caught a train this morning and were destined to wake to find machines keeping alive an inert body, their futures shattered in an instant. His job was to help those who had survived; move them away from this nightmare. Concentrate on that!

Information continued to reach them over the airwaves, warning them what to expect. Ambulances and police vehicles were being impeded by cars which ghoulish onlookers had left in the narrow lanes while they tramped over fields to gawp at tragedy for entertainment.

'What is it with people like that?' Chris growled.

Randal's thoughts wandered again, this time to memories of the spectacular death of a Harrier pilot at an air show. A talented young man rejoicing over being selected to fly with the Red Arrows had lost his future in a ball of flame, and spectators had fought each other to get the best view of his funeral pyre while Maggie, who loved him, had stood paralysed with shock beside her helpless colleagues.

'Yes, I can see the bloody radar mast, Chris,' he snapped, pushing away that visual memory. 'No need to bawl the info in my ear.'

'Just checking,' soothed the man beside him. 'Passes the time.'

'If you've got nothing to do, get an okay on our route. The air space around the crash'll be humming with aircraft of every size and shape. They're the only means of access. And you can bet the media slugs'll be fouling everything up while they record death for the front pages.'

Chris was told they had priority clearance, which upheld their belief that non-casualties were hampering recovery of the injured and the dying.

Randal discussed with his crew their probable routine on arrival. 'We'll put down in the best available spot to give unimpeded passage from the rail cutting. I don't believe anyone'll be marshalling the operation yet; it's too soon to get that organised. The poor buggers called in to these accidents never know where to start . . . And here comes the bloody rain an hour earlier than forecast,' he added, as it began beating against the windows.

Hampton called them up with the news that an emergency reception centre would be set up in the gymnasium of a private school set back from a main road. All uninjured passengers would be dealt with there. A large playing field adjacent to the school buildings was ideal for them to land and offload the people. Chris marked the grid reference for the school on the chart on his knees.

'What d'you bet we arrive to find no one there but kids in posh blazers?' he commented to Randal. 'It takes hours to set up something like that.'

'Yeah, but it might take us hours to set up our side of it. These people aren't going to be queueing in neat lines to file on board.'

For the last ten minutes they had been overflying one railtrack running through a cutting, and watching for the other which ran in from the west to the junction three hundred yards before the bridge that had been destroyed. Open country lay in every direction with farms, rural communities and a network of narrow roads, but the haze of rain reduced their distant vision so that the low range of hills five miles to the east was no more than a dark, looming shadow.

'No problem finding somewhere to land,' mused Griff from his place at the rear of the cabin. 'Take your pick. Fields, fields, and more . . . Oh Christ, just look at that!'

Randal had already spotted evidence in the grey distance of the mammoth pile-up, both in the cutting and spewing over the banks on either side. His blood ran cold once more as he visualised the trains converging to be crushed into each other as forward momentum drove them inexorably through a gap that could not contain them. Closing on the area he gradually took in the full scale of the disaster. Wreckage was jammed solid between the low banks, making it surely impossible to reach trapped passengers until cranes had lifted some of it. The leading carriage of one train was embedded in the stone arch of a bridge; another stood on end against a bank smothered in wood, broken seats and chunks of metal. Most of the rolling stock was practically unidentifiable as such. People were thick on the ground and looked to be milling around aimlessly. In the surrounding fields stood police and rescue helicopters, along with several marked as media aircraft.

To his silent crew Randal said grimly, 'Let's get down there and do what we can. I'm going for that field beyond the ploughed one. We'll have to get people across the mud to load them, but it'll leave the immediate vicinity clear for the rescue operations. They'll need more help than they've got, so I guess aircraft will be flying in all the time. However do they make a start on something like this? We'll search out the senior guy on the ground and work with him, so he'll know what we're doing.'

He circled the area, and his crewmen talked him down to the wet meadow some fifty yards from a five-barred gate. When they climbed out rain beat in their faces as they walked against a chilly wind towards the railway. As they drew nearer, the chaos they had seen from above became more starkly real when sounds were added – screams, shouts, hysterical sobbing and . . . *singing?*

Halfway across the ploughed field they found survivors standing oblivious of the rain and staring blankly in the direction of the cutting. There were others, mostly women, crying uncontrollably or sitting hugging their knees tightly while rocking back and forth. Several policewomen moved among them offering comfort in vain. A few men in city suits were standing hunch-shouldered amid human suffering, talking into mobile phones (I'll be late in. Train's delayed!), and some yards from them grouped youths were singing a rousing football supporters' chorus. Shock affects people in varied ways.

Randal and his supplemented crew drew near enough to appreciate the scale of the problems facing rescue teams. Beside ambulance helicopters paramedics were dealing with minor cuts and wounds; police in yellow jackets were dragging people away from the wreckage at the top of the bank, only for them to run back the moment they were released, in their desperation to reach friends or loved ones buried somewhere in the cutting. Not only were they endangering themselves they were hampering the limited number of officers trying to marshal all survivors to a safe distance.

Randal lost awareness of anything save the appalling sight before him. Stretching away into the dreary distance lay a carpet of splintered wood, smashed glass, twisted metal, torn and crushed seating, carriage wheels, washbasins and lavatory pans. This was festooned with soggy sheets of paper spilling from briefcases, ripped holdalls, women's handbags, plastic cups and sandwiches from the buffet car, and football scarves galore. Staring into the cutting where he could hear moans and sobbing from within the compressed coaches, Randal's gaze was caught by a small patch of grass showing between the destruction where a cluster of primroses had survived untouched. They somehow made the horror of the rest almost more than he could accept. How many people down there would never see primroses again? How many had hurtled into that same blackness he had experienced? How many would waken to wish they had not?

Chris materialised before him, also an ashen-faced man in a yellow coat. Coming from his old nightmare, Randal simply stared at them.

'You're the pilot?' asked the man in a voice roughened by shouting.

It was an effort to respond. 'That's right.'

'Well, you see the situation. We've more men on their way – police and fire service – and lifting gear is coming up the line. Can't do much until it arrives.' He glanced back at the cutting. 'God knows how many are under that. No passenger lists for trains.'

Seeing the man's exhaustion, Randal forced his brain into work mode. 'I was told you want us to move out the non-casualties so you can concentrate on the rescue. A reception centre is being set up at Linwood School. From there I imagine your people will contact relatives and check out anyone known to be still in the trains.'

'Both of them were packed,' the police officer said heavily. 'There were hundreds on the football special. We've had a tough time restraining lads trying to pull their mates out. They've no idea of the danger if they start moving anything.' He shook his head. 'I've not seen anything as bad as this in all my years.'

'The first thing to do is to shift to the far side of this field everyone we've to fly to the school. We have seats for thirty, and we can start a shuttle service as soon as your men get going on a bit of one-man-and-his-dog activity. We'll give you a hand with that, then take over from there.' Wiping rain from his face, Randal nodded to where press photographers and TV cameramen were recording the catastrophe on film. 'Aren't you going to kick that lot out?'

'We'll shift them when they get in our way. They've got a job to do. You're a godsend right now. We've been promised more helicopters, but they're coming some distance and won't arrive until mid-afternoon. They'll not take as many as you can, and we'll have casualties piling up soon, so whatever you do will be invaluable. Just getting people grouped by your aircraft should be enough to calm them; make them feel something is being done. Let's get going.'

The RAF men crossed to join a body of men and women

who were strung out in a line trying to stop the football fans from approaching the bank. Some of the youths were on the verge of hysteria, and Randal there and then decided to fly them out first. The stunned and silent, and even the quietly sobbing, were less of a problem than overexcited young men trying to be heroes. He said as much to Chris, who agreed.

Slowly, patiently the police persuaded the agitated and distressed survivors to leave their friends and relatives to experts trained in rescue skills.

'Please go across to the big helicopter in the next field. The crew will fly you all to a centre where police staff will contact your families and help you in any way they can. Please clear this area. Please move away so we can start to search the wreckage. Yes, your families will be notified of your safety. Please go across to the aircraft in the next field.'

Repeating these phrases, the cordon of police finally got through to the shocked senses of everyone who had managed to crawl from the rear carriages physically unharmed. The Chinook provided a focal point to rally to; a means of taking them away from horror to a place where they could telephone anxious relatives. Ahead of the yellow-coated line they moved over the ploughed furrows now turned to mud by the relentless downpour, very much like a flock of sheep being rounded up by dogs. Only then did Randal grow aware of just how many they had to deal with.

He turned to Chris as they trudged towards the Chinook. 'I offered to fly a shuttle service, but we'll be working flat out at this rate. There're a few hundred here to shift.'

'And we'll have to go into Coventry for fuel.' Chris was silent for a moment. 'Still, I'd rather be doing this than what those poor devils will have to face when they start digging. How the hell could it have happened?'

'Mechanical or electrical failure, human error. Same

reasons aircraft crash. Mankind has invented its own catastrophes. When the horse was the only means of transport
the worst that could happen was you got thrown.'

'That can kill you.'

'Safest to walk, then.'

They reached the gate leading to the meadow and indicated that their potential passengers should remain on the
other side of it. While police officers continued to reassure,
Randal discussed with his men their best plan of action.

'I feel it's best to ship out the more volatile ones first, yet
I'm not happy about an entire load of teenage football fans.
Some of them are *too* volatile. They might treat the flight as
a macho adventure and cause problems. Any input?'

'It's only a short hop to the school,' Chris pointed out.
'Let's get them there and hand them over – if anyone's
actually set up the reception centre yet.'

'I agree,' said Griff. 'Any one of them tries anything, I'll
sort him.'

Randal glared. 'This is a rescue mission. They're all
scared and badly shaken. None of us is going to "sort"
anyone.'

Dave spoke up. 'Some of these people might seem docile
enough but they could be in deep shock. Once aboard they
could panic. They've just crawled from one travelling tube;
being shut inside another could set them off.'

'Good point, Dave,' Randal agreed. 'You're the expert
on the medical aspect. So we take them first and leave
the lads?'

'Why not half and half?' suggested one of the volunteer
sergeants. 'Get the youngsters to keep an eye on the rest.
It'll concentrate their minds on helping, which they were
desperate to do back there.'

'Dave?' asked Randal.

'Aye, sounds good.'

'Right.' He beckoned and one of the policewomen came

over. 'It's now midday. This is going to take most of the afternoon unless we get help fairly soon. These people are going to become soaked to the skin. Any chance of you organising oilskins or a batch of those coats you're wearing?'

She looked too delicate for the work she was doing, but there was total confidence in her manner. 'We've blankets here, but they'd get wet through and we need them for casualties. Tents are being flown in with field hospital equipment and a team of doctors. Once we begin pulling people from the wreckage, on-the-spot intensive care will be needed.' Her pale blue eyes clouded momentarily. 'We were unprepared for anything on this scale. I'm afraid people getting wet is the least of our concerns.'

He put his hand on her shoulder. 'Sorry, didn't think. Will several of your lot stay with them while we go back and forth? My crew will sort each group, get them aboard and strapped in, then check them in at the other end. Keep them all behind the fence. The downwash from our rotors is fierce.' He began turning away. 'We'll shift them as fast as we can.'

Dave, Griff and the extra men organised the boarding of the first thirty passengers while Randal and Chris started up for take-off. Visibility was poor, so although it was little more than a gigantic hop across country, Randal climbed above the height of any wires and cables. Dave and Griff would have their work cut out watching for any in the vicinity of the school. By the time they had done two or three runs they would all be familiar with the terrain and its obstacles. So, while the volunteers wrote down the names and addresses of survivors on board, the B Flight crewmen were noting details of everything they passed.

'Chris, get on to Hampton and fill them in on the situation,' said Randal. 'Then contact Coventry. Tell them we'll need priority clearance to refuel at around thirteen

75

thirty. Ask if they have any info on the other helicopters on their way.'

'Will do.'

The open fields gave way to small estates of red brick houses, shops and factory buildings. A river wound through the minor town; there were a number of leisure boats tied up along its banks. The streets were filled with moving cars. At the school to which they were heading the pupils would be following their regular curriculum. Life was going on as usual here, while for anyone who caught either of those trains this morning it would never be the same, Randal thought yet again. People had continued to drive along the motorway chatting, listening to music, thinking about sex, while he lay on the brink of death in the tangled metal of his car. The whole world did not stand still in tragedy; just individual worlds hung in the balance.

'There's the school.'

He pulled himself together. 'Got it, Chris. There are a couple of police vans on the gravel, guys, so I guess they're already in business. Once we're down, get them all off and across to the school buildings. They'll hear us arrive and come out to meet you. When you've handed over to them one copy of the names and addresses, get back here fast. The weather isn't going to improve and I want to make the turnarounds as speedy as possible.'

He had a good crew, so they made two more trips before heading for Coventry airport to refuel, grab something to eat and down some hot drinks. The two officers had dried off fairly well in the cockpit, but the crewmen had been in and out of the rain at both ends of each trip. They took the opportunity to change into dry clothes from their emergency bags and stood around the radiators in the busy snack bar.

Randal asked for news of the relief helicopters and was told that two had refuelled and just taken off for the scene of the disaster. Two more were due to arrive within the hour.

Normal flights in and out of the city airport were badly disrupted – some being diverted – because of the heavy additional air traffic likely to continue all night and next day. Drinking his third mug of coffee as he walked up and down to stretch his legs, Randal's thoughts returned to the overwhelming human disaster and that clump of primroses. When he had woken after his crash there had been banks of bleeping machines, a bag of blood slowly dripping into his vein, and a vice clamped on his head. Nothing to explain the terror it brought; nothing to indicate what had happened. No primroses.

'You okay, Rip?'

He turned in a daze. 'Eh?'

Chris looked concerned. 'Everything all right?'

'Everything's bloody fine.' He stopped and challenged the man. 'Come on, say it! Put it into words. You don't think I'm up to the job, do you? Like Jeffries. Like every-bloody-one else. You're watching my every move, my every sodding breath, waiting for me to crack up.'

Frowning, Chris said, 'If I shared Jeffries' opinion nothing would have got me into the cockpit with you. If *you* shared it you'd never have asked to return to Six Four Six. You won't crack up. You're the steadiest man in the air I've ever flown with. But, yes, I'm checking on you. For two reasons. This is a demanding task and you've no second pilot to take on some of the flying . . . and seeing that appalling pile-up must be even more disturbing for you than for the rest of us. It's my job as your Nav to give you every assistance. Playing nursemaid is part of it, whatever the circumstances.'

Letting out his breath slowly, Randal said, 'Yes, sorry. You're right, it has resurrected memories. Not of lying trapped and in pain. That part's a complete blank, but it's as though I'm now seeing the other side of it, seeing the rescue I knew nothing of at the time. Some of those poor devils in the train were conscious and crying for help. That's what got to me.' He forced a smile. 'It's good to bring it in the open. Thanks.'

'Any time. We're a team, remember.'

Putting his mug on a nearby table, Randal said, 'Let's get the team back on the road, then.'

When they returned to the disaster scene more help had arrived. Several large tents had been set up, and the wreckage appeared to be swarming with an army of yellow-coated men armed with cutting equipment. Arc lights were being positioned ready to continue into the night, and a large mobile canteen was now in operation. Over in the meadow a Sikorsky rescue helicopter was loading people for the reception centre, and the number still waiting had been somewhat reduced. Waterproof ponchos had been distributed and they had been given hot drinks.

Chris was delighted. 'The other aircraft must be already at the school so, with their help, we'll be able to clear the rest away in no time.'

Randal nodded. 'We'll have to work in relay with them so that we all know what we're doing. The school staff'll go crazy with the noise of three of us coming and going.'

'But I bet it's the kids' most exciting day ever.'

After a conference with the pilot on the ground and with his colleague just arriving at the school, a flight plan was agreed by all three. It went without a hitch through deteriorating weather as the afternoon progressed. By now able to concentrate on the job by keeping in constant radio communication with the pair of smaller aircraft, the haunting memories faded to the recesses of Randal's mind.

The Chinook undertook the final run because the huge helicopter could carry the remaining twenty-eight. When they eventually set down Randal left his seat to express his regret over the survivors' long wait, thanked them for their patience, and told them they would be given a hot meal at the school along with any help they needed. They gazed at him wordlessly. Reality had not yet sunk in for them. It probably would not until they reached their homes and watched TV pictures of their ordeal. Then it would hit them with a vengeance. Randal was thankful he had not seen the mangled wreck of his Porsche.

Their job finished, they were invited to join the other crews for tea and hearty sandwiches in the school staffroom. His four crewmen looked wet and weary, but Randal was amused to see them soon chatting up the younger female teachers. Aircrew never could resist a pretty, admiring girl. Before long he dragged them away because they had to refuel before reaching Hampton. He telephoned Ops to report the situation and requested a stop at RAF Lyneham for a 'hot' refuel with engines running. He then thanked the headmaster for his tea, and rounded up his crew.

On their way from the school building they were suddenly confronted by a group of boys in grey shorts and red blazers. They pushed forward one of their number and stood waiting. Despite his heightened colour, the boy's dark eyes gazed up unabashed.

'Excuse me, gentlemen, but did you come in one of those helicopters?' he asked in an ultra-polite upper-class voice.

'Yes, the big one,' said Randal.

'Are you the pilot, sir? There are wings on your suit.'

'That's right.'

'Go on, *ask*,' hissed the boy behind him.

'In that case . . .' He cast a nervous glance at his friends. 'In that case, I'd like to ask if we could have a look – go inside.'

Randal squatted to the lad's level and said gently, 'This isn't a good day. I'm sure you've been told why we've brought all these people to your school; why the police have taken over your gymnasium.'

'Yes, sir.'

'Then don't you think it would be better to wait until another time for something like that?'

The boy screwed his face into a reasoning expression. 'Ye-es, but you won't be here another time.'

'No, we won't, but how about if your headmaster arranged a trip to our station some time in the summer? You could look over the Chinook and everything else, too; speak to all kinds of people about anything you want to know. We might even fix you up with Coke and burgers.'

'Ye-e-es!' they all cried with gusto.

He stood. 'OK, I'll see what I can do.'

Once outside Chris said, 'Bit rash, weren't you?'

'No, the CO'll wear it. The school put up with us today. It's one way of showing our appreciation. Good PR. Besides, those lads are tomorrow's recruits.'

'Not for my bloody job, they're not,' snorted Griff. '*Are you the pilot, sir?*' he mimicked in over-posh tones. 'For that little lemon-sucker it'd be fast-jet officer's tabs or nothing. They weren't bloody interested in our stinking great workhorse. It was just a chance to show off.'

'Stop waving your red flag, Griff,' said one of the volunteers.

'Yeah, well, can you see any of those little—'

'Pack it in, Griff. They were young boys chancing their arm to get a closer look at the Chinook,' put in Chris wearily. 'They're no different from any kids their age.'

'Aah!' Griff said in disgust. 'They're officer material. They wouldn't work their guts out in the cabin.'

'Dave does . . . and he resigned his commission in order to do it,' Randal pointed out sharply, which should have closed the subject.

'And took a job away from some other puir sod who'd never get the chance of what he threw away,' countered Griff. 'Some blokes want it all ways.'

Randal halted beside the Chinook. 'The way I want it

right now is a quick, uneventful flight to Hampton. Back in that cutting there are men and women – kids, too, perhaps – who are suffering and terrified. They may be there all night. Some will possibly die before anyone can reach them. So cut out the petty whingeing and count yourself lucky not to be one of them.'

No one said a word as they followed him inside the aircraft but as he began the start-up checks with Chris, Randal realised the pugnacious Griff could be a real troublemaker if he was allowed to be.

Throughout the flight, the extended debrief and a substantial hot dinner Randal did all he had to, but his usual habit of unwinding over a few pints at the end of the day was more than he could face. He would admit to no one but himself that he felt totally shattered, mentally and physically. He needed to get to bed and sleep. Yet, when his head hit the pillow, a succession of thoughts and doubts rushed through his tired brain.

Had he taken on more than he could handle? Had he been too clever this time? Maybe the medical board and that smug redhead were right. No, it was just bad luck that his first op had been so demanding and there had been no other pilot to share the flying. *That's no excuse*, his brain argued. *When you wangled yourself back to 646 you knew damn well what you'd be taking on. You'd done the job before. It's no picnic.*

Chris had been tactful; claimed his nursemaiding had nothing to do with lack of trust. They had been together in the old days. They knew each other well. Chris was a steady, supportive team member. He had brought his pilot's wandering thoughts back to the job in hand several times.

Randal's head moved restlessly on the pillow. Had he been irresponsible to fast-talk his way into a command he had before handled with ease? However much he might kid himself he was not the man he had been then. How could he be? Self-confidence once had come naturally. It was now the result of constant inner boosting. (I *can* do this. I *am* able to move my legs. I *will* walk again.) He had been talking himself into the seemingly impossible for the past year. If he were not so dispirited and exhausted he would do so again now. It was good therapy, but much easier with a pretty girl urging him on.

He thought of the times Maggie had encouraged him when he had felt defeated. Her room was a short way along the corridor, but she was in Northern Ireland. Not that he could go to her if she were here . . . and she had asked for a transfer, anyway. Not all the boosting therapy in the world would solve things in that direction, but to hell with Pam Miles' offer of impotency drugs. He had heard that the rule for pilots on them was the same as alcohol. No sex for eight hours before taking off? He wanted no part of that nonsense.

His troubled mind focussed on his suspended marriage, which had been as lusty as a relationship could be. Fiona could excite him in an instant with one glance, one endearment, one erotic movement. His obsession with her had more than satisfied her selfish desire for slavish attention at all times, but he had eventually seen the light. It seemed incredible that he was now incapable of satisfying any woman's desire, selfish or otherwise. Good thing Maggie was leaving. He was of no use to her.

For a while he lay tormented by memories of hectic sexual encounters in his past, but mostly of wonderful times with Fiona when their marriage had been good. Then, inevitably, he dwelt on the joy of his children. That small boy in shorts and a red blazer had reminded him painfully of Neil, who was about the same age. He yearned to see his son, and the little girl whose big, blue eyes could cajole anything from her daddy, but he had to face the fact that they were lost to him, along with the prospect of fathering other children.

Some while later he told himself the one thing he did have was the job he loved, so he had better concentrate on making certain he could hold on to it. With an effort he began silently chanting: 'I *can* command B Flight. I *am* able to handle days like today. I *will* succeed.'

When he slept, the nightmare returned after a break of two months. It was slightly different. Instead of hurtling into a fiery furnace and on into blackness, he lay beneath the crushed body of his car unable to move. When he shouted for help no sound came from his mouth and he knew he would be there for ever.

Four

A fter two and a half months with 646 Squadron Dirk recognised his room when he woke with a hangover. Not that he had slept in it often. Of those ten weeks he had spent two in Bosnia, one under canvas on Dartmoor with the Army, and three supplying troops on emergency standby in the Gulf. He was marked down for a three-day refresher course on biological warfare at Hampton next week, so he looked forward to a comfortable bed tonight after adding quite considerably to his bar bill.

As he left his room he saw Maggie come from hers and he decided to test her response to him. They had not flown together since that eventful trip to Shawbury. Their duties had taken them in different directions after he recovered from concussion, so he had not seen her to explain, even apologise if she would accept it with any measure of grace. Two crews had returned from Northern Ireland late this afternoon, along with his own and another headed by Nick Lorrimer, glad to leave desert heat for spring in England. It was the season when young men's fancies turned to . . . whatever they fancied. For Dirk it was certainly not Maggie Spencer, but she presented him with a challenge he could not resist so he quickened his pace and fell in beside her.

'Please don't bawl me out, ma'am. I'm in my humble mood.'

'Do you have one?' She walked on towards the stairs without looking at him, but her tone was pleasant enough.

'When you get to know me you'll find I have far greater depths than you give me credit for.'

They started down the staircase. 'That's you being *humble*?'

'You'd know if you'd ever heard me bragging.' He stopped in the panelled entrance hall to appeal to her. 'Look, we got off on the wrong foot at the start, then our first flight ended badly. If I'd had any hint of a problem I'd never have set out for Shawbury. It hit me amazingly suddenly. You were absolutely marvellous.'

'Don't overdo it! I did what we're trained to do, that's all.'

He wagged his head. 'Maggie, Maggie, you're a very tough cookie.'

'I have to be, living and working with men who get their lives in impossible tangles and think the solution is to drink themselves insensible.'

'Never any tangles in your life?' he asked, knowing about the boyfriend who had been killed before her eyes.

She shrugged. 'Occasionally, I suppose.'

'But you don't drown your sorrows?'

'Not in alcohol. Too much gives me a debilitating migraine. It's bed, with cocoa and a paperback instead. It's cheaper, leaves no hangover . . . and I never end up in a ditch,' she added pointedly.

'Cost me an arm and a leg to get the MG back on the road.'

'And three days in the sick bay with concussion. Was it worth it?'

When she moved away Dirk followed. 'There was a reason.'

'Sure. I've heard it from almost every man in B Flight at some time or another,' she said over her shoulder. 'Just let me know when she does it again and I'll keep well clear of you.'

He caught her arm to halt her. 'You're so sure it was a woman?'

'Isn't it always?'

He studied her for a moment or two. Without the green unisex flying suit she was no longer the professional pilot, just an attractive girl in a black silk blouse and a blue skirt. A girl who had also watched someone close die in an air crash. He softened his approach.

'Haven't you ever thrown a guy over?'

She sighed. 'One just recently, but I hope he didn't react as drastically as you did or I'd be afraid to date anyone again.'

'No point in my asking you for one then?'

'None whatever.'

He smiled. 'Can we at least declare a truce until your transfer comes through?'

'Oh, I . . . I've binned it for the moment.'

It was the first time he had seen her disconcerted, and his interest flared. 'Oh?'

Avoiding his eyes, she said, 'They could only offer me an instructor's course and three years at Shawbury. It's not what I want after only two years operational.'

Dirk pursued the subject as they entered the room filled with laughter and the fast chatter of young men and women starting to relax at the end of a strenuous day. 'When did this happen?'

'A week or so ago.' She glanced up at him as they were halted by a group holding full glasses who were making their way to a table. 'Guy Briscombe, head of Personnel at Aldergrove, understood my decision and dealt with it speedily. I told him I thought our revered boss was somehow responsible for the move, but he naturally wouldn't comment on that. I hope he mentions it off the record, all the same.'

'I shouldn't think the Judge was responsible. He sent you

to Shawbury specifically to demonstrate the unisex nature of Six Four Six Squadron. You heard him say as much. He's not likely to get shot of a good PR asset.'

Disparagement clouded Maggie's eyes. 'Borrowing a phrase from your cocky little pal Perry Newman, who has a hang-up about people getting more attention than himself?'

They moved carefully across the crowded room, trying not to jog arms holding full glasses, and enlightenment began to dawn on Dirk as he put together several slight incidents which added to an intriguing supposition. Maggie had been reluctant to visit Shawbury, but she fired up at Perry's comments on her former boss and had been deep in conversation with the man in the bar. On her return she had applied for a transfer. Rip Price was now back with B Flight; Maggie had turned down a transfer to Shawbury. Well, well!

'Perry's okay,' he said as they reached the bar. 'He's had a bit of a raw deal, that's all. Always in the wrong place at the right time. You know how it sometimes goes.'

'Yes. The man he held in contempt was in the wrong place when four tearaway kids dropped an anchor from a bridge. Deals don't come much more raw than that.'

Well, well, *well*! The woman was not as tough a cookie as she made out. They ordered their drinks and, before they were drawn into the general homecoming verve, he continued the theme.

'You heard about the rail pile-up, of course. I wasn't there, but Chris was on it. He told me Rip found it rather difficult. I didn't know him before his accident, but I must say he seems rather tense and withdrawn. Is that usual?'

'When you've been here longer you'll find out,' Maggie said crisply. 'And I'll find out if driving into ditches and trying to open the wrong bedroom door is usual behaviour for you. So far, apart from collapsing on the job, that's all I know about you.'

She moved away to join Jeff, Chris and a pilot named Steve Clarkson who had flown in from Aldergrove with her, leaving Dirk convinced his hunch was right. The truce had lasted barely five minutes.

'You're wasting your time. She never gets involved with anyone on home ground . . . And if you really don't know your rating with her let me enlighten you.'

Dirk turned to see Nick Lorrimer beside him, flushed and loquacious. 'I thought you were going straight home to wife and carpet slippers.'

'Left something out. *And* flaming mother-in-law!' Nick shifted closer. 'Got inside the door and wham! There the old bat stood asking why I didn't ring when we stopped for the last refuel. Clare was upset and worried, she said, and that's bad for the baby. Was I totally insensitive; didn't I care? Then Clare came downstairs all red-eyed and calling me every name under the sun. What a bloody welcome! They don't understand, do they? Got no idea.' He emptied his glass and ordered another beer.

'You'd better go easy on that if you're driving home tonight,' Dirk advised.

Nick grinned. 'Might end in a ditch?'

'The divorce court more likely. Walking out's not the answer. Send her mother packing. I keep telling you that.'

'She won't go. Says someone's got to be with Clare during this difficult time. And *I'm* never there.' Over the rim of his glass he asked sarcastically, 'Ever heard that cry before?'

'No, I'm not married.'

'Wise man.'

The Mess Sergeant came up to Dirk. 'Excuse me, sir. The switchboard's got a caller on the line asking to speak to "Uncle Dirk", who's a pilot. Kid called Sam. Seems upset. Make any sense to you?'

Dirk put down his glass and started for the door, his heart racing. 'He's my godson. You say he's upset?'

'According to the girl on the switchboard.' The man caught up with him. 'Would you like the call put through to your room?'

'No. No, I'll take it here.' Something had happened to Paula. He needed to know as soon as possible. Sam must be alone in the house with his mother and she must be unconscious or she would tell him to dial 999 for help. Poor kid must be terrified. Got some guts to work out how to contact him here. Mike's kid to the hilt!

Dirk snatched up the receiver. 'Flight Lieutenant Marshall here. Put Sam through.'

'One moment, sir. Go ahead, young man. Uncle Dirk's on the line,' said the girl with a touch of amusement.

'Sam? Sam, what's wrong?' Dirk asked urgently. 'Is Mummy ill?'

'She's out.' How young he sounded, how warmly familiar.

'Out? Out where?' She must already be in hospital.

'At the Odeon with Grandma.'

Dirk counted to five. 'So Mummy's all right, is she?'

'S'pose so. She's always out doing something or other.'

'Is Grandad with you?' Maybe the old boy had collapsed.

'He's watching football. He's always watching football . . . or cricket . . . or snooker.'

The wistful note in the four-and-a-half-year-old's voice tugged at Dirk's senses, and his voice thickened with emotion. 'How did you know where I was, old son?'

'Mummy said you'd gone to a place called Hampton, so I asked the lady on the telephone to find you. Uncle Dirk, why don't you come and see me any more?'

Dirk counted to five again. 'Is that what you wanted to say to me, Sam? Just that?'

'Why don't you?'

'I . . . I've been away a lot. Been very busy.'

89

'You're always busy. So was Daddy. But you still came. Now you don't.'

He cast around for the right words. 'Mummy forgot to give me your address.'

'It's twenty-seven Glenwarden Street, Bristol,' the small voice recited importantly. 'So there's really no excuse for you,' he added in words probably often quoted to him by adults.

'No . . . there's no excuse. Sam, how are you doing?'

'All right, I s'pose. I start big school after Easter. Mummy's got a job and she says it'll be easier when I start school full time. When're you coming to see me?'

'Soon. I'll . . . I'll arrange it with Mummy.' He hesitated. 'Does she still cry about Daddy sometimes?'

'No. She says the best thing she ever did was get away from the Air Force, but Uncle Tim's always coming here so she didn't really get away and I miss my friends and our house and you. Uncle Tim never plays games like you did. He takes Mummy out and I'm left with Grandad and his wretched football.' This last was clearly an echo of Grandma's impatient words on the subject.

Seared by jealousy of Tim Ferriday, a twice-divorced navigator who was chancing his arm with Paula and apparently succeeding, Dirk could not help asking, 'Does anyone else take Mummy out?'

'Sometimes. Grandma says she's playing the field, so I s'pose Mummy's into wretched football now. Football's all right, but I like the bobsleigh and racing boats, same as you. Uncle Dirk, when you come to see me can we go out on a fast boat again?'

Dirk took too long over a reply to that and the boy added in a small, scared voice, 'Have you stopped loving me?'

'*No!* Oh God, no, Sam. Never think that. No matter what anyone tells you, I'll always love you. And Mummy. Tell her I said that when she kisses you goodnight,' he added recklessly. 'But shouldn't you be already in bed, lad?'

'I was. Grandad tucked me in, then got his beer ready for the football. So I got out again and came on the landing to talk to you. He doesn't know I'm up. He never knows what I'm doing when he's watching the telly.'

'I think you should go back to bed, Sammy boy. It's late. What I'll do is write you a letter each time I'm away and talk to you on the phone when I'm here at Hampton. Now I know your address we can keep in touch, can't we?'

'And see each other?'

'Yes. I'll talk to Mummy about that.'

'*Great!* I love you as high as a mountain, Uncle Dirk.'

'I love you the same. And Mummy. Don't forget to tell her that, will you?'

'And don't you forget to come,' the boy urged with increased wistfulness. 'Goodnight, Uncle Dirk.'

'Goodnight . . . and God bless you, Sam.'

He replaced the receiver slowly, deeply upset by the contact with a little boy he had fully expected to make his stepson this year. Had Paula no idea of the hurt she had inflicted by writing that letter and cutting all contact?

'Everything all right, sir?'

Dirk turned to the Mess Sergeant who was watching him curiously. How much had the man overheard? He tried to make light of it. 'Not yet five and he gets this number from the operator. Kids today! They'll have computers in their cradles next.'

'Shouldn't wonder,' the man agreed with a laugh.

Returning to the bar, Dirk stood irresolute. It seemed even more crowded than before. He needed to get drunk very fast, but he had had enough of Nick's griping about his mother-in-law and he could not face the usual macho jokes that accompany serious boozing.

'I know most of B Flight came in today, but I didn't

expect them all to congregate here. Some must have wives and families to go to.'

Coming from his dark thoughts, he turned to find Pam Miles beside him surveying the noisy drinkers with a wry smile. She glanced up. 'Care to act as a battering ram to clear a path through to the bar for me?'

She had hair as red as Paula's and large, lustrous eyes. Her breasts were moulded by a fine wool shirt, and she smelled fragrantly feminine. She would not talk about flying or how size does matter. She was exactly what he needed right now.

'Why don't we go to the Bird in Hand instead? Have a meal, a few drinks, and get to know each other better.'

Although her colour rose very slightly, her gaze was clear and frank. 'Have you been stood up by someone?'

'Not since January. How about it?'

'All right . . . but I'll drive.'

'Suits me. Then I can get plastered.'

'Better book a room for yourself, in that case. I always leave when the going gets rough.'

'Not with me, you won't,' he murmured, following her to the main entrance and appreciating the shape of her bottom in her well-fitting skirt. How easy would it be to get her into bed? If Paula was having it off with Tim Ferriday, why not play the same game?

'Hey, see what I see?' said Jeff, causing heads to turn in the direction of his nod. 'Are those two getting cosy?'

'Perhaps he wants to ask her about the ongoing pain he's getting between his legs lately,' mused Chris.

'We've all been getting that,' put in Steve heavily. 'It comes of spending so much time doing bloody uncongenial tasks like transporting crates of root vegetables or drums of petrol, when it's pissing down and you find the ground handlers have hoofed it off to lunch because they expected you an hour earlier.'

Maggie laughed. 'Who's fault was that? You'd forgotten we'd put the clocks forward, you mutt.'

'There are four in a crew, matey, and the other three went along with it,' he countered. 'Anyway, what about Dirk and the Doc? Has she let on anything to you, Maggie?'

'I haven't been here, *remember*?' she said with emphasis.

Steve studied her face, nose to nose. 'Ah, you were the guy in the cockpit with me coming over from Aldergrove. Thought I'd seen you somewhere before.'

'All Pam has said to me about Dirk Bogarde is that he's very biddable when he's concussed.' This was greeted with a knowing *oooh* from her companions, which she countered with a reminder that they were doctor and patient at the time. 'No hanky-panky allowed, lads.'

'Oh yeah?' they chorused in disbelief.

'But,' Maggie added with a chuckle, 'she thinks he's rather like Tom Cruise, only bigger.'

'Ah, a doctor would be perfectly ethical in checking *that* out,' pronounced Chris with a knowing grin.

'But she wouldn't have checked out Tom Cruise to make the comparison,' reasoned Jeff.

'You can't be certain,' Steve insisted. 'She's only been with us a few months and who knows what she got up to before that?'

'Or *who* she got up to,' added Chris. 'I read that Tom Cruise spends a lot of time in London. Picture the scene: Our Tom passes out in a crowded restaurant. Up goes the cry "Is there a doctor in the house?" Perky Pam's there on the job and gets his pants down before he knows it.'

'Ask your glamorous grannie about it. She might know,' said Jeff.

Maggie stopped listening to their nonsense because Randal

had just entered the bar with Jim Hewson, a senior controller. At Shawbury he had spoken of his longing to be back with 646 and she had been astonished to learn soon afterwards that he and Andy were swapping jobs. It made great sense for Andy, but Randal was not a man to spare himself so there was little likelihood of his taking the easier tasks each time. Maggie did not doubt his ability to resume command, but she questioned the effect it might have on his physical well-being.

The rail disaster with its heavy death toll had been headline news, and at Aldergrove they had heard that a Chinook of B Flight had helped evacuate passengers. Dirk's revelation that Randal had been the pilot was Maggie's first indication of his involvement. A crash scene, people trapped in wreckage and doctors wearing bloodstained coats would be upsetting for any witnesses. For a man so recently recovered from his own disaster it must have been almost traumatic. Of course he had found it 'rather difficult'! Dirk's implied criticism had angered her so much she had to walk away in the hope of questioning Chris on the subject. It was a vain hope. Just back from three weeks in the desert, the lively navigator was set on booze and bawdiness with the lads. They were all impossible to pin down on their first night back at Hampton.

Jim Hewson was cornered by one of his cronies, and Randal crossed to join Maggie's group, smiling a general greeting. 'So all my wandering chicks are safely back in the nest . . . but what are you doing here? Haven't you read the squadron notice about using the sports facilities during your off-duty periods?'

'We read it, but it doesn't say what we should use them *for*,' said Jeff with a wide grin. 'Bonking on the badminton court? Spanking on the squash court?'

'Permissiveness in the pool?' suggested Steve, as wound-up as the others.

'Cuckolding on the cricket pitch?' offered Chris.

'And I can guess the variations for the football field,' said Randal with a laugh. 'Maybe we should pin up a list so that everyone understands what the notice means.' He ordered a beer, then turned to Maggie, his amusement fading. 'Hi.'

'Hi, yourself,' she said quietly. 'Welcome back.'

'Thanks. How was Aldergrove?'

'Same as always. Where've you been?'

'Night flying in Scotland. Saw Rusty.'

'How is the randy bastard?' put in Jeff. 'Bet he's got some besotted lassie keeping the sheets warm for his off-duty periods. Never saw him engaged in any other kind of physical recreation.'

Talk centred around the pilot who had been Jeff's drinking and whoring partner before promotion to squadron leader had led to Rusty's transfer to a Search and Rescue squadron. Maggie drank her gin and tonic in silence while her colleagues grew even more noisily relaxed. Very soon, two more B Flight officers who had also been night flying in Scotland joined them, and exchanged news of their exploits.

With what was left of his second pint in his hand, Randal angled away from the group to concentrate on Maggie. 'So you changed your mind about a transfer.'

'All they could offer me was instructing at Shawbury.'

'Which didn't appeal to you?'

'It didn't to you, did it!'

He gave a faint smile. 'No.'

'How did you manage to get back here?'

'I'd done the job before.'

'But I thought they'd ruled out anything operational.'

'They did.'

'Then how—'

A shout of laughter drowned the rest of her question. Frowning, Randal nodded at the door. 'Let's walk.'

Unsure how to interpret his suggestion, Maggie never-theless followed him to the hall, then was surprised when he continued to the main entrance and went outside. Still uncertain of what this was about she joined him at the top of the steps, but they had only moved a few feet from the foot of them when it became apparent there was fine rain falling.

'Oh hell! Let's sit in my car.' He headed to where it was parked, giving Maggie no choice but to follow. Once they were inside, he said with irritation, 'It's hard luck when you have to sit out here to have a private conversation.'

'The bar's always hopeless but we could have used the ante-room.'

'Where ears flap behind open newpapers?' He started the engine. 'This is ridiculous. Let's drive.'

Disconcerted by his strange mood, Maggie said nothing as he drove from the Station on to the road running alongside the cliffs. A short way along it he pulled over to a viewpoint popular with summer visitors, but thought better of it and swerved back to the road. 'Let's go to the Bird.'

Maggie was totally mystified. He had been much like his old self joking with Jeff and Co., yet he now seemed tense and uncertain. This was a virtual hijack, and she was growing angry over his high-handed assumption that whatever he did was all right by her. Caution led her to keep her tirade until he had reached the village pub and brought the Porsche to a halt.

The Bird in Hand had a dining area; Randal led the way through to it. Although she had eaten there many times Maggie never entered without recalling her first evening with Mark, and the impact he had had on her. That had been two years ago. The memory no longer caused her pain.

'Oh Christ!' said Randal, pulling up. 'Look who's here. Let's go.'

'*No,*' she said firmly, spotting Pam and Dirk drinking at a corner table. 'I've had enough of your bossiness, and I'm hungry. Go if you want to, but buy me something to eat before you leave. It's the least you can do.' She made for a vacant alcove, sat and began studying the menu with great purpose.

His shadow fell across the table. 'What'll you have?'

'Chicken and asparagus pie, and a glass of white wine while I'm waiting for it,' she said without looking up.

He returned with the wine and a pint of beer. 'So you've decided to stay?' she challenged as he sat opposite her.

'You can drop the heavy stuff. I've got the message.'

'I haven't got yours. What's this all about?'

He seemed back in control. 'It's about catching up.'

'On what?'

'Things we can't discuss with the rest of the team around.'

'*I* haven't any secrets from them.'

'Maggie, don't let's have one of our famous tussles. Much as I often enjoy them, let's skip it for tonight.'

Her pique melted away as she sensed he was curiously troubled. She picked up her glass. 'Go ahead; catch up!'

He drank his beer, taking his time. 'At Shawbury you dropped hints about being unhappy with a new crewman, and of preferring any task but flying with our chum over there in the corner. Was it one or the other of them, or both, who made you apply to transfer?'

'You could have asked me that in your office. It's part of a flight commander's job to see that his subordinates are kept happy.'

He sighed. 'I'll shake you in a minute.'

'It would be more profitable to tell me what this is really about.'

'It's about the fact that because you won't be leaving Six Four Six after all, I've become your boss again.'

'And?'

'And so I have to sort out your problems, as you've just said.'

'Over a pub meal?'

Their food arrived at that point. During the interruption Maggie again reasoned to herself that this could have been done in his office – the normal procedure. The certainty she had had at Shawbury that he was somehow holding something back now returned more strongly. There, she had tried to play it cool, pretend his inexplicable silence once he was back on his feet had not happened. Tonight, whether he liked it or not, one of their 'famous tussles' was on the cards. She wanted some answers.

The girl who brought the meals expressed the hope that they would enjoy them, and departed. Maggie ignored her pie and launched into Randal instead. 'I'm on stand-down until Monday morning, so you're not my boss until then. Forget about crewmen and that bonehead in the corner. I have a major problem you can sort out as someone I thought was a good friend until last November. Just explain in simple words your reasons for pretending I didn't exist once you were up, walking and declared fit to fly. I rang your flat to be told by some woman that you'd gone and left no forwarding address. In January I read in a newspaper of your "heroic arrival" at Shawbury to train as an instructor. I read that your parents were "overflowing with pride at your courage" and that your wife was "extremely emotional" over your return to the life you love. No mention of how your friends felt. You know I know your parents and wife don't give a damn about you.' Now she had begun, the words spilled out with growing heat. 'They weren't there when you were desperate to end it all. They didn't cry with you. They didn't rejoice and share your excitement on the day you were told the paralysis might be reversible. They didn't follow your progress throughout the last harrowing year, did they? *Did they?*' she demanded hotly.

'No.'

'Who did?'

'Maggie—'

'So don't give me all that about sorting out my professional problems,' she stormed on. 'Just explain why you turned your bloody back when I was no longer needed.'

Realising that her voice had risen and people nearby were looking their way, Maggie gulped the rest of her wine while glaring across at Randal, who now seemed deeply disturbed. He said nothing for some moments as he played nervously with the serviette-wrapped cutlery the girl had brought.

'I've done some pig-stupid things in my time, Maggie,' he began heavily, 'and that was one of them. It didn't occur to me that you'd see it in that light.'

'What other light could it possibly be seen in?'

He threw up a hand. 'How the hell do I know? As you said, you knew the situation where Fiona and my parents were concerned. Several of the guys came to Headley Court once they discovered I wouldn't be disabled for life, and that was great. You were faithful and visited whenever you could manage it.'

'And got sworn at for my pains, once or twice.'

'You gave as good as you got, as I remember.'

'Our famous tussles?'

'Our famous tussles,' he agreed quietly. 'Look, you know what an opinionated bastard I am – you've told me often enough. I didn't find it easy to work my way back. I wanted it to happen overnight. I sometimes gave the therapists hell, and you more often than you deserved. When you left, I felt bad about it, then bloody well did it again the next time you came.' He paused for a moment. 'You helped me through those bad months. When Dave came to see me he said you had told him it was because I'd helped you when Mark was killed. I'm glad I was able to . . . but once you'd got over the initial shock you didn't expect me to continue supporting you. You got on with the job, determined to stand on your own feet.'

'Go on.'

'That's what I did. You'd devoted too much of your precious leave days to coping with my tantrums, so I thought it was time I let you off the hook. I obviously made a hash of the whole business, but you know what we men are like. No finesse.'

Maggie studied him thoughtfully. She had grown accustomed to his highs and lows, his forthrightness, his volatile expressions. She could read him with ease. 'Why have you decided to become a liar as well as an opinionated bastard?'

The girl appeared beside their table and asked with some concern if there was something wrong with their meals. Randal looked up at her in relief. 'I'm afraid we've let them grow cold. Our fault. Would you bring us the same again?'

'And I'll have another white wine,' added Maggie, cursing the interrruption. Knowing Randal would race on with a new topic, she spoke quickly as the girl took away the cooling meals. 'Don't think you were saved by the bell. There's another round coming up.'

'No, there isn't. I concede defeat. The tussle's over.'

'You're going to let that lie stand?' she demanded fiercely.

He adopted the familiar steadfast expression that brooked no opposition. 'So was it Griff or Dirk who upset you enough to ask for a transfer?'

For a moment she considered telling him to go to hell and walking out, then she thought better of it. They had come in his car and she was damned if she would fork out for a taxi because he was being so infuriating. Besides, she had not finished with him yet.

'Should I stand to attention to answer that, Boss?'

'Just tell me the reason, Maggie,' he said, the light of challenge in his eyes as they faced up to each other.

The waitress came with two fresh meals and a glass of wine.

She smiled at them both. 'Don't leave this to get cold.'

Randal unwrapped his cutlery and began eating. 'Come on, get started. I'm not buying you a third portion.'

Starting on her own meal Maggie asked, 'What about a third glass of wine?'

He grinned. 'I'd buy you any amount of that if I thought I'd succeed in finally getting you thoroughly pissed.'

'So you could crow to the rest of the team?'

'So I could collect my winnings. You know we've all got a long-standing bet on it. I'd collect enough to cover an expensive night like this ten times over.'

'We could have stayed in the Mess car park and it wouldn't have cost you a penny.'

'But we'd have been cold and hungry.' He ate in silence for a short while, then he looked across questioningly. 'So which one of them was it?'

She wagged her head in exasperation. 'You never give up, do you?'

'No.'

'I wasn't enjoying being with B Flight. Some of the old team had moved on or left. Those two didn't fit in. At least, I didn't think so. I felt it was time to go elsewhere.'

'Then changed your mind.'

'You came back; I hoped things would improve.' She sipped her wine. 'I heard you found it difficult at the rail crash.'

'God, was that Chris making the understatement of the year? I damn near accepted that I wasn't up to the job when I got to bed that night.'

'I'm glad you didn't.'

'I have something to prove. An opinionated bastard, remember?'

'And a barefaced liar, to boot.'

His eyes narrowed. 'That's something for *you* to prove.'

'Should be easy enough.' This was her opportunity to force from him the truth about the present state of his marriage, which she was certain was really behind his decision to drop contact with her in November. 'Is Fiona still "extremely emotional" over your return to the life you love?'

There was no time to assess his reaction because someone sat at their table and offered an apology for intruding. 'I'm afraid the situation is getting rather out of hand,' said Pam. 'I saw you both come in a while ago and hoped you were still here. Dirk's been drinking steadily for the past two hours. He won't leave and, frankly, if he has any more I'll never manage him on my own.' She addressed Randal. 'If you're going soon perhaps you'd help me get him in my car and out at the other end. The alternative is to book him in for the night.' She glanced at Maggie. 'He's deeply depressed over a phone call from the son of his friend who was killed. I'm reluctant to leave him alone, under the circumstances.'

'I'll deal with it,' offered Randal. 'We were pretty well finished.'

Oh no, we weren't, thought Maggie furiously.

'If you'll give Maggie a lift back, I'll bring Dirk along later and put him to bed.'

Pam smiled and got to her feet. 'What a bit of luck you were here. Thanks for helping out.'

Randal then stood. 'You seem to have everyone's weaknesses neatly pigeonholed. I'm sure you'd have coped.'

Both women were silent as they left the pub where Randal had bought two pints and walked to join Dirk. It was not until Pam was driving along the cliff road that Maggie trusted herself to speak.

'You knew what that moron's like. Why get into a situation with him?'

Pam said calmly, 'He's not a moron, he's a very sincere person who's struggling with personal problems.'

'So are we all.'

'He needs to get things out of his system; talk to someone.'

'Then talk to him in your surgery. Better still, send him to the psycho boys.'

Pam rose to that. 'His close friend was killed in an air crash. You, of all people, should understand how that affected him.'

'Mark wasn't a close friend; he was a man I was in love with. There's a subtle difference.'

They did not speak again until they arrived at the Mess and parted at the top of the stairs leading to the bedrooms. Pam offered a tentative apology. 'It seemed the best way to deal with him. Sorry if it spoilt your evening . . . but it wasn't a romantic date, I imagine.'

'Not in the least. We were discussing the problems I have with the latest recruits to B Flight – one being your outpatient you couldn't handle. There appears to be a new trend for holding professional consultations in pubs.'

If Pam detected the sarcasm she ignored it. 'I admit I was surprised when I saw you walk in with him. Isn't he still tied to the delectable daughter of racehorse breeders?'

'I'm sure you know the answer from his medical record. Isn't that what he meant when he said you have everyone's weaknesses neatly pigeonholed?' As the other girl turned away Maggie relented. 'Pam, whatever your motive was tonight I should consider it carefully. He may look like Tom Cruise, but he's no Top Gun. I'd rate him dangerously near the bottom.'

Five

On Monday morning B Flight was gathered in force before the Wailing Wall, the name they had given to the huge board showing the present whereabouts and upcoming assignments for every member of the Squadron's aircrew. Like every flight commander, Randal had had some difficult moments sorting out crews for the tasks in hand and there were the usual gripes as his team checked their names.

'Surely it's not time for me to do a stint on the simulator?' 'Oh God, not a biological warfare refresher! Four bloody days galumphing around in an NBC suit in a hut full of poisonous bugs!' 'Hilary's mother's getting married on Saturday and she'll kill me if I'm not there. Who'll do a swap? *Pleeese!'*

Randal's careful planning had to be rearranged to allow navigator Tom Shepherd to attend his mother-in-law's remarriage ceremony. His penalty for this would be four days galumphing around in a hut full of poisonous bugs, while Vince joyfully prepared for mountain flying in Bavaria in Tom's place.

Randal had put himself on a three-day combined services exercise requiring two Chinooks. Crewing these with him would be Jeff, Chris, Dave, Jimmy, Sandy, Griff and Maggie. They had all handled landings at sea save Griff, so it would be good experience for him. Randal also intended to sort out the man's attitude with regard to Maggie. Unfortunately, the evening at the Bird in Hand had not sorted out hers with regard to himself, so he vowed to restore their old relationship before his hospitalisation. Concentrate on the job; forget women!

The good thing about the coming exercise was that they could return to Hampton at the end of each day. The downside was the Met report. When the sea was smooth, visibility was perfect and there was no more than a light breeze, landing on a carrier was a doddle. When the ship was ploughing through heavy seas, with fine rain hampering vision and a brisk wind blowing, it could be tricky because the landing surface was not only undulating but was also moving steadily forwards. The pilot had to hover alongside the ship then move in sideways, acting on instructions from a deck marshal and his crewmen who could see clearly when his sight of the deck was restricted. What the pilot could not fail to see, however, was a huge superstructure rising to his right as he closed towards it. The crew of a helicopter the size of the Chinook had to be fully on the ball and have total faith in each other in situations like that.

They all dispersed. Those who were going to be flying grouped around charts to discuss routing, refuel stops and accommodation at their destination – would it be service billets, hotels or the dreaded tents? The eight on the sea exercise clustered together for their individual briefing. They had first to make a short hop to the Naval airbase at Yeovilton, which was to act as Central Control over the three days. From there they would fly out to the ship in the English Channel to pick up supposed invasion troops and take them to a mock battle zone on Dartmoor, then ferry supplies to them as the dummy war progressed.

With the essentials settled, Randal said, 'We're programmed for nine forty-five. Today's crews will be Jeff, with Chris, Dave and Jimmy. I'll fly with Maggie, Sandy and Griff.'

There was a significant silence after this announcement and, as Randal turned away, Griff appeared beside him.

'Did Wing Commander Jeffries no' mention to you about not putting me with a woman, Boss?' he asked urgently.

'Ah yes, the family superstition.'

'Aye.'

'Because they're all seamen.'

'Aye.'

'Except you and your brother, who I heard is in a Fusilier regiment,' said Randal casually. 'And your father, according to your service record, is a welder very much on dry land.'

Griff's eyes darkened. 'My grandfather and his two brothers went to sea. The superstitiion is very strong with all of us.'

'The myth that a woman aboard brings disaster?'

'It's no myth. They do.'

Randal leaned back against the wall, arms folded. 'Griff, last month you crewed with me to airlift passengers from the rail crash. During that day we must have carried near a hundred women from the scene to the school with no trouble at all. And I don't believe you've never taken a commercial flight where cabin crew are nearly always women.' His tone hardened with determination. 'I can't accept that crap about superstition. If you're in my flight you become one of a team. Maggie's in that team. She happens to be one of my best pilots, which means I give her the more challenging tasks. If you persist in your sexist attitude you'll be down for all the grotty jobs, day after day. By your own choice,' he emphasised. 'You can think it over while Maggie flies us to Yeovilton.'

He walked away, ending the discussion. If Griff should be crazy enough to maintain his stance there would be no alternative but to get him posted elsewhere. No way would Randal allow any one of his team to dictate to him with whom they would or would not fly. There were occasional personality clashes, temporary quarrels, but the lads had never so far let private differences affect their work. There were no ejection seats in a helicopter, for obvious reasons, and they did not carry parachutes. If a crew member was careless or bloody-minded in the air they could *all* end in a heap on the ground. For that reason Randal was confident Griff would present no problem during the short flight to Yeovilton.

Walking out to the aircraft half an hour later, Maggie glanced up at Randal to say quietly, 'Thanks. How did you manage it?'

'Called his bluff.'

'Ah, your favourite solution to awkward situations. I should know,' she added with an intimate smile.

Concentrate on the job; forget women. 'He might call mine when we reach Yeovilton. You won't be so cocky then.'

Griff flew with them all day. He looked sullen and had little to say during refuelling or snack breaks, but he gave concise, competent instructions to the pilot at sea and on shore. At the end of the day they flew back to Hampton satisfied that their side of the exercise had gone well.

On the second day Randal followed his usual practice of switching crews around, replacing Maggie and Sandy with Jeff and Dave. This meant he still kept an eye on Griff, who would be working in tandem with Dave – another person he resented. Aside from putting a slight damper on the banter that was normally exchanged between crew members, Griff's mood did not affect their efficiency.

Towards the end of the day, however, things began to go wrong. As sometimes happens, the wrong batch of supplies was loaded and Maggie delivered them where they were not required. This brought angry radio messages from Army officers waiting for vital supplies on the battlefield.

Central Control attempted to sort it out by sending Maggie back to pick up what had been dropped off then deliver it to the correct sector, and by changing Randal's schedule to fly the right consignment to where it should be. B Flight's commander countered the expletive-scattered radio instructions with some choice expletives of his own and a reminder that they were not actually fighting World War Three that day. Jeff, who knew Randal of old, smiled with the contentment of knowing all was right with his world. When Rip Price clashed with anyone over a member of his team, the other stood no chance. When the antagonist was from another service the contest was formidable.

Their problems increased. Already behind schedule over the error, the two Chinook crews were faced with worsening weather conditions by late afternoon. Cloud began thickening ominously and the wind was rising to presage a coming storm as Randal returned to the ship for his final run of the day.

'I don't like the look of that sea,' he murmured to Jeff as they approached the carrier.

'I never like the look of it, which is why I didn't join the Navy.'

Randal spoke to Dave and Griff. 'We'll have to watch this one very carefully, guys. That deck'll be moving more than before and there's a marked increase in wind velocity. Let's take it nice and easy.'

He made his approach over the dark grey-green sea with white flecking the crest of giant waves, feeling the power of the wind combatting the power of the aircraft. The two crewmen began their talkdown patter as he turned alongside the ship and cut his speed to that of the vessel. The marshal on deck was giving manual signals, the legs of his suit flapping wildly in the wind.

'Forward five and right,' said Griff as the aircraft began to drift.

Randal made the adjustment, his eye on the marshal but now unable to see the edge of the deck and relying completely on his crewmen. The Chinook was taking a buffeting from the wind and was difficult to hold in position.

'Right three, descending,' called Griff, hanging from the front door. 'Steady down. Forty . . . thirty . . . twenty.'

As Randal concentrated on maintaining a steady vertical descent, a vicious blast of wind hit the aircraft broadsides sending it across the deck. The marshal threw himself flat in panic as Randal found the grey superstructure growing too close. Immediately increasing power he practically stood the Chinook on its side as he gained height and turned left away from the hazard.

'That's it. This has got too risky,' he ruled as they flew out over the sea. 'We're going home.'

In radio contact with the ship, he announced his decision and it was mutually agreed that conditions were now unsuitable for operations to continue.

'The Captain sends his compliments and wishes to remind you that you are far too large to attempt a landing on the crow's nest,' said the voice over the radio with dry amusement.

Randal scowled. 'It wasn't so bloody funny from where I was sitting.'

Heading for Hampton, Randal contacted Maggie, who was just leaving Dartmoor. He gave her the picture and suggested they race each other home. 'Losers buy the beer,' he ruled.

He then conducted a very crisp exchange with Central Control. The man was eventually persuaded to agree that 'the poor sods out in the ocean doing the flaming job' had a better idea of what constituted a hazard than he had 'sitting on his bloody arse, snug and dry'.

Randal walked from his aircraft on home ground feeling relaxed, professionally fulfilled and ready for a meal and a few beers before bed. He was only half-listening to Jeff's delight over getting back early enough for him to have a long hot shower before driving to meet his latest girlfriend, so he overheard an aside from Griff to Dave walking just behind them.

'If it hadn'a been for the cock-up by that bloody woman, we'd ha' been back even sooner.'

Maggie and Chris flew in ten minutes later and so, when they met up in the bar before dinner, they were both obliged to buy a pint for Randal. His offer to drink two more on Jeff's behalf was turned down flat. They then sat and talked for a while about the day's work and the loads that got mixed up.

Maggie appeared to be in sparkling form. 'The guy who got equipment to set up a field kitchen instead of spares for armoured cars was a pompous little bastard like Perry Newman. While he jumped up and down, I told him it wasn't my job to open everything before lifting it to check the contents. It's the responsibility of the ground handlers to attach the correct load, I said, and more often than not they were wearing khaki.' She grinned. 'He didn't like that and rattled on about this being a Navy cock-up, adding that *they* had everything easy with all they wanted on board and no worries about moving from A to B in foul weather in vehicles needing spare parts sent to the wrong places.'

Wiping froth from his mouth, Chris said, 'When we left we flew low over his tent and flattened it.'

'Quite unintentionally, I suppose?' asked Randal.

'Of course. Still, you know how erratic women are in the cockpit.'

Maggie poked him in the ribs. 'For that piece of sexism you *will* take me to that first night. I keep telling you I'm the obvious choice.'

'You're not "a nice young man",' Chris insisted.

'Neither are you . . . nor anyone else on the team.

And that includes you,' she said to Randal with another grin.

'I've never claimed to be,' he protested, enjoying being with her despite his resolution to avoid moments like this. 'Who wants one?'

Chris leaned across the table as if divulging secret information. 'Gran has two tickets for the first night of the new musical based on *The Prisoner of Zenda*. One of her former protégés is playing Rupert of Hentzau.'

'It's *Anthony Dillane*,' breathed Maggie with girly awe.

'And?' prompted Randal, looking totally unimpressed.

'Gran always stipulates that any friend I introduce to her should be a nice young man. Maggie maintains I don't know any and should take her instead.'

'You've always claimed I'm one of the boys, and I'm *very* nice,' she urged.

Randal decided to stir things. 'Where did that idea come from? Anyway, you'll be of no use because I reckon Gran has invited two gorgeous girls to even up the numbers.'

'Phoo, Chris can cope with them single-handed. He's always boasting about his virility.' She stroked Chris's hand and made big eyes at him. 'Come on, sweetie. You've never let me in on one of those invitations . . . and I *should* be the only one in the team who gets turned on by Anthony Dillane.'

Chris sighed and gazed pointedly at his empty glass, until Maggie said, 'All right, but just one pint, you bastard.'

'What happened to *sweetie*?' he asked in hurt tones.

'Do I get the ticket?'

'We-ell, we're invited to dinner after the show to meet some celebrities. Could you tart yourself up enough?' he asked with evident doubt.

Her eyes glittered. 'You want tarted-up, I'll give you the whole shebang. So is it yes?'

'Make it two pints and I guess—'

'Whee!' she cried with excitement, leaning across the table to kiss him full on the mouth with great enthusiasm.

Chris was startled. It completely ruined Randal's evening.

Maggie was somewhat surprised when, for the final day of the exercise, Randal arranged things so that she flew with Jeff, Dave and the pugnacious Griff. The latter had been reasonably damped-down with their commander in the crew, but Jeff was a happy-go-lucky person preferring to avoid personal clashes and Dave, as a Highlander with noble connections, was the personification of all the Glaswegian detested. However, she trusted Randal's judgement. Having himself flown with Griff on the previous two days he must feel confident that all would be well.

Still excited over the prospect of the glittering first night with Chris and his grandmother, the glamorous Evelyn Montrose, a musical comedy star of the fifties and sixties and present director of a well known stage school, Maggie faced the day in cracking form. She loved to fly with Jeff and Dave – two good friends – so Griff could be tolerated.

The overnight storm had cleared the air. There was still a lively breeze with sunshine and flying white clouds, but these conditions should present few problems for them. Maggie and Jeff took off forty-five minutes after the other Chinook to head out to the ship from Yeovilton, where the tasks for the day were outlined by the Navy coordinator. He made little attempt to disguise his opinion of RAF aircrew who not only picked up the wrong loads but threw in the towel as soon as it grew rough out at sea. Randal would normally have countered this attitude very effectively, but he seemed unusually distracted. Maggie could not believe his aborted landing yesterday had unsettled him. So what was on his mind?

Their first task was to pick up troops as supposed reinforcements to the invading army. These men had been in cramped conditions on the carrier from day one, and most had been violently ill during the night's storm. They could not embark on the Chinook fast enough; the prospect of a mock battle on muddy Dartmoor being infinitely preferable to shipboard life. Maggie laughingly told their two officers that one of their colleagues had yesterday claimed the Navy had it good compared with what he was putting up with.

'Give us his name; we'll enlighten him,' replied a lieutenant with camouflage smears over his face.

'He was a cocky little bastard,' she added.

He grinned. 'Couldn't be one of ours. We're not like that.'

He accepted Jeff's invitation to occupy the centre seat and proceeded to chat up Maggie as they crossed the sea. Jeff was flying and kept throwing in outrageous comments about how she was just along for the ride to see what the *men* in the Air Force did. Her usual job was to cook their dinners, he declared.

They reached the grid reference they had been given, landed and offloaded a platoon of soldiers glad to get their boots on firm ground again; but they were soon piling back in the cabin. An Army coordinator wearing a chunky yellow armband informed them that the advance had been more of a rout and the reinforcements should be taken to a new position eight miles to the east.

Maggie consulted her chart and marked the revised setdown point. Then she turned with a smile to the young officer in the centre seat. 'They're doing so well they don't really need you.'

He smiled back. 'Might as well stop on board with you for the rest of the day.'

She indicated her chart. 'We'll get you as close to them as we can, but it's scrub around there and we'll have to find a clear area.'

'Take as long as you like,' he said warmly.

They were on the ground again within ten minutes and the mock battle was so intense it could have been a real war under way. They could hear the clatter of machine-guns, the staccato rattle of rife fire and the deep thud of anti-tank artillery. A pall of smoke overhung the entire area. Through it they caught odd glimpses of light tracked vehicles and huge blundering tanks making good the advance. It was open country so the troops had to crawl on their bellies, or risk a forward rush through the smoke. It might be an exercise, but these men were highly trained and treated it seriously.

As Maggie stared at the mock battle she vividly recalled a snowy morning in the Balkans when they had airlifted British peacekeeping troops sandwiched between battling Serbs and Albanians. The bullets, the shells, the missiles had been live and the killing had been for real. She had shared the cockpit with Jeff on that day, too, and Dave had manned the cabin with Sandy. They made a good crew. They had all risked their lives by overflying the hostile area and landing in the midst of it, but they had successfully plucked the soldiers from danger and been strengthened by the experience.

'Thanks,' said a voice in her ear. 'If you cook dinners as well as you do this job I'll be along for one when this is over.'

She returned from her vision and turned to the bright-eyed lieutenant. 'Take care.'

He grinned at her intensity. 'It's only a game. We'll all get pissed together tonight.'

Forcing a return grin, Maggie said, 'That's what I was referring to.'

They lifted off as soon as the men were all out. The Chinook was part of the action so could be counted as a target if the 'enemy' locked on to them. Once clear of this hazard, Maggie contacted Control to report that the men had been offloaded at the advanced position. Control told them to return to the ship to pick up the last of the supplies, along with three soldiers who had inadvertently been left behind.

Jeff cast Maggie a wry glance. 'Your admirer can't count.'

She set a course to cross the coast and then rendezvous with the carrier's new position. They passed the other Chinook en route for Dartmoor and exchanged updated information. Chris told them the three men had been left aboard because they were laid out by seasickness.

'The ship's doc has confined them to the sick bay. They're out of the war, Maggie.' He laughed heartlessly. '*Mal de mer* will be nothing to what they'll suffer when they return to their mates.'

With the ship now visible Maggie received a message telling them a Sea Harrier had requested a priority landing due to shortage of fuel, so they were to wait and follow it in.

'Tell him to speed it up. We're low on fuel ourselves,' said Jeff, and Maggie radioed accordingly. 'I also need my lunch,' he added.

'I wish they did kids' meals. I can't face their man-sized portions.'

'I'll finish up anything you can't manage.'

'Greedy guts!'

They watched with professional interest as the Harrier pilot rotated the thrust nozzles to switch from forward to vertical movement, so that he could gently settle on the deck much as they did themselves. As the jet fighter hovered alongside the carrier and moved slowly into position, Jeff prepared to follow him in. Then something went wrong. The Harrier dropped dramatically, crashing down to slew into another aircraft parked nearby.

'Bloody hell, that's all we need!' cried Jeff, veering to the left and gaining height over the sun-sparkled sea.

Maggie's ears were ringing with the terse radio direction

to hold off until the deck was clear, even as Jeff had taken evasive action.

'Tell them *our* fuel situation is critical,' he shouted at her.

'They already know that,' she snapped, watching the ship's crash crew racing into action to spray the two tangled Harriers with foam and to ensure the pilot could climb from his cockpit. It was impressive the way an entire team of men appeared as if from nowhere to counter the deadly fire hazard and to pull the obstruction clear of the landing area in the fastest possible time.

Concentrating on the business of aiding Jeff to set down slightly to the rear of the spot where the Harrier had dropped uncontrolled, and maintaining radio contact with the ship, Maggie was thankful when they completed the shut-down procedure and received clearance to leave the aircraft.

They had a scheduled ninety-minute break for a meal and a rest. Maggie headed for the aircrew lounge below, while the three men lingered to watch the activity around the damaged Harrier. Walking alone in to the large room where men in flying gear were eating, lounging around yarning, or reading newspapers, she was greeted with loud invitations ranging from the offer of a seat being kept warm for her by a sexy bottom, to a vacant bunk being kept warm for her by a panting pilot. By this third day she knew some of the Navy fliers, and she normally met their randy comments with words quelling enough to bring laughter from their fellows. Today, she found the sexual innuendo deeply irritating and walked through without a word to the washroom to clean up.

This was one of the occasions when being the only woman in a room full of extrovert, bragging, one-track-minded males made her yearn for gentler feminine company. It was that time of the month. By now she was used to coping with what women so aptly named 'the Curse' in difficult, inconvenient situations surrounded by men who considered menstruation something to joke about. Any one of the brotherhood could have an off day, be worried about his marriage/love life, feel jaded or under par, and he would get rough sympathy, but if a woman was forgetful, uncommunicative or irritable it was loudly declared by all and sundry to be PMT and she was ostracised. Growing up with three brothers, followed by six years in the RAF, had taught Maggie that many men tended to ridicule anything they could not understand or experience.

Returning to collect her meal, Maggie took one look at the giant steak with mounds of vegetables and knew she could not eat it. Not only that, she felt she might soon be sick if she did not seek fresh air. Scrambling to her feet she quit the atmosphere of baritone laughter, male aggressiveness and the smell of healthy sweat mixed with avgas, passing Jeff as if she had not seen him. He had food on his mind and did not stop to question her.

Personnel were allowed on the flight deck only if they had a reason to be there, so Maggie huddled against the bulkhead, staring along the dark landing zone at the damaged Harrier, which was still surrounded by men in protective suits. The pilot, miraculously on his feet and in one piece, was explaining with nervous hand gestures to one of the air accident team.

As she watched, Maggie felt something tickling her cheek. She put up her hand to discover that it was wet with tears. Useless to blame the time of the month for the way she felt. When she had seen that distinctive aircraft smack down on the deck she had expected flames to consume it; expected to witness another eager young man burned to death in a Harrier. So much for the belief that she was over Mark. Right now she wanted to hide away somewhere and cry her eyes out.

A hand fell on her shoulder. 'Are you all right?'

She could not look at Dave. She just nodded. He had been with her at that August air show and now guessed her reaction to what they had seen here. He stayed alongside, saying nothing more but comforting her by being there. They had joined 646 on the same day, but relations between them had not been warm until that air show. Maggie sometimes suspected Dave of having deeper feelings for her, but he kept them well hidden. Unlike the rest of the team he was a relatively private person; a man as tall and striking as Dirk yet as modest as the other was flamboyant.

Eventually she turned to him. 'Don't you want your lunch?'

Dark eyes studied her shrewdly. 'Aye. And you'd do well to eat something if you're now ready for it.'

She sighed. 'I suppose I'll have to face them all again. There are times when I wish I'd joined a convent instead of the Air Force. This is one of them.'

He grinned. 'They'd never have you in a convent, Maggie. Six Four Six is far less choosy. Come on, let's get our snouts in the trough.'

Jeff glanced round as Maggie sat beside him. 'Didn't think you wanted your meal. Someone's eaten it.' He grimaced at the dish of stewed fruit and custard she had in front of her. 'That won't put hair on your chest, *or* boost your pecs.'

She smiled fondly. Dear Jeff was a good friend, but he had little idea of women's frailties despite having two sisters. From what Maggie had heard, it had been Jeff and his father; the women of the family being a separate unit. Maybe that was why Jeff never stayed with a girl for long. Apart from sex, he had no understanding of them.

He now continued his theme. 'I suppose you're having one of your slimming bouts so you can get into a posh frock for the first night of *Zenda*, and the theatrical piss-up afterwards.'

'Can anyone go?' asked an eager pilot opposite.

A lively conversation about West End shows ensued. Maggie was grateful for it while she ate her pudding. It took her mind from dark memories. They were revived when the Harrier pilot, after being debriefed and looked over by the doctor, entered just as she and Jeff were leaving. He was greeted with good-natured jeers and comments about it being time he learned to read altimeters so that he wouldn't think he was on the ground when he was still in the air. Although he looked pale, he grinned and took the ribbing in good part as he went to clean up. Maggie knew the intense professional discussion about what had happened would come later. It was all in a day's work for these men, but it could so easily have ended in tragedy to remind them all that flying was a risky business. Maggie suddenly longed for this day to end. It had turned sour.

On the way to the flight deck Jeff asked quietly, 'Are you okay to fly this leg?' showing Maggie she had been wrong to think he had not guessed why she left her meal and fled.

She smiled up at him. 'Yes, I'm fine now. Thanks, pal.'

'Any time.'

In the cabin they carried a light load: basically the stuff the troops had not needed. The war would be over tonight, so the surplus supplies had to be returned to the Army. Dave and Griff talked Maggie into the air, and Jeff set a course that had varied considerably because the carrier was now heading back towards Plymouth. Clouds were again massing way out to sea, but they should be back at Hampton before the bad weather reached the coast.

They were well out over the sea when Jeff suddenly asked, 'So what are you going to wear to the bash with Chris? He's deeply concerned about it, you know. Not that anyone'll notice you in a bevy of glamorous stage stars.'

'You know, Jeff, it's a mystery to me what women see in you when you're so bloody rude.'

'Honest, Maggie, *honest*. They can't resist my little boy

119

truthfulness and as I've never tried to chat you up you're unfamiliar with my devastating— Hey, there's a warning light come on,' he said with abrupt change of tone. 'Engine transmission. Failure in number two.'

'*Hell!*' Maggie swiftly checked the temperature and pressure gauges and saw irrefutable evidence of why the light was on. 'What a time to go bad on us! Problem, guys,' she announced to Dave and Griff. 'I'm shutting down number two engine. We're at the point of no return, so we'll carry on and re-evaluate the situation once we're over land. Keep me posted on things back there. Should reach the coast in twenty minutes.'

They shut down the faulty engine and flew on monitoring the behaviour of the aircraft, all levity gone. Maggie was tense. The Chinook was vulnerable over the sea. It was possible to land successfully on water that was reasonably calm, but on a choppy sea the top-heavy aircraft was likely to turn turtle. When things went wrong solid earth below was the preferable option for all Chinook aircrew.

'There's a noise back here I don't like,' said Dave over the intercom, calm but precise. 'A high-pitched whine and a scraping sound. Can't exactly locate it, but I shouldn't be hearing it.'

'And I shouldna be smelling burning,' put in Griff in a more excitable manner. 'There's something very wrong back here.'

Maggie tried to analyse the problem. If Dave at the front could hear alien noises, and Griff smelled burning at the back, they were in real trouble. Then the Chinook began to vibrate, not violently, but enough to indicate the wisdom of getting out of the air. The coast was still around fifteen minutes flying time away.

'We'll have to ditch, Jeff,' she said.

'Looks like it. What's the situation back there, guys?'

'The scraping noise is worse. I'm not happy,' said Dave.

'I can see smoke. Get us down, woman!' yelled Griff.

'Stand by to lower the ramp and inflate the dinghy,' Jeff instructed. 'As soon as we hit the water, get out fast.'

Maggie began to lose height, her heart thudding. They had all been taught how to escape from a submerged aircraft, but still she dreaded it. Things could go drastically wrong. The sea was green, white-flecked and deep. The hell of it was that they could see the coast as a darkish haze in the distance. So near and yet so far.

When the surface was no more than twenty feet below them Maggie recalled something Randal had related to her during a visit to Headley Court, and she spoke swiftly to Jeff.

'What's the nearest landfall?'

'A small sandy bay just west of the MoD Danger Area. I've sent a mayday signal.'

'I'm going to have a shot at taxiing on the surface while we still have an engine operating. The nearer we get to the coast the better chance we'll have. The forward movement will prevent us from capsizing. It's an option we have to take.' She spoke to the crewmen. 'Don't lower the ramp yet, guys, but stand ready. I'll need continuous reports on what's happening back there and yell at the first sign of serious trouble. Close your door, Dave, we're about to hit the deck!'

As when landing on snow or sand, the rotor down-wash violently disturbed the surface to raise blinding spray as the Chinook dropped close to the huge, undulating waves. Unable to see clearly the exact moment of touch-down, Maggie prayed Randal had not been spinning her a yarn about his successful taxi over water a few years ago.

'Think it'll work?' asked Jeff shortly, watching the warning panel for further signs of trouble.

'We're about to find out,' she replied as a thud indicated

contact with the sea, and she shifted into taxiing mode as if they were on firm ground.

Half expecting to feel the cockpit tip sideways into the water, Maggie stared through the windows cleared by swishing wipers and tried not to think about the dark fathoms passing mere inches below her feet as they ploughed towards the coast. Biting her lip in concentration she was aware of Jeff reporting to Control details of their intention and present position, and of the comments of her crewmen on the situation back in the cabin. Throughout, she prayed they could keep their one engine alive and the rotors turning for as long as they needed.

'We're taking on water by the gallon through the ramp,' warned Griff. 'I'm moving up with Dave.'

'Keep going,' urged Jeff, as Maggie cast him a glance. 'Another eight minutes or so'll get us to that beach. If we have to take to the dinghy let's do it at the last possible moment.'

'How's the noise, the smell of burning?' she demanded over the intercom.

'Only noise we can hear now is the thunder of waves against the sides,' Dave told her. 'Can smell only what we normally smell. No smoke visible, but it's very dim with the door shut. How far to go? It's bloody scary back here.'

Jeff answered. 'Six minutes, and it's bloody scary up here. We can see more than you can. Take a good look around the cabin, Dave. If there was smoke just now it must still be there. I don't want to risk anything at this point.'

'Aye, but we'll have to slosh around down by the ramp.'

'Here come the Yellow Hats,' said Maggie, spotting the Search and Rescue helicopter heading towards them. 'They were quick off the mark.'

Jeff switched frequencies to make contact with the other crew and outlined the situation. 'We have one engine shut down and we're taking on water, but we hope to reach that cove dead ahead and beach there. Stick around in case we need you.'

'Will do. Listening out.'

Maggie began to relax. They had been forging over the waves for more than ten minutes; the small bay was now clearly visible and the SAR boys were overhead ready to pluck them from the deep, if necessary. If they made it to dry land there would be no dreaded inquiry into how a hugely expensive aircraft came to be lost at sea. As the pilot at the time, Maggie would be held ultimately responsible for whatever happened.

It was possible to see figures on the beach. There was a cluster of people staring and pointing; dogs racing over the sand; children at the water's edge – the hardy British braving the April chill at the seaside who all at once see a great green beast with whirling rotors speeding over the sea towards them!

'Those idiots look set to stay where they are and risk being mown down,' cried Jeff.

'Run the buggers down if you have to, but get us on that beach before we go under, woman,' snarled Griff from the rear.

Maggie ignored his outburst, concentrating on keeping afloat for the length of time it would take to get to the beach. The watchers would surely run back when they saw the Chinook about to land. Her estimation was wrong. As the aircraft closed with the strip of sand, the onlookers surged forward in excitement towards the clear area Maggie was heading for.

'God, are they *mad*?' she cried, tensing further.

Jeff said crisply, 'They'll soon halt when the downwash hits them. Keep going! The shoreline's only sixty feet away. The wheels'll be making contact any time now.'

When it became obvious the Chinook was going to rise from the sea on to the beach, the hurrying spectators checked, but Maggie was by then more concerned with the prospect of wet, yielding sand strewn with seaweed. What if the wheels stuck fast?

The next few minutes demanded all her skill and attention as they surged from the water sending sand flying in a vortex to obscure her vision from the windows, but beneath her feet she saw solid ground. Yielding sand or not, it was a welcome sight. She let out a long sigh of relief at returning to earth, and silently thanked Randal for the tale that had saved them today.

Dave had opened the side door and was able to give Maggie a commentary on the state of the beach and any obstacles. She slowly moved the Chinook clear of the tideline and brought it to a standstill. Then she and Jeff began the shut-down procedure. The engine was cut, the rotors gradually stilled. The flying sand settled. It seemed blessedly quiet.

A cheery voice came over the airwaves from the circling Sea King. 'The walrus has landed! If you don't need us, we'll get back to our game of chess.'

'Yeah, thanks, guys. Sorry to spoil your afternoon's pleasure.'

'Maybe no one told you those ugly great things are meant to travel through the air. Comes in lesson two.'

Maggie was leaning back in her seat taking deep breaths to ease her aching stomach muscles when Jeff tapped her arm. 'I'll recommend that you be promoted from cooking our dinners,' he said with a grin. 'That wasn't half bad.'

She gave a weary smile. 'Thanks, but right now cooking dinners sounds like a very restful occupation.' Her attention was then caught by the sound of raised voices, and she gazed from her window to see Dave and Griff out on the sand engaged in an aggressive confrontation watched by awed spectators. 'Trouble! We'd better get out there, Jeff.'

They swiftly clambered from the cockpit to a brisk, salty

breeze and the pungent smell of seaweed, in time to hear Griff say forcefully, 'C'mon, man, we could now be at the bottom of the sea because of that bitch.'

'It's because of Maggie we're *not*,' Dave argued hotly.

'It's bloody fantastic *luck* we're not! Another few minutes and we'd ha' gone down like a stone.'

Dave pointed at the massive rotor blades now drooping motionless. 'With that power holding us up? Don't be a fool. Calm down, Griff!' He glanced past the man at the interested onlookers, then added in an urgent undertone. 'And for God's sake, *shut up!*'

Griff was furious. 'You eat your sodding tongue! You're no' an officer any longer.' He began to poke Dave in the chest with his finger to add force to his words. 'I've been watching you. You kiss the arse of anyone with rank just to keep in with them – even that commissioned cow who should never be put in control of anything, much less a helicopter. She's disaster. I said so all along, but the Boss willna have it. He's as besotted with her as the rest of ye.'

Dave grabbed the Glaswegian's arm and tried to pull him further down the beach away from the earshot of the clustered civilians enjoying this unexpected drama. The powerful Griff threw Dave off and up against the side of the Chinook. 'Aye, you're all panting for her, especially Randal bloody Price, ye puir fools!' he said, thrusting his face close to Dave's.

Fully aware of the attention they were attracting, Dave said through gritted teeth, 'If you want a fight I'm ready for it, but we'll settle it inside the cabin.'

At that point, Jeff walked the few paces to them and spoke with quiet authority. 'Okay, guys, break it up! You're playing to an audience.'

Griff's pointed face flushed darker with anger. 'This is between me and this bastard who thinks he's a better man because his folk live in a bloody castle. I know my job well

125

enough and *I'm* not going into orgasm with gratitude because we're not lying on the seabed. What about that Harrier? When *she's* around there's disaster wherever you look.'

By now really annoyed, Jeff pulled rank. 'This is between the entire crew and I'm the senior member of it. If you've anything more to say, get inside the aircraft and say it to me. *Now!*'

Griff gave an evil smile. 'I'll say what I need to when we get back to Hampton, *sir*. I want out of B Flight. The boss of it was smashed up by four yobbos who dropped something on his car. With him *and* her in the ranks there's a double jinx on the whole lot of us.'

After dinner, Randal was drinking with Chris in the bar. He was not relaxed. Dirk and Pete had taken the standby Chinook to bring the stricken one in, and he was on edge waiting for first-hand news of what had happened. Jeffries had hinted that the crew could just as well have flown to the shore if one engine had been functioning throughout. He was unhappy over a helicopter of his squadron taxiing up to a public beach surrounded by luxury holiday homes. Randal had asked if he would have preferred a landing in one of the gardens, taking off the roof of the luxury holiday home, and they had exchanged heated words.

'He's impossible, Chris, although there was never much rapport between us when I was here before. It seems to have vanished altogether now. He fails to back us when anything doesn't go according to plan, and you know how often that can happen. Christ, they couldn't help an engine malfunction.'

Chris made a face. 'I keep praying he'll be offered promotion and go off to plague some other poor devils. Ah, forget him and drink up.' After a moment he said gloomily, 'D'you think Maggie'll find something decent to wear to this first night next month? You know what these affairs are like – women turn up in the most outrageously sexy outfits. I don't want to be the only man with—'

The Mess Sergeant had appeared beside Randal and clearly wanted him urgently. As Chris broke off abruptly, Randal asked, 'They're back?'

'Not that I've heard, sir. The Station Commander's on the phone.' His tone mirrored his thoughts; good news could always wait until morning. This meant trouble of some kind. 'I'll get the switchboard to patch it through to your room.'

'Right.' Randal headed out to the stairs and took them two at a time, deeply worried. Something had gone wrong! There was a spring tide which would practically flood the small bay by midnight. It was essential to lift the damaged Chinook well before then, but it would take time. The rotors had to be dismantled before chains could be attached and the handlers would be working in poor light created by the steady rain which had now reached the area. Dear God, surely both aircraft had not come to grief during the return flight!

Leaving the door of his room open in his haste, he snatched up the receiver. 'Squadron Leader Price.'

'Connecting you, sir,' said the girl, then Martin Ashe spoke from his home.

'Did you watch the early TV news this evening?' he began without preamble.

'No, sir.' Randal's mind raced. Had some overseas military coup put them in emergency mode?

'As usual in these cases no one on the Station appears to have seen what Joe Public did,' he said heavily. 'My dinner has been disrupted by telephone calls from radio and TV stations, national newspapers and Group Captain Marchant at Strike Command, all asking me to comment on something I knew nothing about. Something bloody awkward to gloss over with any credibility.'

He sounded tetchy rather than geared for an operational emergency, but Randal was disturbed by the media and

Command interest even though his fears over the safety of his aircrew and the Chinooks seemed unfounded. Sinking on the bed, he asked, 'What was on the TV, sir?'

'Footage from a video film taken by a pensioner living in a bungalow overlooking the bay where one of our Chinooks fetched up this afternoon. The old boy apparently saw it taxiing over the water and rushed for his camcorder. He filmed the beaching and the shut-down.' Ashe's voice grew harsher. 'Unfortunately, he kept the camera running to record a punch-up between the crew.'

'*What?*'

'A brawl. Watched by a dozen or so fascinated civilians. Our excited senior citizen then rang the local TV station offering to sell his exclusive film, whereupon they sent a reporter and cameraman to get the full story. I imagine they're all set to record the removal of the military invader of their peace, too, but that won't be as titillating as the sight of RAF aircrew exchanging insults and grabbing each other by the throat.'

Randal was immediately defensive. 'I find that hard to believe.'

'*It's on film*, Rip. Viewers saw it on their screens.'

'But—'

'Onlookers filled in what the video didn't record. They claimed the fight was over a woman in the crew who was responsible for what had happened to the aircraft. One of the men was overheard to say he would never fly with her again, because she had also caused a Harrier crash.'

'*What?*' cried Randal again, growing uncomfortably aware of who was probably behind this.

'When questioned, Flight Lieutenant Jeffrey Norton said they had just dealt with a potentially hazardous situation and were simply letting off steam to ease their tension. He would not allow the reporter to speak to the woman pilot, or to the two men who had attacked each other.' Ashe allowed time for that to sink in. 'Sound tactics on Jeff's part, thank God! I imagine the crew has been under siege inside the Chinook ever since.'

'Sir, it's—'

'One more thing. During this alleged punch-up, mention was made of their boss being the victim when four boys dropped something on his car along a motorway. The details of your accident were dug out and mentioned on the TV report to highlight the declaration by Sergeant Griffin that there is a double jinx on B Flight, Six Four Six Squadron. From the tone of the calls I had this evening, that will be the gist of the piece in the seedier tabloids tomorrow.'

All this was so far removed from what he had expected to hear, Randal could think of nothing constructive to say. His deep aversion to media attention overrode any other reaction.

'I need to get to the bottom of this before morning,' said Ashe crisply. 'I've just spoken to Gerard. He said he warned you of Sergeant Griffin's attitude over flying with a woman aboard, and you ignored it.'

'No, I discussed it with Griff,' he corrected, driven to his feet again by anger over Jeffries' passing the buck. 'I pointed out to him many instances when he had flown safely with women in the aircraft, then gave him the option of becoming a full member of the team or of operating at a disadvantage. We all come across men like him with various chips on their shoulder. They try it on wherever they go. I can't have my aircrew telling me who they'll fly with and who they won't.'

'So you overrode your squadron commander's advice and deliberately crewed the pair together for this flight.'

Randal sensed that he was becoming deeply involved with this entire issue, and further justified his action. 'Sir, Sergeant Griffin has a strong dislike of Dave Ashmore because of their disparate social backgrounds. If I had given in over

Maggie, he would next have refused to fly with Dave . . . then someone else, until *he* was commanding B Flight.'

'It was Ashmore he was brawling with. Was putting them together another of your psychological stratagems?' The Station Commander changed direction. 'Can you explain the reference to Maggie being responsible for a Harrier crash?'

Disturbed by laughter as two men walked past his door, Randal kicked it shut while trying to marshal his wild thoughts. 'I can only imagine Griff has heard talk of the Harrier that blew up during a flying display at an air show the year before last. Maggie was present as one of a crew manning a static Chinook.' He paused to control his anger. 'She was in no way responsible for it. She was in love with the poor devil flying the display.'

Martin Ashe asked curiously, 'You're talking about Mark Hascham? I was stationed at Wittering when that happened. He'd just been selected to join the Red Arrows. There was no serious entanglement with a woman, so far as I was aware.'

'He hadn't advertised it . . . which helped Maggie escape media harrassment after the tragedy. If the tabloids somehow now get hold of that information the poor girl will be *hounded*,' he said explosively.

'That "poor girl" is a professional Air Force pilot trained to cope with the unexpected,' Ashe returned dryly. 'If she can resolve an emergency the way she apparently did this afternoon, I think she's well able to ride out tabloid sensationalism. From what I've seen of her she can hold her own without any mollycoddling from you.'

Randal felt his colour rise at this clear hint that he had put personal interest before professional considerations. In the face of his silence, Ashe wound up the interview. 'I'm about to drive back so I can speak to the crew when they fly in. I'll brief you and Gerard in the morning, once I've concocted a suitable comment for the media. The kind of exposure this brought us is very unwelcome. These bloody people fasten on the slender titbits supplied by excited civilians and play down the fact that one of our crews dealt admirably with a crisis at sea, salvaging an expensive aircraft that might otherwise have been lost. And Rip, whatever arrangement you had with your previous station commander, *I* wish to be made aware of any serious problems between your aircrew. When you joined the Squadron I was prepared for you to need bigger boots than Andy, but don't get too big for your own. Goodnight.'

Returning the dead receiver to its stand, Randal knew he had just had his knuckles rapped. It was not the first time in his career, but this was over something he could not possibly have forseen. He remained unshaken in his belief that he had dealt with Griff intelligently. The man's attitude had not endangered lives, or the Chinook, and it was pure bad luck that an amateur had filmed the aggression that often resulted from tricky situations. He still believed Griff was more of a troublemaker than a real danger, because if he was professionally obstructive in the air he would be putting his own life on the line with the rest of the crew. Griff was purely flexing muscle and pushing things as far as he could within the limits of his rank. He would almost certainly be posted elsewhere now, and he would play his power game with another flight commander.

There was now little point in being around to meet the incoming crews; Martin Ashe intended to do that. He had taken a Flight situation out of Randal's hands. While understanding why the man was deeply annoyed at being tackled as he had over a tiny incident that had been inflated into a juicy story about a squadron jinx, Randal nevertheless recognised that his CO had a steely side in contrast to the bonhomie normally in evidence when they met up. He would have to bear that in mind.

Returning to the bar, Randal attempted to drown his sorrows without success. Everything pointed to the details of his car smash being in newsprint again, and if some enterprising slush seeker now connected Maggie with Mark Hascham the tabloids would have a field day. Why Griff should have said what he had about Maggie being the cause of the Harrier tragedy Randal could not fathom. It happened almost two years ago. Griff would not have been in the Air Force then, so it was curious that he should have raised that particular point in a moment of stress.

Sure, Maggie was a professional pilot trained to cope with all manner of hazardous situations, but it was hardly 'mollycoddling' to regard her as a person with normal human emotions. He would behave the same way towards any member of his team. Randal had seen her minutes after Hascham's aircraft had exploded and dropped in flames. Ashe had not, or he would be more understanding.

Soon under the influence and maudlin, Randal told himself he should never have twisted Mark Grainger's arm to get back to B Flight. Maggie had reversed her request for a transfer because he was returning and she thought things would be better. How bloody wrong she was. He was making a mammoth cock-up of everything.

Taking himself off to bed before someone would be obliged to do it for him, he lay in the darkness, muttering, 'I *can* command B Flight. I *am* able to handle days like today. I *will* succeed.'

Morning newspapers bore banner headlines heralding the shocking details of the discovery in a hotel room of the naked bodies of a member of parliament and his black mistress. Both had been shot at close range. The MP had been involved in a recent secret arms deal. Was it political murder, a racist killing, the vengeance of a scorned wife, or a suicide pact? The story of an RAF squadron jinx was nothing compared with this sensational development, so it did not even warrant a small paragraph on the pages mostly taken up by adverts.

Six

On an Olympic bobsleigh run Dirk had been fearless. Scaling a tricky rockface his hands and feet were steady and sure. He explored subterranean caves with total confidence, and he drove a fast boat with skill and daring. Why, then, did he feel in need of Dutch courage when about to face Paula?

Of course, he might not face her. Caution – or cowardice – had led him to decide on a surprise visit to Bristol during a three-day stand-down. That way, if she was not at her parents' home when he called he would know she was not deliberately avoiding him. If she was there she would hardly slam the door in his face. Or would she? If she could write that bruising letter out of the blue maybe she could do that.

Sam's phone call had revived feelings Dirk had tried for four months to subdue. Overnight his fighting spirit returned, making him wonder how he could have tamely accepted Paula's advice to back off and get on with his life. She and Sam were a significant part of it. So was Mike. A friendship like theirs did not end because one of them was no longer around.

In a small wayside pub Dirk drank a large Scotch and thought about those eight years when he and Mike had been dubbed 'the terrible twins' by parents, teachers and neighbours alike. Only the advent of Paula had changed that. Dirk recalled how he had drunkenly released the bridegroom who had been confined, naked, in the village stocks at the end of a riotous stag night, and somehow got Mike and himself to the church on time with buttons and zips decently fastened. They had stood side by side, suffering from mammoth hangovers, while Paula pledged her fidelity and her beautiful body to that one of them she had chosen. They had stood together in church once more for Sam's christening. Had Mike ever appreciated how much it had cost his pal to be there in a subordinate role on those two occasions?

The advent of Sam had heralded a new aspect of their friendship. Fatherhood had banished Mike's wilder impulses; he even threatened to become boring on the subject. There had never been a baby the equal of Sam. Gradually, almost imperceptibly, Dirk had also sobered over the next three years. The marriage became a threesome inasmuch as the men shared its problems and successes – until the night Dirk took things a step further and shared Mike's wife.

Staring moodily into a second large whisky, Dirk reflected that it had seemed perfectly natural at the time. With Mike on relief in Northern Ireland, he and Paula had presided over Sam's birthday party trying to control seven little demons. They had together put an overexcited Sam to bed then gone downstairs to face the messy clearing up, just like a married couple. Ninety minutes and two bottles of wine later they had begun to make love on the settee, then decided bed would give them greater scope and comfort. Just like a married couple!

When Mike returned five days later a deep sense of betrayal then smote Dirk, so he volunteered to replace a pilot granted compassionate leave from Bosnia. Mike arrived there on normal duty two weeks later and resumed his former wild ways. Although he displayed no animosity towards Dirk, their rapport was absent. Mike had been in a world of his own; drinking heavily and bedding any willing woman. Only during those few minutes before his final flight had Mike revealed his intention to divorce Paula and abandon his beloved son along with her.

Resuming his journey, Dirk remembered being once again in church with Paula, this time as one of Mike's pall-bearers. For almost a year Dirk had been true to his vow to care for his friend's widow and son through the terrible grief. Paula had stayed in the house Mike had bought and continued working part-time with a travel agent, saying it kept her from thinking. During that period of mourning Dirk had not attempted to be more than a good friend to the girl he loved. A curious sense of culpability had persuaded him it would be unacceptable until they were married. He had assumed Paula shared his feelings, until her letter had shown him he was wrong. Putting his foot down on the accelerator, he now headed for Bristol with the aim of getting to the bottom of her shattering rejection.

The Martins' detached, mid-fifties house was one of a long row of similar homes. The short drive was occupied by two cars, so he parked his MG alongside the kerb and took a deep breath before heading for the front door carrying several packages: chocolates for Paula and for her mother, a toy boat for Sam.

Jean Martin came to the door, a plump woman with fading red hair. Her face lit with pleasure. 'Dirk! What a lovely surprise. Come on in. Stan'll be very pleased to see you.'

'Is Paula here?' he asked, stepping inside.

'We all are.' She kissed him heartily. 'Why didn't you let us know you were coming?'

'You know how it is. We can't predict where we'll be from day to day. Hopeless to make plans.'

She studied him in motherly fashion. 'You look very tired. Where've you been since we last saw you at Christmas?'

'I'm with a new squadron.'

'Yes, and they must be working you too hard.' On the brink of saying more, she instead turned and led the way through to where a door stood ajar. Pushing it fully open, she announced, 'Look who's here.'

Dirk only had time to register the shock on Paula's face, and the fact that his old squadron colleague, Tim Ferriday, was beside her on the settee, before a small tornado rushed at him shrieking, '*Uncle Dirk!*'

All Dirk's attention was taken by this wild greeting. 'Hey, I'm not a brick wall. I can be knocked down by speeding kids.' He lifted the boy, hugging him close before holding him away again to study the round, flushed face and blue eyes sparkling with tears. 'How's my best mate?'

'You came. You *came*,' Sam said thickly.

'Didn't I say I would?'

'Mummy said you'd gone away for a very, *very* long time and wouldn't be able to visit any more.' Sam flung his arms around Dirk's neck, mumbling into his collar, 'I've missed you *heaps*.'

With the child clinging as if he would never let go, Dirk glanced across at Paula. Although her face was pale it now wore the expression he knew well. She was never less than fully in control of any situation, he recalled. He had not been there when they broke the news of Mike's death to her, but her emotions were mastered by the time the body was released and Dirk arrived from Bosnia to attend the funeral.

'How did you know this address?' she now demanded.

Sam twisted to face his mother. 'I told him. The lady on the telephone found the place called Hampton and Uncle Dirk was there. I talked to him. He *hadn't* gone away. He didn't come because he didn't know where I was. Why didn't you tell him, Mummy. *Why* didn't you?' he demanded tearfully.

Stanley Martin, like many fathers of daughters, who took

refuge from feminine behaviour beyond their comprehension in the only way they knew, did so now by offering beer. 'Sure you could down a pint before lunch, eh?' he said in his familiar pipe-and-slippers way. 'Jean, there'll be enough of that pie you've made for one extra, won't there? Even one with Dirk's appetite,' he added with a chuckle as he disappeared to the kitchen.

'Of course,' his wife replied, exchanging a significant look with Paula.

Dirk explained hastily, 'I was intending to take Paula out to lunch.'

'Then you should have phoned first,' Paula said with perfect poise. 'Mum's arranged a meal here.' She came to him and the scent of Opium washed over Dirk to bring tantalising memories. 'Get down, Sam, and let Uncle Dirk drink his beer.' She took the boy and set him on his feet, telling him to wash his hands before lunch.

'I've a present for you,' Dirk said. 'Better open it before you wash.'

Sam tore off the paper with eager hands. 'Wow! *Thanks*, Uncle Dirk. Is it just like yours?' he cried, examining the model powerboat from every angle before looking up. 'Will you take us to sea again? *Please.*'

'*Wash your hands,*' ordered his mother. Sam went.

Dirk put the chocolates on the coffee table. 'Something for you and Jean.'

'You shouldn't have,' Paula said tonelessly, turning away. 'Come on, Mum, I'll help you set the table.'

Left in the room with Tim Ferriday, Dirk tried to smother his jealousy by asking carelessly how his former squadron was faring. Also determined to rise to the occasion, Tim offered news of scandals and successes in similar throwaway manner. They both forced laughs and attempted to revive the cameraderie of men who had flown together many times, all the while knowing they were predatory males after the same mate. Stanley came with beer for them all, then led the way down the garden to show off the begonias he intended to enter in the flower show. His single-minded insensitivity to the situation probably saved its deterioration into raw aggression, but the two young men ate lunch with it smouldering beneath the surface.

Dirk studied Paula across the table with mixed feelings. She looked younger, less strained than at Christmas, which was understandable. The first anniversary of Mike's death had passed, and she had left that area that held memories of her four years with him. Time to get on with her life, as she had written. Yet there was a brittle quality about her, a curious suggestion of aloofness. Paula had always been a generous, outgoing person whose eyes sparkled with teasing lights whenever she was enjoying herself. An undeniable flirt, Dirk admitted, but not now. Although Tim had had his arm across her shoulders on that settee there was no life in her when she looked at him, no intimate message in her glances across the table. Nor was there for Dirk. They might never have been close; never have been lovers one night.

As the difficult meal progressed Sam chatted non-stop to Dirk, Stanley visibly bored Tim with a monologue concerning the judging at flower shows, Jean fussed over extra helpings of vegetables and gravy, but Paula ate in relative silence. Thrown by her attitude, Dirk wondered how to get her on her own to say what he needed to. Yet even that seemed unwise in the face of her coldness today. How could he tell this distant girl to follow the obvious course and marry him, as Mike would surely want? As *he* most certainly wanted.

They all determinedly munched raspberry meringue, then drank coffee while Sam continued to update Dirk with all that had happened to him since he arrived in Bristol, and Stanley moved on from flower shows to enthusiastic descriptions of match-winning goals he had enjoyed over a lifetime of watching his favourite game.

'You and your wretched football,' Sam said after a while.

'Don't speak to Grandad like that,' snapped Paula.

'Grandma does.'

'That's different.' She threw a glance at Stanley trying to smother a grin. 'It's not funny, Dad.' Getting to her feet, she said, 'If we live here much longer he'll be impossible to control. Go to your room, Sam!'

The boy's eyes filled. 'I want to stay with Uncle Dirk.'

'That's a bit harsh,' Stanley protested, and Jean added stiffly, 'He's overexcited. He's barely five, Paula.'

Into the awkward silence Tim got to his feet, saying, 'I ought to get going, honey. We're flying out at dawn tomorrow and I've yet to get my stuff together.' He turned to Jean. 'That was a delicious lunch. You're a super cook. If you ever grow tired of Stanley and fancy becoming wife number three, give me a call.'

With pink anger spots still on her cheeks, Jean could not reply to his joke in kind. 'You'll be after someone younger and more flighty than me, a girl with *no* responsibilities.'

'I'll see you off,' said Paula, apparently impervious to that strong hint.

Tim kissed Jean's cheek, shook hands with Stanley, then nodded at Dirk. 'Cheers. See you around.' He ignored Sam.

After the pair left, Jean gave an apologetic shrug. 'It's a difficult time for her, Dirk.'

'Did she really not tell you she was here?' asked Stanley.

After a glance at Sam, who appeared engrossed in the model boat, Dirk told them about the letter Paula had written after Christmas. 'I respected her wishes because I thought she needed time to sort out her feelings for me. Then Sam telephoned the Mess, very upset because

I had stayed away. When he mentioned that Paula was dating Tim, and others, I thought I should come and sort things out with her.' He moved from the table, wondering how long a goodbye she was going to give the randy navigator. He knew more about Tim Ferriday than she did.

'Fancy Sam making that call to you without knowing the number,' marvelled Stanley. 'He's a smart kid. Just like his dad.'

'Shh!' warned his wife, inclining her head towards the boy.

'It's good to talk about Mike,' Stanley insisted. 'It's not as if the poor lad's in prison or done something bad. Sam's got to be proud of his father and understand that he died doing something really worthwhile. You and Paula sweep the truth under the carpet, but someone's got to do the right thing by young Mike. Don't you agree, Dirk?'

Dirk was presently more concerned about what Paula and Tim were doing, but he hastened to make this couple his allies. 'I know it must have been hell for Paula since the crash, and it's probably good for her to be with you for a while, but you know how I've always felt about her. Mike and I . . . well, the best man won. I might only be second best, but I was all set to—'

Paula entered to end what he had intended to confess. 'Is there any more coffee, Mum?'

'In the pot.' She stood. 'Where's that blue begonia you were going to show me and Sam?' she demanded of her husband.

'What blue begonia?' Tardily interpreting this suggestion that they make themselves scarce, he got up. 'Ah . . . yes, a blue begonia. Come on, young Sam, this is something you have to see.'

'I want to—'

'Uncle Dirk'll still be here after you've seen this rare

flower,' put in Jean, firmly propelling the boy ahead of her through the French door leading to the long garden.

Paula glanced up from pouring coffee. 'They've no tact.'

'Maybe they want this cleared up as much as I do.'

She sipped her coffee. 'Want what cleared up?'

'Oh, for God's sake what's got into you, Paula?' he demanded. 'For six years we've been as close as friends can be – too close on one occasion. You can't end something like that with a short letter saying we must get on with our lives and goodbye.'

She gazed at him frankly. 'I thanked you for your support, didn't I?'

Dirk counted to five. 'Why d'you think I gave it? It wasn't just for Mike's sake, you know. He was the lucky one you chose, but I thought there was enough caring left over for me. That night . . . we were pretty good together, weren't we?'

'I don't remember much about it.'

Growing hot, he studied her curves outlined by tight jeans and a clinging yellow shirt. 'You didn't exactly lie there with your eyes closed.'

Setting down the cup and saucer she said calmly, 'Dirk, we were both pissed; you were there, Mike wasn't. Don't make a major issue of it.'

'It *was* a major bloody issue for me. It still is. Mike was like a brother but I loved you as much as he did.'

She pushed back her rich red hair with a hand tipped by scarlet nails, and sighed. 'That was the trouble. You two were so close you hadn't lives of your own. At that wedding reception you both spotted me and began a game of one-upmanship. When Mike started getting serious, so did you. When he married me you convinced yourself that was what you wanted. We could have been a *ménage à trois* if the Air Force had allowed it. You didn't betray Mike that night, you simply substituted for an absent buddy. As I said, it wasn't a major issue for me.'

'Something bloody was for poor Mike,' he said with heat. 'I've kept quiet about this because I didn't want to hurt you, but perhaps you should know. When he came out to Bosnia he was tense and withdrawn. I couldn't get through to him at all.' He glanced away through the French door, seeing nothing of the garden but only that green Balkan valley. 'If you'd told him about that night you claim to remember very little of he'd have half killed me, so I guessed it wasn't that on his mind.' Turning back to her he said, 'As we walked out to the Chinook he told me I could have you and Sam soon, because he was getting shot of you both the minute he arrived home. Why, Paula, *why*?'

Her calm control vanished; she looked deeply upset. 'It's water under the bridge, Dirk. Mike's gone. Why rake up things that no longer matter?'

'They matter to me.'

'I know. I *know*,' she repeated more gently. 'You still can't adjust to life without him.'

'You clearly can,' he accused bitterly. 'It didn't take you long to get Ferriday on the go.'

'Tim's no hassle. He just wants sex.' Before Dirk could comment she asked, 'Has it ever occurred to you that I didn't know Mike very well? In the five months before we married I guess we had only a dozen or so dates. Don't look so caustic! You know damn well what squadron duties are like. Here today, gone for several months tomorrow.'

'He saw you often enough to put you in the club.'

'After the wedding I spent more time alone in our new house than I did with him there, but you were with Mike day in, day out. You flew with him, went wherever he went. You worked, relaxed, ate, went on the town with him and even slept in the next bed more often than not. When you came home you even arrived at the house with him.'

Disturbed and angry, Dirk hit out. 'Hang on! Who kept

asking girls to the house to make up a foursome? Who said I made life go with a swing?'

'I did . . . and you did.' She sighed heavily. 'It didn't take me long to realise Mike was going to take parenthood very seriously. When I was seven months pregnant he called a halt to full sex in case the baby was damaged. After Sam was born he drove me mad checking that I was doing all the right things at the right time for his precious boy. It was a relief when he was away.' She gave a bitter smile. 'Even when he rang from wherever you happened to be at the time, he used the call to ask about the baby. You said yourself he became a bore on the subject.'

'But I was just—'

'You so often hear of husbands going off the rails because their wives concentrate on the children to their exclusion. We had that situation in reverse. I didn't go off the rails, I instead invited sexy girls for you and tried to create some fun. I'd had parenthood up to my ears while Mike was away. I needed to be young and crazy with him when he got home, but he wanted to do the daddy act.' She waved an arm at him. 'You know. You were there.'

Dirk studied her for a moment or two. 'What's this all about?'

'It's about *me*. About wanting to be a person in my own right, not merely a nursemaid and nanny for Sam. All Mike's hot passion that refused to take no for an answer when we were dating, vanished somewhere beyond recall. When we did have sex half his attention was on listening for crying or shouts from Sam's room. At the first sound of a whimper he'd be out of bed like lightning, leaving me in the middle of orgasm as like as not. Selfish bastard!'

Shocked, Dirk voiced a protest. 'The poor guy's *dead*, for God's sake!'

'And I'm a widow. *A twenty-five-year-old widow!*' she cried. 'I need something more from life than that.'

'I was offering it, but you gave me the brush off,' he countered hotly. 'Ferriday just provides sex, you said. I'd provide that along with a whole lot more. I want us to get married, have a house together – a home to return to. I want to look after you, have fun with you. Spend the rest of my life with you.'

She was already shaking her head before he finished speaking. 'You won't see it, will you? Mike's gone, so you're trying to live his life for him. You want to take over where he left off, that's all. You'd be forever talking to me of the old days with him; what you used to get up to together. Oh God, can't you understand? You'd be wearing the same uniform, working the same deadly routine, flying the same bloody aircraft and coming home knackered after rampaging through the bars and nightspots of wherever you'd been serving.' Her voice rose with tension. 'Marrying you would be like living with Mike's ghost.'

'*Paula!*'

She was losing control now. 'You think you're offering marriage for *my* sake? Wise up, Dirk. You're doing it for him.'

'And for his son.'

'Sam isn't Mike's son.'

The silence between them was so total it seemed impossible to break, until Dirk managed to say, 'What the hell are you talking about?'

Paula looked stricken. 'I shouldn't have said that.' Turning away to gaze down the garden she said wearily, 'Why couldn't you do as I said and get on with your life without us? Why did you have to turn up here and bring it all to the surface again?'

Dirk was too shaken to respond and, for a while, he thought Paula would say nothing more. Then she began speaking in a curious, faraway voice as if just to herself.

'When you and Mike came on the scene I was desperately

trying to keep alive an affair with a married man. I was seriously in love and I thought dating other men would make him jealous enough to arrange a divorce. What a fool! When I told him I was pregnant he backed off. Advised me to have an abortion.' She paused a moment before adding reflectively, 'Men can't be humiliated that way.'

'There are other ways of doing it,' he said harshly.

'Mike was getting demanding, so I slept with him. We married. He was adoring. I really needed adoration right then.' She gave a bitter laugh. 'My bid to avoid being an unmarried mother rebounded on me. Sam became the kingpin in our relationship, and the irony . . . the irony was that Mike doted on a kid who wasn't his. He bored on about how much Sam resembled pictures of himself at that age – even his mother said so – and he claimed "his boy" was more intelligent, more advanced than any other on the Station. There were times when I longed to scream the facts at him just to shut him up.'

She turned back to face him, and there were tears on her cheeks. 'I thought he'd grow out of it in time, but every stage of Sam's growth brought further adulation and bloody ridiculous pride at having sired such a prodigy. On the night before he flew out to Bosnia we had a flaming row and I— The truth came out before I could stop myself. I thought he'd lay in to me. Or Sam. But he just walked out; snatched up his bag and left. That was the last time I saw him, and I'll never forget the look on his face when the truth hit him. I've lived with that from the moment the Squadron Commander and the Padre came to tell me Mike had been killed.' Her voice finally broke. 'Every time I see you the knife twists. *Now* d'you understand?'

He walked out on her, as Mike had.

The Squadron had an obligation to hold one aircraft and crew on emergency standby night and day. When Dirk returned to Hampton the Wailing Wall showed his name against the task for the coming twenty-four hours. With him would be Maggie, Dave and Jimmy: three squadron stalwarts. Were they expecting something big to break?

Dirk went from there straight to his room, bypassing the bar. He was in no mood for company after trekking through the Welsh hills alone for the past three days. He could not yet come to terms with what Paula had confessed; could not begin to accept that Mike had died knowing he had been duped into marriage to provide a father for some other bastard's child. Terrible enough to lose his life at twenty-nine, but to go out after being told the boy he adored was not his own son! Paula's treachery surely diminished Dirk's own. That night had meant very little to her because she felt loyalty to no one but herself. Dirk had actually stolen nothing from Mike.

He slept badly and was awake when the alarm buzzed. Slamming a hand on it he grunted,' Yeah, I know the bloody time. I've been looking at you for most of the night.'

He showered, shaved and dressed in depressed mood, then walked morosely to the Briefing Room where the standby crew was waiting to hand over to them. They seemed unreasonably cheerful. He scowled at their rude comments on how best to pass the time when emergencies failed to materialise. Maggie countered them expertly. She would. She had an answer for everything! Women were not high on Dirk's list of favourite people as of four days ago, and he cursed the fact that this particular one had been dumped on him.

They went up to the Crew Room where they made coffee and toast, then settled with newspapers to await breakfast. The other three soon began a lively debate on press reports of possible human cloning. Dirk took no part in it until Maggie turned to him.

'You're quiet. You normally give an opinion on everything under the sun, even when you're not asked for one.'

From behind his paper Dirk muttered, 'Why fabricate people? There're too many kids coming into the world already.'

'Five are mine,' Jimmy reminded him.

'They're legit— with the right parents.'

'There's some doubt about that,' joked Dave. 'There are dark rumours about the pizza delivery guy.'

'Give it a rest,' said Jimmy, swiping Dave with his folded paper.

Dirk tried to concentrate on reading while they progressed to speculation on whether a community of clones that would tolerate life on another planet could be created.

'Introduce the right genes and I can't see any problem,' concluded Dave. 'And if we sent home-produced humans into space they'd be programmed not to be hostile to earth dwellers. Lessen the threat of attack by wee green men with two heads, wouldn't it?'

Conversation soon turned to the swift departure of Griff, and of the poor unsuspecting team he would be joining. 'Let's hope his replacement'll be more reasonable,' said Maggie with feeling. 'He'll surely be from your old squadron, Dirk. Any misfits you know of?'

He glowered at her. 'Don't you ever shut up? I agree with Griff. Women should be refused aircrew status and kept on the ground, where they can cluck like hens to each other all day long.'

'Dear, dear, has she turned you down again?' Maggie taunted.

He moved to a chair in a far corner, making a great show of studying the newspaper while the others muttered about *all* members of their rival squadron clearly being misfits.

Moods and attitudes were forgotten five minutes later when the loudspeaker summoned them for a briefing, and they headed along the corridor speculating on the nature of their emergency task.

147

'A military coup in Latvia! Our man and his entourage have to be brought out under heavy artillery fire,' suggested Dave dramatically.

'Nah,' countered Jimmy. 'Spain has invaded Gibraltar and we've to go in and rescue the Barbary apes.'

'Speaking of apes, perhaps one has driven his MG into a ditch and needs us to pull him out,' suggested Maggie slyly.

Dirk hit back. 'More likely some woman's got her Chinook stuck on a beach and wants to be airlifted out before her crew do her in.'

Maggie cast him a level look. 'My, she must have put up the *strictly verboten* signs this time. I suppose you'll be seeking another counselling session in the Bird with our friendly station doc.'

'Let me know when you're set for another cosy-up with our boss in there and I'll pick a different evening,' he snapped.

Dirk was surprised to find Gerard Jeffries waiting for them. He lived very near the Station, but was not normally in his office until eight to eight-thirty. What had prompted this early start to his working day? The Squadron Commander gave no clue on that, merely told them in the testy manner they knew well to sit down. He was clearly more annoyed than hyped-up, so Dirk's ideas of a major military disaster began to fade. The senior man was sharply on the ball when it came to national security.

'We've been called on because we happen to be in the right area,' he began, still testy. 'Four days ago Jeff and his crew picked up air cadets from two public schools and flew them to Exmoor to begin a survival exercise. Nothing too demanding. Springtime, reasonable weather. Each boy had three days' rations and was expected to find whatever he could to eat on the other two. With them was an ATC officer and a physical training instructor from one of the schools.

Late yesterday afternoon all contact with the group ceased. An SAR crew was sent to the area they ought to have been in, but found no sign of them. Although conditions were dicey last night they kept up the search while their fuel lasted. Land rescue groups prepared to go out until the advent of freezing fog made the operation futile. A Sea King resumed the air search at first light. Soon afterwards, SAR Headquarters received a call from a Group Captain Soames who reported that his grandson had contacted him on a mobile phone borrowed from a passing motorist. This boy gave the approximate position of the group and said they're all ill.' Jeffries' eyebrows rose. 'The whole bloody lot, including the adults in charge.'

'How come not the grandson?' Maggie asked.

Deeming that irrelevant, Jeffries continued. 'Half an hour ago the second Sea King took out extra medics to join the search. They've just located three boys who had left the main group in a bid to fetch help. They're in a bad way – food poisoning, dehydration, hypothermia. There was a sharp frost on the moor last night, and they felt too ill to find shelter. SAR are flying them to Barnstaple hospital, but they can't cope with forty or more emergency casualties. You're to collect the bulk of them and fly them to Exeter. A fleet of ambulances will be on standby to drive them to hospital. I've contacted Squadron Leader Miles. Two of her orderlies are on their way over here with additional medical equipment.' He swept them with a cold glance. 'The parents of these boys will be out for someone's blood. Thank God it won't be ours!'

'Will SAR work with us?' asked Dirk.

'Naturally. These bloody lads have ignored the first rule of survival and split up, apparently. Their approximate location is here,' he added, circling the wall chart with his finger, 'but it's only approximate. The three who've been rescued were too disorientated to give any useful info.' He turned back to face them. 'Here's the bad news. Although the temperature has risen four degrees the fog is persisting in low-lying areas. SAR say visibility is tricky. Don't forget how boggy those low areas can also be,' he reminded Dirk unnecessarily. 'Get one of your crewmen out there on foot before attempting to land. All right, get going, and for God's sake find those boys before a tragedy occurs. Someone's made a balls-up of this affair and the Press'll be gunning for them. Make sure they get nothing on you.'

It was not by chance that his gaze rested on Maggie for those final words before he left the room. She was furious. 'There are kids out there suffering and scared to death, but all he can think of is keeping clear of the headlines. His guts are made of steel.'

'Which earned him a medal in the Falklands bash,' Jimmy pointed out.

Having taken on board all relevant details regarding Met conditions and the state of the aircraft when the crew had handed over to him forty-five minutes earlier, Dirk brought the two medical orderlies up to date while Maggie swiftly found the relevant charts and worked out their course on take-off.

They were in the air with professional speed, conscious of the gravity of the situation. Maggie sat beside Dirk, studying the charts that plotted all the hazards they faced when flying low. The moors were harsh and testing for those who left the roads and headed across country. All aircrew undertook survival courses in similar terrain throughout their service years, and Dirk well remembered two occasions on which he believed he would not make it back to the living.

He said to Maggie when she sat back, 'Before any-one's sent on these treks they're told what not to eat – berries, fungi and so on. Surely these lads, and more so their instructors, had studied the subject before set-ting out.'

'What I haven't got straight is why one boy was able to walk for help when everyone else is incapacitated.'

'Maybe he got it wrong and only one or two are sick. Kids turn everything into a drama.'

'But why didn't one of the adults use his radio to get SAR on the job when things began to go pear-shaped? They must be responsible guys.'

'My guess is it's been blown out of proportion. That call might have been from some kid trying to be clever; get some attention.'

'Rot! No boy keen enough to join his school's squadron would pull a stunt like that.'

He turned on her. 'You know all about schoolboys and what makes them tick, do you?'

'I've three brothers. One's my twin. Of course I know what makes them tick. You clearly don't,' she replied, annoying him further.

'Okay, as you're so bloody knowledgeable about the little buggers, study that chart and work out where we'll find them.'

It was impossible to do that, and the Sea King pilot emphasised the point when Maggie made radio contact. 'The three we picked up were probably the last to collapse as they attempted to reach help. I'd guess the others are scattered along a line to the north-east of their position, falling by the wayside as their guts gave up the ghost. Should have stayed together; made our job easier.'

'How's the visibility where you are?' she asked.

'As dense and grey as a badger's arse.'

Grinning, she said, 'Give me your bearing. I'd hate to meet up with you in a place like that.'

It was not long before Dirk had evidence of the lingering fog as he flew above it towards the map reference he had agreed with the other pilot would be his starting point for a systematic search. It was essential that the two aircraft stayed on their designated flight paths to avoid risk of a collision. When the other Sea King rejoined them from Barnstaple there would be three helicopters combing a small area, unable to see each other. It was not a situation any of them much liked.

Dirk told Maggie to keep in constant contact. 'I want to know where he is the whole time.'

She glanced up from her chart to look from the window. 'There's a cairn at two o'clock. Turn right just past it and I'll set the new course.'

Dirk spotted the cairn on a rise revealed by a break in the grey blanket. 'Any power lines in the vicinity, guys?' he asked of the sergeants in the cabin, and received a cheerful negative. 'The chart shows that the area is mostly low-lying with no appreciable high ground to worry about, so when we begin the search I'll go down to rock bottom. If we can't see the ground the whole thing's pointless. Agreed?'

'Yeah.'

'I'll take it real slow, so keep your eyes peeled and for Christ's sake yell the minute you spot anything. I don't want to balls around here all day.'

Dirk was not happy about flying no more than twenty feet above the ground in poor visibility, but the charts showed an area free of obstructions and it was notoriously difficult to see inert bodies in camouflage overalls on bracken-covered terrain. They had been faced with the job frequently enough on exercises but it was more vital now when doing it for real. The medical orderlies joined Jimmy and Dave by the open doors to add four more eyes in the effort to find up to forty suffering boys. Dirk cut his speed as they descended into the eerie greyness, both he and Maggie keeping a close watch on the altimeter until the ground finally became visible through the murk.

'Okay, guys, we've got it in our sights now,' Dirk said calmly. 'Pull out all the stops.'

Taking the aircraft forward into the swirling fog he activated the windscreen wipers to clear the dampness forming outside, ready to act quickly if an unexpected obstruction loomed. Beside him Maggie maintained low-voiced contact with the Sea King, and his crewmen gave reassuring comments on the absence of hazards from their positions hanging from the doors. Dirk could not help feeling sorry for the boys who had run into serious trouble on what should have been a 'fun run' at this time of year. This fog added further to their predicament. If they had inadvisably split up they must be lonely and desperate for any kind of help, not knowing where their friends were.

'Three o'clock! Something moving,' said Dave suddenly.

Two wet and bedraggled sheep.

For twenty more minutes they continued sectioning the area, their eyes straining for a sight of human life on the grey-green moorland that shone with dampness. Within their limited vision nothing was there that should not be. The SAR pilot was having no better luck.

'You sure that boy who phoned in really knew what he was talking about?' Dirk asked him.

'My pal picked up three in the right vicinity. The rest can't be too far away. If this bloody fog would lift we'd see 'em right away. I'm watching my fuel. Thirty minutes then I'm heading home. Our other Sea King should be back here by then.'

'Gottem!' declared Dave triumphantly. 'Boulders at four o'clock. Looks like a fair group of them beneath an overhang.'

'Well done! How come we missed them?' Dirk demanded of Maggie, as he circled to take a look himself.

'Dave's got X-ray eyes,' she murmured.

One of the medical orderlies said,' Looks bad. They're not moving.'

153

Maggie was reporting the news to the SAR pilot as Dirk spotted a straggle of boulders almost straight ahead. There appeared to be a flat stretch some twenty-five yards to the left and, sticking to the rules, Dirk told Jimmy to test the surface as he hovered a few feet above what looked to be a barren, desolate spot. Their thunderous arrival created no reaction in the huddling bodies in the lee of the rocks.

'I don't like the look of this,' Dirk murmured as Jimmy signalled the all-clear and he set the Chinook down. 'Get over there fast, guys, and do what you can for them. Tell Jimmy to report back on the situation.'

There were fifteen lads suffering from hypothermic inertia and dehydration. All about them was evidence of diarrhoea and vomiting, Jimmy said when he returned to the aircraft. 'They're too far gone to understand they're being rescued. We won't get any info out of them.'

'Okay, bring them aboard fast as you can. The others must be within a few miles' radius of here. If they're as ill as this lot they won't have gone far beyond this point,' Dirk reasoned. 'Christ, I wish this fog would lift!' He spoke to the SAR pilot. 'Do we have an exact number to look for?'

'Forty cadets, two adults. We picked up three; you've found fifteen. Two dozen left.'

'We've got to get to them fast. This is a major emergency.'

After a swift discussion they decided on a plan of action. The smaller aircraft could fly tighter manoeuvres than the Chinook so it would start circling the immediate area while Dirk searched in wider sweeps in case the other boys had remained on their feet longer than expected. So, with the fifteen casualties in the cabin being given basic emergency treatment, Dirk took off on a course that would take them well clear of the incoming Sea King.

Within ten minutes the other crew had located and picked

up the two adults and four boys who were sheltering in a hollow.

'I'm taking them to Barnstaple,' the pilot radioed. 'The kids are in a bad way. So's their teacher. The other guy – in his mid fifties, I'd say – is a goner. Looks like a heart attack. After I've dropped them off I'll refuel, grab a sandwich, then come back, if needed. Our second aircraft will rendezvous with you in ten minutes. Good hunting!'

Dirk shot a glance at Maggie. 'A guy dead? Questions are definitely going to be asked. What the hell's behind it?'

'Something that didn't affect one of them,' she reminded him.

She had a point. Dirk tried to fathom a solution, continuing the systematic search. He was starting to feel the strain of precision flying in difficult conditions. His eyes ached from staring into the shifting greyness; his reflexes were tensed to react the moment any obstruction loomed. The charts showed none, but there was always the fear of the unexpected when visibility was restricted. The general heaviness of his spirits increased his creeping tiredness.

Checking the fuel gauge, he said, 'We're getting low on juice. Unless we find these lads soon we'll need to—'

'Three o'clock,' said Dave sharply. 'A large group in some shrubs.'

There were ten, all very weak and largely incoherent, but one managed to say that their companions had headed due east where they thought there was a road. Dirk discussed this with Maggie while the boys were being carried aboard.

'The kid can't say how long ago the others left, so they could be miles away or very close.'

'I'd say reasonably close,' she guessed. 'The symptoms would surely have disabled them swiftly. It appears to be a pretty violent bug.'

'Yeah,' he said slowly. 'Eight more out there somewhere due east, if we can accept what a delirious boy says.'

'Seven more. One reached the road and a passing driver, don't forget. How the heck did he escape this?'

Dirk was staring from the window. 'You can ask him. If it didn't seem completely loony I'd say he's just appeared out of the mist.'

A lanky boy in camouflage overalls was walking unsteadily towards them from an easterly direction. His face was ashen and it was clearly an effort for him to put one foot before the other. Seeing the men clustering round the casualties he veered towards them. Dave then spotted him and swiftly crossed the few yards to hold him by the shoulders. From their seats Dirk and Maggie watched a pantomime of gestures and pointing hands before Dave left the boy to run over and climb aboard.

'Don't tell me that's the kid who phoned,' demanded Dirk, twisting to Dave in the doorway.

'Aye, he is.'

'But he was picked up by a motorist.'

'No, he went back to tell his mates help was on the way. According to him, the rest are only two hundred yards away. He heard us come in and followed the sound of our rotors, scared we'd leave not aware that they were so near.' Dave wiped his damp face with the back of his hand. 'He didn't know these ten were close by or he'd have checked on them.'

'He must be some kid,' said Maggie with feeling.

Dave's dark eyes glowed momentarily as he gave a weary grin. 'Aye, he's a Scot.'

Dirk glanced out at the boy still on his feet. 'How come he didn't get ill?'

'Dunno. Says he's okay. Wants to show me where the others are. Reckons he marked the way back with pebbles.'

'Right. Go with him and check if we can put down beside them, in which case we'll hop over as soon as this lot are on. If the site's too risky they'll have to be carried back

156

here.' As Dave turned, Dirk added, 'Make it snappy. We don't want anyone dying on us after his heroic efforts.'

Dave nodded. 'Will do, but he's pretty well dead beat.'

'Leave him with his pals when you report back. And Dave, give the kid a blanket. He must be dangerously chilled.'

Ironically, as Dave wrapped a blanket around the boy's thin shoulders the mist thinned and began to melt away. At the same moment, the pilot of the second Sea King announced his imminent arrival to take up the search. In a frenzy of activity beneath strengthening sunshine the crew of the Chinook collected the remaining casualties, while Maggie radioed to ensure the ambulances were standing by and passed on their assessment of the lads' condition given to her by one of Pam's orderlies. Then she turned to Dirk.

'You look tired. Want a switch?'

He considered her offer and allowed common sense to prevail over his personal resistance to her. He had slept badly and was feeling the lack of rest after a tricky couple of hours in the air. He moved out to allow her to climb in the right-hand seat, then dropped heavily on the one she vacated. It had been a successful rescue, yet he felt no sense of elation or even of satisfaction. Just extreme weariness.

After setting the course he sat back to survey the moor that had been cloaked in fog on the way out. It now looked reasonably benign washed by early morning sunshine; wildly beautiful but hazardous to those who crossed it unprepared for rapid changes.

A flurry of movement behind his right shoulder caused Dirk to glance round. Dave was fixing the jump seat in place; the white-faced boy was with him.

'I think Duncan's had enough of sickness,' Dave explained. 'All right if he sits up here with you?'

'Sure. Make yourself at home,' Dirk shouted. 'I'm Dirk and this is Maggie.'

She turned to smile. 'Hi, Duncan. Flown in one of these before?'

The boy shook his head as he slumped on the canvas seat, clutching the blanket round his shoulders and drinking cocoa from Dave's flask. It was impossible to conduct a conversation with someone not plugged into the intercom, so it was not until they landed on a rugby pitch where a fleet of ambulances waited that Maggie began questioning Duncan.

'How is it you're the only one of a large group to escape whatever hit the rest?'

Dull green eyes gazed at her. 'I've thought about that. It's bizarre, but it's the one answer I can come up with. I'm the only one in my group who didn't eat the packed rations we were given. Everyone was okay on the first two days. Yesterday a couple began throwing up, and so on. The rest soon followed. I didn't realise the whole group was ill. We'd split up, you see. That was part of the exercise. Cranbrook – the leader of our group – had a radio to keep in touch with Squadron Leader Barnes, but he lost it during one of his spasms. Vomiting and diarrhoea, you know. It must have fallen from his pocket.'

He glanced at Dirk. 'There was no way of telling when it had happened, so it was a dead loss. I decided to go on to the rendezvous. I know the rule is to stay together, but leaving them was the only way to get help.' A frown deepened his pale brow. 'I'd no idea *everyone* was ill.' he said again. 'It was only when I made the rendezvous and no one turned up that I got seriously worried and decided to reach a road. It was dark by then, and very cold, but walking kept me warm.'

'How did you know where the road was?' asked Maggie.

'I had a compass, and I'd mugged up the maps before-hand.'

'Even so . . .'

'I spend holidays with my grandparents in the Highlands. I'm used to finding my way about on moors.'

'You should talk to Dave about that,' said Dirk quietly, impressed by this fourteen-year-old's resourcefulness.

'A lorry driver let me use his mobile.' He gave a ghost of a smile. 'I must have been a bit dopey by then. The only number I could think of was Grandfather's. He wasn't too pleased to be fetched out of bed at that early hour, but he said he'd get on to Search and Rescue when I gave him the details.' The faint smile again. 'His bark's worse than his bite. I knew he'd sort everything.'

Dirk asked why the boy had gone back across the moor instead of getting a lift with the driver. 'You must have been pretty well at the end of your tether by then.'

'I had to let them know help was coming,' he explained simply. 'Cranbrook was full of guilt about losing the radio, and the others gave him stick over it. They needed some sort of boost to keep them going.' He bit his lip. 'I also thought I should be there to signal our position when SAR came. Didn't realise that fog would hang around so long. It was jolly frustrating knowing helicopters were overhead and being unable to show where we were.'

Maggie smiled at him. 'It was jolly frustrating for us, too.'

Duncan half glanced back at the cabin as victims continued to be offloaded. 'They *are* going to be all right, aren't they?'

'Sure to be,' Maggie said. 'Tell me, why didn't you eat your rations?'

He pulled a face. 'I'd had an upset stomach the day before we set out, would you believe? I was so afraid I'd be ill and have to drop out, I took a load of dry bread and bottled fizz to settle my innards. I chucked the other stuff away when no one was looking.'

159

'And that's all you've had for four days? You must be starving!'

'The lorry driver gave me a massive bacon sandwich. It tasted great.'

Dirk studied the boy's drawn face and lustreless eyes. 'You're quite something, young Duncan. Your dad'll be cockeyed with pride when he hears about this.'

'He's dead,' came the stark reply. 'His Tornado crashed during a test flight last year. That's why I was scared I'd be ill and miss out on this exercise. It's so important that I make it into the Air Force. It's . . . it's a family thing, you see.'

'I think you'll make it okay,' Maggie told him.

Dave came up just then to grip the boy's shoulder. 'Your turn, Duncan. They want to give you the once-over at the hospital, and something to eat. Then you can sleep for as long as you like. You look about ready for that.'

Duncan scrambled wearily across the seat, then turned to the cockpit. 'Thanks for coming for us. Maybe I'll do the same for someone else one day.'

Maggie watched through the window as Dave walked with Duncan to the remaining ambulance. 'He should get some kind of recognition for this . . . and he's sure to earn a sponsored commission. His leadership potential sticks out a mile.'

'But is it what *he* wants, or just because it's a "family thing"?'

She turned. 'Surely the two go together in his case. Why else would he have done what he did?'

'Struggling to live up to his father?'

'That's understandable.'

'Just so long as the dead hero *was* his father.'

'What?'

He turned away from her puzzled gaze, saying bitterly before he could stop himself, 'How does any kid know who his father is, apart from a name on a sodding birth certificate? That doesn't mean a thing.'

Maggie fixed him with a long look and wisely said no more on the subject, but the anger that had resurfaced when the boy spoke of his father's death in an air crash stayed with Dirk for the rest of the watch. Because they were on standby he could not drink to dull his senses, so the day dragged past. It was difficult to concentrate on reading or the daily crossword, and the light-hearted conversation of the others irritated him as he continued to brood.

Paula's father had protested that the family should speak freely about Mike; that young Sam should grow up proud of his father and understand that he died doing something worthwhile. No. *No!* He should be told that his father was a cheapskate who cheated on his wife for kicks; a man who had suggested his son should be snuffed out in the womb. That would ensure that Sam never did anything as courageously risky as Duncan to prove himself worthy of his parent. An adulterer's bastard could never be worthy of a man like Mike.

Seven

They drove to London in Chris's battered RX7. He refused to go in Maggie's Fiesta, saying an old sports car that could not be updated due to heavy child support payments was still preferable to a staid hatchback. She kept quiet. This fabulous theatrical invitation was too important to her for verbal sparring, and she had suffered enough already at the hands of the team. They had made the macho most of their chances to exaggerate the glamour of women who attended these dos, which she could never match in a hundred years. Oil-stained hands and a perfume of avgas would lead to Maggie being barred from entry by the bouncers at the door. She should pull out now, they said, and allow one of them to take her place. Cinderella should *not* go to the ball. The ribbing spread to the ground crews, and Maggie coped with it by falling back on the belief that most men never outgrew the Billy Bunter stage and should be pitied.

Randal was as bad as the rest, but his jibes included Chris. Those aimed solely at Maggie concerned things discussed between them during her hospital visits to him. They irritated her more than the basic blokey humour. He had played his ace yesterday by listing Maggie for a three-day refresher course on night flying in Wales. She had momentarily fallen for it. Her cry of protest had been met by his insistence that records showed she was overdue for it and MoD rules must be observed. His hands were tied. Recovering

162

her wits, she told him she would like to tie up more than his hands.

Assuming the mock innocence she knew so well, he had said, 'Okay, I'll put my career on the line and let you off. But if you start getting magic messages about Anthony Dillane I'll have to ground you for safety reasons.'

The trouble about being one of the boys was that Maggie more often than not dressed like them, so she did not possess a wardrobe of glamorous clothes – certainly nothing sexy and showy enough for a glittering gala occasion – but there had been so much ribbing on the subject it had posed a serious problem. Chris had openly expressed his doubts about her, and there had been instances of provocative pictures from girly magazines being left in her locker, under her plate and even affixed to the cockpit window. One enterprising male had got hold of one of her flying-suits and stuck red sequins to resemble a fan-dancer's breast patches. Certain Jeff was the culprit, Maggie vowed to get back at him in kind when he had a hot date.

Even with such 'ho ho' pressure on her to confound them all, Maggie had neither the opportunity nor the inclination to blow a year's salary on a dress to match those of showbiz personalities. Flight Lieutenant Margaret Spencer was a down-to-earth helicopter pilot, not a candidate for the casting couch, yet she did badly want to give Chris a facer after his hints about her ability to tart herself up. Luckily, Maggie had three sisters-in-law, and one of them owned the perfect dress. Maggie had tried it on at Christmas and knew it fitted her well. A begging telephone call and a request to send the parcel to Jill's address had settled the matter. Maggie's friend had promised, on pain of death, not to allow her adored Arnie, the Great Dane, anywhere near it nor to breathe a word to her husband Pete. Maggie did not trust a single member of B Flight. Neither did Jill!

Chris's grandmother, Evelyn Montrose, had an apartment

in Chelsea where they were to sleep after the late dinner party following the performance. Evelyn's other personal guests were to assemble there for cocktails prior to the show, and Daimlers would transport them all to the theatre. Chris grumbled that Gran could surely have made it a stretch limo for her immediate family.

'As someone who drives around in a scruffy, clapped-out wreck, stop being so picky,' Maggie told him, getting back at him for his insult to her Fiesta.

The 'clapped-out' car took them smoothly to London in good time, however, and Maggie's anticipation rose further when Chris buzzed the security panel and his grandmother's rich voice invited them up. The huge apartment was furnished like a stage set for a play set in the home of a film star, Maggie thought with amusement, and the walls were covered in studio portraits signed by the eccentric and famous.

Evelyn Montrose was a surprise, however. Maggie's visions of mauve-tinted hair, trailing chiffon and graceful, melo-dramatic arm movements fled on meeting a rather plump, silver-haired woman in a black, jet-beaded dress and jacket, who seized Chris in a hearty, grandparently hug and told him if he could not be bothered to pick up a pen and write to her he could, at least, pick up a telephone receiver more often than he did.

It was then the confusion began. Evelyn might not fit the popular image of a former star clinging to youth, but she certainly loved holding centre stage. Her classically beautiful face wore an approving smile as she greeted Maggie.

'My dear, I'm delighted Chris has finally recovered from that painful divorce and found someone else to love. You're a great improvement on that *dreadful* Chloe. I told him at the outset he was throwing common sense to the winds, but he's very pig-headed, as you've surely already discovered. He's nevertheless a darling boy and I love him dearly. You'll need to start getting ready. Oodles of time, really, but you won't want to feel pressurised. Carla has prepared your usual room, Chris, but Maggie can use the dressing-room and bathroom across the corridor right now. She won't want you under her feet while she makes herself even more beautiful.' She clapped her hands. 'Off you go, children!'

Not having managed to say a word, Maggie found plenty as Chris led her to the far regions of the apartment. 'What the hell have you told her about me? *Someone else to love?*'

Chris looked amused. 'I didn't tell her you were my girlfriend. She's simply made an assumption.'

'Which you didn't contradict.'

He threw open the door to a lavish, velvet-hung bedroom. 'Gran never likes being interrupted in full flow.'

Carrying the dress in a zipped bag, and a holdall containing everything else for a grand occasion, Maggie followed him in. 'Does she know what I do for a living; that we work together?'

His eyes were still full of laughter. 'I thought it best to keep that quiet. She wouldn't understand. Anyway, introducing you to her friends as a Chinook pilot would downgrade my pulling power with the sexy birds tonight.'

'Bastard!'

'Would you honestly want to bore Gran's guests with talk of positive stick gradient or optimum rotor speed?'

'I'm strongly tempted,' she threatened. 'If you expect me to act as if we're an item, think again. Right, where's the room I can use to escape you for a while?'

He pointed across the corridor to a door with a crystal handle. 'There's an en suite bathroom. Maggie,' he added, as she crossed to it, 'I'll let you have the bed tonight and doss on the floor.'

'You'll doss over here,' she responded. 'You'll know by now that I'm also pig-headed, "darling boy".'

As she showered and washed her short hair Maggie reluctantly conceded that Chris had probably been wise. Too often she had seen the glaze cover people's eyes when told that she flew helicopters for the RAF. In tonight's arty crowd that would be far better left unsaid. Evelyn's error about their relationship would have to stand, but Maggie was determined on one score. She might well have slept in a tent with Chris, among others, when there was no alternative, but she was going to have the plush comfort of that bedroom all to herself tonight.

Swiftly drying herself, Maggie then applied a lot more make-up than usual for this special occasion. On went silk underwear given at Christmas and not worn until now. It was fun to be feminine for once. The borrowed dress slipped on easily, and she crossed to a full-length mirror. The deep red clinging gown left her right shoulder bare and had a knee-high side opening to allow freedom of movement. High on the left shoulder a double bar of rhinestones glinted with rainbow lights, and round her right wrist was the matching bracelet Sheila had sent with the dress. A Chinook pilot? Maggie smiled as she thought of the song performed with such touching gusto by Shirley McLaine, 'If my friends could see me now'. Pity B Flight could not!

Chris, dinner-jacketed and with a drink in his hand, was chatting to a middle-aged couple. He half-turned as Maggie came up beside him, his impersonal, social smile slowly fading as it dawned on him who she was. More guests arrived, drinks were circulated, laughter dominated conversation. Maggie's enjoyment was heightened by the knowledge that she had truly thrown Chris off balance. Girl power at its most potent!

Zenda took the audience by storm with its lavish costumes, sword fights and spectacular sets. The kind of musical that had gone out of fashion was brought back in overnight, Anthony Dillane's wickedly rakish Rupert of Hentzau undoubtedly stealing the greatest applause.

During the many curtain calls Maggie turned to Chris. 'You're quiet. What's up?'

'Can't compete with *that*,' he murmured, nodding at Dillane.

She grinned. 'Please keep quiet at the party about your being a Chinook navigator. It'll reduce my pulling power if I get a chance to meet him.'

A scowl darkened his pleasant face. 'He's sure to be gay.'

'Then he might take a fancy to you, "darling boy".'

As they made their way down the stairs, jostled by the crowd, Chris said in her ear, 'You're not seriously turned on by that chocolate-box uniform and choreographed swordplay, are you?'

Highly amused by his attitude, she ladled on feminine gush. 'Not half! Polished boots and tight breeches put shivers down any girl's spine. And when he stripped to the waist in Act Three . . .'

'Yeah, no need for an orgasm,' he growled.

On a laugh, she said, 'Next time you'd better bring a "nice young man" as Grannie dictated.'

Chaos reigned at the party venue as people mingled effusively, making certain they were 'seen' before walking to their tables. As Evelyn charmed her way through the crush like the adored leading lady she once had been, Chris held Maggie back.

'Why don't we miss out on this and go somewhere quieter on our own?'

Surprised, she shook her head. 'Not on your life. I'm enjoying every extravagant moment.'

Two minutes later she had cause to change her mind as they approached a circular table, and Chris whispered urgently, 'Christ, there's Rip's wife.'

Fiona Price was with a bronzed, beefy man introduced by Evelyn's friends as Seth Nicholls, one of the show's backers. 'My grandson Chris and his girlfriend Maggie' was sufficient for Evelyn before talk centred on *Zenda*. Randal's wife gave no sign that she recognised two members of his squadron whom she had met before, and Maggie had no doubt she truly did not remember them.

Beneath the theatrical eulogising Chris asked Maggie, 'Aren't they supposed to be divorcing?'

'How should I know?' she replied shortly. 'Hasn't he confessed all at a lads' booze-up?'

'Uh-uh . . . but what man could break the ties that bind him to *her*?'

'One who was utterly let down on the "in sickness and in health" clause? If he can possibly see beyond taut boobs and endless legs, that is.'

Chris's eyes narrowed. 'Claws out?'

'Not against talons like hers.'

The focus of the evening changed for Maggie as she studied Fiona. Huge sexy eyes, blonde hair in an expensively designed waterfall, full pouting mouth, and a slinky black dress that revealed a sensational tanned body. No one could deny she was stunning. And irresistible? Did Chris have a point? Despite her heartless desertion, could Randal still find it impossible to sever the bond? It would explain that unresolved hiatus in their own friendship forged during his illness. It might also account for his surprising lack of interest in women lately. They were invariably attracted to Randal's charismatic personality, and even when he was besotted with Fiona he had responded. Now he seemed to avoid social contact with them. Did he know his wife was running around with an obvious playboy?

After a while Maggie began to grow bored. The talk was all of people she did not know, or theatrical news that meant very little to her. Curiously, this party seemed more artificial than the Ruritanian dramatics on stage a short while before. Even Anthony Dillane was a disappointment when he came to their table to kiss Evelyn and tell her that she was *entirely* responsible for his success tonight. Posing for a retinue of photographers throughout the conversation, he failed to instil in Maggie the excitement he had generated on stage. That wicked smile, the silken voice, the bravura personality had vanished to leave a lacklustre peacock.

When the actor's gaze slid past Fiona to rest on her muscular companion, Chris muttered, 'Told you so. You'd be far better off somewhere quiet with me, Maggie.'

She took up her purse. 'Okay. I'll visit the loo and meet you in the lobby.'

As Maggie was touching up her lipstick in the pink and cream luxury cloakroom Fiona Price walked in. She smiled vaguely at Maggie before entering one of the cubicles, but ignored her when she reappeared to wash her hands.

'Your friend must feel his injection of cash was a sure-fire gamble after the rave reception of *Zenda*,' said Maggie.

Fiona shook out a starched hand towel. 'Seth only backs winners.'

'He must be very astute.'

'Mmm.' She took a gold-cased lipstick and a slim bottle of perfume from her jewelled purse, and added tangerine colour to her full lips. When she realised Maggie was making no attempt to leave, Fiona applied perfume with a tiny glass stopper, asking without real interest, 'You're linked to show business?'

Bingo! The perfect cue. 'No, I fly with your husband.'

It shook her as much as Maggie hoped. The self-assurance that had been evident all evening failed Randal's wife as she gazed back speechlessly, perfume stopper in hand.

'Chris and I are with Six Four Six Squadron. Did you know Randal has taken up his former post as B Flight commander?' At the other's silence, Maggie said, 'Oh, you wouldn't, of course. You walked out on him when you learned he was paralysed. Well, he's right back on the ball now and loving it as much as ever.' Into her stride and enjoying every moment of an opportunity she had never expected to be given, Maggie added, 'I suppose I shouldn't be surprised that you've forgotten when we met before, because you were so wrapped up in your own importance that evening you'd never have noticed anyone else. It was at an important dinner dance in the Officers' Mess. All was well until the VIPs left and Randal was dragged out by us to lead the Flight's own Middle Eastern version of the conga, and the limelight moved from you to him.' She gave a savage smile. 'As I recall, you tried to walk out on him then, too – with my boyfriend Mark. When that failed, you let forth your opinion of your husband, his friends and the Air Force in general, in a voice loud enough to be heard by everyone in the vicinity. I imagine you meant publicly to humiliate him, but it rebounded on you. Everyone who was there that evening remembers you; not as the belle of the ball but as the selfish bitch you clearly still are.'

Picking up her purse, Maggie went in search of Chris.

They returned to Evelyn's apartment, having had enough of crowds. Maggie kicked off her high heels and draped herself over an antique chaise longue, while Chris shed his jacket then brought a bottle of red wine and two glasses from the discreet bar. Maggie glanced up as he returned. 'Faded glory.'

'Who, me?'

'This room. Seems to have been bequeathed by Noel Coward.'

'Who's he?'

It was the standard B Flight teasing response whenever she spoke of anything cultural. 'I'd forgotten that even a man whose grannie was a famous actress has a one-track mind when there's alcohol available.'

He settled beside her with a grin. 'Two tracks. Booze *and* sex.'

'Then you should have stayed at the party and tried your pulling power with braless Fiona.'

'And have our boss on my back? Anyway, *I* don't fool around with married women.'

Maggie watched him pouring wine, understanding the bitterness in his voice. Station gossip had it that a chemist from Dorchester had consoled Chloe during Chris's frequent absences, yet he had not demanded DNA proof of paternity of the child born before his divorce was finalised. Maggie had never shared a social twosome with this man she knew so well on a professional level, and it now occurred to her that Evelyn might be wrong in believing Chris had 'finally recovered from that painful divorce'. No single girl had featured in his life since the split with Chloe.

'That bronzed hunk who invested in the show doesn't share your scruples,' she commented, taking up one of the glasses. 'I can't believe he hasn't a hands-on relationship with that high class bitch.'

'He has. I watched him massaging her thigh when you moved away from the table. Had a perfect view of his undercover foreplay. Coupla minutes later she got up, cool as you like, and walked off as if he wasn't there. Our muscle-bound chum resembled a dog who's lost his bone.'

'Bloody idiot! What is it with you men and women like her?'

'Same as you women and beefcake like Dillane,' he returned, scowling.

'He really got to you, didn't he?' Maggie sipped her wine reflectively. 'Are you going to tell the Boss she was at the party with one of the show's wealthy backers?'

He shook his head. 'No point.'

'She's still his wife, so far as we know.' Chris continued to shake his head. 'She came to the cloakroom while I was

171

there, so I reminded her that we'd met before and when. By the time I left she had a pretty good idea of our opinion of a wife who would walk out on a man facing the end of his flying career and a future as a paraplegic.'

Chris drank for a moment or two in silence. 'Rip's tough enough to fight his own battles, Maggie.'

'What does that mean?'

'That you should leave other people's relationships well alone. I know you did a lot to help him through his months in hospital, but he's back on his feet now. He might be angling for a reconciliation – she'd be hard to give up, I reckon. You might have aborted his chances.'

She was instantly angry. 'Then I'll have saved him from a second dose of humiliation at her hands . . . And if he's planning to buy her back into his bed with another country mansion, I'll also have saved him a cool million.'

'It's his money. If he wants to spend it on—'

'Oh, get stuffed, Chris,' she snapped, losing patience with his short-sighted masculine reasoning.

He leaned forward and topped up their glasses. 'And there was I thinking we were getting on so well.'

'We were, but anything to do with that woman has me spitting fire.' She tried to douse it with wine, then she said, 'I really did enjoy the show and all the glitzy pizzazz. Thanks for bringing me.'

'Had no choice. You twisted my arm.'

She grinned. 'Might have known you'd come back with that.'

'But it's worked out okay, hasn't it?' After slight hesitation, he added carelessly, 'All that ballsing around by the guys – sexy pictures and stuff – well, I did express doubts about being crazy enough to let you talk me into it. But none of us has ever seen you all—'

'Tarted up?' she finished.

'Not on this scale.' He began to run a lazy finger along

her bare arm. 'I had no idea you could look such a knock-out.'

'So you're going to tell that to the guys tomorrow, are you? *Are you hell!* You'll play it for laughs. I've been around you long enough to know what makes you tick, Chris Foley.'

'Not when I'm on a date, you don't.'

'We're not on a date. You had no choice. I twisted your arm, remember?'

He gave a sleepy smile. 'You're an expert verbal fencer, Maggie.'

'I have to be against overwhelming odds in B Flight.'

'So why hasn't it turned me on until tonight?'

'Because you're never half-pissed on the job.'

His fingers had reached her shoulder and began travelling towards her neck. 'I'm not now. You've seen me legless often enough to tell the difference.'

Maggie recognised the signs, but was uncertain of her reaction to such a development. She had shared a cockpit with Chris many times during a period of almost three years. They had played bruising squash together and worked out in the gym side by side. They had argued and played tricks on each other. They had slept in the same tent on manoeuvres. During those years he had suffered an acrimonious divorce, she had seen her lover killed, and both of them had received support from the team to help them through. They were utterly familiar with each other in a warts-and-all relationship, but they had never shared a situation like this one. Maggie knew she had achieved her aim in proving she could look as glamorous as any woman and she was now faced with the outcome. Chris was an attractive, lusty man, they were alone in a luxury apartment discreetly lit, and the wine was potent. Her body was sending undeniable signals to her brain, which was holding them at bay.

'You smell good enough to eat,' Chris murmured, edging closer as he caressed her ear.

While doing nothing to stop him, she said faintly, 'I don't really think this is a good idea.'

'I do. It's the best one I've had in ages.'

His mouth was pleasantly warm and hard on hers, and his hands aroused a leaping response in her as they fumbled with the zip of her dress. She lay back against the cushions ready to take things further, then she began to resist, thrusting him away and getting to her feet in a semblance of panic.

'Christ, Maggie, what's the problem?' Chris demanded as he sprawled back in frustration along the seat.

'I . . . maybe I'm just not drunk enough,' she said, hugging herself tightly.

'We can soon remedy that.' He stood up beside her with the bottle in one hand and her glass in the other. In silence he filled and offered it to her. She took it and drank most of the wine in one draught, still hugging herself with one arm.

Eventually Chris asked, 'Is it about Mark?'

She glanced at him in confusion. 'I don't know. I just don't know. It's a long while ago. I thought I was over it . . . yet when I watched that Harrier slam on the deck recently I *dissolved.*'

Chris charged his glass and drank thoughtfully. 'It takes a hell of a time to forget. Chloe and I had some awful fights; said absolutely foul things to each other. Yet I still hanker for the good times, now and again. Must be worse for you. You and Mark ended on the good times.'

She gazed into her glass and found herself expressing her private thoughts. 'We didn't meet very often, as you know. He was giving Harrier displays all over the country; I spent a lot of time abroad. But when we did get together we were firing on all cylinders. He fast-jetted into my life . . . and he left it the same way,' she added hollowly. 'I think that's part of the problem.' The bottle hovered over her glass; more ruby wine filled it. She sipped, conscious of the man beside her to whom she was confessing something no one else had been told.

'Mark had just been invited to join the Red Arrows: three years of intense, superlative flying which would leave little time for an intense, superlative love affair. I was no wife with kids for him to return to for brief intervals, I was a career pilot with heavy commitments of my own.' She glanced up at Chris's familiar face. 'At that dinner dance when Fiona gave her prima donna act we talked about the penalties of Mark's selection for the aerobatic team. He regarded it as the pinnacle of his career, and I was thrilled for him. We said the usual things like if we felt the same when his term was over, we'd think about getting married. But we both knew the score.'

She took another swift gulp from her glass. 'During those three years the fire surely would have slowly died. We were both young, ambitious and surrounded by the opposite sex, with little hope of fanning the flame by meeting up. By now – almost two years on – we would probably both have been in new relationships. Mark would have slipped out of my life almost painlessly.'

'Mmm, it's possible.'

'Instead, he burned to death while I looked on,' she said thickly, seeing in her mind's eye that flaming ball hurtling from a cloudless August sky. Fighting the horrific vision, she continued as though to herself. 'We hadn't known each other long enough to exchange presents, so I've nothing of his to cherish. We always phoned each other, so no love letters tied with ribbon. I can't even visit his grave with flowers – he's buried in South Africa near his widowed father who doesn't know of my existence. It's as though Mark never was . . . and I've begun to wonder since that recent Harrier incident if it's the way he died that I can't forget, not Mark himself. Have I got a hang-up over the crash rather than him?'

Chris looked out of his depth and muttered something about fetching another bottle from the bar. Maggie followed him and looked on while he drew the cork. His silence frustrated her. She needed a response to her confession, yet he was pursuing the usual male solution to awkward situations by getting drunk.

'*Do* you think I have a hang-up over the crash itself?' she demanded again.

'How the hell do I know? I'm not a shrink,' he said irritably. 'Go and see Pam when you get back tomorrow. She'll arrange counselling.'

'I don't want counselling, I want your opinion as a good friend,' she cried.

'Why me?'

'Because you've got a hang-up over that baby you're supporting, so I thought you'd understand. I know why you won't try to prove he's yours, but I don't know why I panicked with you just now. Why, Chris?'

He said bitterly, 'I suppose I didn't turn you on. According to my ex I've lost the knack.'

'You were starting to, that was the trouble,' she told him quietly. 'I took fright, for some reason.'

'Oh.' He studied her for a moment or two, interest rekindling. 'Why don't we finish off this bottle while we discuss our hang-ups and how to beat them? After all, you don't want to become a frustrated old hag, do you?'

Maggie was woken by Carla bringing tea on a tray, then departing discreetly. The red dress and silk underwear lay on the floor with Chris's discarded clothes. His blond head was on the next pillow; his body was warm against hers. She slipped from the bed, wrapped herself in her bathrobe and went to the adjoining bathroom. After splashing her face with cold water she noticed her reflection and paused with the towel in her hands. Her face was bright with life, there was that après-sex glow in her eyes. Her body felt wonderfully relaxed; her movements were dreamy. She felt a surprising sense of freedom and she pushed away her doubts on the wisdom of what had happened. They had to fly together, work as members of a team in the days ahead. There might be problems, but sexual release had been long overdue and it would not be an ongoing habit.

Back in the bedroom she sat on one of two velvet padded chairs beside a low table, and poured herself some tea, gratifyingly contented. Before long, Chris groaned, rolled over, then raised his head to look around.

'Good, tea,' he mumbled sleepily. 'Where's mine?'

'In the pot.'

'Bring me some over,' he coaxed.

'Why, have you lost the use of your legs?'

He gurgled sexily. 'Get back in here with me and you'll find out.'

Maggie stayed where she was.

After a series of loud, exaggerated yawns and a deal of grunting, Chris arrived in a T-shirt and underpants to pour some tea. He downed it in two gulps, then filled his cup again before flopping in the other elegant chair to leer at her. 'Too scared to get back in bed?'

'Tea was a better prospect.'

'I'm hot stuff in the morning,' he boasted.

Maggie eyed his crumpled clothes, tousled hair and stubble-covered face. 'You look it.'

He began to run his right foot up and down her bare leg. 'We proved two things last night, you don't have a sexual hang-up, and I haven't lost the knack. It was pretty good, wasn't it.' It was a statement not a question, so Maggie made no comment as he stretched lazily then resumed caressing her leg with his foot. 'Just so long as you didn't fantasise that you were doing it with Anthony Dillane,' he teased.

Maggie slowly lowered her cup to the table, contentment

fading as she remembered with a shock that somewhere along the way she had imagined the man possessing her was Randal Price.

They returned tired and hungry to Hampton at daybreak. The hours of darkness were presently so short they had had to fly during the dead of night to test the new goggles. Crews from stations at home and abroad were also guinea-pigging and giving reports to be analysed by the MoD.

Randal had taken the flight because he was highly experienced in night flying, as was Dave. With them were John Caine, a young pilot with only six months' service in Chinooks, and Brad Lovell, Griff's replacement straight from qualifying. They gave the new goggles a unanimous thumbs up: better definition and clarity aiding recognition at greater heights than previously possible.

They had worked well as a crew. Brad was a friendly, laid-back walking encyclopaedia on the subject of footballers past and present, who good-naturedly accepted that as Dave was a rugby man, Randal an avid follower of motor racing, and John exclusively interested in the honeymoon from which he had just returned, much of what he said about strikers, keepers and cup-winning aggregates fell on deaf ears. Tall and wiry, with a talent for mimicry, the new loadmaster had made himself instantly popular with a wicked impersonation of Gerard Jeffries.

On the last leg of their flight there was little intercom chatter, each man becoming engrossed with his thoughts. The testing part of the flight had taken their full attention, but Randal now let his mind wander where it would. Inevitably, although unwillingly, he dwelled on the fun Maggie must be having among the celebrities. Those star-studded arty parties lasted well into the early hours, so she was more than likely just falling into bed right now. Alone, he hoped. Pure dog-in-the-manger thinking!

Pursuing that line of thought, he told himself he must answer James Kitchen's letter regarding the terms of settlement of his divorce. It was being handled by the Price family's solicitor and that of Gerald Holland; two high-powered legal men employed by two even higher-powered millionaires. Randal's parents were betraying their usual lack of interest in his affairs – James must surely have informed them that the marriage was legally about to end – but Randal was sure Fiona's father had taken the sad burden off his 'little girl's' shoulders to 'save her any pain'.

It was the question of access to his children that was holding up Randal's reply to James's latest letter. Believing he would be permanently disabled immediately after his accident, Randal had not doubted the wisdom of his decision to spare a very small boy and an infant girl the distress of seeing what their father had become. Eighteen months on, he felt that they must be so used to the situation, demanding access now would be disturbing for them. A part-time daddy after no daddy would give them few advantages, if any, and knowing Fiona's immense sexual attraction Randal felt there must be a new father waiting in the wings for the opportunity to take up his role.

Every third weekend? Twice a month? How often would squadron demands make mincemeat of any access arrangements? Randal could rarely bank on where he would be on any given date. Was it fair on Neil and Lydia to subject them to disruptions to their lives? Being obliged to spend the odd day with a father they had probably forgotten by now would benefit no one.

Even as Randal reached that conclusion for the umpteenth time, that inner voice so often with him these days reminded him that those two had his genes and must have inherited some of his ways. He had created them; he was an indisputable part of them. Could he stand by and let another man influence them to his own design? It had been one thing to surrender them when he was paralysed and helpless; now he could play with them, chase them, lift them on to his shoulders as before. He reminded himself that he had been capable of doing that since the start of this year. Had he been too busy kick-starting his career again for the question to bother him as it now did? Was it because divorce made the severance absolute, or was it because he could father no more children in a future relationship?

They landed, went to debriefing, then split up to head to their respective Messes. After showering and dressing in fresh clothes Randal went down to breakfast. Being Sunday the room was empty. People were either sleeping in late after rowdy Saturday night excesses, or were enjoying a weekend at home. Taking a newspaper from the hall table as he entered, Randal piled a plate with eggs, bacon, tomatoes and sausages from the heated containers then settled at a corner table.

John entered several minutes later, taking his food and newspaper to the opposite corner. The resulting silence was broken only by cutlery scraping on plates and the crackle of pages being turned. Randal banished his thoughts by concentrating on weighty world affairs, until the peace was shattered by a loud exclamation from the other pilot.

'Wow! Rip, have you seen the arts supplement? I can't believe it's Maggie, yet she's sitting with Chris and his gran is mentioned.' John became revitalised, reading aloud with enthusiasm. '"Anthony Dillane pictured at the celebration party with former darling of the musical theatre, Evelyn Montrose, who groomed him for stardom at her Stage School." There are other pictures. Says here it's a block-buster hit.' There was a lull as John absorbed more, then added almost to himself, 'Never thought our Maggie could scrub up so well!'

Having discarded the travel, fashion and arts supplements of his own newspaper, Randal had a choice of retrieving them from the hall or crossing to John. He walked to look over the other man's shoulder at the double-spread feature on *Zenda*. First to catch his eye was a large picture of Dillane in costume, with headline references to 'out-swashbuckling' Errol Flynn. Randal grunted disparagingly. Was that what turned Maggie on?

'Reckon Chris was made to eat his words when she appeared in *that*,' John remarked, pointing to a group picture at the bottom of the page. 'Won't she crow when she gets back tonight!'

Randal heard no more as he recognised Fiona. He had not seen or had contact with his wife since the day he had been brutally frank about her future tied to him, easily achieving an end to their disintegrating marriage, but this picture nevertheless made him inordinately angry. He had long ago stopped wanting Fiona, yet he hotly resented the tailor's dummy with a smile over-full of dazzling teeth who was sitting beside her with his arm along the back of her chair. Was that what she admired these days? Was he buying her a country house to play in while he jetted around the world creating, breaking or merging companies? Dear God, were Lydia and Neil going to be taken over by a smoothie who would spend no more time with them than their pilot father had?

'You okay?'

He glanced at John. 'What?'

The younger man grinned. 'Always suspected you had a deeper interest in Maggie than you make out. How much d'you bet Chris edged you out by scoring with her last night?'

Randal would normally have offered expletive-filled advice on what John should do next. This morning he simply returned to his table to drink cooling coffee without tasting it. John had never seen Fiona so he had no notion of the impact the picture had made on Randal, who had not

181

even noticed Maggie and Chris at the same table. He burned with an emotion he could not identify. Fiona had constantly complained of the absences demanded by his job; was it more acceptable to her if the absences were caused by the drive to be king of a boardroom rather than king of the skies? Could an Armani-suited whizz-kid with a year-round tan thrill her as much as . . . ? What if he does? he asked himself savagely. You can't thrill *any* woman now.

Abandoning breakfast he went to his room, stripped off and dropped on his bed. After a period of tossing and turning with no hope of sleeping, he dressed again and went out to his car. He drove along the clifftop to a place he knew where he could pull off the road. It had turned into a beautiful morning, and people were enjoying the early summer heat down on the sands. Randal sat for a long time watching the happy beach activity as unexpected yearning invaded him.

If those boys had not dropped that anchor on him, would he have arrived home that day and upheld his decision to keep the marriage going for the sake of the children? Would they still be together as a family? His gaze lingered on a young couple making a sandcastle with a small boy and girl, envying them. Then he realised life would never be that simple for Neil and Lydia. They were 'rich kids'; the grandchildren of two very wealthy families. Watching the group on the beach, he longed to build sandcastles with his children even as he acknowledged that Fiona would hate it.

That was the true barrier between them. At heart, he was an ordinary working pilot; she was at all times a wealthy socialite. He drank beer; she loved champagne. He was happiest having rowdy fun with aircrew; Fiona adored upper-crust parties. He had had wealth and rank, and had known how to excite her in bed, but that was not enough when weighed against the rest. Sandcastles would not have featured in any future he might have contrived for his family if that anchor had not been dropped when it had.

Starting the engine, he drove off telling himself it would be pointless to demand access rights. He had stopped being of any use to his children when his Porsche had left the road and slammed into a high bank studded with concrete blocks.

The morning began badly and the day grew steadily worse. Gerard Jeffries accosted Randal in the corridor as he headed for his office.

'Ah, glad I caught you,' he said with a perfunctory nod by way of a good morning. 'Will you let me have the crew's reports on the new NVGs?'

Randal continued walking. 'As soon as we've had time to write them.'

'You had all day yesterday, man.'

'We were catching up on our sleep.'

Jeffries appeared in the office doorway as Randal reached his desk and spotted the page of newpaper pictures of *Zenda* someone had kindly put there. His mouth tightened as he glanced up. 'Dave and Brad start the two-day Internal Security refresher course you insisted they attend, and John's due for his six-monthly flight check today. I have to see Doc Miles at ten for my compulsory medical, and this afternoon I'm taking up a couple of cameramen who're working on that recruiting film. Tomorrow—'

Jeffries interrupted testily. 'We're *all* under pressure, you know, but paperwork still has to be done.'

'It will be. *When we find the time to do it*,' he repeated harshly. 'It's not as if our recommendations will be acted on in less than six months – even that would be unusually swift – and it's not a top priority matter.'

'That has nothing to do with it,' Jeffries snapped. 'When you're given new equipment to test you write up your report while everything is clear in your mind. If you're so all-fired busy you've no time to do your job properly, you should give it to someone who has.' He paused significantly. 'You've been back at Hampton for just three months and the facts speak for themselves, man. I had my doubts about your reappointment, but I was overruled.'

Randal regarded him with narrowed eyes. 'What are you hinting?'

'I heard you were not fully on the ball during the airlift of the rail crash survivors.'

'You didn't hear that from Chris,' he countered swiftly. 'Or from Dave. Ah, the garrulous Griff. A pal of yours.'

'I treated him with the same fair-mindedness and tolerance I show to every member of this squadron, and I resent your tone.'

'I resent any crewman still wet behind the ears telling my boss I'm not up to a job I've been doing for more than twelve years. The unspoken rule is that if any member of a crew is unhappy over his pilot's actions he has it out with him. He *never* goes over his head without tackling him first, even if he feels his life was endangered. If that's what Griff suggested to you he was bloody lying.'

Jeffries' thin face hardened. 'You handled that man badly throughout. Had you had the slightest understanding of the situation, that appalling business with Maggie last month would never have happened. An aircraft beached, pictures on TV of of our crewmen brawling—'

'You read the reports of the crew, for God's sake. Griff became aggressive and pushed Dave away when he tried to calm him. That doesn't constitute a brawl. And what "appalling business"? The Chinook could have been lost altogether if Maggie hadn't had the cool sense to have a long shot at saving it. That she did had nothing to do with my handling of a man who was anti-social, anti-women, anti-everything save himself.'

'The Station Commander didn't see it that way. He shares my concerns over your capabilities.'

'Then he should talk to me about them. As he hasn't they can't be as strong as yours.' He looked at the clock. 'Briefing is in ten minutes and I must clear these memos first. Paperwork, you know.' He sat at his desk, adding as calmly as he could, without glancing up, 'You'll have the reports on the new NVGs as soon as we've written them, Boss.'

Walking into the Briefing Room the first thing to hit Randal's eye was a huge, fuzzy enlargement of part of a news picture showing a slim young woman in a striking dress that left one shoulder bare. Maggie wore a butter-wouldn't-melt-in-the-mouth expression, and the others were reacting in typically male fashion to this nose-thumbing. Chris looked like a cat who had had a whole jug of cream. Ignoring the picture, Randal called them to order.

'Right, you've all seen the Wailing Wall. Who's not happy?'

For a quarter of an hour he addressed the problem of switching crews around to suit Ray and Pete, who had legitimate reasons to change tasks, then he began on briefing details. Only when each crew had grouped to discuss routing and Met information did Randal draw Maggie aside as she passed.

'Everyone's seen the newspapers, Maggie, but if you felt you still had to make a point you should've stuck that sexy blow-up in the Crew Room. This isn't the place for it. If the Boss sees it he'll go spare.'

'As you are?'

'I'm quietly telling you to take it down. Now.'

'Yes, *sir*,' she snapped out with military exaggeration.

'Don't play up. I'm not in the mood.'

'Why? Didn't Fiona tell you she would be at the party? Ah, I see she didn't,' she added slyly. 'The guy she was with was an angel.'

'A what?'

'One of the show's backers. Name of Seth Nicholls. Know him?' He gave no answer, so she continued in an undertone. 'I ran into Fiona in the cloakroom and couldn't resist reminding her of where we last met. She'd forgotten, of course. I doubt she had even noticed me that evening; she was more interested in Mark, who was giving her the attention you had snatched from her. But she was genuinely shaken when I told her we were flying together again. Does that mean you two are still incommunicado?'

'Go to hell, Maggie,' he said in quiet anger.

'Can't,' she returned with infuriating calmness. 'You've just tasked me to fly to Boscombe Down. Incidentally, I told your wife exactly what we all thought of any woman who would walk out on a man facing a future as a paraplegic. I hope it spoiled her evening, but it probably didn't. To give her her due, she turned a little pale beneath her designer tan. You're better able to assess the significance of that than me. I barely know her, thank God!'

Randal watched her walk away to tear down the photographed image that had surprised them all. In her flying suit and heavy boots she was fondly familiar, but the girl had many facets to her personality and she had just keenly disturbed him on more than one count. Damn her for accosting Fiona in that manner! Why had fate put the pair so unexpectedly in proximity?

He made coffee in the Crew Room. There was an hour to pass before his appointment with Pam Miles. Time enough to write that report on the NVGs, but he was in the wrong frame of mind to be clinical and concise on paper.

Gazing from the window he reviewed what Maggie had told him. So this Seth Nicholls had money enough to risk investing in a lavish theatrical venture that could just as well have flopped as been acclaimed a blockbuster. Show business would undoubtedly appeal to Fiona, who had never even tried to understand the raw excitement and danger of flying. And what might Maggie have said to that bronzed side of beef during the course of the evening, in her misguided championship? He conveniently pushed aside recollection of his dependence on her during those darkest days of his life, as he told himself he was well able to sort out his marriage without her making the situation worse.

Thirty minutes of frustrating paperwork later, Randal drove across to the Medical Centre. The Medical Board had stipulated that he have quarterly health checks for the first year of his return to active service. While accepting the wisdom of this, he, like the male majority at Hampton, was not comfortable with a female MO. She knew her job, but it was irksome to be intimately examined and questioned by a curvaceous redhead with a soft Cornish accent that managed to sound sexy even when uttering medical mumbo-jumbo.

Randal had not encountered her professionally since his look-in on arrival at Hampton. She had then annoyed him by asking unwelcome questions. Today, he would have to submit to a thorough examination. While he stripped to his underwear she chatted in friendly fashion, making the status quo even more repugnant to him. After checking his sight and hearing, sounding his chest and recording his lung capacity, testing his reflexes and general mobility, she told him to lower his pants.

'You're very quiet today,' she commented as he did so. 'It's unusual for you.'

'I rarely talk while a woman's studying my balls.'

She stiffened, but managed to say lightly, 'The strong, silent type? Cough, please! And again! Right, that all seems fine.' She glanced up at him. 'Any signs of sexual response returning; stirrings of an erection, however slight?'

'Carry on feeling around and you might get lucky,' he drawled.

187

She straightened as he covered himself, her eyes bright with anger. 'This is a medical consultation, Squadron Leader. Don't take that line with me or I shall have to have a word with the Station Commander.'

'What about, sexual harrassment? I'm the one who's been ordered to strip, and you're doing all the touching, *Squadron Leader*,' he pointed out crisply.

'You can dress,' she snapped, turning away to sit at her desk.

He swiftly put on his clothes, by which time Pam was writing up her notes. 'Is the consultation over, ma'am?'

Without looking up, she stated, 'You're an amazingly fit man. If the spinal injuries from your accident had been even marginally lower you'd still be in a wheelchair. At best, shuffling along with the support of sticks. Do you appreciate your good fortune?'

'Every time I climb into the cockpit, believe me,' he told her with sincerity.

She fixed him with a long, level look. 'You accepted every available medical aid to get yourself back there, but you refused my offer of impotency pills. You've been made fully aware that there's no guarantee your system will return to normal only that it might, in time. Drugs could give it a helping hand in the meantime.'

'No, thanks. Can I go now?'

She exclaimed in irritation, 'The impotency is a legacy of your injuries, Rip. It doesn't make you less of a man, you know. Don't get so uptight!'

'Isn't the problem the fact that I can't?' he countered.

'Yet you refuse my advice. Why? Don't you want or need full sexual satisfaction these days?'

'What I want in my free time is my own affair. I told you that before.'

'But the mental welfare of personnel on this station can affect their efficiency, and that becomes *my* affair.'

He let fly. 'Christ, is everyone on the bloody station spreading it around that I'm not up to the job?'

'Calm down! I've merely noticed that it's all work and very little play with you. I've only known you for a few weeks, but you have a repuation as a colourful character up to every trick in the book, and a few that aren't. I've heard stories of your past exploits and been waiting in vain for evidence of a few more.'

'Ha! If you're already concerned about my mental health, you'd have me in a straightjacket if I began larking around the way I used to.'

'I'm serious, Rip,' she insisted gently. 'You worked like a Trojan to get back to flying, but you're still driving yourself hard now it's no longer necessary and risking a setback.'

Growing tense, Randal asked, 'Is all this going in your report to the Board?'

'Of course not, it's just a touch of friendly advice. Believe it or not, I'm on your side.' She smiled. 'It doesn't take a doctor to know that every man needs to let off steam in one way or another, or head for trouble. I heard you used to be a hot favourite with the girls. There's no better way of relaxing than with the female of the species.'

'So we're back to that,' he declared angrily. 'I've never been an advocate of pill-popping, and I've read stories about poor bastards staying erect for hours at the most embarrassing times. There's no way I'll accept your bloody sex aids and risk resembling a teapot during briefing, or at any other time. And what made me "a hot favourite" with girls wasn't my knob value. I was never a mere stud,' he ran on furiously. 'Thanks for your agony aunt advice, Pam, but I'll wait for my impulses to return when they're ready.'

As he reached her door, she asked, 'And what if they don't?'

He gave a savage smile. 'I can always dip it in starch if I get really desperate.'

All through lunch Randal brooded, and when he led his crew out to fly two cameramen wanting footage for their recruiting film, he glowered at Chris walking jauntily beside him. 'What're you looking so bloody bouncy about?'

The Navigator gave a wicked grin. 'You saw the picture Maggie put on display before briefing. If you get her alone, away from the rest of you crude, insensitive guys, she—'

'Give it a rest,' he snapped. 'We've all had a gutful of that damn musical show.'

Chris unwisely pursued the subject. 'I was referring to what happened *after* the damn musical show.'

Randal climbed through to the cockpit trying not to believe the broad hint. Maggie was still too much affected by Mark Hascham to start playing around with anyone else. He should know. Yet Chris looked remarkably cocksure.

They began the pre-flight checks without preamble, and were soon under way, heading for the hills that would provide the right conditions for the manoeuvres required by the film makers. What they saw as ideal from a filming angle the crew might find impossible or too risky, yet they were obliged to give full assistance within reason. Randal had had no option but to deal with this because his medical check had prevented his taking any other task, but he allied these men with the Media who he hated unequivocally. This added to his depression as he heard Sandy and Mitch in the cabin outlining the problems of landing in small woodland clearings.

When they neared the hills Randal spoke to his passengers, trying to sound friendly. 'When we do the low flying I suggest we first put one of you down on the hill so you'll get our "brow-hopping" from inside the aircraft and below it simultaneously. We'll go through that sequence first. Then, when you've got all you need, we'll move on to one of our practice areas for the vertical landings. You must appreciate that we'll then be operating in a very tight space surrounded by dense woodland. I doubt if you'll be able to get long shots there, but you know your business better than I do. What we as a crew can do is limited by lack of clearance for the rotors, but you said you wanted to film teamwork necessary for precision landings and take-offs and you'll certainly get that. If any of it doesn't work for you, we'll try something else that will.'

As they followed the course set by Chris, the aircraft cast a long shadow over green, undulating countryside dotted with sheep and lambs. Then they overflew a line of hikers who gazed up and waved.

Chris said, 'I'd rather be down there on a day like this.'

Randal looked at him in surprise. 'Never knew you were keen on rural marches.'

'Not to pound the sod in hobnailed boots! I was thinking more of a picnic, a few cans of beer, and an inventive girl.'

'Quadruple that and we'll all join you,' said Sandy.

Randal added nothing where once he would have topped that with a comment to bring howls of laughter. Pam had apparently heard of his reputation as a colourful character up to every trick in the book, and a few that were not. Had he lost his sense of zany fun along with his virility? Was he slowly turning into another Gerard Jeffries?

The afternoon dragged past as they flew standard manoeuvres until their passengers had all the shots they needed from the air and the ground. At one point Chris asked if Randal was OK.

'Yep,' he said crisply. 'Let's get this wrapped up quickly then head back. I've things to do tonight.' These were to write to James Kitchen disclaiming visiting rights, then to get drunk.

The cameramen were not as demanding as the crew had feared, and they appeared delighted with how smoothly the plan had been executed. Even so, as he took off for the last time from the tiny forest clearing Randal reflected sourly that the whole business had been as boring as he had feared. Then a new worry hit him. Was he losing interest in flying? Had he fought a long, hard battle against disability to return to the great love of his life only to find it starting to pall?

As if in answer to that, when they landed twenty minutes later, the cameramen thanked Randal and the crew for a fantastic experience, adding, 'You guys get to live life in the fast lane. We held our breath once or twice, but you've got good judgement off to a fine art. Can't wait to come back for another session on load-lifting. We understand you can actually pick up another Chinook and transport it somewhere else. That we have to film!'

'The rotors are removed first,' said Chris with a grin. 'Or we'd be in real trouble.'

'Will you be flying the second session with us?'

'Unlikely,' put in Randal. 'We never know where we'll be from one day to the next. The Gulf, Bosnia, Ireland, Kosovo . . . or Salisbury Plain.'

'Like we said: life in the fast lane. Cheers!'

They walked off with their equipment leaving Randal prey to his thoughts again. Those men saw his own job as he had always before seen it. The work had not changed, so it must be him. Pam had said everyone needed to let off steam in one way or another. Did Rip Price's volatile personality find life too mundane without a constant challenge: a rocky marriage, a near-impossible goal to strive for, a mid-air emergency to deal with?

This premise stayed at the back of his mind throughout the short debrief, nagging at him, urging him to take some action. As he passed Jeffries' office with Chris he noticed that it was empty and surprisingly tidy.

'Where's he scuttled off to? It's not like him to lose an opportunity to check on us, and he's invariably much in evidence when civilians are around.'

Chris grinned. 'Maybe they told him they wouldn't need to film him playing the Big Boss.'

'It's still unusual for him to leave this early.' They walked on towards the Crew Room and Randal said on impulse, 'How about rounding up some of the guys for a few jars at the Bird tonight? According to Dave, there's a jazz group there on Thursday nights now.'

'Since when?'

'Last week. He wasn't happy. Hates jazz.'

'Christ, it must've shaken the cosy yokel ambience!'

'So are you on?' Randal asked, pushing open the door.

'I thought you had things to do.'

He grinned. 'Drinking's one of them.'

The room was fairly full and buzzing with the uninhibited chatter of aircrew. They headed for the tiny kitchen to make coffee, needing the stimulus of caffeine. When they emerged, mugs in their hands, Randal again suggested an evening at the Bird in Hand.

'I've plans of my own,' murmured Chris, smiling across the room.

Randal followed his glance and saw Maggie leave a small group to cross to them. He spoke quickly, outsmarting Chris.

'Some of us are driving to Heyhoe tonight. How about it, Maggie? Dave says they have jazz on Thursdays.'

She shook her head. 'Not any longer. Complaints apparently flooded in about not being able to hear themselves speak, about catering for tourists instead of the regulars who spend money there all year round, and about getting too trendy simply to please the youngsters. I suppose we fall into that category. According to Pete and Jill, who took Arnie there for a pint on Saturday night, there was a petition and posters urging support of the campaign to save our traditional country pub.'

'I'll wager Dave stirred it all up,' put in Chris darkly. 'I

193

worry about that boy sometimes. Unless it's bagpipes, it's not music to his ears.' He gently flicked the bars of rank on Maggie's shoulder with his finger. 'So where are we two going tonight, ma'am?'

'I don't know about you, but I'm going to be studying. I'm on a nav refresher course next week, and the new instructor's reputed to be a total sadist. Ask Steve.'

Chris smiled, but could not hide his disappointment. 'If you need help with revision, come and get me.'

He moved away and, after a swig of his coffee, Randal asked, 'Was that a brush-off?'

'It was a statement of fact,' she said levelly. 'I do need to put in some work before that course. If the guy's a misogynist as well as a sadist he'll give me a bad time.'

Pleased that she had not leaped at the chance to spend an evening with Chris, who must have lied about what happened between them after *Zenda*, Randal cocked an eyebrow. 'Now who would ever give you a bad time?'

'Short memory, Boss?' she asked smartly. Then, after a moment or two, added, 'What kind of mood are you in now?'

'As sweet as always.' When she hesitated he sensed that she was not responding to his teasing tone. 'What's wrong, Maggie?'

She glanced around to check that no one was near enough to overhear, then faced him with curious tenseness. 'Do you want the bad news, or the bad news?'

'Is there a level of badness to chose from?'

'Not really. Jeffries' promotion has come through. He'll be leaving next month.'

'That's *bad* news?'

'It is when you know who's replacing him.'

Randal frowned. 'Go on.'

'Perry Newman. Dirk had the fact straight from the bouncy little bastard's mouth.'

He swore. 'That's all I bloody needed.'

'Bad day?' she asked softly.

Seeing the concern in her expression he recalled how often she had studied him this way, how often she had been there to hear his expletives and frustrated ragings against life. How often she had returned for more! He gave a faint smile.

'I've had a lot that were a damn sight worse, haven't I?'

'No one's happy about the appointment . . . except Dirk Bogarde, of course. The news has actually brought him out of the dumps he's been in lately.'

'Glad it's given someone a boost.'

After a moment, she said, 'If you still want to go to the Bird *sans* jazz – I could work on my nav later.'

He shook his head. 'I'll get pissed here. Won't have to worry about driving back tanked up.'

After showering and dressing in a grey shirt and trousers, Randal doggedly pursued his plan to write to James Kitchen. It was pointless to delay what he knew would be best for everyone. He sealed the letter, stuck a stamp on it and prepared to go downstairs with the intention of dulling his depression with beer. And if Pam Miles appeared he would start horsing around like a maniac, throwing her into medical confusion. Was he mad, or simply a 'colourful character' again?

As he closed the door the telephone in his room began to ring. Let the bastard call in vain, whoever he was! He made for the bar to drink a few pints before he tackled dinner, but he had not even managed to get one before the Mess Sergeant appeared before him, his expression carefully schooled.

'Telephone call for you, sir. Your wife.'

Conscious that those nearest to him had fallen silent, Randal challenged him. 'My *wife*?'

'That's right, sir. Will you take it in your room?'

Momentarily tempted to tell the man to say he would

ring back when he was free, he merely nodded and headed for the stairs. How long since they had last spoken to each other? Eighteen months? Even longer. She wanted to get on with the divorce so she could marry Seth Nicholls. Well, he could tell her he had just put with the outgoing mail a letter removing the last hitch to completion.

He lifted the receiver. 'Squadron Leader Price.'

'I have your wife on the line, sir. I'll put her through.'

A moment of silence, then, 'Randal? Thank God you're not overseas! You have to come right away. You're the only one who can deal with this. Please, *please* get here as fast as you can. Oh God, I don't know what to do. Mummy and Daddy have gone to pieces, as usual, and I *need* you. *We* need you. Oh God!'

She began to sob hysterically, and it was not an act. The coldness of apprehension began to creep over Randal as he struggled to absorb her words. He had twice to repeat her name before she was calm enough to respond.

'*Fee*, what's happened?'

'They've snatched Lydia from ballet school,' she cried in anguish. 'They're demanding a ransom . . . or they'll . . .'

Apprehension turned to an emotion more savage than any he had ever known. 'I'm on my way.'

Eight

As Randal took the Porsche up the long drive to the Holland stud his inner rage intensified. The last time he had come to Marylands Neil had been in a coma after being thrown from a pony here. The time before that had been his vain attempt to persuade Fiona to return to their quarter at Hampton and start afresh. And the time before that he had stormed into this mansion to remove his children from grandparents who had coaxed Fiona to leave them there 'in a stable environment'. On that occasion the slumbering enmity between the racehorse breeders and the pilot accused of too often abandoning his family while on overseas duty reached the point of no return.

A mild truce had existed while Neil was in hospital – mainly because of the Hollands' culpability for the accident – but hostilities had returned with a vengeance when Randal had brutally outlined to Fiona what her life would be like tied to a paraplegic. Holland had taken his weeping 'little girl' away, heaping curses on the crippled pilot for his insensitivity. Now, another crisis had brought Randal here; a crisis that had him questioning how he could ever have relinquished his children.

Eleven p.m. but the house was ablaze with lights. Randal saw the lads grouped in the stableyard nearest to the mansion, shifting restlessly as they talked. The car's full beams swept over them and came to rest on the ornate front door before Randal killed the engine. As he climbed from his seat the front door opened and Fiona ran to him. He caught her shoulders and held her steady, shocked by the extent of her terror. Dear God, had Lydia already been harmed?

'What's the situation?' he demanded hoarsely.

Her lovely eyes were now huge with fear. 'They want three million by tomorrow night, or else . . .'

'We'll pay. *We'll pay!* How did it happen? Why wasn't someone looking after her? Christ, Fee, how could she be taken, just like that? Where were *you*, for a start?'

Fiona began to tremble, and Gerald Holland strode from the house to put a protective arm around his daughter.

'Haven't you done enough harm to her, you bastard? I wasn't aware she'd called you until half an hour ago. She can't think straight in this horrifying situation. It has nothing to do with you.'

'It has everything to do with me,' Randal snapped. 'It's my child whose life's in danger.'

'The child you *abandoned*. You surrendered any responsibility for both of them to Fiona and dropped out of their lives like the selfish bugger you've always been. You don't give a damn about that precious little girl.'

Professional experience of dangerous situations allowed Randal to stay focussed. This man would never understand his actions when facing his shattered life, so he instead turned to Fiona.

'Let's go indoors. I need to hear the details.'

'I won't have you entering my house,' raged her father.

'For God's sake get your priorities right for once, man,' he returned, leading Fiona inside and across to one of the four sitting rooms. She was still trembling badly as he took up the decanter containing brandy and poured some for her. 'Drink this up. It'll steady you. We'll sort this out. Trust me.'

'That's why I called you,' she said, her teeth chattering

against the glass as she drank. 'Daddy's blaming himself, Mummy's in Lydia's room crying, but you've always known how to deal with a crisis.'

He refrained from pointing out that the job she hated had trained him to do that. Instead, he asked what had happened. Her eyes swivelled to look at her father who was standing just inside the room.

'Didi, the au pair, usually goes to fetch Lydia from her ballet class, but Daddy had to go over to Riversmead to talk to Colonel Boyer about his mare so . . . so he said he'd pick Lydia up on his way home.'

'So why didn't he?'

Holland crossed to them, his face working with emotion. 'There'd been an accident. Traffic was jammed solid for half an hour. I was stuck in the middle of it. Nothing I could do. *Nothing.*'

'He rang to tell us but . . . well, Mummy and I were in the middle of having a massage,' she confessed jerkily. 'So Didi set out right away.'

'*And?*'

'The road was jammed in both directions,' Holland explained with nervous impatience. 'The damned ballet studio was almost exactly where the accident had happened. No one could get there. *No one!*'

Randal thought fleetingly that the helicopters this family so despised could have got there, but he said, 'So none of the parents could collect their children?'

'I've just said so,' snapped the other man. '*It was a solid jam!*'

Turning his attention back to Fiona, Randal asked,' Who runs this ballet class? Surely she keeps an eye on the kids until they're collected.'

'*Of course she does,*' put in Holland explosively. 'You don't think we'd send our little princess anywhere without thoroughly checking it out.'

Randal rounded on him. 'Kids are snatched from anywhere. Hospitals, mansions with sophisticated security sys-
tems, public playgrounds, even prams. In every instance
they've been left unattended, if only for a few seconds.
This woman you checked on so thoroughly must have done
the same.'

'Adela swears she didn't,' cried Fiona. 'They were all in
the studio playing guessing games. Parents had all phoned
from their cars saying they couldn't get there. Lydia wanted
the toilet. It's just across the hall and the door's visible from
the studio, but she was a long time so Adela went to check on
her. The door leading to the garden was open – it's usually
locked – and Lydia had vanished.'

'I'll close her down; get her prosecuted,' vowed her father
brokenly.

Randal ignored that. 'Then Lydia must have gone into
the garden, Fee. Is it walled?'

'A very high hedge. But just a wire fence at the end.
Quite low because of the view of the downs at the back
of the house.'

'Oh God, that means that anyone walking there could have
enticed her away.' He flung Holland a look. 'You needn't
close the woman down. After this, no one will leave a child
in a place so easily accessible. Have the police any leads?'

The older man licked his lips nervously. 'By the time
the wreckage of a multiple accident had been sufficiently
cleared to open one side of the road, and I'd eventually
filtered through the bottleneck to reach the house, it was
an hour later than the time the lesson usually ended. There
was pandemonium. Older girls were arriving for their lesson
and parents were milling around collecting or dropping off
their daughters and the ballet paraphernalia. *That woman*
took at least five minutes before detaching herself to take
me to her office. She was highly agitated, of course. Said
she had left her young assistant minding the rest while she

and her housekeeper searched the extensive garden. Said she then went through to the front garden giving on to the road. Asked if anyone had seen a little girl. The police, firemen and paramedics were all coping with the casualties trapped in the cars, and bystanders were more interested in that than a wandering child.'

His face paled further. 'I let rip at the woman, and rang Mary telling her to check Didi's car phone in case she had seen Lydia wandering along the pavement and picked her up. None of us had any idea of how near to the house Didi had managed to get before meeting the jam of traffic. Then I searched the garden very thoroughly thinking maybe Lydia had initially hidden somewhere for fun then found she couldn't get out.' His voice cracked with emotion. 'She can be a little scamp.'

Memories welled up to thicken Randal's throat, too. 'I know.'

'Mary called back to say Didi didn't have her. She sounded frightened. I went to the road to question the policemen sorting out the crashed vehicles. They'd been too occupied, they said. I then went to the neighbouring houses for two or three hundred yards in both directions, thinking she might somehow have pushed through to another garden.'

There was such an air of desperation in his voice now that Randal felt a stirring of sympathy. Whatever else the man was, he worshipped his grandchildren.

'When I returned to the studio I insisted on searching it from top to bottom. That woman had seen the open door and assumed Lydia had gone through it. Hadn't looked indoors! I went through every room, searching the wardrobes and cupboards.'

Randal broke into the other man's attempt to prove he had done all he could to find the child. They already knew someone had snatched her and was demanding money in exchange for her safety. How it had happened could be gone into later. He got down to essentials.

'Who's in charge of the police team? Is he keeping in touch?' Seeing the expression on his face, Randal turned in rising alarm. 'Fee?'

She shook her head helplessly. 'We were told not to inform them . . . or else.'

'You mean you haven't brought them in on this? Not even when you'd searched everywhere and realised she must have been abducted?'

'There wasn't time,' she confessed brokenly. 'While Daddy was still at Adela's the man phoned saying he had Lydia. He insisted on speaking to *me*. He said if I . . . if I wanted her back alive I must keep the police out of it. He's going to ring at eight tomorrow evening to check that we've got the money, in cash. Once he's counted the money, we can fetch Lydia from the place she's in.' She gripped the thick wool of his sweater with feverish pleading. 'Do whatever he asks, Randal, but please get her back. *Please!*'

Closing his arms around her, he said, 'We have to bring the police in.'

'*No!*' cried Holland.

Randal turned to study the man's drawn features and knew he was close to cracking. 'It's obvious this devil means to squeeze money out of you. It's also obvious that he's familiar with this family or he'd never have made his demand so quickly. Someone with a grudge. Someone wanting to get at you. There are quite a few, I imagine,' he added harsly, knowing the ways of the racing world through his chaotic marriage to Fiona. 'Once we hand over the first payment there's no guarantee we'll get Lydia back. He'll ask for more; aim to bleed you dry. It could last for weeks. We *must* get police help.'

'No,' the older man cried again. 'No, *no!*'

Fiona pulled at Randal's sweater. 'He warned us not to.'

Holding on to his control Randal confronted her. 'You called me to come and sort this out. Because I know how to deal with a crisis, you said. Well, for Christ's sake *let* me. If we don't get Lydia in exchange for the cash, the only way to find her will be to follow whoever picks it up. None of us is equipped to do that. Trained men can do it without being spotted. They have all the equipment and a backup team at their headquarters.' He gripped her arms to emphasise the importance of what he was saying. 'A military operation is rarely conducted by one person. It takes planning by experienced men who work together. This is much the same, believe me. We need the professionals.'

Turning from his wife's reluctant nod, Randal challenged her father. 'Lydia is my daughter, so I'm entitled to overrule you on this. If you attempt to stop me using the phones in your house, I'll call the police from my car.'

After a long, tense moment Gerald Holland turned and walked from the room.

The two detectives did not leave Marylands until three a.m., after intensive questioning. They applauded the decision to put the matter in their hands and assured the family they had men who were greatly experienced with abduction cases.

Gerald had been hostile and uncooperative; Mary too upset to participate. Once the decision had been taken Fiona went along with it and stayed close to Randal during the long, harrowing session with the detectives who would return that evening to record the ransom call at eight o'clock. It had been agreed that Randal would take the bag containing the money to the rendezvous. His distinctive red Porsche would be easy to follow, and the bag would contain a tracking device to facilitate the police pursuit when the ransom was collected. After a heated argument on the weight of responsibility, Randal and his father-in-law agreed to supply half the sum each. They would that morning be arranging for their respective bankers to provide the money in notes of large denominations.

Fiona claimed she needed the reassurance of his nearness and, unexpectedly, Randal found he needed to give it and willingly stetched out on top of his wife's bed. Whatever the gulf between them, nothing could ever change their mutual parentage of the little girl presently undergoing a terrifying ordeal. It drew them close, transcending bitterness from the past.

Lying wide-eyed with exhaustion while Fiona sank into a drugged sleep, Randal tortured himself with memories of a beautiful, provocative toddler who could wind her podgy arms around his neck and coax anything she wanted from him. Dear God, how could he have abandoned her? What kind of a brute would turn his back on a sweet, vulnerable child who might now be . . . The thought was so unbearable he could only banish it with action. Going downstairs to make coffee he discovered it was already morning. In the kitchen the nightmare hit him anew. He had been scared in dangerous war situations; he had been afraid when Neil had lain in a coma three years ago; he had been so terrified by his own paralysis he had longed to die. Yet he had never felt such fear as this before. He wanted to kill with his bare hands the man who had Lydia; *would* kill him if he got to him the minute his daughter was safe. By tailing the police car tonight he could . . .

His violent thoughts were scattered by the sound of someone behind him, and he turned to the door ready to deal with Mary or Gerald. A boy in pyjamas stood gazing at him with wide brown eyes, an expression of disbelief on his square face. Randal gazed back at his son, who had grown beyond belief!

Neil said, 'They told me you weren't coming back any more.'

Randal had never been readily eloquent, and the boy's words smote him. 'Did they? Well . . . I'm here, aren't I?'

'Because of Lydia?' At Randal's nod, he asked, 'Do they know where she is yet?'

Knowing Neil had been told by the Hollands that his sister had gone home from the ballet class with someone and had not told Miss Adela who it was, Randal chose his words carefully.

'I'm all set to fetch her back tonight.'

'She's often naughty,' he replied with the matter of factness of a six-year-old.

Father and son continued to gaze at each other across ten feet of sea-green floor covering, unsure of each other. Then Randal said, 'I'm going to make coffee. Would you like some?'

'Ugh, no thanks. I usually have a kind of milkshake in the morning.' He walked to the refrigerator. 'They make some really cool flavours like peppermint ice and tangerine cream.' He looked over his shoulder. 'You should try them.'

'Perhaps later on.'

While Randal plugged in the kettle and spooned coffee into a cafetière, Neil poured milk and flavouring into a mixer with the ease of long practice then switched it on. When the drinks were ready they sat side by side on tall stools at the breakfast bar. Neil opened a tin filled with biscuits and began to eat with the single-mindedness of small boys.

'Don't you want one?' he asked with his mouth full.

'Just coffee.' Randal was marvelling at his son's self-possession and deeply regretting the many months of his development he had missed. He had even been planning to bail out of his life for good.

Silence fell again while Neil devoured biscuits and drank the curiously-coloured mixture he had concocted. Suddenly, without looking up at Randal, he said, 'I won the long jump and throwing a cricket ball on sports day.'

'Well done!' On top of his fears for Lydia this suspended emotion between them was proving too much to take. Pushing his mug aside, Randal asked gently, 'Did anyone explain why I wasn't coming back, Neil?'

He mumbled into his glass, 'You'd been sent overseas for years and years.' Turning his face, still pressed to the rim of the glass, he looked accusingly at his father. 'You didn't say goodbye and you didn't telephone like you usually do when you go away.'

'That's because I didn't go away.' He knew the boy must now be told the truth, and he began carefully to tell it in a manner Neil might understand.

'Remember when Lydia was a small baby? She couldn't do anything for herself. When she dropped things one of us had to pick them up and give them back to her. She could only go out if we pushed her in a pram, and she couldn't run about and play with you however much she wanted to.' Neil was frowning with incomprehension, so Randal moved on swiftly. 'The good thing was that we all knew she would soon grow and be able to do what everyone else could do, didn't we?'

Neil nodded, still unsure of where this was leading.

'Remember the day you started school? I had to fly to Poland for an exercise. It lasted ten days. When I got back I set out to drive home to see you all, but somewhere along the way my car left the road and went into a wall. It was well and truly smashed up.' He put his hand on Neil's shoulder. 'Remember when you fell off that pony and woke up in hospital wondering where you were?'

'I didn't like it in there. I kept hurting.'

'I woke up in hospital, too. And I was hurting. The crash had damaged my back so badly that I'd become very much like Lydia used to be. I couldn't walk and had to be pushed in a wheelchair. If I dropped things I couldn't pick them up, and other people had to do everything for me. But here's the worst part, Neil. Unlike Lydia, they told me I would stay that way for ever. You've never seen me cry, have you?' The boy shook his head. 'I did then. You see, I knew I wouldn't be able to play games with you, pick you up on to my shoulders, swim with you, chase you around the garden – any of the things we used to do. You wouldn't be able to brag about your dad at school; you'd probably feel embarrassed, instead.'

He let his hand drop from the pyjama-clad shoulder as he recalled those desperate days. 'And Mummy would have to look after me the way she looked after Lydia . . . always.' Gazing into the boy's dark, puzzled eyes, he said quietly, 'I didn't think it would be very fair on any of you, so I decided you would all manage better if I stayed away and you came to live here at Marylands. It wasn't because I didn't love you, Tiger,' he added, using the pet name unconsciously. 'I loved you *too much*.'

Neil thought about it for a while, a half-eaten biscuit still in his hand. That last comment was clearly too deep for him to understand, and the rest made little sense to him, either. Eventually, he said as if challenging a schoolfellow who had told him a whopping great lie, 'There's nothing wrong with you.'

'No, I was lucky.' Randal poured more coffee for himself as he searched for words to explain that no one had waved a magic wand to make him better. Would a six-year-old be able to accept the extent of pain and frustration endured to recover full mobility? Almost certainly not.

'You see, Neil, the hospital doctors gradually realised that my back could be mended. It took a very long time, but they managed it and I can do everything again.'

'Is that why you've come back?'

207

What to say that would not alarm him! 'I've come because Mummy asked me to.'

Neil frowned. 'Why did she say you'd gone overseas for years and years?'

That was a tough one. 'I expect she thought it would be easier for you and Lydia to understand.'

'Now she's asked you to come.'

'Yes.'

The boy decided to finish the biscuit, asking through the crumbs, 'So are we going home now?'

An even tougher one. 'I have to bring Lydia back first, then Mummy and I will talk.' He made a show of looking at the clock on the wall. 'Isn't it time you were getting ready for school?'

'S'pose so.' He slid off the stool. 'You *will* be here when I come home, won't you?'

'Promise.'

The boy paused at the door and sighed heavily. 'I don't know whether to believe that bit about you being a baby again. It sounds weird. I couldn't tell that to my friends. But I *wish* you hadn't stayed away. We used to do some cool things together.' He began to wander through to the hall. 'I think I'll stick to saying my dad's been flying secret missions no one must know about. Yes, that's best.'

Randal watched his son walk up the stairs, and fought the desire to call him back and hug him tightly. Neil was not yet ready for that. But he needed and wanted his father, he had made that clear. Choked, Randal watched through the open door the lads engaged in their stable chores, seeing instead a cavalcade of images of himself and his children as they grew from baby to child.

Out of a sense of shock and despair he had withdrawn from marriage and parenthood while yearning to withdraw from life itself. That he had allowed the status quo to remain might be due to his own non-relationship with his parents.

They had never been there for their small son, so Randal had swiftly grown self-sufficient. Neil was different. He had just revived a rapport Randal had smothered as relentlessly as he had fought back to normality, revived it just as he had sent a letter to James Kitchen renouncing rights of access. He must ring the man as soon as this nightmare ended.

Gerald Holland came in just then to make tea for his wife, who was still too upset to leave her room. There was a brief skirmish between father and grandfather over whether or not Neil should be sent to school under the circumstances. Randal clinched his argument by asking if the older man wanted to subject the boy to the stresses and traumas of the coming hours.

'Fiona and Mary are weepy and emotional, you're at the end of your tether, and I've turned up out of the blue to further confuse him. You and I have to organise and collect three million by tonight, and a police engineer's coming this morning to connect a recording device to the phone. So far Neil's been given a fairly acceptable explanation for his sister's absence, which was very astute of you, but if he's kept home from school for no obvious reason he'll be drawn into the fear we're all feeling. Aside from doing what's best for Neil, we don't need the additional problem of having him around the house today.'

So the boy was taken to school by Didi, as usual. The Danish girl was calm but untalkative, plainly upset by the kidnap of a child she was fond of. Fiona was also calm and quiet when she came downstairs, making clear her continued dependence on Randal to bring the crisis to an end by saying nothing to her father.

For the second time that year Randal plundered his 'frozen food' money. His bank manager did not ask outright why such a large sum in cash was needed so immediately, and Randal blocked his loaded comments. Gerald was a close friend of his banker and was frequently involved in high-flying deals, so little curiosity was shown at his request. Both men arranged to collect the money after the close of business that day. The police inspector had said the kidnapper might be watching their actions and would be encouraged if he saw each of them drive off and return with heavy briefcases. Halfway through the morning a police engineer arrived in a truck bearing the logo of a well known animal feed supplier to doctor the telephone. Apart from that, the hours dragged for a group of people each locked in introspection.

Randal spent much of the morning around the paddock area, gazing unseeingly at the horses. The confusion of being in this house of unhappy memories and the hostility of its owners mingled with the unreality of being suddenly thrust back into roles he had surrendered so precipitately. He had taken charge, was making all the decisions. The police treated him as the husband and father he had not been for many long months; he was himself acting as such. Yet a sense of living a disturbing, frightening dream ruled him. When this present appalling situation had ended, what then?

At three thirty, as Didi was leaving to pick up Neil, the telephone rang. Gerald was in his office struggling to deal with an owner who had called unexpectedly to check on his two mares, so Randal took up the receiver, saying automatically, 'Squadron Leader Price.'

'Inspector Miles here, sir,' said the calm voice. 'A short while ago one of our sub-stations got a call from a woman who simply said they would find the Price child at the lost children's centre in Eastermain Mall. We rang the centre and the manager confirmed that a girl giving her name as Lydia Price was brought in by a middle-aged woman who claimed she had found her wandering along the upper level having no idea where her mother was. Several announcements over the loudspeakers asking for her parents to collect her have

210

met with no response. Now, sir, this may very well be a false alarm, but a car is on its way to pick up you and Mrs Price. Please warn your wife to prepare for possible disappointment, yet the description given by the childcare woman closely matches that of your daughter. This is a very curious development in this case, but I sincerely hope you will shortly have Lydia safely back with you.'

Randal replaced the receiver, his heart thudding. It made no sense. If a woman had taken her yesterday, who was the man demanding a three million ransom? What was behind it all? He hardly dared to hope, and yet unless someone had found a lookalike child and coached her to give a false name the little girl at the mall must be Lydia.

Crossing swiftly to the conservatory where Fiona was sitting listlessly, he drew her to her feet. 'The police are sending a car to take us to Eastermain Mall to identify a child who could be Lydia.' Seeing the sudden terror in her eyes, he said, 'No, she's alive and unharmed. Miles warns that it could be a false alarm, but the description matches. It's crazy . . . but I think it must be for real, Fee.'

Finally giving full rein to her fear and misery Fiona began to sob, clinging to him as if to a lifeline.

It was painfully familiar. Two children having a bath, the boy so like his father, the girl a miniature of her mother, and everyone getting very wet. Neil was bubbling with exuberance, clearly delighting in Randal's presence and seeing Lydia's return as nothing unusual. The little girl had now emerged from the dream-like state she had been in when they collected her, and she seemed none the worse for the ordeal she had suffered.

A policewoman trained to deal with child kidnap cases had gently questioned Lydia, with little success. All she revealed was that she had ridden a horse and had had porridge in a teddy bear bowl. The family doctor had examined her. She had been mildly sedated, but appeared to be fine otherwise. The police psychologist was due to call in the morning for further questioning of the child in the presence of the doctor, but right now Lydia Price was behaving as if nothing abnormal had happened. She happily accepted Randal as a person called Daddy who could be coaxed into doing whatever she wanted, like all other men she encountered.

For an hour or so Randal wholeheartedly reverted to the family man he used to be. Laughing, willingly getting soaked to the skin, he indulged in the delight of bathroom battle using sponge animals, water pistols and dolls' teaset cups as weapons. Then he wrapped Neil in a huge warm towel and wrestled with his son in the process of getting him dry. Fiona, also very wet, treated Lydia more gently and her laughter contained remnants of the strain she had been under for the past twenty-four hours.

Lydia was allowed to stay up later than usual, so both children were put to bed at the same time, and it was not surprising that they demanded a story from Randal rather than their mother.

'I'm no good at making up tales like Mummy is,' he confessed. 'But I'll read to you, if that'll do.'

'It was always the same one about the little red bus that was too rusty to be driven to market,' said Neil, bruising Randal with evidence that he remembered it so clearly.

'Aren't you too old for that one?'

'No. You always did funny voices. Do them again.'

When the children had finally settled, the make-believe atmosphere drastically vanished and Randal confronted his wife across the playroom, knowing facts must be faced before he returned to Hampton. 'We have to talk,' he said quietly.

She walked to the door. 'Right now I need to shower, put on a robe, then get very pleasantly drunk.'

'We have to talk before I go back,' he insisted, following her.

'But you're not leaving tonight. Change into dry clothes then come and get drunk, too. No beer, of course, but plenty of everything else,' she said airily, entering her bedroom.

Randal showered and changed in a guest room. He had no desire to get drunk. He was almost dropping with weariness, and there was an outside chance that the eight o'clock call could come and he would have to take a bag containing blocks of paper to the designated drop zone where the police would arrest whoever came to collect it. He could not begin to fathom the truth of it all. His brain was woolly with stress, lack of sleep and emotional confusion.

Inspector Miles was suggesting that the ransom had been demanded by a man who knew Lydia had vanished and was simply cashing in on the fact. If so, he might be one of the lads, which Gerald found unpalatable. There were flaws in that theory, but as yet nothing to support the belief that he was in any way linked with the woman who had surrendered Lydia. She had been caught on the mall's security cameras entering with the child, so a police team was questioning shoppers and sales staff in the hope of gaining identification.

Mary Holland produced a chicken curry which she persuaded the detective constable waiting by the telephone to share with them. Now Lydia was safely home Mary was again the society hostess, who nevertheless managed to avoid speaking to her son-in-law. Gerald was the same. It suited Randal. He ate while kaleidoscopic thoughts still turned around in his brain, unable to get to grips with any of them.

Eight o'clock came and went with no ransom call. At eight thirty the constable was called on his mobile and given information that a sales assistant had recognised the woman as a divorcee living in a farm cottage near her home. The lead was being followed up. The interesting aspect was that the informant claimed a man had recently taken up residence in the cottage, so he might possibly be connected with Lydia's abduction. Deeming it advisable that the constable should remain at Marylands until the pair at the farm cottage had been interviewed, Inspector Miles then spoke to Gerald Holland to check that all was well. The young policeman tactfully withdrew to read in the conservatory from where he would hear the telephone, should the ransom call still come through.

The minute the conservatory door closed the Holland attack began. 'You'll be off first thing in the morning, then we can get back to our normal peaceful routine,' Gerald said. 'Fiona should never have contacted you. You weren't needed, and what happens in this family is no concern of yours.'

Randal refused to fuel the man's implacable hostility. It would get them nowhere, and he needed to marshal his wits for the discussion he was determined to have with his wife before he slept. Amazingly, Fiona challenged her father's comments with some heat.

'*I* needed him here. You're a whizz on anything to do with horses, Daddy, but you can't cope with a crisis to do with the children. If I hadn't got him here we'd be sitting around with three million in cash, waiting for some weirdo to tell us where to take it. Meanwhile, the police would be trying to trace the mother of a lost child in the mall. How many Prices are there in the area? And I'm not listed in the directory; you are. It's only because Randal insisted on bringing in the police that Lydia's back with us now.' She got to her feet, the heavy satin robe falling to her ankles in deep folds. 'Let's have some champagne and count our blessings instead of this ridiculous aggressive post-mortem.'

Her outburst prompted emotional blackmail from her doting parents. Mary began a hearts-and-flowers speech about how they had stood by their daughter through the many crises in her heedless marriage, but if she now felt no further need of their support perhaps she would prefer to take the children to live elsewhere. Gerald then begged his 'little girl' to remember all they had done when her husband turned his back on her and the children, suggesting that she was overwrought and would see more clearly who she really needed once things reverted to normal.

At that point Randal left and went up to Fiona's room to stretch out on the bed and wait for her. He lay marvelling at the single-mindedness of these people. They had last seen him lying in a hospital bed with his head in a clamp, both arms in plaster and paralysed from the chest down. Gerald had referred to that time as 'when your husband turned his back on you and the children'. As far as they were concerned it had been the callous, selfish act of a man relinquishing responsibility. Had they no idea whatever why he had done it, and what he had gone through to regain a full life? Fiona herself had last seen him lying helpless, immobile and in terrible pain, yet she had behaved as if it had never happened from the moment he last night stepped from a car that was a replica of the one in which he had crashed. He had been the person she needed right then. All else was forgotten. That was the kind of woman she was.

When Fiona appeared ten minutes later it was with a bottle of champagne and two glasses. She smiled and walked across to sit on the bed. 'See how impossible they can be?'

He sat up and swung his legs to the floor. 'Why haven't you moved out?'

'Where to?' She offered him a glass of champagne. 'Let's celebrate.'

He shook his head, then watched her drink, watched her throat move as she swallowed, studied the contours of her face, the long lashes over her large, sexy eyes, her blonde hair falling softly to her shoulders. The satin robe clung to her shapely shoulders, and to her breasts whose nipples were prominent, but the rose-coloured satin fell away to reveal one of her long, beautiful legs crossed over the other. She was undeniably a breathtakingly lovely woman; wealthy, classy and totally motivated by her own desires. She did not so much love others as love making them love her. The Hollands had put their enchanting only child on a throne and that was where she meant to stay. A large number of people were willing to keep her there. That fool Randal Price had been one of them.

'Wouldn't Seth Nicholls offer you a home?' he asked dryly.

Her mouth curved into the wide, knowing smile he remembered so well. 'So you saw the press pictures of the *Zenda* party! Jealous?'

'Not in the least. I'd like to know if he's going to be dealing with my children before long.'

'*Seth?* He can't stand kids. Too messy and noisy, he claims. He's also too fond of himself for my liking. Two of his mares are here about to foal, and Seth fancies himself as a stud. Hence the invitation to see *Zenda* but I spent the night alone in our Chelsea apartment. He's not my type.' She ran the tip of her tongue around the rim of her glass, directing the full magnetism of her eyes at him. 'You should know what I go for.'

'Yeah, a worshipping, stay-at-home guy with no ambition,' he replied cuttingly. 'I hope you find him one day. Look, we need to get a few things straight before I leave.'

She pouted. 'You're not still determined to have a heavy discussion! I'm not in the mood for it after all I've been through these last two days. I need to relax and lose myself in enjoyable things like champagne, low lights and sweet talk.'

How typical that she should speak as if only she had

been stressed over the drama. She had been lazily enjoying a massage while Lydia was being abducted, but he had been flying precise manoeuvres for film makers. With that in mind he tried to get back to the vital subject of the children's future.

'Fee, are you planning to remarry after the divorce?'

'God, no! Once was enough. Are you?'

'No.'

It came out sharper than he expected, and Fiona read into his bitter tone what she wanted. 'I see. Well . . . in that case . . .'

Her lips were full and yielding, tasting of champagne to further heighten his sense of recollection. She wore the same perfume he used to bring her from his trips to Europe. While her mouth ate hungrily at his, her hands were unbuttoning his shirt. When they began to caress his skin he instinctively reached for her. The robe fell from the upper part of her body as she pushed him down on the bed.

'Let's celebrate,' she murmured, sexual excitement flaring in her eyes as she fumbled with the zip of his trousers.

A sudden surge of violent desire revived in him the old urge to dominate. Struggling free of his clothes he rolled on top of her, driven by overwhelming lust.

'I'll give you something to celebrate, you sexy bitch,' he panted triumphantly. 'It'll last all sodding night long.'

Later, as Fiona lay asleep across his chest, Randal finally succumbed to exhaustion. Lying with his eyes closed, revelling in the sensation of soft breasts against his skin and the satiny heaviness of a leg over his that had not so long ago been paralysed, he offered up a prayer of deep gratitude. Then, just before he slipped into sleep, his mouth curved in a faint smile. He would put the fear of God into that medical redhead the next time she asked about his need for full sexual satisfaction.

*　　*　　*

At RAF Hampton two items of current news had everyone talking. Despite attempts to keep them quiet, details had been leaked to the Press of Lydia Price's abduction from the dance studio of a woman giving ballet lessons to the daughters of the wealthy racing set. Alongside that meaty story ran reports of the inquiry into the exercise on Exmoor that had resulted in the death of one of the organisers and the serious poisoning of forty schoolboys and their teacher.

The crew that had flown to their rescue were particularly interested in the official findings. It seemed the exercise had been doomed from the moment the ATC officer had collapsed. Telling one of the boys to radio for help, their teacher attempted desperate resuscitation, but the lad was so agitated he failed to locate the correct wavelength. His companions argued over how to operate the radio and, between them, put it out of action.

Ineptitude and blunders followed. Inadequately trained in military operations, the teacher then sent off a small group of more senior boys to get help, almost immediately suffering severe stomach cramps and vomiting. The younger boys thought he was also about to die and panicked. Unable to agree on the right thing to do, some refused to leave their teacher, the rest divided into groups of three or four to follow their own plans to effect rescue.

One by one the boys succumbed to food poisoning. Then, freezing fog descended over the moor. The cause of their illness was traced to the survival rations. All packs in the same batch had been called in, and the premises of the company producing them were being inspected by health and hygiene officers. Some parents had withdrawn their sons from the school's air cadet corps and all were demanding action against the teacher who, in their opinion, should have been trained to cope with the emergency.

The hero of the hour had been nominated for a young person's award for courage. His grandfather, Group Captain

Harry Soames DFC, said it was only what he expected of a member of a family with a proud record of service with the RAF.

On reading this, Maggie accosted Dirk as they relaxed in the Crew Room. 'That lad told us it was a "family thing" but you sounded off about kids not knowing who their fathers are so shouldn't try living up to them. According to the grandad it was an inbred quality that led Duncan to act as he did.'

'Yeah, yeah,' grunted Dirk from behind his newspaper.

Maggie wondered yet again what had provoked Dirk's savage reaction to the boy's words that day. The only reason she could come up with was that someone had had his baby then married another man. Or maybe the woman causing him so much grief now was bringing up her child alone and refusing to acknowledge Dirk as its father. Maggie's attempts to get to the truth prompted from him a brusque command to shut up.

The kidnap of Randal's daughter was a bizarre affair. A stable lad dismissed by Gerald Holland for carelessness resulting in slight injury to a mare in foal, had been riding over the downs when he spotted Lydia wandering alone, apparently lost. His evidence was that he had taken the child up with the intention of contacting his former employer, and it was only when he neared the cottage of his girlfriend that he saw a way of hitting back at a man he felt had treated him too harshly, and getting rich at the same time. He had not intended to hurt the little girl.

Initially excited by the plan, the young woman's fear that it was too risky led her the next day to return the child by a means she believed would not incriminate anyone. When two detectives called on her with video evidence of her complicity they found her shaken and bruised from the violence of her lover on learning what she had done. He was now in custody; she had been arraigned as an accessory to the crime of abduction with menaces.

Randal had remained with his family for three days, and no one in B Flight doubted that his renewed exuberance was due to a reconciliation with the fabulous Fiona. The men might mutter that he was a glutton for punishment, but they all envied his access to a woman who would make any man yearn for her kind of punishment. On Maggie it had a more devastating effect.

The notion of leaving 646 Squadron seemed an attractive career move once more. Next month Perry Newman would be taking command. That brief meeting at Shawbury told her she would fare no better with him than she had with Judge Jeffries. All in all, men were proving more difficult than usual to work with. Dirk was moody and bad-tempered, Chris had read too much into that night at his grandmother's flat, Jeff was behaving suspiciously like a man who has finally met his female Waterloo and Dave, another of B Flight's stalwarts, had applied for pilot training and would go off on a course before long. There was nothing to encourage her to stay. She was due some leave which would give her a week away from Hampton in which to get to grips with what she really wanted from life, but first the Flight had a commitment in Kosovo to fulfil.

Nine

M aggie was quiet during the flight to the Balkans, thinking of the time two years ago when she had taken part in the rescue of a small British peacekeeping force. It had been her first experience of real war after so many mock battles, and only when they were back at Base had the shock hit her. She had seen men being being shot, blown apart by shells, burning in armoured vehicles. At the time of rescue she had been intent on landing, loading the endangered troops, then taking off with the urgency of knowing her aircraft was in the line of fire.

That memory would stay with her for years to come: white ice-gripped valley, dark figures stumbling through the deep snow, orange flames, black belching smoke. She could still remember the strain on the faces of the British troops who had been ordered to hold their position in a devastated village offering them scant protection against the severe winter weather, or against the hostile irregulars who massively outnumbered them. Even now Maggie could recall the young captain whose successive reports on the explosive nature of the situation had been met with airy assurances that a diplomatic solution was practically on the table. She had often wondered what he had said to his superiors after the eleventh-hour rescue. He was mighty angry.

The tragedy that had had its beginnings at that time was nowhere near over – the diplomatic solution never happened. Ethnic hatred was rampant; thousands were homeless and living among ruins with no fresh water on hand dreading the inexorable onset of another winter. Covert executions were being carried out almost beneath the noses of the multinational occupying army forbidden to support either of the antagonists.

For once, the men and women who operated in the air above this devastated country felt sympathy for the ground troops who were witnessing first hand the horror of vilification and murder. Theirs was an unenviable duty. It shredded the nerves of even the most hardened men on peacekeeping patrols.

Kosovo in summer must once have been quietly beautiful: gentle hills, wide green valleys, pretty villages, orderly towns. There were still some areas untouched by the violence, but the British troops operated amid the rubble and deprivation. The crews of support helicopters caught glimpses of the gentler aspects as they ferried supplies to many points around a large area, but the ground forces only saw them as they thankfully flew home.

The four crews of B Flight were housed in a tented area mainly occupied by the logistics element of the Army. The Chinooks operated from a field that had been churned up during the spring thaw to destroy any but the hardiest growth. The stifling summer heat had then dried the surface so that crossing it disturbed spirals of dust, and the downwash from rotors created veritable duststorms. Although the aircraft were parked far enough from the tents to obviate total collapse of the camp when their engines sprang into life, dust covered everything anew each time they took off or came in to land. The military contingent moaned non-stop. Off-duty aircrew also moaned, but not in the presence of soldiers. There was enough friction between the two services without adding to it.

Maggie spent a lot of her off-duty time alone in any shady place she could find, grappling with the problem of what she would do when they returned to Hampton. It was on one of those occasions in her second week in Kosovo that she was approached by a beefy Infantry sergeant wearing an expression she knew well.

'Had enough of those lazy, arrogant sods you cohabit with?' he asked smoothly.

'No, I'm after some solitude so I can think.'

He dropped to the ground beside her, grinning. 'Now I wonder what a sexy girl like you thinks about on a hot sultry day. Me, I prefer doing it to thinking about it.'

In a level tone Maggie said, 'I'm considering applying for a transfer; moving on. As you prefer doing it to thinking about it, move on, chum!'

He laughed. 'So you like to play games first, do you?'

Showing her anger she said, 'You wouldn't like the games I play. I've thrown bigger boys than you and bruised more than their egos.'

Still amused he leapt to his feet and adopted a tackling stance. 'Come on, then. Lock on! I'll enjoy grappling with you.'

'For God's sake grow up,' she snapped. 'Those "lazy, arrogant sods I cohabit with" are intelligent enough to know when they're not wanted. Go and find another dimwit like yourself to grapple with . . . *sergeant.*'

His mouth tightened further when his smouldering glance was caught by something beyond her. 'I guess the only thing he also pulls is rank . . . *ma'am!*'

Maggie turned and sighed with exasperation at the sight of Randal sauntering towards her. Was there no solitude to be had?

'Everything okay?' he asked, watching the other man walk off.

She glared. 'I don't need a guard dog.'

'I don't recall going woof, woof.'

'I came here to get away from everyone.'

'I know that.'

'So why follow?' His silence goaded her further. 'If you must know, I'm sick of the overwhelming odds. Sick of all the stupid macho posing.' The heat with which she said this surprised her. 'You're all such shallow, arrogant bastards, and to do the job I love I have to be one of the boys. That means I have to listen to all the bloody knob jokes by day and your drunken snores at night. Then, when I seize the chance of a little solitude, you come and invade it.'

After a long moment he asked, 'Anything more to say?'

'Just piss off.'

'The number of times I said that to you and you took no notice!' He sat on the ground near her and gazed at the distant hills. 'The atmosphere here is the same as in Bosnia, isn't it: menacing. No, more than that: lingering evil. A few miles away, not visible from here, there are burnt out villages, mass graves and orphaned children traumatised by what they witnessed only a few months ago. Christ, what a world we live in!' The silence lengthened until he asked quietly, 'What's your real problem, Maggie?'

She sighed. 'In the face of what you've just said, nothing.'

He turned to her. 'I was only trying to get things in perspective.' He gave a faint smile. 'I'm a right one to give advice. I never listened to yours, did I?'

This second reminder of the closeness they had once enjoyed renewed her anger. 'You're two different people, aren't you? You switch from one to the other as it suits you, and to hell with anyone else. When the outlook was too black to face you were glad of my involvement; my support and encouragement. As you just said, the number of times you told me to piss off and I took no notice. I kept going back for more, didn't I?'

'Maggie—'

'But as soon as you were back on your feet, and the out-look was sunny again, *you* bloody pissed off. No forwarding address, no "thanks but goodbye", no sign that there'd ever been anyone named Maggie in your life.'

He threw her the optical challenge she knew so well. 'We settled that point at the Bird one evening several months ago.'

'Wrong! We didn't settle anything. You simply switched persona to being the Boss again. And now you're right back where you started.'

'But I learned a hell of a lot along the way.'

'Ha!' she cried dismissively. 'Then forgot it all two weeks ago.'

He frowned. 'Is that what you think?'

'Didn't you?'

'No.'

She got to her feet. 'You'd better tell the rest of the team, because they all seem pretty sure of what's behind your return to the crazy guy you used to be. Those knob jokes I mentioned; some of them have your name attached.'

He stood to face her and she was momentarily taken aback by the anger in his eyes. 'My name's been attached to a number of things over the years, but what happened to Lydia compelled me to remove at least one of them. I saw I'd been wrong to believe my children would be better off without me. I made that decision when, as you just mentioned, the outlook was too black to face. Then the lapse of time away from them fooled me into maintaining that belief. I was on the point of severing the bond altogether when that . . . that *bastard* played his filthy trick with a helpless little girl as his bargaining pawn. Maggie, I wanted to kill him, choke the life out of him with my bare hands.' He appeared to be seeing something beyond her imagination. 'The love I have for my kids resurfaced in a rush. I know now I need to see them, watch them grow, guide them. And they need me, Maggie. Whatever else, they're part of me. I'm their father.'

'And she's their mother,' Maggie countered hollowly.

'It's a *package* you've taken on again. I said you're two different people, and I don't understand this one.'

He moved closer. 'Does it matter that much to you?'

This was getting dangerous so she hit out. 'That you're making a fool of yourself all over again; that she only has to make big, sexy eyes at you and you turn into a besotted idiot? You wanted to know my real problem. I've had enough of B Flight, of the Squadron, everything at Hampton. When we get back I'm going to apply for a transfer, and this time I'm willing to go anywhere so long as it's well away from *you*.'

She walked away before tears blurred her vision and her image as one of the boys dissolved in front of him.

On the following morning Maggie recklessly agreed to Chris's suggestion that they take a drive to the river for a swim before their flight at fifteen hundred. The encounter with Randal had accentuated Maggie's restlessness, her yearning for something more in her life. Mark had fast-jetted into it then left her bereft. Peter McGrath had offered marriage, but she did not love him enough. The man who had slowly and unexpectedly become all-important to her had now surrendered his soul to his heartless wife a second time. It hurt unbearably.

Her twenty-eighth birthday was looming. She lived and worked surrounded by men, yet they all regarded her as one of the boys. Except Chris. He had broken her sexual hiatus and was keen to continue the relationship. He had been good in bed and, right now, she needed that kind of release. Just until she got her transfer and found a new direction. She did not believe Chris was looking for a heavy commitment, just a pleasant episode to drive away the final bitterness left by his failed marriage. So Maggie went to the river with him.

Once they left the road, the way through the woods became little more than a dusty track barely wide enough for the four-wheel drive. As they bumped and jolted, dodging overhanging branches, Maggie questioned Chris's navigation.

'This isn't the route Jeff took last week.'

Chris grinned as he swung the wheel around and back, steering between trees at a crazy speed. 'I've found a place that's more secluded. Won't be spied on.' He shot a glance at her. 'It's okay, I told Rip where we'd be. He understood.'

Good, she thought. Let him put two and two together and make whatever sum he likes.

It was an ideal place for what Chris had in mind. A low grassy bank lined a horseshoe bend in the river's course forming a haven that could be overlooked only from the other bank where the dense trees were practically impenetrable.

'Wasn't I right?' Chris demanded, throwing down two blankets and his holdall.

Maggie silently studied the sylvan scene: the way the sunshine shimmered on the river, how it flickered through the branches, how its warmth on her skin failed to melt her inner chill. All at once, the contrast between this tranquil beauty and the vicious destruction of life and civilisation that she had flown over sharpened her sense of personal isolation to a painful degree. She swung round to hug Chris tightly, seeking comfort.

The big brother role was not welcome when he had other plans for the morning, so Chris eased her from him, asking warily, 'What's up?'

Maggie shivered. 'Sorry, something spooked me. It's too quiet, too cut off from that other reality.'

'That was the idea. To get away from it for a while.'

'I know. Don't worry. I sometimes get curious sensations. I used to think it was due to being a twin – most of them concerned Phil – but I occasionally get a freaky feeling about other things, too. It's the reverse of déjà vu. An unsettling sense of looming disaster. Or I get an undeniable impulse to go to a particular place without delay.' She gave a faint smile. 'Our boss calls them magic messages.'

Chris began pulling off his shirt and shorts. 'Nothing magic about it. It's your monthly cycle. Chloe used to get moody and irrational halfway through it. All women are the same,' he said with masculine dismissiveness, then took a great leap into the river.

Maggie stripped to her black swimsuit, trying to shake off her uneasiness. Monthly cycle be damned! She recognised a magic message when she experienced one. Oh, for God's sake, she must forget about the man who gave them that ridiculous name!

They swam and splashed in the river, enjoying the activity that seemed comfortingly normal against their work in this tragic country. Chris soon indulged in the usual macho tricks that delight men when they are in the water with the weaker sex. One of the boys or not, Maggie could not match his strength and was roughly handled in what she knew was a brand of sexual foreplay. She had her revenge all planned, however.

They eventually scrambled on to the bank, water running from their hair and limbs, to grab towels and vigorously dry off. Maggie's spirits had risen, and she delighted in the predictability with which Chris offered to dry her back and came over with his towel suggesting that she should slip her swimsuit from her shoulders. As soon as he was near enough Maggie stepped forward, seized him in an expert karate grip, and had him on his back before he knew what had happened.

'Walked right into that, didn't you,' she taunted as he rose, bent on retaliation. 'If I were you I'd surrender.'

'You're not me, and I *never* surrender,' he warned grittily.

Maggie countered his second advance easily, flinging him

to the ground the way she had bigger men than he. Then she forgot that this was not a real karate contest, with its strict code of behaviour. She was taken completely unawares when Chris hooked one of his feet around her legs as he lay on the grass. She fell alongside him and he immediately pinned her down, breathing hard. '*Gotcha!*'

Chris was as good on a river bank as he had been in his grandmother's guest room, and she discovered that sex in the open air had an abandoned quality lacking in a comfortable bed. She had to concentrate hard to prevent having fantasies of being possessed by someone else, however.

Later, pleasantly fatigued by the water sports and love-making, Maggie pulled on shorts and a T-shirt before flinging clothes across to her lethargic companion.

'Stop behaving like a Balkan peasant, Flight Lieutenant Foley.'

'Okay, come back here and I'll do it like a commissioned navigator,' he invited lazily.

'You imagine? You're right out of fuel, sonny, and I'm more interested in those sandwiches we brought. If you want—' She broke off as the mobile phone in Chris's holdall rang. Her heartbeat accelerated. All was *not* well. She had sensed it!

Chris listened intently for some moments before saying, 'Okay, on way.' He glanced across at Maggie. 'Major alert. Boss wants us back as of *now*.'

She began gathering up blankets as Chris struggled into his clothes. 'Did he give any clues?'

'Urgent bid for two aircraft. Jeff and his crew are sleeping after their night flight, and Steve took one out an hour before the signal arrived. We've got to take this one, and I guess it's a hostile situation.'

Maggie threw blankets and their holdalls in the vehicle, then got behind the wheel. 'Don't tell me the war's started up again.'

'Who told you it had stopped?' Chris flopped heavily on the passenger seat, scowling. 'The perfect anticlimax to a hearty—'

Engine roar drowned his words. Maggie drove fast, thinking more of what lay ahead than of the last two hours. The situation in Kosovo was unstable at the best of times, but an urgent bid for two Chinooks suggested large-scale hostility. She had flown into danger before in the Balkans. Was she about to do so again?

Changing with speed into flying gear, the pair snatched up their emergency bags and hurried to the large tent used as a briefing room. The others were already gathered there.

Randal cast them a sour look. 'Nice of you to join us.'

The comment annoyed Maggie. It was more typical of Judge Jeffries. They had been off-duty and Chris had logged their whereabouts. But her resentment was only momentary, as was Randal's sarcasm. He went straight to the core of the emergency, circling with yellow highlighter a village on the chart spread before him on the table.

'You've flown over this area a number of times; the ground troops have it marked as a possible trouble spot. It's the birthplace of a man who became an Albanian freedom fighter during the height of the struggle. He was eventually captured by Serbs and crucified while his family was forced to watch.'

There were mutters from them all, but Randal remained focussed on his briefing. 'It's now vengeance time. Several thousand Albanians are presently marching to this village which is now exclusively Serb. Our troops on the spot will never hold back a mob of that size hell-bent on bloodshed. There's little more than a handful of them.'

'So we'll be flying in reinforcements,' said Maggie.

'Got it in one. They aim to form a circle around the place.'

'With the usual order not to fire their guns,' put in Chris in disgust.

'Yeah, get yourself spat on, reviled and generally humiliated, but don't show 'em any aggression,' added Dirk with equal disgust. 'You're not trained fighting men, you're simply nursery nannies there to make squabbling children kiss and make up.'

'Have you finished?' asked Randal in quelling tones. 'I'll fly with Chris, Brad and Jimmy to Sector KY to pick up Paras. Dirk will captain the rest of you to Sector BL where some of Dave's countrymen'll be waiting for you. We'll both offload in this field.' He jabbed the chart with his finger, then looked at them all in turn. 'Questions? Right, you're fully familiar with routes and hazards over these areas. Met info is on the board, as usual. The aircraft are fuelled up ready to go.'

Maggie caught his eye as he gathered together his equipment. She was taken aback at being teamed with Dirk on something requiring complete accord in the cockpit. Randal walked past her murmuring, 'The lesser of two evils, I thought.'

It silenced her as she walked to the Chinook, paying little attention to Sandy's quips about Dave being set to exchange 'och ayes' and 'hoots mons' with the Scots they were to transport. Would Randal ensure she did not fly with him again while she remained with B Flight? The thought depressed her. He had never taken her so seriously before.

They were quickly up and away, flying together for the short leg on which their routes matched. Maggie kept in radio touch with Chris in the other aircraft, their romping on the river bank forgotten in the professional routine. Soon, Dirk veered away and Maggie fed him navigational data over an area they knew reasonably well. During a short silence he suddenly said, 'If protesters were on their way to a village at home there'd be bricks thrown, a few car windows smashed, maybe a pile of manure dumped strategically, but here we're talking slit throats, crucifixion and burning alive. Even if we fly in enough bods to stop it today, they'll be back next week, next month. What a godforsaken country!'

The outburst induced silence until Maggie said quietly, 'There's the camp at ten o'clock.' Then she added more urgently, 'Hey, did the Boss know how many we've been tasked to move?'

Dirk began turning towards the cluster of tents. 'He didn't say. That means he wasn't told.'

'There must be a hundred or more.' She studied the large group of men in khaki with blue helmets waiting by an obvious landing area. 'How far from the village is the mob? It might arrive before we can get this lot on the spot.'

'As Rip didn't say, he couldn't have been told that, either. Get on to Chris. See if they know any more. And tell him how many we have here.'

Maggie made contact with the other aircraft and learned that they were already loading – even overloading – in order to get the maximum number to the village as soon as possible.

'The commander here has info regarding the marchers,' Chris told her. 'They're less than four miles from the village as of now. The troops on the spot have set up a road block and spread out thinly on either side of it. They have two Warriors beside the barricade, but these people know very well the guns will never be fired at them so they're of no more use than as protection for the crews inside. The situation's critical, they say.'

Dirk was preparing to land as Chris added, 'The Boss says pack 'em in and fast! Soon as you offload, get the rest. This could get dangerously out of hand.'

'Oh boy, just what's needed on a beautiful summer's day,' muttered Dirk, being talked down by Dave and Sandy.

The laden soldiers clearly shared Dirk's opinion. The

strain of the heavy demands being made on them showed on their faces as they silently filed aboard for the twenty-minute flight. Urged to speed it up by the two crewmen, they were soon filling every inch of cabin space. Dave had not even closed the ramp when Dirk lifted the aircraft off the ground, staying low and coaxing as much speed as possible from the Chinook.

'Dave, just how many have we got on board?' he demanded.

'D'you really want to know?' came the reply.

'*That* many?'

'The Boss told us to pack 'em in,' Maggie reminded him.

'Yeah, but not an entire battalion! Jeez, what a way to earn a living.'

They traversed a valley, their shadow flitting across fields bare of crops or grazing animals and further darkening the blackened ruins of isolated hamlets. There was silence in the packed cabin. Maggie cast a look over her shoulder and met a resigned expression from Sandy hemmed in by infantrymen in camouflage battledress. There was a tense atmosphere throughout the aircraft that transferred itself to her. Faced with a mob bent on revenge one of two things would surely happen. Either the peacekeepers would be trampled underfoot, or they would be forced into defensive action and trigger the kind of incident NATO's opponents would condemn.

After climbing to clear a range of low hills Dirk lost height again, racing over more barren fields amd broken villages where people could now be seen moving among the ruins from which tarpaulins had been stretched by NATO troops to provide some protection for returning refugees. Along dust tracks the occasional rusty tractor crawled and bumped, bringing drums of water and meagre supplies of food to those camping in what remained of their homes. Five minutes later, the aspect changed considerably. They overflew small patches of cultivation, vegetable plots, a few grazing goats, a white church, houses undamaged by shells or bombs.

Maggie studied the chart on her knees, then glanced from the cockpit windows. 'Seven minutes should get us there. That church well ahead at two o'clock marks another settlement similar to the one we've just passed. The village we want is three miles further on. Oh, there are the others coming in already,' she exclaimed, spotting Randal's aircraft approaching. They've beaten us by thirty seconds.'

'Because they're not carrying half the British Army, like we are,' Dirk grunted. Then he instructed his crewmen. 'Soon as we hit the ground get 'em off faster than they came on. I want to be first back here with the second contingent.'

The village hove into sight; a large community where most buildings were virtually intact. A Serb stronghold! If there had been guns or tanks concealed here during the conflict they had been too well hidden from reconnaissance aircraft, so no air strikes had been directed at the area. On nearing it, it was possible to pick out some black patches between the chalet-style houses, where the homes of the few Albanians – former friends and neighbours – had been fired. Maggie resolutely turned her mind from thoughts of what had happened to the families living there.

Dave and Sandy talked Dirk down to the outlying field where blue-hatted troops were already spilling from the other Chinook and streaming across parched grass towards a couple of waiting sergeants. Their own ramp was lowered. Boots thudded on metal, and the cabin emptied as fast as water down a drain while Randal took off and swung away eastwards to where a dark swathe of forest blocked Maggie's view of the horizon.

'Tempest One to Tempest Two,' came Chris's voice

over the airwaves. 'Boss says to make a quick recce at two thousand feet and report present position of hostiles before second pick-up. Orion Leader, the commander on the ground needs up-to-date sitrep.'

Maggie acknowledged then glanced at Dirk. 'Bang goes your hope of getting back first.'

Engaged in taking off, he murmured, 'Might still make it.'

As they overflew the village military activity was very evident. Soldiers were vainly trying to persuade residents to return to their homes, but it was clear the men were armed with all manner of weapons and bent on violent defence of their families and property.

'Poor sods, I don't envy them,' Dirk remarked.

'The Serbs?'

'No, Maggie, our guys. It's humiliating to be carrying high-tech guns only to be pushed aside by peasants with shovels and pitchforks who have no confidence in your powers of protection.'

Sandy spoke from his position by the forward door. 'If I was Orion Leader I'd pull out and let 'em get on with it.'

No one argued with that as they watched the troops they had flown in being deployed on both sides of the road block that had been hastily set up. Flanking the scarlet and white striped barrier were two Warriors beside which a group of officers consulted a map. From the air it was easy to see this limited defence was at a huge disadvantage against superior numbers. Next minute they had sight of the dark mass snaking its way along the only road to the village, and they sensed the full impact of what was happening here.

Maggie called up the other Chinook and reported to Chris. 'Estimated position of hostiles three miles from target. They either halted to discuss tactics, or their earlier position was miscalculated. There's no evidence of arms, but they could be concealed. Shall we go down for a closer check?'

'Negative, Tempest Two. Too risky. Proceed with all speed to Sector BL for rest of reinforcements. Listening out.'

Although the troops were loaded in record time, Dirk could not work miracles. When they arrived at the rendezvous all thoughts of competing were driven away. The situation had worsened. Fearful for their lives, some women had evaded the harrassed peacekeepers to stream on to the field where Randal's Chinook was disgorging soldiers, apparently intent on boarding. The newly arrived Paras were attempting to hold them back, but a cluster of small children ducked beneath their arms and ran on.

'Tempest Two to Tempest One, shall we abort and land elsewhere?' demanded Maggie as Dirk hovered above the mêlée.

'Negative, Tempest Two. Get your guys down here fast,' came Chris's response passed by Randal. 'We need them to hold back these civilians while we take off. You are not, repeat *not*, to allow anyone to board.'

Maggie gazed down at the human panic; the desperation of mothers for the safety of their children, young women terrified of being savaged by men whose own women had been bestially treated by Serbs.

'Dear God, there's no peace here for anyone to keep,' she breathed as Dirk set the Chinook on the grass far from the other aircraft. The soldiers practically ran from the cabin, egged on by sharp words from Dave and Sandy.

Dirk was focussed on the women being dragged away from Randal's aircraft, and swore. 'Where the hell do they think we could take them? *Dave*, get that ramp up,' he added sharply. 'Some of them are heading this way.'

'Can't. Some kids appeared from nowhere and boarded while the army guys were getting off.' Dave sounded tense. 'Fast as I put them off they jump aboard again. Sandy, get down here and lend a hand.'

'Tell me as soon as they're clear and I'll lift off with the ramp down. Tempest One is covered in civilians and temporarily grounded. I want out of here before we're caught the same way. Get it sorted, guys,' Dirk commanded briskly.

From the corner of her eye Maggie became aware that someone was standing beside the forward door, the place Sandy had just vacated. Twisting in her seat she saw a woman had climbed aboard where no one could prevent her. She held a child in her arms and, when she saw that she had Maggie's attention, she indicated the child's flushed face and launched into impassioned speech which no one could hear.

'Dirk, we have an intruder,' Maggie said. 'There's a kid with her. It looks ill and she seems quite desperate.'

'Oh *Christ!*' he exploded. 'We'll have to do something drastic or they'll be all over us. Dave, Sandy, I'm going into the hover just out of reach. Any problem with that?'

'We've got five kids aboard. The rest are just clear enough if you make it quick,' advised Dave.

They made it quick, although Maggie was not happy with the manoeuvre. Another swift glance over her shoulder showed her the woman had moved forward into the cockpit access, her dark eyes full of pleading.

'So what do we do now?' she demanded of Dirk. 'We can't push five kids out to drop eight feet . . . and this woman looks pretty determined.'

'So am I. We're not here to sort out their domestic problems. Get the ramp up, Dave. And you come and sort this woman out, Sandy. I'm going to put them off at the next field where there's no chance of others swarming on. Give me clearance.'

Maggie reluctantly agreed it was probably the only way to avoid what had happened to Tempest One, but she was concerned about the woman and asked Sandy to try to find out what was wrong with the child. It was a tall order, because he was talking Dirk across to the adjoining field several hundred yards away. Only when the Chinook was back on the ground could anything be done.

Dave came up with Sandy and they put the children out through the forward door with no trouble. The youngsters' bravado had swiftly evaporated. They could not wait to get out and run back to their mothers. Several were crying as they were carefully lowered to the ground.

'Now get that woman off,' Dirk directed.

'Hold on a bit,' said Sandy. 'She's gone on her knees as if she was praying. It's not going to be easy.'

'There's two of you, for God's sake,' he cried.

Maggie twisted to see that the Serb woman was, indeed, in an attitude of prayer, and she swung back to challenge Dirk. 'That child is obviously very ill. I think she needs to get him to a hospital.'

'That's not our concern,' he ruled. 'You heard Rip say we're not to take anyone aboard.'

'We didn't. She came of her own accord, and this is a humanitarian emergency.'

'Which the village doctor can deal with.'

'What if he can't? That's why she's doing this.'

'I'm not hanging around here much longer,' Dirk snapped. 'We were tasked to fly in reinforcements, that's all, and we've completed the assignment.'

Dave spoke into the intercom. 'I'd say this wee boy's critically ill, Maggie. The mother speaks English. I can only catch a little of what she says, but I guess she needs to get him to a hospital. I agree. He has a fever. If he doesn't get treatment soon, he'll go into a coma, in my opinion.'

Maggie continued her attack on Dirk. 'What is it with you and kids? This can't be considered as taking sides in an ethnic conflict. With the situation here so grim, can we responsibly dump him and his mother in a field and leave them to it? There's no rule that says we can't give a sick child the chance to go on living, whoever he is.'

'So he can crucify his former neighbours and friends as soon as he's old enough?'

'So what are we doing?' asked Sandy impatiently.

'Madam here's liable to lay a curse on me if we leave them,' Dirk grunted. 'Do what you can for them, Dave. Let's get going.'

As they turned, gaining height, they saw that the second aircraft was still besieged by women and children. The ground troops were now converging at the trot on the road block, abandoning their attempts to drive the Serbs back to their village.

'Their task is to keep the adversaries apart. We have to sort out our own problems,' Dirk observed. 'Ask if we can do anything to help, Maggie. Maybe circle over them and blast everyone clear with our downwash.'

Randal declined this drastic action, and Chris said, 'We've agreed with Orion Leader that the best policy is for us to fly this lot to the wood on that hill backing the village. They'll be safe enough there until the emergency is over. It'll get them out of our hair and give the guys on the ground less bodies to protect. Boss says to return to Base and save some beer for us. Listening out.'

Starting on the homeward run, Dirk said, 'I notice you didn't mention our passengers.'

Maggie frowned at the scene below. 'He's going to shift a cabinful, so he can't censure us over one woman and her child.'

When they landed Dave headed for the hospital tent to fetch a stretcher for the boy, who now looked to be in a coma. Maggie and Dirk left the cockpit to attempt to allay the woman's fears, and they found she spoke quite good English.

Catching at Maggie's hands, she said, 'Thank you, thank you. The Major said no one was to leave. I did not know what to do. Our doctor has gone to a conference. Pavel is so sick, I thought he would die. I saw you and had to take this chance. Not for me, you understand, but for him.' She looked suddenly more stricken. 'If it is not too late.'

Maggie smiled and squeezed the woman's hands encouragingly. 'We'll do all we can for the boy. Our doctor is very good; he has boys of his own.'

The woman turned her large, expressive eyes on Dirk. 'Thank you, Captain. You are a very good man. I shall pray for you and your lady.'

A small soft-topped truck with Red Cross markings drove up. The unconscious child looked so small on the stretcher brought by two orderlies, who slid it expertly in the back of the vehicle. Dave said he would accompany the mother to describe to the MO the deterioration in the boy's state during the flight. He thought the woman might also appreciate the company of someone who had shown her friendly sympathy.

As the truck drove away Dirk gave a dry laugh. 'I think our Dave's testing his chances there. She's quite a looker in spite of the rough gear.'

Maggie scowled. 'Dave's concerned, that's all. He's about the only guy in B Flight who hasn't got sex on his mind ninety-nine per cent of the time.'

'Think what he's missing! Now, would "my lady" care to accompany me to debriefing?'

She collected her charts and her emergency bag, then tucked her helmet beneath her arm as she stepped down from the front access. 'You're remarkably cocky today. What's suddenly pulled you out of the dumps you've been in for the past few months? Don't tell me she's written giving you the green light at last.'

Dirk jumped to the ground beside her. 'You have a very sharp tongue, and little understanding of what makes me tick.'

'Beer?' she suggested slyly as they walked to the nearby tent.

'I suppose you won't believe I feel enormously glad to be free and alive after seeing the drama we've left behind. When all's said and done that's all any of us really wants, isn't it? Thank God we're British.'

Maggie was astonished. She had never heard him sound so serious. Whatever had wrought the change in him? 'What do you think'll happen? Shall we be bringing out our casualties tomorrow?' she asked quietly.

'Who knows! If the Albanians decide to wait until night falls our guys'll have a hell of a job preventing a bloody confrontation.'

They held the debrief without Dave. It was merely a formality, anyway. After cleaning up, Maggie went to the Officers' Mess tent for dinner. She had missed out on the picnic sandwiches with Chris, so she was hungry. Jeff and the others were already there among the majority of Army officers. She sat beside Steve, avoiding the empty chair beside Nick Lorrimer boring on about his mother-in-law who was still at his rented home six weeks after the birth of his bouncing son.

'Okay, so maybe Clare did need her when the baby was imminent and then overdue, but Matthew's fine, and so's she. Other women cope with kids – even three or four – on their own. So why can't my wife manage one?'

'You've got to kick the old girl out,' said John Caine. 'Penny tried the same game when I told her I was coming here, but I put my foot down. Said she knew when she agreed to get married that I'd be away a lot, so she must find friends and things to do instead of inviting her mother over each time.'

241

'Ha! You've only been married a few weeks. Just wait,' Nick warned darkly.

'John's right,' said unmarried Jeff. 'Be master in your own home.'

'Yeah? So what do I say? "Either she goes or I do"? I'm always going. That's no threat.'

Dirk appeared and sat next to him. 'When you get back offer to drive her to the shops, then keep going until you reach her front door. Say you'll send her things on by DHL next day.'

'Why not do what they do out here?' put in Maggie sharply. 'Cut her throat, or nail her to a door. That should solve your problem.' They all turned to stare at her, and she caught herself adding, 'There's a strong chance there'll be some killing in the village we've just left, and you're wimping on about mothers-in-law. You all make out you're so bloody macho. Prove it now and again.'

Nick turned on her with a smirk. 'We all had the idea that's what Chris was doing down by the river with you this morning. Or have we got it all wrong?'

Before anything more could be said Dave entered to weave his way between the tables. He bent towards Dirk but included Maggie sitting opposite when he spoke.

'The kid's got meningitis – a killer strain. The Doc says every child in that village should be vaccinated. Some may already have it and need urgent treatment. He's informed the Camp Commander, who's passing the news to Orion Leader.'

On the point of leaving for the Sergeants' Mess and his own meal, Dave was joined by one of their ground staff corporals with a signal for Jeff, the senior pilot present. He read it, then got to his feet.

'Tempest One has agreed to stay around to assist Orion Force. I'd better let the Boss know the latest update. The Army won't think to inform him.'

242

He went out with Dave and Corporal Bradley, leaving everyone to speculate on how Randal planned to assist in this kind of emergency. After a while Steve said, 'He's a great exponent of "Don't do as I do, do as I tell you." Any one of us would get a bollocking from him if we went out on a limb like that.'

'He's the Boss. Makes his own rules. Always has,' said Pete, who had known Randal for some years.

'Not when he's with Fabulous Fiona. She *definitely* wears the pants,' Nick inserted with a grin. 'But with her sexy arse inside them who can blame him for—' He broke off in surprise as Maggie slammed her cutlery on the table, pushed back her folding chair and went out into a stifling early evening.

The only solitude to be found was over by the parked Chinooks, but they were presently being serviced by ground crew. To walk through the camp to the far side would invite unwelcome interest, so she crossed to their line of vehicles and sat in the cab of one. It was hot, but a hideaway from speculative glances and disturbing sights and sounds. She craved isolation in which to think. It had been quite a day in one way or another.

Those two hours with Chris this morning seemed an age ago. She had only gone with him because of the encounter with Randal yesterday. If she had handled that better she would almost certainly have flown with him today, and still be out there giving voluntary assistance in a tense scenario.

Staring through the windscreen at the sun lowering towards distant hills, Maggie faced the truth. This work fulfilled her. What they had done today was the kind of task that gave her a real buzz; made her feel an essential part of life. The troops could only have been moved to the trouble spot so swiftly by a helicopter. To fly a Chinook was immensely satisfying. It was a vital job with an operational squadron.

243

If she applied once more for a transfer away from Hampton the only other Chinook station was where Griff had been moved to. That sexist aggro again; and there was no way she fancied being an instructor. She gave a heavy sigh. For two and a half years she had coped with being the only woman in B Flight. She had found it occasionally lonely and mildly annoying, but since Fiona Price had reappeared on the scene her own minority state had seemed unbearably irksome. So, was she going to let that selfish society bitch ruin a career she had worked extremely hard to acquire? Maggie Spencer was a female RAF pilot, for God's sake. A relatively rare breed. She was good at what she did. She had made it in a masculine world and survived. Was she going to let *him* mess up all she had achieved?

Now it was in the open. It was not Fiona but her infatuated husband who presently threatened Maggie's future. The Price reunion had shocked her into realising that she had probably been in love with Randal for some time without suspecting it. Could she now continue to work, live and play side by side with him in order to stay with 646 Squadron? To carry on being one of the boys she must laugh when they made crude jokes about Fiona's sexual hold over him, join in the general good-natured male ridicule. She must avoid being alone with him unless they were on duty, and she must reverse his notion that she preferred to fly with anyone but him. Above all she must satisfy her frustrated emotion with someone else. If not Chris, there were enough men around to choose from.

Her thoughts returned to what she had seen this afternoon. The women living in that village faced life and death problems. The one they had brought out had a son who was almost certainly dying. It was time Maggie Spencer pulled herself together and got on with her privileged life in which nothing happened that was comparable with the disasters women all over the world were facing.

The passenger door opened, startling her from her deep concentration. Jeff slid on to the seat beside her. 'Can anyone come on this ride?'

She was surprisingly glad of his company. 'It's the only place I could find to be alone in.'

'Want me to go?'

She shook her head. 'I've finished what I came for.'

'That remark could be badly misconstrued, ma'am,' he said with a grin.

'Did you contact Tempest One? What on earth are they doing?'

He leaned back in the seat, took a large block of chocolate from his pocket, broke off four squares and passed them to her. 'The guys on the ground decided to send the Warriors and a token force forward to negotiate with the hostiles. Rip agreed to circle overhead as a threat to suggest he had a contingent of reinforcements aboard which could be offloaded on the spot. Apparently, he and Orion Leader have established good relations. Chalk that up as a one-off,' he observed with a laugh, familiar with Randal's vocal sparring with members of other services. 'So he had been told about the meningitis before I contacted him.'

Jeff handed her more chocolate and began on another large chunk himself. 'They're playing foxy,' he said. 'Dirk suggested the Albanians should be told the kid might be suffering from a deadly contagious disease, and until it's been positively identified his village should be quarantined.'

'And they believe it?'

'Haven't got that far yet, but Orion Leader is trying to turn things around by suggesting Rip's there to take British troops out as soon as a medical team can be flown in to isolate the place. Dirk's just been called to confirm on air that he brought a sick boy and his mother out this afternoon, and the woman has agreed to speak to the hostiles' leader in their own language. I guess she'll sound convincing. She was pretty emotional when I asked if she'd do it.'

'Poor soul!'

'You don't want any more of this, do you. Think of your figure.' Jeff put the rest of the chocolate in his mouth and crushed the wrapper with long fingers. 'The ruse is working so far. I suspect Orion Leader is playing for time, knowing that if marching people are halted and kept hanging around long enough their fire often begins to die. Throw in strong doubts, a suggestion of deadly contagion, and enough people might throw in the towel and turn back. Even if the diehards won't give up, there'll then be enough of our troops to hold them.'

Maggie nodded. 'There's a strong possibility of that. Good thing we brought that boy out.'

Jeff's eyes rolled to fix her with a stern look. 'Against the Boss's orders, I believe.'

'We might have saved the day, so if he starts anything I'll be ready for him,' she said forcefully.

'Attagirl! That's the only way to handle it. Don't let him get at you.' He smiled at her surprised expression. 'I'm an expert at the testosterone and heaving bosoms syndrome, remember? Luckily, the rest of the guys haven't caught on yet. Make sure they don't or they'll make things difficult for both you and Rip. Drop it before you get deeply hurt, Maggie. You had enough of that with Mark. Have fun with Chris instead. He's still in love with Chloe so you can cheer each other with no harm done.' He opened the door and slid from the seat. 'If you've really done what you came here for, how about a drink?'

Dirk watched the woman as she spoke to the leader of the men ready to ransack her village and beat up the people living there. In her dark skirt and light brown blouse, using a language he could not understand, she looked as foreign as the words she uttered. There was no mistaking her restrained passion, her struggle to remain objective in her bid to persuade the marchers that her boy's desperate illness was a real danger to them. The volume of the voice at the other end of the radio telephone suggested unleashed invective, but she anwered quietly despite the anger in her brown eyes.

Dirk was intrigued as he studied the lines of her sun-browned face, the coil of dark hair held in place by tortoise-shell clips, the swell of neat breasts above her slender waist. On the aircraft he had taken her for a peasant, but he was swiftly revising that impression. In her late twenties she had an air of greater sophistication than had intitially been apparent. Her command of English was unexpected. Why was an educated woman of her quality living in an isolated farming community?

Giving the handset back to the Signals corporal she turned to Dirk. 'He will discuss with his people the danger if they go on.' Flashing a glance at the soldier still communicating with Orion Leader, she looked back at Dirk. 'I think maybe it is over. He was very violent in his words, but perhaps because now he will not be violent in actions.'

Dirk levered himself from his position leaning against filing cabinets and went towards her. 'That's really good. You've been marvellous. It can't have been easy for you.'

She gazed back calmly. 'Nothing is easy in this country.'

Wanting to prolong the encounter Dirk put out an arm to indicate that they should leave, then followed her from the stifling heat inside the huge tent out to an evening atmosphere hardly less stifling. The sky had paled to a threatening silver that suggested a storm in the offing. Good, a deluge should cool the tempers of any firebrands undeterred by the threat of contagion. He thought wryly that it would also turn the dusty landing pad to mud, but servicemen under canvas were inured to that.

They walked through a camp noisy with the sounds of off-duty soldiers: uninhibited laughter, voices raised in contention over football, military politics or women, pop music at full blast.

The woman murmured reflectively, 'You are all so *happy*. I had forgotten how that sounds.'

Dirk found her words unexpectedly moving. There was no melodrama in them, no bid for pity. It was more as if she was unconsciously voicing private thoughts, and it had a more profound effect on Dirk than she could have guessed. He had not been happy since Mike's death. Paula's rejection a year later had worsened matters, and what she had confessed to him at Bristol had taken all lightness from his spirits and renewed grief for his lost friend. Now here was a young woman who had seen and perhaps suffered extremes of fear and loss, about to watch her child die in an Army tent surrounded by foreigners, saying she had forgotten how happiness *sounds*. She was surely more mature than he.

'Why is an educated woman like you living in an isolated farming community?' He smiled down at her. 'I know it's a corny old line, but your English is very good and you don't look as if you regularly work in the fields.'

There was no return smile, but her reply was not unfriendly. 'I am the schoolteacher. My home is Pristina. I taught there for four years and then agreed to join a group sending graduates to village schools to discover the best pupils for free scholarships. We move around, spending one year in each place. The children then grow used to different ways of teaching.'

'And is your husband also a teacher?' he probed as they walked slowly past a cluster of soldiers listening to a radio putting out a live pop concert.

'He was a lawyer, but he abandoned that to fight with our army. Now he does not want the old life. We parted eight months ago.'

'I'm sorry. It's the story of so many marriages.'

'Are you married, Captain?'

'Haven't got around to it yet.' They had reached the small tent beside the Field Hospital in which the boy had been isolated, and Dirk was loath to leave her there alone. 'Can we talk a little longer?'

'I must sit beside Pavel.'

'I could sit there with you.'

'You have duties.'

'Not unless another emergency crops up.'

She faced him frankly. 'I am a Serb, then I am your enemy.'

'If you think that why did you hop on my aircraft?' he challenged.

'It was for the boy only. I told you that.'

'I see. So you were prepared to put yourself in the hands of the ferocious British for his sake?'

Her rich brown eyes studied him carefully for a moment or two. 'You are not so ferocious.'

'Then may I sit with you for a while?'

She gave a small nod. He followed her beneath the canvas, surprised by his wish to stay with her. An orderly was checking the boy's pulse and glanced up as they entered.

'Will you be sitting here for a bit?' At her nod, he said, 'I'm only next door if you need me. I'll pop back in about fifteen minutes. He's still hanging in there.'

As he left she turned to Dirk, her brow furrowed. 'Pavel is *hanging*? What does this mean?'

'He's still fighting for recovery. One of our strange expressions not included in the university course.'

She indicated the folding chair. 'Please sit. I can use the bed.'

'Will you tell me your name?'

'Sophia.'

He offered his hand. 'How do you do, Sophia. I'm

249

Dirk.' Seeing her confusion he smiled. 'Wasn't that your first English lesson; how to greet someone and introduce yourself? It usually comes with the instructions on how to buy toothpaste and complain that your hotel bed is too hard.'

She visibly relaxed. 'Do you speak other languages?'

'Only schoolboy French and German no one in those countries can understand.'

The wooden chair creaked loudly when he lowered himself on it, so he spread his legs wide and rested his forearms along them to ease the weight on the suspect seat. Sophia perched on the foot of the bed with her legs curled beneath her.

'Our boss, the man piloting the Chinook still observing what's happening at your village, is top notch at European languages. I'm sure he'll have a word with you when he gets in.' He frowned. 'Our troops are there to protect the Serbs. We don't regard them as our enemies.'

'You attacked our people.'

'Not now. We're here to help create peace.'

'This is *our* country,' she said with heat.

He let a short silence elapse. 'I merely wanted to get to know you. I'm not here to have a political discussion.'

'I apologise. I am very grateful for your help.'

'And I'm glad we were able to give it. Now, tell me about your family, your childhood in Pristina, the scholarship pupils.'

'This was to be a short talk, I thought.'

'Say it all in short sentences,' he suggested lightly. 'How will I get to know you, otherwise?'

So, sitting in a camouflaged tent in the heart of Kosovo, Dirk heard about a culture vastly different from his own, told to him by a woman to whom he felt drawn in a manner that was new to him. The orderly came and went several times, and torrential storm showers brought with them a refreshing breeze to cool the air, but nothing stopped the flow of conversation between them. Even when a night orderly brought cups of tea and a lamp to provide pale light, Dirk made no move to leave. By then he had spoken of his friendship with Mike which had lasted more than twenty years. She understood his pain so well.

He had been unable to pour out his grief to his mother, or to Mike's mother, and certainly not to Paula. He had been strong for her sake, playing the role of male comforter to the widow in the belief that she was as devastated as he over Mike's passing. He had tried to ease the blow with Pam Miles at the Bird in Hand, but she had countered his words with clinical practicality and he had instead got drunk. This Serbian woman who was familiar with the destructive power of loss listened quietly and said only, 'I know, I know,' when he finished speaking.

The Medical Officer brought an end to the intimacy when he came to examine Pavel, still in a coma. He gave his opinion that the child's condition remained critical, and said Sophia should try to get some sleep on the camp bed which would be brought for her shortly. Dirk was then forced to leave, but promised to return in the morning.

The storm had left the ground covered in surface water unable to soak through the rock-hard earth. Dirk walked to the tent he shared with Jeff, Chris and Steve, heedless of the puddles and the noisy mopping-up activities of soldiers used to all weathers under canvas. His tent was unoccupied. Disinclined to join his colleagues for a late drink, he stood in that darkness swiftly returning to the pre-storm clamminess, enjoying a new mood of calm, a curious sense of having shed a heavy burden. Time passed unnoticed by him, until the familiar thwack-thwack of approaching Chinook rotors told him Tempest One was back.

B Flight, particularly those who had manned Tempest Two, was keen to learn the latest situation so they all converged on the Briefing Tent as the weary returning crew tramped across the waterlogged ground illuminated by the landing lights strung around the dispersal area.

Dave came up beside Dirk and studied what could be seen of the crew's expressions. 'What d'you reckon?'

'I'd guess they got away with it for the time being,' Dirk said. 'Just so long as the ruse hasn't started panic among the villagers that a deadly virus is about to kill them all.'

'Mmm, but better that than the massacre we tried to prevent.'

Dirk called to Randal as he neared, 'Is all quiet on the Western Front?'

'Quieter than it was, thank God.' Randal entered the large tent and dropped his bag and helmet before sinking on one of the folding chairs. 'How's the kid?'

Dirk tilted his hand to suggest that things could go either way. 'The mother's been given a camp bed beside him for the night. They're doing all they can.'

'I'll check before I turn in. Your ruse pretty well saved the day. All the same, it's a poor little beggar's life.'

Dirk recalled being told that the Price boy had several years ago been thrown from a pony and injured badly enough for the RAF to fly Randal home from Bosnia. Hence his present concern?

'The kid was ill before today's trouble blew up,' he pointed out.

'Yeah. Let's make this quick, guys,' said Randal as the rest of his crew sat, dropping their equipment at their feet. They all looked tired and stressed. 'The hostiles were starting to disperse when we headed back, stopping for a hot refuel on the way. Orion Leader's confident of holding the determined minority with the reinforcements at his disposal.' He smothered a yawn. 'We went to fetch the women and children from where we'd offloaded them on the hill, but they bloody refused to go back to the village with us. That's their choice, so our participation is over for now. On the assumption that the crisis has been averted, we'll be tasked to return the troops to their units as and when the Army sees fit.' He yawned again and stretched his arms over his head. 'If there are any calls for an emergency crew tonight, it won't be us. Jeff, you'll take Nick, Brad and Ray. Okay?'

The four nodded glumly, so he added, 'I know you were out last night, but you've been asleep all day while the rest of us were working. Just pray nothing comes in until morning.' He got to his feet and nodded at Dirk. 'Thanks for your backup and for the bright idea about the kid's condition.'

'What a good thing we ignored you and took them aboard,' said Maggie airily.

Randal cast her a glance that fuelled Dirk's ongoing suspicion that there was something between the pair despite Chris's presence on the scene. 'Just goes to show how easy it is to misjudge *any* situation, Maggie,' Randal said. He picked up his gear. 'Sleep well, folks.'

There was no emergency during the night. Dirk slept well and awoke with a continuing sense of well-being. While he was shaving Maggie stepped from a shower cubicle dressed in knickers and the T-shirt worn beneath her flying suit, towelling her hair.

Dirk grinned at her. 'How's "my lady" this morning?'

'None the better for seeing you unwashed and black-jowled,' she returned smartly.

He waved his shaver at her. 'You women are spared the curse of having to do this every day.'

'We have other curses, Bogarde.'

Obeying sudden impulse, he said, 'Isn't it time you dropped that jokey name? I was pretty well pissed that night.'

'Nothing unusual for you.'

Maybe it was his new light-heartedness that held at bay

the irritation her attitude usually aroused in him, or maybe it was that she presented an unexpectedly alluring image with newly-washed hair fluffing around her face, and her breasts moulded by the shirt against her damp skin. And why had he never before noticed what good legs she had?

'Look,' he began, lowering the shaver to the washbasin, 'we got off to a bad start and that flight back from Shawbury worsened it, but things haven't improved despite flying successfully together over the past six months, have they?' When she said nothing, he continued. 'I suppose it's mostly my fault; being moody. Trying to get over the death of a friend of twenty years. You can understand that, can't you? There was also a sense of guilt because two men died and one was severely injured, while I survived practically unscathed. It's not a good feeling, Maggie.'

He moved closer to her and could smell the apple-scented shampoo she had used. 'I tried to atone by marrying his widow, but she was wise enough to see it wouldn't work. It's taken me much longer to recognise that she's right. It wouldn't. She's now out of my system.'

'Until the next woman creates havoc in you.' She shook her head in exasperation. 'You guys are all the same. If it isn't wives or girlfriends, it's mothers-in-law. I listen to all your gripes day in, day out. None of you seems able to handle women.'

'Least of all Rip,' he put in slyly and watched her colour rise, but if he thought he had disconcerted her he was mistaken.

'Least of all him,' she agreed. 'He's the biggest fool of all, returning for a second dose.'

'Yet you accept his weakness. Why not mine?'

She frowned. 'He and I go back a long way.'

'Then you've done a hell of a lot of accepting.'

'Mmm, haven't I,' she murmured reflectively.

Dirk was more than ever sure his theory was right. Why

was the girl wasting herself on a remote hope? Randal Price was a colourful character, if station gossip was to be believed, and he had certainly lived up to it in recent weeks, but B Flight descriptions of Fabulous Fiona suggested it would take an exceptional woman to woo him away from her. Unsure of the state of play where Chris was concerned, Dirk found himself considering entering the arena. Paula was well and truly out of his future plans. It might be stimulating to make a play for Maggie. He was better-looking than Randal, and had just as much else going for him. More, in fact. There was no wife and two children tied to *him*.

'So what about it?' he asked.

Coming from a reverie, Maggie asked, 'What about what?'

'Shall we kiss and make up?'

'I thought you were doing that last night with our Serbian mother. Spent a couple of hours closeted with her, didn't you?'

He sighed. 'You're a hard, hard woman.'

'No, just used to being outnumbered by men since child-hood. I'm immune to plaintive tales like you've just spun. Forget the kissing . . . but Pam Miles assures me you're quite biddable under certain circumstances so,' she repeated his own words with a knowing smile, 'I'm prepared to accept your weakness.' She pulled on her flying-suit. 'Better remove that beard and get across to breakfast pronto. The Boss might not be so accepting of it if you're late for briefing.'

After that unsatisfactory skirmish Dirk dressed and headed for the Field Hospital. Another scorching day was forecast. The storm puddles were fast evaporating, but the air still smelled damply semi-tropical. The camp was busy as the troops stacked their bedding and kit ready to go for breakfast: the start of another day as peacekeepers in a foreign country.

Halfway to his destination Dirk encountered Randal coming towards him. 'The kid died at three twenty-four,' he revealed. 'Poor little bastard never stood a chance, but he at least went out easier here than he would have in a threatened village. He also happened to avert a menace to stability in the area. What little there is of it,' he added heavily. 'When hatred is so deep-rooted situations like yesterday's can blow up any time.'

'Any idea of the latest sitrep on that?'

Randal nodded. 'The diehards are still there vowing vengeance, but the majority drifted away. Orion Leader has control and is prepared to sit it out until they give up. The Army plans to fly the woman and the child's body back in a Medivac aircraft shortly. The sight of an ambulance helicopter landing at the village might strengthen the suggestion of a serious medical emergency and further diffuse the danger. I think it's unlikely we'll be tasked to take the guys back to their units yet. They'll play safe for a day or two.'

'And pray they're not suddenly needed somewhere else,' Dirk observed as they parted.

Sophia was slowly walking beyond the tent they had sat in last night. Through the half-open flap Dirk could see the small sheet-covered shape on the bed, and he slowed. Maybe he should not intrude on a mother's grief. Yet Sophia then turned, saw him, and approached as if glad he had come.

'This is so good of you, Dirk, but you must have duties and your commander has been here just now. He made the gesture to speak to me in my own language.' She cleared her throat. 'I think he has made some practice first of what to say, but it was so kind of him. Everyone has been . . .' She searched for words.

'We haven't treated you as an enemy?' he suggested.

She sighed. 'If only all people had more understanding of each other.'

'There would still be wars; for power, territory or industrial wealth. There never has been universal peace. Human nature makes it impossible. But that doesn't prevent understanding between people like ourselves.'

The Medical Officer emerged from the tent, carrying a large envelope. He came over to them and addressed Sophia. 'We're ready to drive you to the helicopter now. Here are copies of the death certificate and my report on the treatment given. The padre who administered the last rites has also written a note to your own priest. If he or anyone else in the village wishes to contact us about the case they are welcome to do so.' He gave her the envelope as a covered jeep pulled up to collect the body being brought out on a stretcher. Sophia tried to thank the doctor, but she seemed too upset to be coherent. Then she turned back to Dirk.

He swiftly eased the situation. 'There's no need to say any more. It's been a privilege to meet you, Sophia. And an enlightening experience. I only wish we could have saved your son.'

She shook her head. 'Pavel is not my son.'

'But I thought . . .'

'I teach him at the school, that is all.'

He was totally taken aback. 'You've done all this for one of your pupils? Where are his parents?'

She had regained control now and spoke softly to him. 'The mother is raped by many men after a carnival. She will not have Pavel; she will not know him. So he lives with the old schoolteacher, who could not bring him to the helicopter yesterday. I have made this little boy my friend.' She gazed at the passing stretcher with sadness. 'The family will be glad of this. They will say God has taken the fruit of sin.'

'Do you also believe that?' demanded Dirk.

'Oh no, he was just a child like any other. Each child must be valued and loved; it is their right. I have loved him in my way for a few short months, and he was

257

happy with that. It was important. Goodbye, and thank you.'

She climbed in the jeep and looked back through the open window to raise a hand in farewell before the driver headed off towards the waiting aircraft.

Dirk remained where he was for some moments before moving away, only half-aware of his surroundings. Once more Sophia had touched his own life with the simplicity of her creed. What of his own? He had walked out on young Sam who looked up to him with love and admiration, because he had been told he was not Mike's son. The boy did not know his true father had abandoned him at the embryo stage; did not know the man he had adored as the parent who had been there for him from birth had been about to desert him when he was killed. He could not guess that Uncle Dirk, who had promised ongoing devotion, was set on punishing him for his mother's sins.

The death of a small Serbian boy had changed all that. He would arrange to see Sam on a regular basis from now on, no longer for Mike's sake but because he was a child wanting to be loved by someone who had also been there from his birth. A series of Paula's lovers would not satisfy that need.

Dirk remained thoughtful during his breakfast, which was soon interrupted by Randal.

'Make it snappy. I've been warned to have you available for interview by Mitch Stirling in fifteen minutes.'

Dirk knew the defence correspondent of a popular daily from past dealings. He was a good journalist who, unlike some, had no axe to grind with Britain's fighting forces. 'I guess it's about bringing out the kid.'

'Yep. The medics will give him the ins and outs of their involvement, so all you'll have to do is say why you picked them up and no one else. Keep it short and strictly impersonal in the best peacekeeping tradition. He's probably already got the juicy details from Orion Leader, so don't attempt to trespass in that area.' He glanced at his watch. '*Twelve* minutes. In the Briefing Tent.'

As he walked away, Dirk asked, 'Is Maggie coming in on this?'

'He asked specifically for you. One of my team tied up like this is enough. If she makes an issue of it, I'll calm her down.'

Dirk finished his last piece of toast wondering gleefully how the Boss intended to do that. Not in the manner she would like, that was certain, but being left out of this interview would not further his own bid to get on a better footing with her.

Mitch Stirling was chatting to Randal when Dirk walked in. The journalist shook his hand, greeted him in friendly fashion. 'Haven't heard your name mentioned in any recent sporting contest, Dirk. You haven't given up top line competition, surely.'

'Too many other things on the go,' he returned vaguely, unwilling to admit to himself that Mike's death had even robbed him of the desire to participate in the things he had once done with skill and enthusiasm. 'I gather you want to talk about the sick child whose only hope of treatment was to fly him back here to our Field Hospital.'

'I've already heard about that from Rip,' he replied easily.

'What I really want from you is a comment on the allegations by Clive Fielding about your handling of the crash that killed two of the crew and permanently disabled him.' He held out a copy of a sensationalist tabloid. 'You *have* seen this, haven't you?'

Dirk took the paper folded to an inner page. The headline underscored in red made his blood turn cold.

CRIPPLED SERGEANT CASTS DOUBT ON CAUSE
OF CRASH

It was appalling. The words came at Dirk like a guided missile, shattering the peace he had just found. He could not accept that Clive, who had been one of a good, close-knit team, could be doing this to him.

Dirk was a heavy drinker even by normal squadron standards, and there were hints flying around that he was too friendly with Mike Steadman's wife. All three of them were far too close. It was almost unnatural. Sure to cause problems. Just as we were boarding for the return flight that day, he and Mike began a heated quarrel. Jake and I overheard Mike say, 'I don't want you sniffing around her until I've moved out and seen a solicitor. Then you can take over, if you've got the stomach for it.' It was pretty obvious Dirk had caused a split between Mike and Paula, and divorce was on the cards. Well, Dirk grabbed his arm and said he couldn't do that, and they went at each other again. When they got aboard Dirk suggested he should fly the return, but Mike says, 'I'm not getting pissed until we're back on the ground. I'll fly.'

Jake and I wondered about the meaning of that remark and we were glad Mike was doing the handling.

Once we were in the air they didn't talk and laugh together like usual, so we grew even more concerned. Fifteen minutes into the flight Jake and I heard Dirk say something about a warning light coming on, but the intercom connection was playing up and I didn't catch just what the problem was. Next thing I knew we were dropping like a stone. I went out like a light and woke up to find my career was over and I'll never be able to run or play sports again.

I know no one can back me on this; Jake and Mike are dead. All I'm saying is you're in the hands of the guys up front, and if they're not fully on the ball they can make mistakes. In a Chinook there's no time to compensate if one of them pulls the wrong lever or jabs at the wrong switch. It just falls out of the sky and guys get killed. Or permanently disabled.

As Dirk stared at this printed condemnation he vaguely heard Randal demand to know what was going on. Mitch told him.

'In Tuesday's TV documentary detailing how servicemen cope with disabling injury, the other survivor of that crash in Bosnia apparently suggested friction between the two pilots led Dirk to make a fatal error during an emergency. He can't prove anything, but it's pretty damning and the tabloids are making a meal of it.'

'My God, I thought *you* were above this kind of dirty trick,' Randal snapped. 'If I'd known what you were after I'd have told you to go stick your head up your arse.'

'Cool it! I simply want Dirk's comment.'

'He has none to make . . . and you can piss off p.d.q. You're no better than the rest of the vultures. Don't expect any cooperation from me or my team from now on.'

As the journalist left, Randal gave his usual unexpurgated opinion of people who dug up scandal. After a short silence, he asked, 'Can I read that load of garbage?'

Dirk glanced up at the man who had just proved his loyalty as a commander. 'Everyone else will . . . if they didn't hear it on TV.' He handed over the folded paper. 'Ever since that fatal day I've often wished I'd died instead of Mike. Now I know why.'

Ten

'**I**'m sorry about this business, Dirk,' Martin Ashe said. 'I've asked Perry to join us, not only as your new Squadron Commander but because you've served together before and are personal friends. However, this meeting will be on a purely professional level to discuss how Fielding's comments affect the Air Force, and you merely as a member of it. I had several in-depth conversations with Strike Command and agreed with them that it was best to ground you and bring you home.'

'Because Fielding is believed?' Dirk asked woodenly.

'You know better than that. No pilot who is dealing with heavy personal problems is allowed to fly. You were of no use sitting around in Kosovo, an easy target of keen reporters.'

'And Price is notorious for antagonising them into writing vindictive articles,' put in Perry Newman. 'At Shawbury he was downright abusive to a PR woman wanting a piece on his recovery and return to flying duty.'

'That's irrelevant,' said the senior man. 'Our concern is how best to handle this PR crisis. It's likely to run until the next big news breaks.'

'Or until they reopen the investigation into the crash,' said Dirk.

'That's not going to happen. The accident report stated positively that a rare double engine failure occurred over

262

snow-covered mountains, giving the pilot zero chance of landing safely.'

'But Clive is claiming I killed the wrong engine when one failed.'

'He said nothing of that during the inquiry,' Perry reminded him. 'His evidence was perfectly straightforward.'

Martin Ashe gave Dirk a straight look. '*Did* you kill the wrong one?'

'Of course not,' he cried. 'I knew exactly what I was doing.'

'Then stop acting as if you now have doubts.' He adopted a gentler tone. 'As Perry said, Fielding stated at the time that his intercom was playing up and he didn't exactly hear the nature of the emergency. In fact, he's still saying that. As he was in the cabin unable to see what action was taken in the cockpit, his evidence at the initial inquiry was of no great import. Nothing has changed that.' He frowned. 'What we're concerned about is his hint that one of the pilots could have been drinking before that flight, and that both were in the middle of a violent argument over the wife of one of them; an argument that affected their ability to handle the emergency.'

Dirk was silent for a while beneath the scrutiny of his CO, remembering his drunken arrival at Hampton in January. Ashe would not have forgotten that, and he clearly expected some kind of response to Fielding's damning comments. All the way from Kosovo Dirk had been trying to see a way out of this appalling situation. He had been haunted for almost two years by the catastrophic events of that day he would never forget. To be publicly reviled as the possible perpetrator of the fatal crash was almost more than he could handle. Yet he must.

'Of course I'd not been drinking,' he claimed in a monotone. 'Ask anyone who knows me and they'll say I'm far too professional ever to do that. As for the quarrel . . .' He spread his hands expressively. 'Clive's misquoted Mike and me. As we walked out to the aircraft I suggested that we spend our leave at my parents' place on the Isle of Wight, where I keep my boat.' He looked from the CO to Perry and back, and sighed. 'The poor bastard's dead. It's bizarre to talk about his private life like this.'

'I agree,' said Ashe. 'Nevertheless, we have to. Strike Command will give you a thorough grilling tomorrow, and I want to know all there is to know before they do.'

Dirk's inner vision returned yet again to that valley in Bosnia. He saw the tents, the supply dumps, the Warriors and the Jeeps; he saw men in camouflage khaki moving around beneath the sun. He saw Mike in bitter mood.

'We often spent our leave together. Mike, his wife and his s— and Sam. But my suggestion that day brought a shocking response. He more or less told me he was going for a divorce.'

'What does "more or less" mean, Dirk?' asked Perry. 'They'll need something more positive at Command.'

Feeling that he was betraying Mike with every word, Dirk said, 'He told me he was getting shot of Paula and Sam as soon as he got home. That he would get a solicitor on it . . . and that he didn't want my advice or any interference. I naturally tried to reason with him. Anyone as closely linked to them all would have done the same. It wasn't a quarrel, sir,' he explained to Ashe. 'I wanted to talk about it; he didn't. That's all it was.'

'Mmm, but he was very worked up?'

Realising where that was leading, Dirk answered carefully. 'He was coldly determined, sir, and he was fully in control of the aircraft when we took off. How many of us have *never* flown with something at the back of our mind? Girlfriend trouble, wife grumbling about being alone so much, kids with measles, mother-in-law stirring things. But we're perfectly on the ball in the cockpit. So was Mike that day. Anyone who says he wasn't—'

'No one is saying that. It's you Fielding is pointing the finger at.'

'And he's wrong,' Dirk insisted heatedly. 'I saw the light come on. I announced the problem to the crew, and I shut down the inoperative engine.'

'*Now* you sound totally convincing.' Ashe leaned forward to emphasise his next comment. 'Two men died because of a rare dual malfunction. Sergeant Fielding was disabled because of it, not for any other reason. What you and Mike Steadman said to each other prior to boarding is a matter of your word against Fielding's, as is his hint that you had been drinking. The first can't be proved either way, but anyone with a grain of sense will see the second as arrant nonsense. You would have been jeopardising your own life along with the rest of the crew's. It was pure luck that you were the only one to emerge whole from that pile of wreckage.'

'I'm not so sure I was the lucky one.'

The CO was furious. 'I'll pretend you didn't say that.'

'Sorry, sir. Stupid of me.' Dirk sighed heavily. 'Clive's evidence after the crash was professionally straightforward. Why's he decided to do this to me?'

'Because he's now a civilian. He knows the service can't touch him,' put in Perry sourly. 'He was in the limelight on TV and he made a meal of it by telling a story that would bring him certain additional limelight; possibly with some financial reward. He's been offered a chance to hit out at the Air Force and life in general. You happen to be a convenient patsy for a man grown bitter over his disablement.'

'That's what Rip said, and he should know. He's been in a similar situation.'

'I wouldn't say that,' came Perry's quick response. 'He wasn't involved in a tragic air accident. If he hadn't been

265

driving a flashy scarlet car those kids wouldn't have been tempted to drop something on it.'

'Shall we return to the subject in question?' prompted Ashe coldly. 'So far as the service is concerned, Command has put out a media statement reiterating the official findings of the AAI and declining to comment on the TV programme. Group Captain Mark Grainger will see you at eleven tomorrow morning at Command Headquarters. After that, you'll go off on fourteen days' leave. I suggest you stay clear of any place where reporters and cameramen are likely to be watching out for you, but if you do get waylaid you repeat as many times as it takes "No comment." That's not advice, Dirk, it's an order.'

'Yes, sir.'

'However, this *is* advice. It was probably wise thinking to ground you for several months after the crash. There's no professional cause for it now. You've been granted leave only to get you out of circulation while the fuss dies down; then you'll resume your flying duties. Here's the advice. Get out and enjoy the future you were granted two years ago. The thing happened. You were in no way to blame. Life goes on. Stop drowning your sorrows night after night and get back to those sporting heights you were on.'

The interview with Mark Grainger, who began by asking after Randal, was infinitely more penetrating. It ended with the same advice given by the Station Commander.

'In the past you've brought prestige to the Air Force in inter-service and international competition, as well as representing us in the Olympics three years ago. The best way you can deal with this storm in a teacup is to dump it where it belongs and work back to peak fitness so that you can enter the lists again.' A brief warning concluded the meeting. 'In the scramble for promotion a man can lose out by his own hand. Friends die. Several of mine were blown to the four winds in the Gulf. It's one of the penalties of our job. If you can't accept that you shouldn't be doing it. Here at Command we take account of that.'

Further depressed by this very heavy hint, Dirk drank a couple of pints in a pub filled with noisy young bankers while he decided what to do during the next fourteen days. The obvious way to get out of circulation was to put to sea. He would then have time to think out his future. Maybe Grainger was right. If he still could not get from his system Mike, Paula, Sam and the bastard who had begun the roundabout; if he could not survive Clive Fielding's public accusations with total confidence, he should not be doing what he did.

He rang his parents, wondering how they were taking it. His father answered the call. 'Hi, Dad, I flew back yesterday because of this Media nonsense.'

'We were told about that by a young hack from the local rag who's more or less camping out on our mooring.'

'Oh hell!'

'I saw off with a boathook some smart alec from the *Sun* two days ago. Then Bill Thomas showed me the paper when I went in for my Independent, and the creep had printed that your mother and I were so distressed we had bolted indoors rather than speak to him.'

'It makes a better story.'

'So why'd they bring you home? Surely they're not going to reopen the case.'

'No. It's just . . . They've given me two weeks' leave and advised me to make myself scarce until the dust settles. I thought I'd take the boat. Maybe head for the Hebrides, or the Channel Islands. If someone's watching the mooring could you take *Skyhigh* round to Cowes, and I'll pick her up there.'

'I can do better than that. John Yateley's going over to Poole tomorrow to pick up a new deckhand. He'd bring me back if I took *Skyhigh* over first thing. Suit you?'

'Great! Thanks, Dad. How's Mum taking this?'

'On the chin, as she always has since you and Mike were first brought home by Constable Bates for letting down his bicycle tyres.' Sadness touched his voice. 'Young Mike's death was the exception. He was like a second son to us.' When Dirk made no comment, he said, 'There's no way Mike would be considering a divorce, as this blighter claims. He was devoted to Paula and that lad of his.'

'That's right.' What else could he say?

'Don't let this rubbish get to you, Dirk. It'll blow over. Now here's your mother determined to wrest the receiver from my hand. See you tomorrow. Usual place, around eleven?'

Helen Marshall was a redoubtable woman who would surely have been a suffragette in an earlier age, but her present concern was apparent despite her crisp manner.

'You're very wise to go out in *Skyhigh*, dear. If the ghouls from the Press come after you, ram 'em then scat. How are you?'

'Fine. You sound fighting fit, as usual, Mum.'

'We read about the little boy you rescued from that threatened village, then they straightaway printed libellous stuff quoted by a man clearly determined to blame someone for his present sad situation. He knows air accidents happen, and you could have ended up the same way after that crash. Or like our dear Mike. I'm so thankful you—' She broke off, then continued in her normal firm voice. 'You will speak to Claire, won't you?'

'Of course,' he said obediently. 'I'll ring her next.'

'And Paula. Dad forgot to tell you she got on to us after the TV programme. Very upset. She knew how you'd feel about what was said. Begged us to tell you to ring her as soon as you made contact.'

He hesitated. 'I'm not sure that's a good idea.'

'Yes, dear, you must. She spoke out in your defence when they interviewed her. Denied the suggestion of a divorce. Said you and Mike had never had a row in all the years you'd known each other. Dad and I can testify to that, too. Paula apparently gave them an earful when they referred to the hint that you might have been drinking before the flight. That's *infamous*, Dirk. How dare he say such a thing? I remember you talking about Clive Fielding as a good sort of man. One of the lads.'

'Yes. I don't know, I suppose he had his reasons for doing this. I was the only one who got out of the wreck in one piece. I guess it rankles.'

'Well, he's said it and can't take it back, so he'll have to live with his lies as well as his disability. Keep in touch, dear, and bring *Skyhigh* home. Let me know when you're on your way and I'll push that scruffy hack into the water just as the tide's turning. He'll need to catch the hydrofoil back from Portsmouth.'

It brought a faint smile as Dirk said, 'Nice thought, Mum, but we don't want your name in the papers as well. Take care. Thanks for everything.'

The call to Claire Steadman was practically one-sided. She was deeply upset over the suggestion of a pending divorce at the time her son was killed, and she barely referred to the accusations made against Dirk. Mike's mother had grown introverted after her husband walked out to live in Australia with a twenty-year-old dancer he had met on a business trip. The loss of Mike then deprived her of the little self-assurance she had retained, so she had become an elderly woman at the age of fifty-eight. Dirk need not have worried that she would now blame him for the crash. Clive's hints of that appeared to have gone over her head. She was obsessed with the 'lie' that her son could be preparing to walk out on his wife and son the way his father had. Dirk concluded the call thankfully.

He drove to Poole, booked a room for the night and ate dinner before forcing himself to ring Paula at her parents' home. He had almost decided not to make contact, then he decided that by doing so he could touch base with young Sam.

After a very long time Stan Martin picked up the receiver to shout, 'Who is it this time?'

'Dirk.'

'Oh, I thought it was another of those sharks. Where are you?'

'Out of circulation. I'm sorry you're being pestered over this, Stan.'

'I'd like to wring that bastard's neck! Speaking ill of the dead. Our girl's taken it badly, especially the bloody suggestion that you and Mike were fighting over her. *Too close*, be damned! In the forces men always keep an eye on the wife and family when their pals are away. It's common practice, and a jolly good one. It's not the same in industry. When I was sent out for six months to Namibia to set up that communications centre, no one from the company called to see Jean was all right. There was a big freeze here at home. She had to cope with frozen pipes and several feet of snow; couldn't get out for days, and she was still breastfeeding Paula.'

Dirk interrupted before Stan could get well into his stride. 'Is Paula there now?'

'Where else would she be?' he demanded, still indignant. 'They waylay her if she so much as puts her nose out the door. Young Sam hasn't been to school this week. She's afraid someone'll start asking him questions.'

'Oh, surely—'

'I'll get her to the phone. She's dying to talk this over with you. *Paula, it's Dirk, love,*' he called out. 'She's coming. Get over to see us when you can, Dirk. Pity you were called away so urgently last time. Sam was upset when he found you'd gone without saying goodbye. He thinks the world of you.'

'Don't rabbit on so, Dad!' Paula then spoke into the receiver. 'I knew they'd bring you home and give you leave, Dirk. When can we meet and talk this through?'

He unconsciously stiffened at the sound of her voice. 'It isn't a witch-hunt, just a nine-day wonder. If something big breaks before that, it'll die even sooner.'

'But we need to get things straight; agree on what we'll say,' she insisted. 'They know there's no smoke without fire.'

'You started the fire, not me. My people, yours, and Mike's mother all think Clive's lying about the divorce. We know different, but I'm keeping *shtum* and so must you. There's nothing to talk through.'

'But that bastard hinted that we'd been having it off.'

'A lucky guess better ignored,' he said coldly.

She grew angry. 'I supported you when they cornered me. What happened to friendship, pal?'

'It died very abruptly earlier this year. I only rang tonight to say I want to keep in touch with Sam.'

'And have everyone casting you as his father?' she snapped.

'Would you prefer to name your married lover?'

'Would you care to admit you killed the wrong engine?'

As he drew in his breath with shock, a young voice full of excitement came on the line. 'Uncle Dirk! I was asleep, but I heard Grandpa tell Mummy it was you on the phone. Where've you *been*? Why'd you go without saying goodbye last time?'

'Put down that phone and go back to bed, Sam! Dad, get upstairs and sort Sam out, for God's sake. I can't take much more of this,' Paula yelled against the sound of a distant TV programme.

271

Dirk spoke quickly. 'Sam, how about spending a day together?'

'Y-e-a-h!' he cried in drawn-out delight. 'Can we go on your boat?'

'If you like.'

'Y-e-a-h,' he cried again. 'Triffic!'

Dirk heard Stan arrive beside the first-floor extension. 'Now come on, young Sam, Mummy's having a very important conversation with Uncle Dirk. It's rude to interrupt other people talking. You've been told that umpteen times. Say goodbye and come back to bed, lad.'

'Oh, *must* I?' the boy moaned. 'Bye, Uncle Dirk. Come very, very, very, *very* soon, won't you. I love you as high as a mountain.'

'I love you the same,' he replied thickly.

For some moments all that could be heard were the fading voices of Sam and his fond grandfather. Then Dirk caught himself saying, 'That Serb boy we picked up died in our camp in Kosovo. He was around Sam's age. He hadn't had much of a life with his own people, and it ended among men they regarded as enemies. It made me think, Paula.'

'What's this leading to?' she asked wearily.

Dirk sighed. 'I don't know. I didn't mean to say it but hearing his voice . . . After you told me the truth I was as angry, hurt and disgusted as Mike had been. Any love I had for you was killed stone dead, but watching that poor kid's body being loaded in a Jeep to be taken back to a village where he'd been ostracised for being a bastard brought home to me the fact that I was treating Sam the same way. He's a person in his own right, no matter what you did. I intended to write to you about seeing him, perhaps taking him to stay with my parents now and again. Then this affair broke.'

'The affair you're blaming me for.'

'Just now you accused me of pilot error that killed Mike

and Jake. If you truly believe that, any personal contact between us is impossible from now on. I'll deal with Stan over Sam.'

'He's got no say in it. I'm his mother and can stop you from seeing Sam.'

'You'd better not,' he told her heatedly. 'Mike loved that boy dearly until you confessed how you'd cheated him. For more than four years Mike adored him as his son. I can give Sam the kind of steady relationship he won't get from Tim Ferriday and a whole succession of others like him.'

After a curious silence Paula spoke through tears. 'My life's a total mess.' He decided not to comment. 'Dirk, I think I made a big mistake in not marrying you.'

He rose to that swiftly. 'The same uniform, the same deadly routine, the same bloody aircraft, coming home knackered and half-pissed: it would be like living with Mike's ghost, you said. And you were right. I've finally stopped living with it and I'm getting on with my life, as you advised. You'll have to do the same. I'm taking *Skyhigh* to sea for a week or so, then I'll be in touch with Stan about having Sam for a day.'

'Dirk!'

'Yes.'

'I didn't mean that about killing the wrong engine.'

'Goodbye, Paula.'

'Can't we be friends, if nothing else?'

'It's too late for that.'

After he disconnected he sat staring at the beige walls, feeling drained. He had been in a great many hotel rooms over the years. Hectic sex with promiscuous girls, rowdy binges with the lads, lying awake before important exams with facts whirling around in his brain, crashing-out after exhausting flights and sleeping like the dead in the bed next to Mike's. Tonight, he must say an overdue farewell to someone who had shared his life from the time they had let down the tyres of Constable Bates' bicycle. He crossed to the minibar. He would bloody well make it a farewell worthy of the 'Terrible Twins'.

Eight days and nights of solitude. Eating and sleeping on the boat, fighting the swell, drifting lazily along the leeward coasts of islands rich in bird life, lying at anchor to eat double-decker sandwiches and watch seals at play on sun-warmed rocks, and all the time discovering that it was *not* painful to do these things he used to enjoy with Mike, activities he had shunned for almost two years.

By publicly airing details of those last unforgettable minutes before take-off, Clive Fielding had forced Dirk to confront them again. Newspaper headlines questioning the cause of the crash now brought surprising freedom from the burden of being the only one to emerge from it whole. Media doubts had dispelled his own. Mike, Jake and Clive had been victims of a tragic accident, nothing more. The official inquiry had proved that. Yet Dirk had metaphorically buried himself with the friend who had been as close as a brother, subduing the gift of remaining young and alive with a subconscious sense of guilt. Fielding's vindictive hints had banished it.

It was time to live life to the full again; enter *Skyhigh* in competitions, challenge a difficult rock face, explore the unknown depths of a pothole. It was time to revive his sex life. Paula had never been really his – or Mike's, apparently – yet she had dominated his thoughts for six years. No longer. He was all set to play the field. And there was Sam. A child bearing Mike's name, but a person in his own right needing guidance and affection. To Sam he could give all the things young Pavel had been denied. By so doing, it might balance the account.

He went ashore full of confidence that evening, eating a

hearty meal in a pub and drinking in company with other amateur sailors passing through. Conversation was purely nautical and he returned to his bunk reasonably sober. He would reach his parents' place in a couple of days, and he lay before sleep making plans to inspect his climbing gear then take it back to Hampton. Dave Ashmore was a mountaineer; he had been one of a Highland rescue team before joining the RAF. Maybe they could team up. Although Dave was leaving 646 Squadron soon for pilot training, that would not prevent their getting together during leave periods.

The morning was sunny and warm with a lively off-shore breeze. After an early breakfast of boiled eggs and toast Dirk left his mooring and followed the spectacular Cornish coast, enjoying the surge of power as he gave *Skyhigh* her head past the dark, towering cliffs. He and Mike had made one or two hairy ascents in this area, roped together and drenched by sudden high spouts of water thrown up as it crashed against the rocks below. The thrill, the risks had been irresistible; the elation on gaining the top unbeatable. It would be great to tackle a sheer face again.

Hot on that thought he spotted two coloured blobs against the grey wall of rock, showing that someone was doing what he planned. Interest made him slow and alter course for a closer look at a climb he and Mike had intended to have a crack at one day. Known as the Funnel, it was normally only undertaken by experienced climbers in reasonably moderate weather. Squadron demands had limited their own chances of being free when conditions were right, so they had done no more than study the Funnel on paper.

As *Skyhigh* cruised gently landward Dirk saw through his field glasses why it was thus named. A narrow fissure split almost three hundred feet of bare rock, ending below sea level. From reading about it Dirk knew the cleft was rough and tortuous, offering hand and footholds only first-class climbers could negotiate. After inching through several sections barely wide enough for a human body, and scaling the hundred-foot vertical rise which inspired the name, they then had to face a daunting overhang where the fissure widened dramatically at the cliff top. Not a climb for the faint-hearted!

There was no beach or cove, so this pair must have abseiled to a spine of rocks presently exposed by a sea eddying benignly around them. Dirk had often seen this coast from the air on wilder days, and he now imagined how the water would pound and fly high with thundering savagery in gale-force winds with lashing rain. He envied men whose lifestyle enabled them to pursue their sport whenever the right opportunity offered.

Dirk cut the engine and followed the progress of the lead man as he edged his way through a steeply sloping section leading to the foot of the funnel. Storms must have sent stones down to collect in this stretch, for the second man shielded his face with his arms as his partner set them rolling. It was slow going, but both men eventually stood gazing up the vertical chimney deciding how to proceed.

Taking *Skyhigh* even closer Dirk then appreciated just how awesome this fissure was, and he acknowledged the skill being displayed here. The last two crazy years would have taken their toll of his own expertise, but his enthusiasm swiftly revived as he watched.

Their discussion over, the lead climber began on this most difficult section. He tested each hand and foothold carefully before using them; his partner watched patiently. Climbing was not a rushed sport. One slip could prove fatal. The sun warmed Dirk's arms and back as he watched progress through his field glasses, and it was easy to see how the climber searched for any slight ridge or indentation he could use to gain height.

Dirk had lowered the binoculars momentarily to wipe sweat from his forehead when he heard a faint cry. Glancing up sharply, he saw the man was now spreadeagled against the rock face while his feet sought some kind of purchase. Then he dropped, knocking his partner sideways into the section they had just traversed, where he slid helplessly on a mini-avalanche of shale until coming to rest on a narrow ledge. The second man was swept down to join him. Their cries of pain and alarm echoed between the cold walls, adding to Dirk's concern. He studied the figures for signs of movement. Both lay still, perilously near to falling through the lower confines of the fissure to the sea.

Dirk snatched up his radio and called the local coastguard, detailing the situation concisely. The response was daunting. The helicopter and inshore lifeboat were dealing with an incident at sea, so the RAF Search and Rescue station would be called. The news that Dirk was a helicopter pilot with knowledge of rock climbing was greeted with enthusiasm, and he agreed to remain at the scene to give any assistance. He was soon in radio contact with the crew that had been scrambled at RAF Chivenor.

The Yellow Hats had some choice words to say on learning the location of the emergency. They had flown to the aid of climbers in the Funnel before and were well aware of the overhang preventing a straightforward rescue. Dirk said he would take *Skyhigh* to the edge of the rocks and attempt to discover the condition of the casualties. The SAR crew agreed it might help to winch their man to the boat, but would wait to assess the situation when they arrived on the scene.

Wasting no more time, Dirk guided *Skyhigh* towards a large formation well clear of the lofty overhang. Using his anchor as a line he swiftly made her secure and climbed out to cross the long, rocky chain. The water swirling around it was dark and deep, calm at present but deceptively treacherous. It was partly why climbing here was such a challenge.

A clatter followed by a splash made him look up, and he almost lost his balance. One of the men was trying to sit up. Dirk reported this to the rescue team and asked their probable ETA. Fifteen minutes! There was a wide gap between rocks here, and shadowed green water surged through it. This was as far as he could go.

Cupping his hands around his mouth he shouted to the climber now slumped against the rockface. 'Helicopter on its way. What are your injuries?' There was no response, so he shouted at maximum volume.

The man's mouth appeared to be moving but Dirk could hear nothing. The gap was too great. Then gestures indicated their plight. Pointing to himself the man gave a thumbs up, but turned it down when indicating his partner.

Dirk took up the radio. 'One stretcher case, one probable walking wounded. Returning to the boat. Will await your directions.'

Recrossing the rocks Dirk stood beside *Skyhigh* listening for the sound of approaching rotors. The yellow Sea King came into sight five minutes later. It circled while the crew discussed their options, then the winchman descended to *Skyhigh*'s deck. Dirk was ready with a bantering comment on what had taken them so long, but he instead took one look at the face beneath the yellow helmet and said, 'Good God, Chas Whitman!'

'And good God to you, Dirk. What's a pilot doing in a boat?'

Dirk grinned. 'Making your job a bloody sight easier, apparently.'

Chas unhooked the winch line. 'We can rescue *anyone* from *anywhere* without the help of amateur sailors. You just happen to be handy.'

Freeing the anchor, Dirk jumped aboard and started the engine. 'You've grown as cocky as the rest of SAR. How long have you been with them?'

'Six months.' He moved up beside Dirk, studying the figures on the ledge. 'How close in can you take this tub?'

Keeping his eye on the dark masses beneath the surface, Dirk eased *Skyhigh* between them towards the cliffs. 'Up to the point where these guys must have abseiled down this morning, which I guess is that flatish slab abutting the fissure.' He pointed to the transverse section. 'They were already in there when I turned up. I watched for a while and saw the leader start up the funnel itself. He must have fallen some fifteen to twenty feet clean on the other guy. Momentum sent them both sliding to where they are now. Thank God they stopped where they did or they'd have dropped through that lower passage to the sea, which could have proved fatal.' Cutting the engine he let the boat drift up to a serrated ridge providing a secure mooring beside the flat slab. 'How's that for easy access to your casualties?'

Chas checked his equipment, then made a brief study of the initial twenty or so feet of the fissure reaching up to the ledge.

'As you said, that jagged surface could have turned them into mincemeat if they'd fallen further, but it offers good holds to an experienced climber. I suggest you go up there with ropes and a karabiner to secure a line. I'll send up the gear, then join you.'

Dirk looked at the fissure with uncertainty. 'I haven't done any climbing for two years.'

'It's like riding a bike; you never forget how to do it,'

Chas said breezily. 'You and Mike Steadman were rated pretty high when we were all at Shawbury. You'll go up there like a monkey up a palm tree.'

It was not how Dirk had planned to restart his sporting activities, but he knew this was the best procedure. Shouldering the ropes, he stepped out on to the large rock lying almost directly below the ledge. It was cold away from the sun's reach, and far into the depths of the fissure the echoing gurgle and surge of the sea sounded almost menacing. He shivered. Anyone falling could be sucked under and lose all hope of emerging again. Yet even as that prospect chilled him, it brought an undeniable return of the desire to challenge and succeed. He momentarily lost sight of the reason for what he was about to do and surrendered to the old thrill of life in the fast lane.

Chas's simile had been an over-optimistic one. Dirk was soon sweating and breathing hard as he hauled himself upward. There were certainly good holds, but the craggy nature of the rock face also produced some narrow stretches that were tricky for a man of his size to squeeze through. A monkey would have managed better!

When his head eventually rose above the ledge all sense of triumph faded. The climber who had signalled was a girl. She was pale but outwardly calm as she huddled there gripping her partner's hands.

'I think he had a heart attack or something,' she said in a carefully controlled voice. 'He's done this climb seven times. There's no way he would just fall.'

Dirk was dismayed by this news and by the lack of space on the ledge. He eased himself on it and forced a reassuring smile. 'We'll soon have you both safely down. The Search and Rescue guys are medically trained. They'll know how to deal with your friend.'

'He's my father,' she said with rather less control. 'We all told him he was . . . that he should stick to easier climbs. But he was determined to do it one more time. He's never had a fall in all his years at the game.' She glanced down at the man's ashen face and added with a wobbly laugh, 'He'll never live this down, silly old fool.'

'What's your name?'

'Claire.'

'Are you hurt at all, Claire? Have you tried moving everything?'

'I'm okay. Probably be black and blue tomorrow, that's all. Please get Dad to hospital quickly.'

After swiftly checking that the man had a pulse and was breathing shallowly but evenly, Dirk reported to Chas, suggesting that he send the girl down first to leave room for dealing with her father. He set about securing the line as he explained to her what they would do before winching them both up to the helicopter waiting clear of the area. Then he helped the girl to get up, aware of the dangerous drop mere feet away from where they stood, and looped the strop around her to lower her to where Chas waited.

Despite the time lapse since he had done these things Dirk easily slipped back into the routine as he braced his feet on the tiny ridge and steadily played out the rope. He was soon pulling up the stretcher and medical backpack, then the greater weight of Chas, who immediately knelt to assess the man's condition.

'His daughter thinks he had a heart attack,' said Dirk.

'Mmm, so she said. Arthur. *Arthur!* Can you hear me?' Chas demanded. 'Can you speak to me, or move your hand to show you understand what I'm saying?' he added loudly as he carefully examined the man's head.

A soft mumble and the faint flickering of eyelids was

Arthur's response, and Chas gave a slight nod of satisfaction as he continued his routine body check, speaking to the man throughout and receiving unintelligible replies which nevertheless indicated that he was still conscious. Probably because his fall had been broken by landing on his daughter, Arthur's physical injuries were amazingly slight. He had fractured his ankle and several of his ribs, but his semi-coherent state suggested a more serious problem needing hospitalisation as soon as possible.

As Chas rendered what aid he could, Dirk prepared the stretcher then helped to transfer the injured man into it. It was no easy task in the space available, but he and Chas were secured by the karabiner as they wrapped the canvas around Arthur and fastened the straps.

Chas glanced up. 'I'll go down first. You lower the stretcher, then my gear. I'll give my guys the details and tell them you'll bring your boat well clear while we make the transfer. Okay?'

'Sure.'

Lowering Chas was straightforward enough, but the cocooned casualty needed more care. It was during this delicate business that Dirk heard an approaching helicopter. They must have misunderstood Chas's message and were coming in instead of waiting for *Skyhigh* to put to sea. Concentrating on the job, Dirk nevertheless soon recognised the sound of a smaller aircraft than the Sea King and, once the stretcher was safely down, he glanced up to discover who was creating a nuisance by flying too close. For once he shared Randal's violent reaction to airborne media cameramen when he read the name emblazoned on the fuselage. There was apparently a major disaster at sea. Surely they should be covering that?

Dirk was still angry when he reached sea level after lowering the medical pack and the two climbers' gear, but

Chas was coolly chatting up Claire who was responding to him with some warmth.

'Haven't your guys told that prat to piss off?' Dirk demanded, coiling rope.

Chas grinned. 'He's been ordered to keep well clear of our operation, but they're one of the hazards of our job. Right, let's get Arthur aboard. The tide's turning and there's a strong current around the Point. These rocks'll be covered within minutes. You wouldn't guess how often we've had to pick up people in the nick of time all along this stretch of coast.'

With the girl's help they got her father aboard, then stacked the gear before Dirk cast off and started the engine. The incoming surge was very apparent. *Skyhigh* laboured against it, but Dirk could not increase power because Arthur would suffer from the buffeting. It was only a short distance to where the Sea King hovered, and the winch line was lowered at Chas's signal. He hooked himself and the stretcher on it, and up they went.

Claire watched them. 'They're marvellous, aren't they,' she cried above the din.

'Yeah,' Dirk replied somewhat dryly, fighting to keep the boat from spinning in the rotor downwash. 'I'm sure your father will be okay, although his climbing days might now be over.'

Her gaze was on Chas descending. 'He won't admit he's getting too old for things like the Funnel.'

'Maybe when he realises he could have killed you both he'll see things differently.'

She was intent on the man now slipping the hoist around her and gave no reply. Chas made all secure, then shouted, 'Thanks, Dirk, I owe you one.'

Dirk watched them rise to the open door where the winch operator was ready to haul them in, and the helicopter was soon heading inland. The pilot had a final message for Dirk.

'Your help greatly appreciated. If we get a medal for this, we'll give you first look at it.'

'I'll settle for a date with Claire,' he replied.

'No chance. That comes under the heading of Search and Rescue perks, but if you're ever passing by drop in. The beer'll be on us. Cheers.'

Left with a strong current to counter and suffering from a sense of anticlimax, Dirk decided to head for Falmouth and spend the rest of the day on dry land. A sudden need for company made solitary hours at the helm seem more of a penance than a pleasure. He ate lunch in a cosy pub, mingled with tourists buying souvenirs, scored with a couple of girls eating ice cream and arranged to meet them in the same cosy pub that evening. Yet none of it eased his restlessness. He had been a part of the action this morning. He needed to get back to it; make a fresh start with B Flight. Move back into the fast lane.

He bought a newspaper and returned to *Skyhigh* for a quiet beer while the sun went down. The headline jumped out at him from an inside page.

CRASH PILOT HELPS RESCUE PROFESSOR

An account of the tricky rescue of Professor Arthur Troy, a Ministry of Defence scientist, ran alongside two pictures. One showed Dirk on the ledge lowering the stretcher, and the second was a shot of its transfer to the Sea King. The name *Skyhigh* could be clearly seen. From that the reporter could have traced the owner and discovered he had chanced upon a double scoop when returning from filming the tanker blaze at sea. An MoD professor engaged on secret work, and an RAF pilot recently accused of possibly being responsible for a crash that had killed two men and disabled a third were big news. The circumstances that had brought them together made the story even juicier!

They had done their homework. Arthur Troy was a sixty-three-year-old eccentric who indulged in sporting escapades. He had suffered a mild stroke in the Funnel, but claimed it would not stop him from trying the climb again. His stepdaughter Claire refused to comment on his vow. A potted biography of the man followed. Dirk was given the same treatment. How the hell did they dig up such personal details? The Olympic bronze medal for the four-man bob would be well recorded, but powerboat racing, potholing and his other sporting pursuits were no more widely known than any other man's.

As he read on, Dirk began to smile. Two weeks ago the Press had dubbed him a villain. Now they were portraying him as a hero. He had been sent on leave with orders to make himself scarce until the fuss died down. How would Martin Ashe view this unforseen publicity in the face of his warning?

Dirk's smile broadened. Chas Whitman might have got the girl, but he had apparently stolen the man's thunder!

Eleven

The crews returning from Kosovo were given seven days' leave. Randal spent it at a Cornish country club with Fiona and their children. They booked in as husband and wife, although they would not be for much longer. The divorce should come through within a matter of weeks, now visiting rights for Randal had been incorporated in the terms. Fiona had been more than willing to spend time as a family so long as it was at a luxury hotel with a swimming pool, sauna and beauty salon. After six weeks under canvas Randal was happy to oblige her. He was also happy to share a bed. They still made the earth move, but he now recognised it as lust rather than love. A man who had once feared sex would play no part in his future did not quibble over the finer points of passion when it was offered by a sensuous woman, one who knew exactly what turned him on. Reunited with Neil and Lydia who accepted his departure with his promise to see them again soon, he returned to Hampton on top form.

Because his parents were visiting his sister in Australia, Maggie invited Chris to spend a week with her twin and his family in the New Forest. The first few days with Phil, Fay and their twin babies were not altogether successful. Chris was an unenthusiastic small boat sailor, and the little boys clearly upset him as reminders of the child he was afraid another man had fathered in his absence. Maggie suggested forest walks, but two days of rain put an end to

286

that plan. They soon left the Spencers' shipyard cottage and drove to Evelyn Montrose's apartment in Chelsea. Chris's grandmother was in Cheltenham as guest director of a new musical play under rehearsal, so they had the place to themselves. Chris cheered up, Maggie enjoyed the luxury and they went on the town in a big way, arriving back at Hampton relaxed, at ease with each other, but with greatly reduced bank balances.

Martin Ashe had designated the Friday as the annual Open Day, when families and friends could visit the Station for fun and entertainment. The residents of Hampton Heyhoe were also invited as a public relations move. These events were dreaded by some RAF personnel; others enjoyed them no end. Aside from a bouncy castle shaped like an aeroplane, face painting and playground activities for children, there were races and contests for civilians who wanted to join in the fun. For those who preferred spectator sports the Station had organised many, from sky-diving to a tug of war between ground and aircrew – always fiercely fought. There was a huge marquee where teas were served; all proceeds going to the RAF Benevolent Fund. VIP guests would be served in the Officers' Mess.

Maggie was expected to take part in a karate demonstration with seven men, two of whom had also reached black belt status. As they all regularly practised together they knew each other's strengths and weaknesses, although the men were never happy to be bested by Maggie. If she did it in front of an audience they would be even less happy, but she prepared to give it her best shot. Chris had been 'volunteered' along with Jeff for a team event on trampolines, and Dave would partner his friend Sandy for a simulated rescue on a mock mountainside. The day was to conclude with the excitement of go-kart racing. This was always as highly enjoyed by the service personnel as the visitors, and bets were being laid in secret by officers and other ranks on their particular favourites. This year the past overall champion, Randal in his kart named *Demon Hill*, had two new challengers: Dirk in *Go Gettem* and Perry Newman driving *Fast Track*. The odds were changing hourly.

The morning was spent preparing for the flood of visitors when the Station's gate would be opened at 1.30 p.m. From then until six, the personnel of RAF Hampton were virtually on duty. Only the standby crew would be isolated in the Crew Room, whiling away their twenty-four-hour stint and praying for an emergency to liven it up. Those members of B Flight who could manage it had plans to spend the evening in the Bird in Hand giving Dave a worthy send-off to his pilot training course. The Sergeants' Mess would stage their own farewell to the future officer on the following evening: a far rowdier affair!

Maggie watched the trampolining with enjoyment. Her two friends were dressed as clowns with red noses, much to their disgruntlement, and were briefed to make fools of themselves while interrupting a faultless programme by the resident physical training instructors. These muscular men took sly delight in pushing them around until Chris and Jeff staged a skilful comic routine that earned laughter and applause.

Among the crowd was Jeff's girlfriend, Sable. This affair had lasted longer than any other since Maggie joined B Flight, but only because this time Jeff appeared to be the deeply smitten one of the pair. Sable was an aspiring swimwear model and the daughter of an MP. A wealthy socialite, blonde and shapely, she was surely no serious partner for a working pilot. Unlike Randal, Jeff had no private fortune with which to keep the girl loyal, so Maggie foresaw distress ahead for her close friend. Studying the girl in high heels, a cream dress reaching to mid-thigh and a hat more suited to Ascot, Maggie saw another Fiona who would doubtless regard a day spent around hangars and brawny airmen as trendy slumming. Her Sloane Ranger friends would probably shriek with laughter over her descriptions of what she saw today. Maggie burned with brief anger at the thought of Jeff being ridiculed by a bunch of mindless bimbos, but the voice of reason soon asserted itself to remind her that, like Randal, he was willingly laying himself open to it. Fools, the pair of them!

After a forty-five-minute period helping with the children's activities, Maggie went to the tea tent where she had arranged to meet Chris. She arrived first, and grinned as he came up to her shortly afterwards in his flying suit.

'I much preferred you with a red nose. You looked so cute.'

Flicking hers with his fingers, he said, 'You also think I look cute all tousled in the morning. You must have it bad, girl.' He indicated her cup of tea. 'Where's mine?'

'Over there in an aluminium pot, you lazy bastard. Go to one of the girls and offer her fifty pence. That'll get you a cup without having to look in the least bit cute.'

He returned to her side through the jostling crowd. 'Isn't it time for your big moment in the ring?'

'After Dave's done his mountain rescue. We're running late.'

'Hmm, that's about par for the course.' He drank thirstily, then grimaced. 'This tea tastes like coffee.'

'I won't tell you what mine tasted like. While you were doing your clown act I spotted our Sable among the spectators, but I guess Jeff wouldn't bring her in here. She's more than likely got a Fortnum's hamper on the back seat of the BMW Daddy gave her for her birthday.'

'Miaow!'

'He's riding for a fall, Chris.'

'So what? He's broken enough hearts in the past. Do him good to have the tables turned on him. You'd think they'd throw in a few biscuits with this coffee-tea,' he complained.

'Fork out another fifty pence and you'll get some, Scrooge.'

'Can't afford more,' he exclaimed with exaggerated horror. 'I'm being bled dry on child maintainance, and our antics last week put me well in the red. I've no idea how I'll settle my mess bill.'

'So you won't be able to come to Dave's do at the Bird tonight?' she teased.

'Wouldn't miss it. I'm relying on you to subsidise me.'

As Maggie was about to retort she fell silent. Chris's grin had faded to leave a curious expression of shock while his gaze fastened on something over her shoulder. She turned to see a plumply attractive girl in red standing no more than a few yards from them. There was a fair-haired child in the pushchair beside her, and she was studying her ex-husband with pale-faced uncertainty. Chris seemed unable to move or speak, so Maggie took command of the highly charged situation.

'Hallo, Chloe. Long time no see.'

The girl totally ignored her. Although she and Maggie had met only briefly on a couple of distant occasions, this was a deliberate snub. Her attention remained on Chris.

'Hello,' she ventured. 'How are you?'

'What are you doing here?' he demanded huskily.

'Jill invited us.'

'She's got a bloody nerve!' It was said loudly enough to cause heads to turn, and Chloe moved closer.

'Can we go somewhere alone and talk? Please, Chris.'

'There's nothing to say.'

Maggie felt like a mistress when the vengeful wife turns up, except that this woman no longer had legal claims on the man standing between them. The situation grew even more uncomfortable when the child was picked up from the pushchair and held out.

'You could at least say something to Malcolm. He's old enough to understand you now.'

Maggie saw a tiny replica of Chris, who even smiled the way he did. No one could deny they were father and son, least of all Chris himself. Growing anger, and the fact that the scene was causing some interest around them, led Maggie to slip away through the tea drinkers. What a bitch to subject Chris to a public confrontation! Although she felt inclined to stay and give him some support, she knew her continued presence might lead Chloe to create further embarrassment.

Outside the tent the first person she saw was Jill, who was too intent on her surreptitious snooping to notice who was approaching . . .

'What a dirty trick to play! How long have you and Chloe been cooking this up?' Maggie demanded furiously, making Jill turn in swift guilt.

'Oh . . . Maggie! Cooking what up?' she asked in a dither.

'Don't play that game with me. I've just been forced to take part in a soap opera scenario before several hundred assorted civilians. All it lacked was gypsy violins and deep snow as the "wronged" woman thrusts the baby at her seducer.'

Jill was never at a loss for long. 'It wasn't meant to happen that way. She spotted you two in there cosying up to each other, and she left me standing.'

'So how was it meant to happen? Come on, tell me the real plan. When Chris was with all his pals? When the Station Commander was passing by? Or was the kid going to be left outside Chris's room in the Mess?' Maggie paused until several passing family groups had entered the marquee. 'Remind me to remove your name from the list of my friends.'

Jill looked faintly abashed. 'You're not seriously involved

with Chris, are you? Pete swears you're not, and all the guys in B Flight know Chris still has a thing about Chloe. I wouldn't have got her here if I thought—'

'The only serious involvement I have is with flying. It's what you've just done to someone I like very much that I can't understand.'

Jill hit back. 'What about what he's done to her all these months? She had a mild fling when he stormed out after a row and flew to Bosnia for three months. When he heard about it, around the same time she told him she was pregnant, he went beserk, moved to a room in the Mess and filed for divorce. He pays maintainance for the baby because he has no choice, but he refuses to see little Malcolm. Chloe's been struggling along alone since he left her, and she wants more than anything for him to acknowledge the baby as his.'

'How long was it before she knew it *was* his, not her casual lover's?' Maggie asked caustically.

Jill had the grace to acknowledge the point. 'DNA would have proved it, but Chris pig-headedly refused to test.'

'If you knew him the way I do you'd understand why.'

'He surely can't have doubts now he's seen the little kid.'

Maggie sighed. 'What difference will it make? Chloe did the dirty on him while he was away. Nothing alters that.'

Jill sneered. 'Don't tell me he didn't play around when he was out of the country.'

'He didn't, Jill. Some do, but Chris isn't like that. Since the divorce there's been no ongoing affair, either. Why the hell did you have to meddle? Dirk's been mooning around for weeks, Nick bores on and on about his mother-in-law, and as for . . .' She decided not to comment on Randal's second dose of self-inflicted Fiona-itis. 'Now Chris'll be deeply unsettled. We often share a cockpit, but all you see of him is a blip on your screen in the control tower. I can't believe Pete went along with this.'

'I didn't tell him. You know what men are like. Never see what's right before their eyes. I did it for the best, Maggie,' she added on an appeal.

'Certainly not the best for Chris.' Even as she spoke, Maggie saw, with something approaching disbelief, her erstwhile lover leaving the tea tent with his ex-wife. Chris was carrying his toddler son and gazing at him in the way of all proud fathers. Chloe was smiling up at him. They looked like a small happy family.

'She still loves him, Maggie.'

She turned to regard Jill in silence. 'Then why leave it so long before trying to get him back?'

The other girl looked uneasy. 'Chloe and I were good friends when she lived here. We've kept in touch. I happened to mention in a letter that you and Chris were beginning to be an item.' Seeing Maggie's expression, she said gently, 'There'll be another Mark for you one of these days, dearie. Chris was really only second best, wasn't he?'

'I have to dress for karate,' Maggie said tonelessly, and headed for the gymnasium.

Lack of concentration led her to give her demonstration kata with less than her usual skill, and the two black belt men proved that by their faultless performances. When they began the series of real bouts Maggie had got into her stride and won two out of three in which she participated. As the spectators were mostly male the applause was muted. She barely noticed. Dressing again in her flying suit she went to watch the kart races only because the prospect of walking around and coming face to face with Chris and Chloe was too daunting.

Dave came up beside her during the preliminaries that sorted the men from the boys. 'Who've you put your money on?'

'Our boss. What about you?'

He grinned. 'Never ask a Scot about his money. It's going

to be a close run thing this year. Dirk and Perry Newman are unknowns, but I've heard dark rumours about their practice times. And we don't know how good Rip is these days. He's been through a lot since he last raced here.'

Dave's uncomplicated companionship helped Maggie relax slightly. He was a good friend. They had joined 646 on the same day and, apart from some initial ups and downs, there was warm understanding between them now.

'I reckon he's still unbeatable. Those dark rumours you've heard were put around by the bookies to spice up the betting. I'll concede there'll be a fiercer element of one-upmanship today, though. A double dose of media attention appears to have put fresh life into Dirk Bogarde, and our bumptious new squadron boss is determined to prove something – God knows what – by beating the favourite.'

Dave studied her. 'You've got it in for them, haven't you.'

'Not really, Dave,' she said heavily. 'It's just that the atmosphere in B Flight isn't like it used to be. When we first joined it was great, wasn't it? Then Rusty was promoted and posted to Scotland, Simon decided he'd be happier as a civilian, Pete married Jill and became dog-fixated. Oh, I don't know, it seemed to be all change after Rip's smash-up. Now you're going off! I'll miss you.'

'Not half as much as I'll miss you,' he said quietly. 'Why d'you think I've never had a regular girlfriend?'

Unequal to where this conversation seemed to be heading, she said, 'Someone had hurt you deeply. You admitted as much to me one day.'

He ignored that. 'My rank made it difficult for me to do anything about the way I feel about you, then Chris stepped in.'

'Chris has just stepped out again,' she said without thinking, and Dave seized on the implication.

'It's over between you?'

Maggie was weary of the subject; weary of this entire day. She quoted Jill's words. 'All the guys in B Flight know he still has a thing about Chloe, so that must include you. Nothing's over because it never existed.'

There was a short silence as karts shot noisily past in the second semi-final, but Dave's dark gaze remained on Maggie's face. When they could hear themselves speak, he resumed the subject.

'Well, I never saw you look at Chris the way you looked at Mark, and I remember the way you reacted when that Harrier slammed on the deck several months ago.' He took her arm to draw her a short distance from the crowd so they would not be overheard. 'I've never told you this, but the kind of devotion you shared with Mark showed me the solution to a difficult personal dilemma which happily changed my life in a totally unexpected way.'

He offered no more on this mysterious business, and Maggie was so intrigued she failed to forestall his next words. 'When I gain my wings I'll also get a commission, and with this MoD plan to combine Chinook squadrons here at Hampton, I'll almost certainly be posted here as a pilot. That'll put us on an equal footing. We have a lot in common, Maggie, and I'd like to write, mebbe phone you now and again. Nothing hot; just as a friend. As you said, we started with Six Four Six on the same day, and we've been through a lot together.' He gave a swift smile. 'We know each other pretty well, don't we?'

'Dave, I . . .'

'Please listen,' he begged. 'You've always tried to be one of the boys, and it's not unusual to keep in touch with former pals when you're posted. I won't deny I've an ulterior motive, but I promise not to push it until you're ready. When you are, I'll be pushing for all I'm worth. I think you're a wonderful person who deserves—'

Unable to take any more of this Celtic devotion, Maggie

had to stop him. 'I think you're a wonderful person, too, but you're going to be far too busy learning to fly to write or phone. We'll meet up again when you're sent back here wearing your well-deserved wings. Let's hope Napoleon has gone by then.'

Dave looked utterly confused. 'Napoleon?'

Maggie forced a grin. 'He was small and full of himself like our Perry, wasn't he? Oh look, the final's about to start. Let's get a ringside seat.'

Knowing she had handled the issue badly, Maggie wriggled through a gap to reach the boundary of the track. Dave had been sincere, but she could hardly have told him he was wrong about Mark; that she was now even more seriously in love with another man she could not have.

Spectators grew excited as they watched the fiendish rivalry of Randal, Dirk, Perry Newman, two officers of A Flight, three traffic controllers and two flight engineers as they battled it out with scant regard for personal safety. Two karts became entangled soon after the start, another failed to make the second bend and sent its driver head first over the barrier. After the second lap it was clear only four remained in real contention. *Demon Hill* was in second place close behind *Fast Track*. Dirk's *Go Gettem* was third but starting to trail smoke. It came to a sudden halt and *Seat of the Pants* crashed into it, leaving the front pair to go hell for leather around the last lap bringing gasps from those watching. Maggie guessed the sporting element changed to something more devious as they approached the straight neck and neck.

Demon Hill won by a whisker, and Maggie gained fifty pounds. Yet she felt no pleasure as she saw Randal kiss the girl who presented the mini-trophy, then enthusiastically kiss every female within reach before shaking up the bottle of cheap champagne and showering his fellow competitors along with himself. Here was the old Randal; the one who was only fully alive when linked to the woman he could not banish from his system.

Chris was not in his room when the time came to set out for the Bird in Hand, and Jeff was dining with Sable at the four-star Farley Grange before coming to join them. After the session with Dave in the afternoon Maggie would sooner have given the farewell drink a miss, but as 'one of the boys' she felt an obligation to go even if Chris would not be sharing the evening with her. She had just won more than enough to afford solitary splendour in one of Reg Farnaby's taxis.

As she left her room Dirk came from his and hailed her. 'Hope you didn't put your cash on me today.'

'I know too much about your driving disasters, remember.'

He came up with her. 'Oh c'mon, lots of water under the bridge since then. I could've won but for that slight hitch.'

'You reckon?'

'Maggie, Maggie, what can I do to impress you?'

She stopped at the head of the stairs and looked him over consideringly, then said lightly, 'Nothing. Anyway, why should you want to?'

He accompanied her down the stairs. 'I'm a man and you're a woman. The call of nature.'

She laughed in spite of her mood. 'Your line about the back row of the Odeon's a better one than that.'

'No, it isn't; it's too corny for words. I must have been so drunk I dragged it up from the depths that night.'

'You were.'

They reached the entrance hall. 'I'm a reformed character. No one'll have to carry me home tonight.'

'I couldn't care one way or the other, so long as you don't try to open my door with your key when you get in.' She made for the telephone by the wall.

'Are you ordering a taxi? Can I share it with you and Chris?'

'You can share it with me. Chris can't make it.'

'Fair enough.'

She ordered the taxi and replaced the receiver. 'Here in five minutes. He always says that, and it's usually fifteen.'

'So what's happened to Chris?'

'Chloe.'

Dirk's good-looking face registered a series of emotions that reflected his thoughts, but all he said was, 'I see.'

It was only a short journey to Hampton Heyhoe and the driver's account of how much his wife had enjoyed the Open Day prevented any conversation, but Dirk held Maggie back from entering when they arrived at the pub.

'Can I get something straight? A chubby girl in red pushing a pram, who I thought was his sister. That was Chloe?'

'She apparently came to get him back. She got him.'

'So where does that leave you?' he asked quietly.

'Standing outside a pub and longing for a drink.'

'Don't tell me we'll have to carry *you* home tonight.'

She had had enough of Dirk's probing. 'And let one of you win the standing bet by claiming he got me totally pissed? Forget it, sonny. I don't drown my sorrows the way you guys do, even when I have sorrows, and I certainly haven't any at the moment. I won fifty pounds today. Come on, I'll buy you one.'

Dave and Sandy were already in the bar together with other aircrew sergeants, including Jimmy whose long-suffering wife had been left with their five children. These, along with a collection of pilots and navigators, formed a largish group apart from some Heyhoe regulars. They intended to have fun on Dave's last evening with them as a sergeant. Someone had pinned a 'medal' the size of a dinner plate to Randal's shirt, and he was the centre of a laughing group as Maggie walked to the bar to buy Dirk a beer and herself a gin and tonic.

'Rip's in good form,' he commented. 'Another good guy gone back to his wife and kids. Is she anything like Chloe?'

Maggie took a gulp of her drink, her gaze on the merry Randal. 'You've heard enough frank comments from the guys to know she's not. Legs up to her armpits, boobs left as nature intended, eyes like blue saucers with S-E-X written across them. Irresistible!'

'So are you.'

She turned back to him. 'Did you have a drinking session in the Mess before coming here?'

'I told you, I'm a reformed character seeing things more clearly.'

Several loud young men pushed through to the bar, effectively isolating them in close proximity in the corner, a situation Maggie soon regretted as Dirk pursued his theme.

'I know just how long your legs are. I've seen them often enough when we're under canvas. And I know you wear a bra.' He smiled. 'Your eyes are green and often have M-O-R-O-N written across them when they fasten on me. There's more to irresistibility than physical impressions, and I've realised you have it.'

'You *have* been drinking.'

Dirk put his glass down and shook his head. 'I'm serious. From the day I joined this squadron you've been sniping at me over the woman in my life. She's finally out of it.'

Maggie's spirits dropped further. She did not want to hear a maudlin confession. Counselling was more in Pam Miles's line. She was about to suggest this when Dirk spoke of something quite unexpected.

'That business in Kosovo made me think; get things in perspective. Sophia painted a pretty grim picture of life out there. Made me see I'd been wasting mine over the last few years.'

Maggie sighed, half her attention on the jollity at the far end of the bar. 'Isn't that a bit melodramatic? You've been doing a vital job that takes considerable skill, not smoking pot on street corners and collecting weekly handouts at the job centre.'

'That wasn't what I meant.' He was more earnest than Maggie had believed he could ever be. 'There's no secret over the identity of the woman. The papers pretty well splashed Paula's name around in connection with mine, so I won't beat about the bush with you.'

Maggie did not want him to do anything with her; she wanted to join the others. Unfortunately, the laddish group had multiplied and she was not keen on trying to push through them to escape.

'They got it right in one respect. We were all too close, although it didn't cause trouble between me and Mike. What it did was turn me into an idiot for six years.' He made a wry expression. 'Bears out what you've always said, eh?'

'Dirk, this is meant to be a fun evening with Dave.'

'That's the point I'm making,' he insisted. 'While I was cruising around the Hebrides I had time to see where I'd been heading. Nowhere. Now I'm going to go places. The kart racing today was just a start. Dave's agreed to climb with me when we get the chance, and I've brought *Skyhigh* to West Bay so I can get in some speed sessions in her. I'm aiming to compete again, as well as making it across to France for the occasional ooh-la-la weekend.'

Maggie noticed that his eyes were brighter than ever before and that he was brimming with energy. Pam was right. He did resemble Tom Cruise. Renewed life because he had got over his passion for a woman called Paula? Yet again Maggie reflected on the power the female sex had over even these extrovert, super-assured men she lived and worked with. Not as tough as they liked to think!

'I've wasted so much time over Paula it stopped me from seeing what was right before my eyes.'

'Jill told me this afternoon that men never can.' She wondered whether to take the chance and force her way through the rough-looking drinkers to avoid what she feared was coming. It did.

'Maggie, you've probably had some justification for your opinion of me, but this is where everything changes. Can you forget all that Bogarde business while you really get to know me? I think we could start up something good, and now Chris is out of the picture—'

'Chris was never in the picture, as you like to put it,' Maggie insisted, knowing she would have to tackle the louts at any minute.

'I see. Well, you don't stand a chance in the other direction. Legs up to her armpits, did you say? He's no fool.'

Maggie was instantly blazingly angry. 'Neither am I! Nor am I B Flight's camp follower. Who do you have lined up for me when you slide "out of the picture"? Perry bloody Newman?'

The rowdy youths were thrust aside as she headed for the ladies' toilet leading off the dining area. She had the place to herself, and she clutched the rim of a washbasin while she rode out her fury. If Dirk guessed her feelings for Randal, did the rest? Were they all smirking behind her back over her vain hope of competing with Fabulous Fiona? Was Randal himself doing it?

Once she grew calmer Maggie did what all women do in such situations: powdered her nose, defiantly sprayed perfume in the right places, muttered, 'I'll bloody show them!' and sallied forth to do just that. She reached the group just as Jeff entered, so she made a beeline for him, smiling brightly.

301

'Managed to tear yourself away from Sable then. Have a beer on me. I'm rolling in money thanks to our champion over there.'

'So was I, but most of it's gone on dinner,' Jeff said moodily.

'And a room for the night, of course.'

He scowled. 'I booked it, but she had a call on her mobile and drove back to Town for some ritzy party. Never mind that I'd had to put a non-returnable deposit on the room. How about sharing it with me? Shame to waste ten quid.'

'I'd rather give you the tenner,' she said grittily. Although she knew it was only banter he had unwittingly struck the wrong note and revived her bitterness. 'Let's get a drink. I'm in the mood for a real binge.'

Jeff followed her, brightening up. 'Are you? You know we've got a standing bet . . .'

'Yeah, yeah. Tell you something friend o' mine. If I ever get totally pissed it'll be somewhere far away from all of you.'

Maggie did drink more than usual, but Dave was the target for tonight and occasional slugs of whisky were surreptitiously added to his beer as the evening progressed. They were fairly noisy but it was nothing to the rumpus created by the roughs gathered in the corner, who were heckling the girl serving food and making unwelcome overtures to some of the regulars sitting quietly with their drinks. Jean, behind the bar, told Jeff they were lads staying in the beach huts who had been in every night causing a bit of a nuisance. Her husband was ready to order them out if they overstepped the mark.

The bar emptied slightly when several groups went through to the restaurant for a late meal, and it was then that Maggie noticed Randal chatting up a very pretty girl in a pale T-shirt and skirt. She was gazing up at him and laughing delightedly. He had certainly regained his pulling power now he was reunited with Fiona. He soon brought the girl across from the bar to join them. She must enjoy unequal odds, Maggie mused. She was welcome to them tonight!

'This is Moira,' said Randal above the general conversation. 'She's on her own and passing through, so I've taken pity on her. Comes from your part of the world, Dave, so you may have to translate for us.'

The girl greeted everyone with so broad an accent it was hard to understand her, but she had a lovely figure closely outlined by her clothes and that was all Maggie's companions usually cared about. Space was made for her beside Dave, whose eyes were now slightly glazed. Moira immediately began talking to him in her indecipherable Scots accent, which seemed to put Dave in a near trance-like state as he goggled at her.

After a few minutes the girl looked around the group and caused a hush by putting a finger against her very red lips. It was then possible to hear that the background music which was usually kept fairly middle-of-the-road had changed to bagpipes playing lively tunes. Moira jumped to her feet, cried out something, and began to dance a reel with her arms above her head. The irrepressible Randal joined in, leaping around and copying her movements at least five seconds too late. Moira was not impressed and soon pushed Randal aside before advancing on Dave to pull him upright.

Maggie suddenly realised what was going on and turned to Jeff. 'Did you know about this?'

'I knew Rip had something planned.'

Moira had now produced from beneath Randal's chair a tartan tammy and a sporran. These were put on the hapless Dave who was swaying on his feet, then the girl stripped off her clothes to reveal a bright red tartan cropped top with a micro kilt to match. Dave goggled even more, and his fellows gave him gusty advice as Moira began dancing around her bedazzled victim.

'Come on, Dave, show us a real Highland fling!'

'Waggle that sporran, man!'

'Clear above and behind. Forward five. Tail steady,' called Sandy in laughing crewman's patter.

'Back five and left. Now hold your hover,' advised Jeff, enjoying Dave's futile efforts to dance. He was a big man more suited to sports than the light-footed dancing his countrymen favoured. Other customers were amused. The girl's brief outfit was acceptable enough for the more strait-laced customers present, and Dave was more bewildered than incapable. Maggie guessed Randal must have squared it with Jack and Jean Loosemore, and they had put on the music at his signal. They were behind the bar enjoying the diversion. When the music ended Moira guided Dave back to his seat, sat on his lap and covered him with kisses that left his face scarlet with her lipstick. Several cameras flashed, ensuring Dave had reminders of his last night with B Flight.

Then the mood suddenly changed. The beach hut group approached to make lewd comments, asking the girl if she wore anything under her kilt and they had better check to find out. Several demanded kisses and promised her a big surprise beneath their sporrans if she did. Randal took her through the restaurant so that she could dress again in the ladies' toilet, and they were followed by obscene advice on what they should do in one of the cubicles. Then attention was turned on Maggie, by inviting her to strip to 'a tiddly l'il skirt and not much else' and dance.

Dirk, Jeff and Jimmy stood and advised the group to shut up or go home which, when they studied the size of their opponents, made them draw back muttering coarsely. One of them staggered against a table, spilling drinks in the laps of some elderly Heyhoe regulars who told him to watch what he was doing.

'Silly old farts!' he retaliated.

Jack Loosemore came from behind the bar, anger spots on his cheeks. 'Right, that's it! I warned you earlier this week I wouldn't serve you unless you behaved yourselves. I want you all to leave.'

One turned on him. 'Wha' 'bout that lot, then? They're kickin' up nuff row.'

'They're my regulars having a bit of a celebration by arrangement with the wife and me. They're not shouting insults or spilling drinks over people. Come on, take your-selves off before I call the police in.'

The youth sneered. 'D'you 'ave any in this *dump*?'

Jack was equal to that. 'You'll find out if you and your pals aren't gone from here by the time I count to ten.'

Mouthing further rude comments they shuffled out. Jack made a general apology while his wife mopped up the spilt drinks. Maggie went up to the bar to buy pork pies for herself and Jeff. As she waited Randal came up beside her.

'Hi! More drinks?' he asked hopefully.

'The kart race is all you're winning today . . . and when that bet you all have accrues enough interest to make it worth my while I'll make *myself* pissed out of my skull and claim the money. For now I'm buying pies, not drinks.'

'Great, just what I fancy.'

'I'm sure the Loosemores will sell you one, in that case.'

He wagged his head. 'You have a hard heart, Maggie.'

She moved away from that topic swiftly. 'Moira was an inspiration. That pseudo-Scots accent! Poor Dave didn't know what had hit him. Where'd you find her?'

'Through Chris's grannie. I promised the Loosemores I wouldn't get a stripper, or do anything too outrageous, so they went along with it. She's a budding actress and dancer willing to earn fifty pounds. They gave her a free dinner when she arrived, so I guess she's done quite well out of it.'

'Hardly equivalent to a part in *Zenda*, but better than washing up in a Chinese restaurant or delivering junk mail in the pouring rain, which she's probably done often enough.'

'They all have to start that way.'

'Met a lot of actresses, have you?' she asked dryly.

'I've known a few quite intimately in my time, clever boots.'

Jean arrived to serve them and Maggie asked for two pork pies. 'Make that three,' said Randal. 'This woman beside me won a fortune today through my stupendous skill, so she can afford to treat me to a pie, don't you think?'

Jean laughed. 'If she won't I will. That was a good bit of fun just now. That poor lad had two left feet and couldn't believe his eyes when she began dancing. I'm glad to see the back of those louts, though. I hope they're off home tomorrow. Bill Dowsett said they've caused trouble at the beach huts, too. First time he's had a lot like them down there. This used to be a nice quiet holiday place. Retired couples or well-behaved families. Ah well, three pies coming up.'

As she walked away to the kitchen, Randal asked, 'So where's lover boy tonight?'

'Standing next to me,' Maggie returned crisply. 'Didn't you spend your leave with the irresistible Fiona?'

'Didn't you spend yours with the irresistible Chris?'

She studied him with outward calm masking inner turmoil. 'Are we going to have one of our famous tussles?'

His light brown eyes began to dance. 'Why not? Let's live dangerously.'

Jean put down a plate containing three of her home-made pork pies and Maggie absently paid for them, saying to

Randal, 'I'm amazed the news hasn't been buzzed all round the Station, over the length and breadth of Heyhoe village and even down to the vandalised beach huts by now. Chloe turned up today with a small replica of Chris in a pushchair and put on an act that *would* have got her a part in *Zenda*. He fell for it and followed today's popular trend of returning to an erring wife.'

Randal clearly had not heard the news. 'Good God, after all this time?'

'Isn't two years the going rate for staging reunions?'

He let that pass. 'It's the best thing that could have happened. I warned him to ease up with you.'

'You *what*?' she cried in disbelief.

'I can't have personal relationships affecting my decisions when putting crews together.'

'Damn your decisions! Who the hell do you think you are?'

'The guy who had to call you both in from a nude bathing session when an emergency blew up.' His eyes narrowed speculatively. 'Why'd you do it, Maggie?'

'Do what?'

'Don't be obtuse!'

'Go with Chris? For sex, of course. He's hot stuff.'

It really got to him, she was glad to see. 'That isn't worthy of our famous tussles. And it's a flaming lie.'

The laughter and conversation around them faded as Maggie suddenly sensed something she nevertheless mistrusted because evidence disputed it. To counteract her confusion she goaded him further. 'How d'you know it's a lie? Don't tell me you and Chris once had a gay session.'

'Stop trying to be so bloody clever,' he snapped, now as angry as she. 'I know you better than you think. If you just wanted sex you'd be having it with every Tom, Dick and Harry wherever we went. You chose Chris deliberately to rile me.'

307

'Ha!' she cried disparagingly. 'You conceited bastard!'

'I think you finally recognised why that magic message sent you to the hospital on the day they told me there was a chance I'd walk again. Why've you been fighting it?' His voice grew soft and intimate. 'We're two of a kind, Maggie. I knew it long ago. Isn't it time you surrendered to the inevitable?'

'Oh, for God's sake, not you, too!' she cried. 'I've already had Dave *and* Dirk offering to take over from Chris, but they at least don't have a wife and kids at home.'

'Neither have I, you idiot. My divorce will be finalised in a couple of months. I've gone back to my children, that's all.'

This was terrible. How could she analyse anything said in a crowded pub by a man who had been drinking heavily? The hubbub around her, the smell of food and beer, the piped music and the events of that day combined to make escape imperative before she made a fool of herself.

'You can't have personal relationships affecting you when you choose crews, remember? Chase up some of those actresses you knew. They won't get in the way of your work.'

She was shaking as she headed for the door, seeking peace and darkness. It was cooler outside, but the forecourt of the pub was as brightly lit as the bar. Maggie moved around to the side of the building, but it was a moment or two before she grew aware of a scuffle going on in the dimly lit car park.

Moira was being prevented from getting into her car by three or four of the youths who had been ejected by Jack Loosemore. They were telling her to take her clothes off and dance for them, making lewd comments about her body. The girl was clearly nervous. Each time she tried to head back to the pub they blocked her path. Then one grabbed the hem of her skirt and lifted it high enough to reveal her knickers, bringing guffaws and catcalls.

Maggie's overwrought attitude towards the male sex at present caused her blood to boil. They were bastards, each and every one! Crossing the tarmac she cried, 'Leave her alone!' but she had to repeat it before they heard.

They turned and smirked drunkenly. ''Ere's 'nother,' said a podgy one with carrotty hair. 'P'raps she'll strip orf an' dance.'

'No one's dancing and you've been told to clear off,' Maggie said with an air of practised command. 'Let her get to her car!'

'Oooh, let 'er get to 'er cah,' one mimicked to the amusement of his pals. 'We doan wan 'er to. We wan 'er ter dance.'

Maggie advanced. 'Grow up! You think you're so tough, yet it takes four of you to stop one girl from driving home. Go and pick a fight with an equal number of your uncouth pals if you can't find anything better to do. See how tough you are then.'

One of the group came towards her, which was what she wanted. 'You got too much lip, you 'ave. Need a lesson, doancher?'

As he reached out Maggie stepped forward, seized him and sent him crashing to the ground as she had been doing that afternoon in front of spectators. Knowing he would be too winded to move for a while, she concentrated on the others.

'Anyone else want to teach me a lesson?'

There was a short period of inaction before the three started forward in a concerted attack, but during that time Moira had unlocked her car and got in. When she started the engine with a great roar it took their attention. They turned to be dazzled by her full beam headlights before she drove off. Maggie felt retreat might be her best move now, but she had reckoned without the young actress's anger.

Moira turned at the far end of the car park and drove back

at full speed straight at her former tormentors, lights blazing, horn sounding raucous in the country silence. It did not look as if she was going to stop, so they scattered in panic. Moira had not finished with them. She turned again and repeated the motorised charge. This time they were so scared they rushed from the menace and disappeared down the main street of the village.

Maggie sagged against a four-wheel drive, feeling drained. A very small victory! Moira pulled alongside and wound the window down.

'You were terrific!'

'You even more so,' Maggie replied with a wobbly smile. 'Girl power at its most potent! Gives one a wonderful sense of freedom.'

'I'll say. Thanks.'

'Look, could you give me a lift back to the Station? Just as far as the gate. You pass very close to it on the way to the main road. I was going to call a taxi, but that lot might wait for you along the road.'

'Hop in,' she invited. 'I'll be glad of your company.'

They came up with the four straggling across the lane fifty yards from the bus stop, and both girls derived satisfaction from scattering them again before heading on to the cliff road.

'Have a tiff with your boyfriend?' Moira asked suddenly. 'The dark one sitting beside you.'

'Good lord, no. Jeff's just a friend.'

'So which one?'

'You've got it wrong. I fly with them all,' Maggie murmured, gazing at the faint white line of surf breaking on the beach below.

'You're aircrew too?' asked Moira in surprise. 'How exciting. Is that why you learned self-defence?'

Maggie acknowledged the joke, but said, 'I took up karate at university. I'd grown up with a twin to protect me, but when I got out on my own I thought it would be good to learn how to protect myself.'

'I hate to think what might have happened tonight if you hadn't turned up when you did. I think I should take up judo, or something.'

Maggie gave a faint smile. 'It was your demon driving that did the trick. Where did you learn to corner so fast?'

'In that car park tonight.' She laughed. 'It's amazing what anger can make you do.'

Maggie nodded. 'If you'd entered our kart races this afternoon you could've given the macho boys a run for their money.'

'I wouldn't mind entering *anything* with Rip Price . . . and letting him win. He's gorgeous. But I suppose he's married,' she added with a sigh.

'I wouldn't know,' Maggie replied. 'This'll be fine, Moira. I can walk to the gate from here. Thanks for the lift, and good luck. Hope to see your name in lights one day.'

'Ah, if only!' Moira smiled as Maggie left the car. 'I'm grateful for your help tonight. Good luck to you, too, and I hope whichever one of them upset you so much apologises in the morning.'

Nobody apologised. On Monday, after Maggie had spent the weekend on a Devon farm with an old school friend, Randal behaved as if his words in the pub had never been spoken, Dirk enthused about his speed trials in *Skyhigh*, and Chris was in seventh heaven. Over breakfast he confessed to Maggie that he had been an idiot to force through a divorce before he understood all the ins and outs of what had happened while he was in Bosnia. Malcolm was a fantastic child.

'He's so like me it's unbelievable,' he raved, embarking on bacon, eggs and sausages with gusto. 'We're going to call

311

him Mal from now on. I'm not keen on the full version. Can't think why Chloe chose that name. He's so bright it's hard to accept that he's only eighteen months. He chatters away.' He laughed. 'A lot of it's incomprehensible, of course, but you can get the gist of what he's on about. He's a bit slow in walking, but that's quite usual, you know. They either talk early or walk early, rarely both together. But *crawl*! My God, you've never seen anything move so fast on all fours as Mal. Chloe says she has to have eyes in the back of her head. How she copes with him I've no idea. She's marvellous.'

There was no suggestion of 'Thanks, Maggie, it was fun while it lasted.' He told her of his reunion as if she were just one of the boys. He no longer needed her, and she was expected to accept that. Well, she had also used him. No cause to feel hard done by. Not really.

Dirk had apparently given up after her angry response to his overture and resumed a love affair with a boat instead. Dave had departed and been replaced by Alan Chivers, a sturdy married man with three children. Jeff appeared to have ditched Sable, because he was badgering Randal to give him a contact address for Moira. Nick Lorrimer had got rid of his mother-in-law over the weekend and was bragging about it, and Pete revealed that he and Jill had entered Arnie in a dog show where he would surely walk off with all the prizes. Business as usual, thought Maggie.

She flew with Jeff, Sandy and Alan Chivers to collect crates of spares from Boscombe Down, an easy task that allowed them to have lunch there and chat to old acquaintances. In their world there was someone they knew at almost every station they visited. The crates were loaded and they started back in good weather, anticipating a fine late summer evening and how they would spend it. Alan would go home and play football with his eldest boy; Sandy would drive to the model railway club for the meeting to discuss their next project.

Jeff said to Maggie, 'Fancy a fast run to Lyme? There's a carnival and a flotilla of small ships lit from bow to stern. Marching bands, dancing in the street, fish and chips.'

'Shouldn't that be fish and ships?' she asked in amusement.

'Only if you lisp. So are you on for it?'

'A carnival on *Monday*? You sure you've got all this right? It doesn't sound like something Lyme would stage. In any case, these things are normally on at weekends.'

'I heard this one's on all the week.' He grinned. 'We'll get the best of it. By Saturday the whole thing'll be as limp as . . .'

Maggie heard no more. A surge of apprehension engulfed her, painfully accelerating her heartbeat and constricting her throat. This was a magic message far stronger than any she had had for many months so it was all the more distressing.

'I must get to a phone,' she murmured.

'What? Hey, are you okay?' said a voice in her ear.

'It's bad. It must be.'

'*Maggie!* Are you okay?' demanded the voice.

She stared ahead seeing nothing. 'I have to get to a phone.'

'D'you feel ill? Sandy, get up here.'

Another voice reached her ears. 'What's up, Maggie?'

She turned to see two familiar faces beneath helmets. 'It's Phil. Something's wrong.'

'How d'you know?' demanded Jeff.

The initial fear had subsided enough for her to be rational. 'He's in some kind of trouble. I'm sure of it. Soon as we get in I must ring Fay.'

The two men exchanged glances, then Jeff asked, 'You okay now?'

She nodded. 'I'll be happier when I've spoken to her.

313

Should get to Hampton in fifteen minutes by my calculations.'

Leaving Jeff to handle the basic debrief Maggie headed for the nearest telephone, remembering another time when she had done the same thing. Then, Fay had been going through a dangerous miscarriage, and Phil had been suffering for his wife. Maggie sensed that it was her twin now in some kind of personal danger, and she felt sick with dread when there was no answer to her call to the house. That the answering machine had not been activated added to the suggestion of crisis.

She dialled the number of Phil's office at the boatyard. No reply. She then tried the workshop and was about to hang up in despair when one of the men answered her call.

'This is Maggie Spencer,' she said urgently. 'I'm trying to get hold of Phil.'

There was a momentary silence, then the gruff Hampshire voice said, 'This is Andy, Miss Spencer. There's bin an accident. Not too long ago. P'raps you can hear the coastguard goin' over. They're airlifting Mr Spencer to Southampton Gen'ral. S'all I know, I'm afraid. They'll tell you more if you ring the hospital later. I'm very sorry.'

In a curious way it was a relief to know she had been right, but she hesitated over what to do next. If the accident was so immediate their parents had probably not yet been informed. Andy had gone on to say Phil's neighbour was driving Fay to Southampton while his wife looked after the twins, so no one would have had the chance to inform the family. It was then Maggie realised she had the opportunity to do something others could not.

Jumping in her car she raced across to the Control Tower. Thankfully, Jill was on duty. Maggie approached her, putting aside their squabble over Chloe, and her expression must have told Jill there was a crisis.

'Maggie, whatever's wrong?'

She swiftly explained and begged her friend to bend the rules for her. 'You must be pretty pally with some of the Controllers at Southampton. Can you get one of them to question the coastguard rescue guys heading in from the Solent with an accident case? There's surely only one on that route right at this moment. I need to know about Phil. He's my other half, no matter what.'

'Sure I'll bend the rules, ducky. Won't be the first time. I'll have a go, but can't promise anything.'

Jill had been trained to remain controlled and unflurried throughout even the most critical situations and her coolness now steadied Maggie as she waited for contacts to be made and reported back. It seemed an age before Jill expressed her thanks and swivelled her chair to face Maggie.

'A large powered ocean-going vessel sliced through your brother's boat, ignoring the rule to give way to sail. Phil's pretty badly hurt. They're doing all they can for him up there, but his condition is giving concern. Luckily, there's a vacant bed in Intensive Care and the hospital staff are standing by.' She put her hand on the sleeve of Maggie's flying suit. 'I'm so sorry. You have the rottenest deal from life sometimes.'

Maggie shook her head. 'Not me. It's the people I love who get the rotten deals. I must be a Jonah.'

Twelve

The consultant was surprisingly young; fresh-faced and freckled with round blue eyes, yet with an assurance that belied his student appearance.

'There's no doubt you'd be a good match, Miss Spencer. If you gave one of your kidneys to your brother you would both be able to lead a normal life, but you'd have nothing to fall back on should your single kidney become diseased or cease to function. I understand your wish to help, but it's a decision you should consider very carefully indeed. You're a young woman who will possibly want children one day. There's also your career to consider. I've no idea how the RAF would view a continuation of your status as an operational pilot. Aren't you supposed to keep yourself super fit? I think you should go into all that with your medical advisors.'

'But we're talking about Phil's *life*,' Maggie protested.

'Yes. Dialysis is short-term treatment which places great restrictions on the patient's abilities. Your brother is only twenty-nine and should enjoy years of active life ahead.'

'Which I can give him.'

'His details have been entered on the register of patients awaiting a matching organ. When his condition stabilises we can discuss this further; get his views on it, too. Our immediate concern is to combat trauma.' He gave a sympathetic smile. 'I have a twin brother. It's a rather special relationship, isn't it? There's nothing you can do here for the moment. I suggest you go and get some rest.'

At the boatyard cottage they all drank tea, but the sandwiches Maggie made remained untouched. Her brother Rob, who was a doctor, gave Fay and Mrs Spencer sleeping pills and told them to go to bed. Maggie refused the sedative and stayed downstairs even though it was now four a.m. She needed to discuss the transplant with Rob and her father, but they would not listen.

'It's far too early to make decisions of that nature,' Rob ruled. 'There are all kinds of things to consider when taking organs.'

'You mean they might refuse mine?' she demanded.

'I didn't say that. Maggie, I understand your feelings on this but for God's sake calm down. You've given them an option. Leave it at that.'

Mr Spencer sank back heavily against the seat cushions. 'We'll stay with Fay for as long as she needs us. Mother can help out with the twins, and I'll keep tabs on things at the yard. Good thing Jim Hardiman has a good head on his shoulders. He and young Vanessa in the office will keep things ticking over.'

'Really, Dad, who cares about the bloody business at a time like this?' cried Maggie heatedly.

'Phil will care when he's up and about again.'

'Suppose he never gets up and about again?'

'That's defeatist talk, love.'

'Barring some totally unexpected development, he'll pull through,' said Rob. 'Maggie, when we were all young Chas and I envied the bond you had with Phil. It seemed to shut us out. When we heard that you could communicate your feelings to each other without saying anything, sometimes even when you were apart, we grew almost resentful. Use that gift now. If Phil means so much to you, stop upsetting everyone with your urge to tear out your innards and instead sustain him with your absolute confidence in his survival. You sensed his distress when you were flying. He'll know yours now, on that assumption, which won't help him. The rest of us will give him every encouragement and support once he's lucid, but if what you claim is true you can do it for him now. Even Fay can't help him yet, poor girl.'

Maggie dropped on the settee beside her father, feeling empty and very weary. 'Sorry. Didn't mean to be a prima donna.'

Mr Spencer patted her arm. 'We're all stressed, love, but Rob's right. Wait and see how Phil progresses before making major decisions. We're all willing to give him a kidney if ours would be acceptable to his system, so don't feel you're the only one who can help him. Why don't you go and stretch out on the bed as Rob suggested? You've been flying all day, and then you drove down here. You've had no rest at all. Positive thinking will do more good than getting worked up.'

In the small bedroom beneath the eaves that she always occupied during visits, Maggie lay in the darkness haunted by something she had kept to herself downstairs. Surely some terrible pattern was unfolding, something she was powerless to stop. Despite Rob's words she could not influence Phil's present condition. Their 'magic messages' were quite involuntary. At university they had experimented with the deliberate transfer of thoughts or sensations and had failed each time. She could do no more than the rest of her family to help him now.

It was ten a.m. when she roused and went downstairs. Rob was the only one there. He was eating a fried-egg sandwich and speaking to his wife on the telephone.

'Maggie's just got up, so I'll be on my way in around half an hour. Love you, darling. Bye.'

'You're going already?'

'Have to,' he replied through fried egg. 'Antenatal clinic at four, then evening surgery. Dad's taken Mother and Fay to the hospital. No developments, they just needed to be there. You all right?'

She nodded. 'Where are the twins?'

'Neighbour's taken them. Fay gave them breakfast before she left. They like it next door because there's a litter of puppies. Are you having tea? I could do with a fresh cup before I leave.'

Maggie made herself tea and toast while Rob spent ten minutes on the telephone talking to his receptionist. Then he gulped the tea, paid a visit to the cloakroom and took up his bag and car keys.

'Must go. Mrs Whatsit next door is apparently happy to have the kids all day, but I told her you'd be here until lunch time. No point in too many of you sitting around aimlessly at the hospital. Dad reckoned they'd be back around one, unless anything develops. Have to love you and leave you.' At the door he said more quietly, 'He'll be okay, Maggie. I wouldn't be going if I wasn't certain of that.'

He was no more than fifty yards along the road when Maggie picked up the telephone and got through to Pam Miles at Hampton.

'Maggie!' Her surprise was evident; they were not close friends. 'How's your brother?'

'Still on life support. Pam, I need your advice.'

'Surely the hospital—'

'It concerns me.'

'I see. Is it medical, only I've someone with me at the moment.'

'Of course it's medical. Why else would I contact you at a time like this?'

Maggie heard vague masculine tones in response to Pam's as she held a brief conversation with her hand partially over the mouthpiece. Then she said quietly, 'Go ahead, Maggie. I'll help if I possibly can.'

She swiftly outlined the situation. 'If I do this, will I lose my pilot status?'

'They're surely not pushing you into making such an immediate decision.'

'How would it affect me professionally, Pam,' she insisted.

'I'm afraid I can't advise on that. It would probably be left to a medical board to decide. They might consider transferring you from an operational squadron because of the risk of injury to the remaining organ. Sorry, it's the best I can come up with, but I don't understand why—'

'Thanks, Pam, I'll let you get back to your patient.'

To pass the time Maggie went to see how the twins were faring. They were absorbed in play with three black and white puppies, hardly aware of her arrival. Mrs Blake produced coffee and biscuits that Maggie did not want and her friendly attempts to avoid mentioning Phil were merely irritating. Maggie soon escaped on the excuse of preparing a meal for when her parents and Fay returned. It gave her something to do with her hands, but her mind remained deeply troubled.

She went alone to the hospital that afternoon. Mrs Spencer and Fay thought they should spend some time with the children, and Maggie advised her father to take it easy. He had driven down from York the previous evening and had had little sleep.

'I'll come with you for company,' he said.

'No, Dad, you look worn out.'

'So do you, love. Must you go? He won't know you're there.'

'Rob seems to think I can get through to Phil by some mysterious means even in this situation. Maybe I can.'

It seemed unlikely as Maggie gazed at the face so like her own. Phil was lost in a world she could not enter. The friendly consultant stopped by and talked with her for a while about twinship. He promised to contact the family as soon as Phil regained consciousness.

'The man who caused the accident telephones regularly. He's terribly upset.'

'Give me his number and he'll find out what being upset is really like,' said Maggie.

The man smiled. 'You're quite a firebrand, aren't you.'

'I work and fly with twenty-seven men.'

'All the more reason why you should carry on doing it. Uphold female influence in a man's world.'

'That no longer seems important,' she murmured, gazing at her brother.

'Give it time. It will.'

Mrs Spencer produced cold chicken and salad which was eaten because everyone was now hungry. A unanimous decision was made not to visit the hospital again until next morning, unless they received a call summoning them. Maggie was unable to settle and went for a walk. The scent of approaching autumn was in the air and its suggestion of something coming to an end increased the depth of Maggie's sadness. Did nothing good ever go on for ever?

She stood on the little jetty where Phil's own boat was normally tied up and recalled sitting in it with him two and a half years ago, drinking wine and watching the sun go down as he told her Mark's tragic death had given Fay the courage to chance another pregnancy and create new life. One of their twins was named Mark, as they had promised. Suddenly, the sunset became blurred. She was unsure who her tears were for. Maybe for anyone who had ever lost a loved one.

'Hi! They told me you might be on the dock.'

Maggie swung round in disbelief. Randal looked relaxed in grey trousers and a casual sweater. 'What are you doing here?'

'I skipped through my paperwork this afternoon and left early. Thought you might like to talk things through with someone.' He came alongside her and leaned on the rail.

'Nothing as dramatic as a magic message; just happened to be having my quarterly check-up when you rang Pam Miles.'

'She told *you* what I asked her?'

'I have ways of persuading women to tell me what I want to know. You've experienced them.'

'There was no need for you to come.'

'There was no need for you to come when I was in trouble, but you did. Must be a reason why we both do these things.'

She turned away. 'Shall we walk?'

'Sure.' He fell in beside her as they crossed the planked walkway and stepped down to the pebbled shore. 'It's nice here. Tucked away; no twee gift shops, cream teas or minigolf. The perfect place for making custom-built craft, I imagine. Don't know a thing about it but I guess it's a dying art.'

'Not altogether, although demand is dwindling as costs rise. You could afford one, but the average small boat sailor buys mass-produced models.'

'Like Dirk owns?'

'No, he's into power, not sail. An altogether different sport. If he drives a boat the way he drives a car I wonder *he* hasn't chopped someone in halves before now.'

It was almost dark, the tideline no more than a silver gleam in the sunset's afterglow, and Maggie grew calmer in Randal's familiar company. Their shoes crunched the shingle as they strolled, the only other sound being that of an occasional car driving through the village.

'How is Phil?'

Maggie glanced up at him. 'Like you were at the start, I guess, except that he's not paralysed, thank God.'

'But his kidneys have had it?'

'Yep. He'll need a transplant.'

They walked on towards the dark bulk of a yacht under construction on ramps. After a moment or two Randal said, 'D'you recall your first task on joining B Flight? We delivered medical supplies to eight people on dialysis whose homes were cut off by drifts after a couple of days of blizzard conditions. The last of them was young Fiona Hunter, who was then only five years old.'

Maggie stopped. 'Is this leading somewhere?'

He faced her. 'You know damn well it is. Those people had been waiting quite a while for a transplant and were surviving okay. You don't have to make impetuous and emotional decisions over Phil. He wouldn't want that.'

'Oh yes? And how the hell would *you* know what he wants?'

'Because I met and talked with him when Mark was killed. He turned up out of the blue and made nonsense of my cynicism over the bond you two have.'

'You never accepted my word on the subject.'

He grinned. 'I thought it was just emotional feminine nonsense.'

'Bastard!'

'Maybe, but I'd never come across any pilot who claimed to get magic messages . . . and you girls do like to make big issues out of nothing.'

She was furious. 'This isn't nothing, it's life or death.'

'I know, Maggie; I've been there.'

His sudden quiet intensity silenced her, so when he put his hand beneath her elbow she let him guide her to a groyne where they sat in the fast-fading dusk.

'I'm going to tell you something you probably won't like, but you're going to hear it anyway. When Phil came to Hampton sensing that you were in some kind of trouble, I was astonished that he knew nothing about your relationship with Mark. He confessed that there'd been tension between you after Fay's miscarriage. He clearly needed to offload on someone and I happened to be on hand, so I heard how he was striving to be to you and to his wife what each of you wanted

323

him to be, and failing dismally. He was an unhappy man, Maggie. He said something along the lines of if the "other woman in his life" was a cute bimbo he'd deserve grief from both directions. I felt sorry for the guy.'

He was right. Maggie did not like hearing this and she responded with fire. 'And you're blaming me? Did he happen to tell you Fay made him sleep in the spare room after the miscarriage? How could I be responsible for that?'

'I didn't say you were, chum.'

'So what are you saying?'

'That being sandwiched between two loving women is no fun.'

Maggie got to her feet, angry and hurt. 'If you drove all the way from Hampton to say that, you're well out of date. Did your year out of squadron circulation make you forget that Mark's death brought reconciliation all round? Fay and I understand each other and are good friends after sorting things out with regard to Phil.'

He stood up beside her. 'Exactly. She now accepts the twin thing and you now accept that she's his wife. His *next of kin*. That's why you have to ease up on this kidney business. I spoke to your father just now and he says a transplant is something for the future, for when Phil's system is ready for it. Until then it's being activated by machines, as mine was. In my case nobody was particularly concerned, as you often remind me. But if Fiona had been a wife like Fay is, she would have been as distraught as that poor woman is now. And she would have been further distressed if I'd had a twin sister hovering around vowing to sacrifice part of her body because only that would save me. You're diminishing Fay's status by suggesting *you* are his only hope of survival.'

'Because *I'm* responsible for what's happened to him.'

'*What?*'

Words she had been unable to say to her family now spilled from her heedlessly. 'Griff was right. I do bring disaster, especially to people I care for. I loved Mark and he was killed quite horrifically. You came dangerously near to death or permanent disability; now Phil may lose the fight for life.'

In the darkness she heard his sharp intake of breath. 'That's sodding nonsense and you know it! Mark's Harrier had a faulty electrical circuit, I ended up in Intensive Care because four delinquent kids dropped an anchor when they did, and Phil's there now through some guy in a fast boat not sticking to the rules. Only a prize bloody idiot would shoulder the blame for it all.'

'Nobody asked you to come here and give your opinion,' she snapped.

'I give it without being asked, you know that well enough,' he snapped back. 'And here's some more of it. Rob's returned to his busy practice, your brother Charles hasn't flown home from a legal conference in Brussels. They accept that Phil's wife and parents are on hand for when he regains consciousness, and they are the people most closely concerned in this. I think you should come back to Hampton and leave them to cope with it. I'll ensure you're not sent out of the country until his condition improves. Then, if you are called upon to give a kidney, I'll do what I can to sort things professionally for you. What've you to say to that?'

'Get stuffed!' She walked away feeling utterly confused and uncertain. He was right about Rob and Charles: Phil was also their brother. Was he right about everything else? Did Fay resent her being there?

Heavy footsteps on the shingle made her walk faster, but he nevertheless came alongside and halted her. It was too dark to see more of his expression than the glint in his eyes.

'Here's something else I do without being asked. I probably should have done it long ago.'

It was experienced and exciting, confusing Maggie further with the swift transition from colleague to lover, but when

Randal drew back from the embrace he said in the provocative way she knew well, 'You mentioned me in connection with people you care about. What was I to think?'

'You always think what you damn well please,' she responded, but the fight had gone out of her.

He took her hand. 'Let's have a drink in ye olde village pub and talk this through sensibly.'

The Longboat was comfortable and no way trendy, without muzak, just a decor of looped ropes along plain walls. The menu chalked on a small board comprised simple fish and chips, grilled plaice and veg or the seafood equivalent of a ploughman's. There were no concessions for vegetarians or gourmets. In this pub you ate what they had or went hungry.

Maggie knew owners Colin and Mary well, so she was questioned about Phil when they entered. Several locals joined in with eye-witness accounts of the accident and speculated with some relish on being asked to give evidence at the inquiry.

'Young Phil can sue that American for all he's got. They do that over there, you know. Sue everybody for anything,' said Colin. 'Get millions of dollars for nothing more than a broken arm or leg they do, so poor Phil's terrible injuries ought—'

'I'll have the fish and chips,' said Randal, firmly putting an end to the subject. 'I'll also have a pint, with a G and T for Maggie. We'll be at that table in the corner where it's more private.'

The landlord gave him a straight look before concentrating on Maggie. 'Aren't you eating?'

'I had something earlier.'

'The food'll be about twenty minutes,' he told Randal as he put the drinks on the counter. 'It's fresh and cooked to order. None of your frozen rubbish here.'

Maggie could not repress a faint smile. 'You said that to

the wrong person, Colin. This man's father *owns* Price's Frozen Foods.'

She walked to the corner table leaving their host nonplussed, and said to Randal as he settled on the other half of the right-angled seat, 'That'll give him something to gossip about.'

'Until he decides you made it up. *Prosit!*' He held up his glass in the salute he had retained from the Squadron's days in Germany. After quenching his thirst he gave her the frank look that always heralded plain speaking. 'You smiled just now. Was it due to what I did out there on the shore, or because you've reverted to the spunky, level-headed girl I know?'

'What conceit! One clinch and you think you've scored.'

'I'm speaking from years of experience. So which is it?'

The ball was in her court. 'Maybe you've got a point.'

'About what?'

She sighed. 'You're a provocative bastard, you know.'

'Mmm, so I've been told. About what, Maggie?'

'I suppose it is just coincidence that terrible things have happened to people I'm fond of.' She played with her glass, trying to place it exactly central on the circular beer mat bearing a picture of an ornate longboat. 'But I'll be afraid to love anyone in the future.'

'Bollocks!' She glanced up sharply, but he continued before she could speak. 'On that assumption I'd never drive beneath a motorway bridge again. And how d'you imagine Dirk has managed to take a Chinook into the air time and again after that crash? I'll lay you odds here and now that Phil will be back in a boat at his first opportunity.'

She concentrated on the beer mat, but Randal kept at it. 'Tell me honestly, in his place wouldn't you do the same?' When she nodded, he added, 'I'd call you a liar if you'd said anything else. You're a fighter, Maggie Spencer, so this display of defeatism is totally out of character.'

She was driven to challenge him on that. 'My God, you're a fine one to talk! Who told me – told everyone in earshot – that he'd take an overdose if he could reach the drugs trolley? Or jump from the ward window if he could only get to it.'

It was his turn to study the beer mats. He did so for some moments and when he spoke it was in reflective manner. 'One day I drove around a corner and came upon a beautiful girl beside a car with a flat tyre. I couldn't believe my luck. I'm no better than the next guy when faced with the sexiest thing on two long legs he's ever seen, but I married her because I truly believed we could have something good together. For a few years it really was good. Then came Neil and Lydia, two gorgeous kids. When it began to go wrong I couldn't accept it. *Wouldn't* accept it. I made concessions, didn't I? Biggest mistake I could have made.'

When he glanced up Maggie was struck by the sadness in his eyes. 'During that exercise in Poland I grappled with the problem of what to do next. I was driving home to tell her my obsession was over, but I'd stay with her for the sake of our children. As you know, I never got there. When I emerged from coma and found what I'd become I decided Neil and Lydia would be better off if I kept out of their lives. I knew she'd run and keep on running if I painted an impossibly bleak picture of her future with a paraplegic. She ran.'

He appeared to be mentally back in that time, his surroundings forgotten. 'So wife and kids were erased during a five-minute hospital visit. My career had been erased when that anchor hit the bonnet, wham! Everything I loved gone because of four anonymous boys. You'll never know how much I yearned to sleep and never wake again. Lying immobile unable to end my misery only accentuated it.'

He focussed on her again with a deprecatory smile. 'I'm pretty certain I wouldn't have put an end to myself if I'd had the opportunity, but I simply couldn't see a reason for going on. Unlike Phil I didn't have a large loving family to encourage and help me. I had no one . . . until a bossy blonde arrived and told me to stop feeling so bloody sorry for myself. Don't you think I'm entitled to say the same thing to her now?'

Maggie felt as bruised as if he had struck her. His quiet words had revived visions of a strong vital man who had become a gaunt prisoner in a wheelchair, sobbing in her arms because the sight of her had reminded him of the life he had lost.

'Sorry,' she murmured. 'I deserve to be cut down to size.'

His hand closed over hers. 'I wasn't trying to do that. In my usual clumsy way I was getting around to telling you that that searing experience showed me my true feelings for the bossy blonde who gave as good as she got. They haven't changed, and I think you're now ready to admit you feel the same way about me.'

She was unprepared for this. It was the wrong moment. Yet even as she had the thought she knew it was nonsense. He was telling her exactly what she had wanted to hear for a long time. There was something else she had long wanted to know, also.

'So how d'you explain the fact that you cut off all contact with me as soon as you got back on your feet?'

He was typically unabashed. 'That's another story I'll tell you one day when we're in a more intimate place than the bar of a nautical pub. I handled the situation badly. I thought we settled that at the Bird one evening way back.'

'We settled nothing. You simply slithered out of giving an answer, as you often do.'

'Isn't that exactly what you're doing now?'

Maggie's attention was drawn away by awareness of someone swiftly approaching their table. When she saw it was her father a wave of apprehension hit her. She stood, realising she had momentarily forgotten about Phil.

'What is it, Dad?'

Mr Spencer's smile still held a hint of the strain he had been under. 'Thought I might find you here. They've just phoned to say Phil's come round. We're leaving right away. Mrs Blake's offered to babysit so we can all go. It's great news, isn't it?'

'Wonderful,' she agreed thickly, clutching at her father's hand. Then she turned to Randal who had also got to his feet. 'I must go.'

'Of course you must . . . but the fish and chips won't taste half as good eating them on my own.'

Part of her longed to stay. She said softly, 'Thanks for coming.'

'All part of a boss's duties.'

On impulse she gave him a swift kiss. 'I'll drive back to Hampton tomorrow.'

'Is that a promise?' he asked as she followed her father.

'Buy you a beer if I break it,' she said over her shoulder, before going out into the night sensing that all would be well.

The wake-up call came at what appeared to Randal to be an ungodly hour in a room he did not recognise. The same applied to the naked girl beside him: very young, blonde and attractive despite an excess of make-up. His head throbbed, his eyes ached. He must have had a wow of a night before! Groping his way to the bathroom he turned on the shower, taking note of the array of toiletries usual in hotel rooms. Clear thought returned. He was in Bournemouth and had to reach Hampton by breakfast time!

Wrapping a towel around his dripping body he filled and switched on the kettle in the bedroom, then returned to grapple with the tiny plastic razor and minute tube of shaving foam provided for male guests gormless enough to forget to pack their shaver. A quick return, heavily lathered, to make black coffee, then Randal began a determined onslaught on his dark stubble. The lather turned pink, then red. The air turned blue. With scraps of toilet paper stuck on his chin and throat he made another cup of coffee that scalded his tongue. Muttering further expletives he gathered his socks and underpants from the floor and put them on. They smelled faintly of smoke, but he had no others until he reached his room in the Mess. His shirt collar was badly crumpled, his trousers had horizontal as well as vertical creases; they and his sweater reeked even more strongly of cigarette smoke.

While downing a third cup of coffee he scooped his loose change and car keys from the dressing table, his hand momentarily stilling at the sight of silver fish earrings and necklace. A black lace bra and matching thong lay on the floor beside a shimmering black dress. High-heeled sandals had been abandoned several paces apart. The owner of them was still dead to the world. Quickly stifling an impulse to scribble a message of some kind on the crested notepaper – she would not remember who she had slept with, anyway – Randal departed into dark and deserted corridors leading to a dim vestibule where a pimply youth wearing a green apron over the hotel uniform was vacuuming the floor. He regarded with suspicion a casually dressed man without luggage and with bloody paper stuck on his face, who was sneaking out at five a.m.

Randal spent a frustrating five minutes trying to locate his Porsche in the crowded car park, dreading that he might be impossibly hemmed in. When he found it he discovered that some mindless moron had adorned the bonnet with a voluptuous pair of female breats drawn with a spray can of black paint. An explosion of blasphemy failed to ease his anger, and he rocketed from the town along the road to Dorchester loudly questioning the sanity of those who felt compelled to deface everything they came across.

331

Next minute, he was questioning his own decision to stay in Bournemouth for the night.

After Maggie had gone off with her family to visit Phil there had been no reason to stay. Yet his room in the Mess had been no more attractive a prospect than a New Forest village filled with strangers. Restless because, on the point of finally getting things straight with her, Maggie had been whisked off, the lights of Bournemouth had lured. He had intended just to stop for a drink and a little socialising, but a fascinating array of hot-air balloons was in the floral gardens for some kind of festival and he had wandered there caught up in the friendly atmosphere, until he recalled Maggie suggesting that as a paraplegic he could take up ballooning as the nearest thing to flying. He had responded bitterly that he could do a comic turn at village fêtes, dressed as a clown and parachuting down to a wheelchair. He had been cruel to her so many times, and she clearly had not forgiven him for dropping out of her life last Christmas, offering no explanation. He believed no man would care to confess he was of no use as a lover, particularly when he was not even sure the girl wanted him to be. On that point he decided Maggie still had not convinced him.

By then it was so late the best plan had been to stay overnight. He booked in and paid the bill, requesting an early morning call. Then he had wandered to the bar to drown his frustration, knowing he would not be driving that night. He had somehow become involved with a large noisy group of pharmaceutical reps staying at the hotel for a two-day conference, and he entered a discussion on aphrodisiacs with a raunchy blonde already on over-familiar terms with her male colleagues. She gave out unmistakable signals and Randal was in a receptive mood. She was determined to be in some man's bed that night, so why not his? It would be a good opportunity to discover if he could operate satisfactorily with women other than his soon-to-be ex-wife. Essential if he was to wear down Maggie's lingering resistance. Recalling the blonde's squeals and moans he reckoned he had the answer.

His mind dwelt on that satisfying subject while his eyes watched the bends in the road coming up fast as he covered the miles. It was some moments before he grew aware of a siren and blue flashing lights behind him. Where had they come from, and at this hour? He glanced at the dashboard clock and his heart sank. The roads were pretty well empty in this rural district so they were certain to make a meal of catching a lone driver in an expensive speeding car. Oh, *hell*!

One was a girl; both were pink-cheeked and immaculate. Straight from training college? They made him get out and use the breathaliser. They studied his dishevelled clothes, the cuts on his face and the crude paint job on the bonnet. Unmistakable signs of a villain! They gave him a horrendous estimate of his speed, then asked what he had to say to them. On the verge of giving an unexpurgated version he thought better of it and told a whopping lie instead. Showing his service identification he said he had been recalled from leave due to an international emergency. No, he could not divulge the details. They were top secret. All he could say was that it involved the SAS and several world leaders for whom the risk to their safety grew with every passing hour. If they watched the TV news during the next few days they would learn about it.

They let him go, but drove ahead of him with flashing lights at a speed that had him gnashing his teeth until they reached the extent of their beat. When they veered off Randal gave a friendly wave, but it was as well they did not hear what he said under his breath.

It was fully light when he walked into the Mess planning to dress swiftly then grab some breakfast, but luck was still against him. The first person he saw was Perry Newman, who lived in Heyhoe but had breakfast on-station if he came in early.

'I've been looking for you. There's an emergency brief in thirty minutes.'

Before he could stop himself, Randal said, 'Nothing to do with the SAS and several world leaders, is it?'

The Squadron Commander was not amused as he took in Randal's appearance. 'You look as if you spent a night on the tiles.'

He headed for the stairs. 'I did.'

'Someone said you'd chased to Hampshire to see that woman.'

Randal swung round. 'She has a name. Why not use it?'

'What's the latest bulletin?'

'The twin brother has emerged from coma. Maggie's coming back today. I need to talk to you about the ongoing situation where she's concerned.'

'No time for that. You're taking two crews to west Africa tomorrow to join the UN relief effort. The crisis is deepening to catastrophe. We're contributing a couple of Sea Kings as well, and the Army is sending three aircraft.'

Randal frowned. 'We're committed to a night exercise next week.'

'It's been postponed. The PM wants a strong British presence out there.'

'He always does! Pity he doesn't take that into account when making his drastic defence cuts.'

Newman nodded. 'That's something I *do* agree with you on. List of who you'll be taking with you is on your desk. As you were nowhere to be found during the latter half of yesterday I assessed who would be most available and alerted them. You'll have to switch a few guys around to compensate.' He glanced at his watch. 'Briefing in *twenty-five* minutes.'

The Base had been established two miles north of a township

in an area cleared several years before for development by foreign investors, who later abandoned the project. UN engineers had created a makeshift landing pad around which a tented village housed the military of several nations. A swollen brown river bordered one side. On the other three was tropical forest. An uninviting place for an eight-week stay at the best of times, for the members of 646 Squadron it happened to be one of the worst.

Chris had been reunited with Chloe. He longed to cement the new relationship and get to know his son. Frustration made him moody and intolerant. Dirk was annoyed at having to cancel *Skyhigh*'s entry in an important race, thereby forfeiting the hefty fee. He went on and on about his plans for a fresh start being thwarted before they even got off the ground. Sandy was already missing his close friend Dave, and Jimmy was worried because his wife was overdue and might be pregnant yet again.

'She takes the bloody pill, but it seems I only have to look at her and there's another kid on the way. When I get back I'm having a vasectomy,' he vowed.

Nick Lorrimer was certain his mother-in-law would move back in during his absence and was constantly ringing his wife to check. Brad, who had replaced Griff, bemoaned the duty that caused him to miss the European cup matches. His fellow sergeant, Ray, was the only one of them who managed to remain calm and that was because he had taken a dozen lurid thrillers of the kind he enjoyed, and lost himself in them.

Heading this disgruntled team was a man no happier than the rest. He was eager to know Phil's progress and the transplant situation. He had telephoned several times but had been unable to catch Maggie at Hampton. He could not rid his mind of her distressed certainty that she was the kiss of death to anyone she cared for. It had revived memories of arriving at a show ground where she had watched Mark burn to death, and finding a girl in the depths of shock. She had come to him when he had been in much the same state and helped him through.

During the long, oppressive nights in this godforsaken country he lay haunted by something which apparently still hurt her badly. He had severed contact with her once he was back on his feet because it had seemed to him the best way to stop what he sensed was inevitable from happening. Now it had and he guessed it was his pride more than consideration for her that had governed his decision; avoidance of any situation that might reveal his impotency. Surely most men would duck out of that one!

Maggie had been through so much, surviving where many girls would have gone under, because she had courage as well as compassion, but she deserved loving support right now. As it was, there had been no time to settle things between them. He knew she had returned, as promised, because her car had been outside the Mess when he flew out early in the morning. He had pushed a note beneath her door telling her he had written a memo to Perry Newman concerning her need to stay in Britain until a decision on her brother was made, and he apologised for being personally unable to support her on the issue. The nearest to words of love had been his closing comment that he would be thinking of her. He was. All the time.

There were also professional problems. Dirk and Brad had had adverse reactions to the injections given by Pam Miles before they left, so rest periods for the others had been cut to a minimum while they spent three days in sick bay. Mosquitoes were never absent, making for disturbed sleep along with the humidity, and snakes as well as mammoth spiders and other poisonous insects frequently invaded the aircraft. Ground crews suffered more because they lacked the opportunity to take to the air and escape for a while.

The flights were no picnic, however. The terrain was

mostly flat and densely forested, which offered few identi-
fiable landmarks. Clearings in which sat townships, villages
or meaner settlements were little more than liquid mud where
flood water slowly receded. In common with many parts
of the world abnormal weather conditions had prevailed.
A population already on the brink of starvation through
drought then suffered the loss of their remaining animals
and primitive shelters when torrential rains caused rivers
to swell and overflow. On areas of slightly higher ground
small groups had survived on supplies ferried to them in
cockleshell boats by the local militia or any good Samaritans.
The gravely sick and dying were taken back to one of the
medical mission posts set up by foreign agencies. The waters
left havoc and pestilence in their wake. The eternal story
of Africa!

For more than three weeks B Flight's two crews had been
transporting staple foods and medical stores to distribution
points within a wide radius. They were used to distress and
suffering in war or disaster zones, but the debilitating heat,
the abject poverty and the apathy of people who could expect
nothing better from life made this duty more than usually
depressing.

In the early afternoon of their fourth Saturday Randal took
the second flight of the day with Chris, Jimmy and Sandy.
They were all quiet, lost in individual wishful thinking and
planning evening phone calls to the country where they
longed to be. Then, two thirds of the way to their drop point,
Chris suddenly swore.

'Bloody hell, we've had it! Sodding oil pressure's lost.'

Randal glanced swiftly at the warning panel where a
light now indicated something helicopter crews dreaded.
Trouble with any gearbox was dangerous; blockage of the
oil flow required an immediate landing. Even when over
enemy territory they had no choice but to get out of the
air fast.

337

'Christ, we'll never make the village,' Randal said explosively. 'The only place we can set down is on the track leading to it.'

'It's too narrow,' Chris protested.

'It's all we've got, chum. Get on to Base with our position and tell 'em to send someone out pronto. We can't wait here while they have their tea first. And advise them to send out something smaller or it'll never land.'

'But we can?' demanded Chris hotly.

'Got any better ideas?' he countered. Then he spoke to the crewmen. 'This is going to take some fancy footwork. Get us down in one piece, guys. It's all up to you.'

Randal first concentrated on aligning the Chinook with a rough muddy track cutting through the trees – the road to the distribution centre. Luckily, Western engineers had cut a reasonably straight swathe through the forest, but they had never envisaged sixty feet of whirling rotors dropping between the trees. It would be a risky business, but not to do it would bring certain disaster.

In an atmosphere of gathering tension Randal began to lose height, trusting his own wide experience and the judgement of the two sergeants to bring it off successfully. Slowly, slowly they descended, Randal keyed up ready to climb if Sandy or Jimmy yelled 'UP UP UP!' Conscious that the cockpit was now at tree level, his nerves tightened further as he responded to tense calls from the crewmen hanging from the sides of the aircraft. The treetops were above the cockpit now, swaying madly in the rotor downwash. Still no call to climb! Then Jimmy's calm 'Clear below to land.' The wheels touched down on yellowish mud churned up by trucks passing back and forth during the emergency. The two officers in the cockpit went through the shutdown procedure, then sank back in their seats with undisguised relief.

Chris turned a pale face towards Randal. 'Don't ever do that again when I'm on board.'

Randal gave a shaky grin. 'Piece of cake!' He spoke to the crewmen who must also be weak at the knees. 'Best guys in the Flight! Thanks from both me and my guts.'

'You haven't seen the state our guts are in,' said Jimmy in an unsteady voice.

Randal wiped sweat from his face with the back of his hand as he asked Chris, 'Are they on to it?'

He nodded. 'Usual thing. Someone'll be out to us as soon as an aircraft is available.'

'It'll be dark in a few hours, for Christ's sake! What do they think we're going to do while they fool around finding a volunteer?' He climbed from his seat and pushed through to the cabin. 'This is our reward for aiding suffering humanity. Either of you bring a pack of cards . . . or several willing women? Only things to do in a balls-up like this.'

Chris came alongside, scowling. 'Didn't they check this beast out before we left?'

No one bothered to answer. The heat was even more oppressive amid the trees, and mosquitoes swarmed in seeking blood. Crews always carried emergency packs and plenty of fresh drinking water, but tropical forest was inhospitable even to people of the country. To white men from a temperate island it could prove deadly. They did not relish being stranded there for long.

They took off their life jackets and blue UN helmets to cool down as much as possible, then settled on the crates and boxes resigned to a considerable wait. They pooled the contents of their pockets: crisps, muesli bars, biscuits and peanuts and drank liberally from the water containers, all the time silently cursing their luck.

After twenty endless minutes they heard engine noises approaching, but no accompanying thwack of rotors. Randal got to his feet. 'Sounds like a truck. Hope they know another way through, because they ain't going nowhere along this one until we move out.'

He leaned from the door to glance back along the track. A truck was coming towards them. It bore the painted board they all carried when picking up loads from the centre. They all looked so broken down it was amazing they kept going, and this one was no exception. In the back were four men wearing serviceable khaki shorts and shirts. There were two more in the driver's cab. None of them looked surprised by the huge, unbelievable obstruction to their progress, but they were people usually not averse to any excuse to cease work. The vehicle stopped and the man beside the driver got out to slosh his way towards the Chinook, a broad grin on his face.

'You jest takin' a rest?' he asked in amusement.

Randal nodded. 'Looks like it. Can you get to the centre some other way?'

The man was tall and rangy, quite young but full of easy assurance. 'There's plenty other ways. We give you a lift to the village.'

'Thanks, but we have to stay with the aircraft.'

Another of the men had wandered up. 'What wrong?'

'A small problem. Someone's on the way to put it right for us.'

The first one said, 'No man wants to wait here. Too hot. Better we take you to the village. How many you are?'

He put his muddy boot on the step as if to look inside the cabin, but he instead grabbed Randal's left arm and jerked hard. Unprepared, Randal lost his balance and twisted round, whereupon the second man seized his right arm and the pair flung him face down into the mud. With thought suspended, he automatically rolled over and started to sit up wiping the mud from his face. Through the grime he saw Chris and the two crewmen staring in disbelief into the barrels of several rifles.

Randal struggled to his feet. 'What the hell . . . ?'

Something crashed against the side of his head and he dropped into darkness.

Thirteen

Maggie went to the New Forest for the weekend. Charles and her sister-in-law came for the day on Saturday. Judith kept an eye on the twins while the others went to the hospital. Maggie looked after them while Fay saw Phil on Sunday afternoon, but she had declined Fay's offer of an evening meal and was on her way back to Hampton. She had used the stormy weather as an excuse to leave early but, in truth, she had been peculiarly apprehensive the entire time and it was not fear for her brother.

Phil was no longer on life support, apart from regular dialysis, and he was responding well to treatment. His tough physique had enabled him to recover more fully than had been initially feared. His name was on the transplant list with others able to wait for a matching organ. Maggie had mentioned her willingness to donate one of her kidneys when she and Phil had been alone, but he protested so strongly she had dropped the subject. Even so, she reiterated her offer to the consultant. He had replied soothingly that she would be called on if all else failed. She was presently in an emotional limbo where her twin was concerned.

The crisis had turned into a slow, wearying recuperation no longer requiring constant family support. Mr and Mrs Spencer had returned to York after spending a week with Fay, who confessed to Maggie that it was a huge relief to be on her own. Mrs Spencer was a highly emotional woman kept from excesses by her level-headed husband. Occasional overnight visits by her in-laws were bearable, Fay added, but a wife preferred to deal with something like this on her own once the shock had worn off. Maggie took heed, acknowledging that Randal had probably been right to warn her off.

Their brief meeting in the Longboat had left her more uncertain and restless than ever. His absence did not help. The curse of squadron life was that they could be sent anywhere at the worst possible time in a personal relationship. She had been given leave to visit Phil for as long as the emergency lasted; Randal had been granted the same when Lydia was abducted. The Air Force was very understanding in crisis situations, but it was difficult to request time together simply to settle their love life – or to discover if they even had one.

Perry Newman had made snide references to her Flight Commander's commendable concern for her welfare, which he hoped was extended to everyone in B Flight.

'It really wasn't necessary for him to write me a memo on the subject, Maggie. I wasn't given command of a squadron without having proved I was equal to the job. I'm well aware of the facts in this unique case and, although you women loudly proclaim that you don't wish to be treated differently from the men, I was prepared to excuse you from the more demanding tasks to allow for your unusually close relationship with a brother.'

Maggie had responded swiftly. 'I'm perfectly able to take on any task. I'd merely prefer to stay in this country for a while, not only because it would cost more to fly me home if I should be called to the hospital, it would also be quicker. My brother's life might depend on a swift operation.'

Newman had studied her with the disparaging look she had seen in other men's eyes. 'Good thing we're not at war. No time for emotion when it's each man for himself.'

She rose to that unexpressed sneer. 'You've been in a war, have you, sir?'

It hit the target and ended the interview. 'I'll do what I can, but if your family situation continues beyond a reasonable time I shall have to put the demands of the Squadron first.'

'Of course. I appreciate your help.'

Since then Maggie had been given all the boring tasks and had spent a great deal of time on the ground in the simulator, and taking refresher classes in navigation, escape and evasion, and emergency first aid. This had left her with too much time to think, and with two crews in Africa, another two in Bosnia, and the rest, apart from Jeff, married and living off-station, she had been dependent on Pam Miles and Lisa Compton, the 'blonde bombshell of Personnel', as the men named her, for company. Jeff was in hot pursuit of Moira, whose address he had got by brazenly telephoning Evelyn Montrose, so Maggie saw little of him when they were off-duty.

Even allowing for the lack of real professional challenge, and for the rowdy 'boys only' bachelors of A Flight who presently formed the majority of aircrew in the Mess, the root cause of Maggie's restlessness was Randal. Eight weeks had never seemed so long, and only half of them had passed so far. It therefore made nonsense of her sudden urge to return to Hampton early on that Sunday. As she drove through Heyhoe in a heavy downpour, sending water high as the wheels hit puddles, she wondered why she felt anxious to arrive. Had Randal been called home? The notion did little to dispel her gloom, for only another family emergency could be behind it and he had had enough of those already.

The moment Maggie entered the Mess after running through the rain from the car park, she was aware of a buzz of activity unusual for a Sunday evening. The bar looked surprisingly busy; conversation sounded crisply urgent. Unable to go in in her drenched state she went upstairs, her uneasiness deepening. Something was afoot. A military emergency? It could happen at any time anywhere in today's unstable world. Another Kosovo? A fresh Gulf war? A resurgence of violence in Northern Ireland?

Jeff was standing outside his room in deep conversation with a pilot of A Flight. They broke off when Maggie approached. She knew by their expressions that something really awful had happened.

She dropped her overnight bag. 'What's up, Jeff?'

The other man drifted away, and Jeff opened his door. 'Come in here for a moment.'

She walked in feeling coldness sweeping through her as she turned to her trusted friend. 'He's crashed, hasn't he?'

Jeff's normally mobile face was pale and tense. 'There was a problem – gearbox! They managed a dicey landing in the middle of rainforest, and radioed their position. A Puma was sent out to them twenty minutes after receiving their mayday.' He pursed his lips. 'They'd disappeared, along with cartons of medical supplies they were transporting. Their helmets and three life jackets were in the aircraft. Their emergency packs and water supply were also there. Tyre tracks in the mud and a confusion of footprints by the front door suggests that they were surprised and abducted.' He sighed with suppressed anger. 'So far there's no indication of who took them, or why. It's not a recognised war zone. No known rebel guerrillas are operating there. The government's as stable as any African one can ever be. One of them must have grabbed a life jacket with the personal locator, because its signal indicated their position was in a small settlement. Some army guys investigated, with no luck. We don't know where they are now.'

Forcing the words through her lips, Maggie asked, 'Who, Jeff?'

'Chris, Sandy, Jimmy . . . and Rip. Their wives have had

to be informed, and Sandy's parents. Jill has rung Chloe.'
He put his hand on her arm. 'They'll be okay, Maggie.
Whoever's behind it wanted them as hostages, or they'd
have been killed on the spot. Sooner or later there'll be
a ransom demand. Efforts to locate them are continuing,
of course, and a crew from A Flight is going out there
tomorrow.' He gave a strained smile. 'Our Special Forces
will already be on this, you bet. They'll get them back all
in one piece.'

She turned and fled. In her own room she leaned back
against the door and began to shake. Had it been the kiss
of death she gave him when they parted in the Longboat?

The Royal Engineers captain faced Dirk frankly. 'Four days
and still no bloody clue! You've flown over it so you know
what it's like out there. Most of my men have had jungle
training, but I haven't enough of them for the job. It'd take
weeks to comb the whole area. In any case, whoever took
out your crew would move around while we searched.'
His youthful, sunburned face was troubled. 'I'm up the
creek on this. It's not a recognisable scenario. We're here
on humanitarian issues, to rebuild bridges, repair roads,
re-establish communications – all standard demands of our
job. War I also understand. I know the rules on taking
prisoners. Rebel forces, military coups, guerrilla tactics, all
those I can deal with. But a helicopter crew vanishing into
thin air along with crates of medical supplies in a friendly
country is really a police matter.'

Dirk stiffened with protest. 'You think the local, slap-
happy constabulary is better equipped to trace them than
your jungle-trained British troops?'

The man's blue eyes hardened. 'They're more likely
to understand what's happened. As I see it, the nub of
this business is plain and simple theft. Medicines, drugs.
They'll fetch a packet on the black market in a country like

this. Some venal guys came along in a truck and – surprise, surprise – there's a stranded helicopter bung-full of valuable stuff just waiting to be lifted. They jumped the unsuspecting crew and dumped their bodies somewhere inaccessible to us to give the impression they had taken the stuff themselves, then scarpered. That makes it theft *and* murder. A job for police, not Army Engineers.'

Dirk was furious. 'So you're calling off the search?'

'I am, yes.' He sighed. 'Look, it's a needle and haystack syndrome. We ransacked that settlement pinpointed by the locator, and nix! There's no guarantee your guys were ever there. The signal could have been activated by some crack-head playing with it like a toy. Four days of silence since that signal was received. My men are exhausted and demoralised. It's no doddle scouring rainforest day and night unsure what you're looking for or what you might be up against. If, as seems most likely, they're already dead we have to accept that the chances of finding them are very remote.' After a brief, tense silence, he added, 'I know how you feel. If they were my men . . . I'm sorry, but I've been told to get back to the work we were on before this happened.'

If the soldiers were demoralised it was nothing to the way the men of 646 Squadron felt. A Puma had flown out a team of technicians to deal with the Chinook, and they had been shocked by what they found. The sense of shock was now augmented by a desire for revenge. Violence, possible death, were accepted as standard risks of their profession, but there was something *un*acceptable about this. Rip Price and his crew had been unarmed and engaged in international relief for disaster victims. What had befallen them and who had perpetrated the outrage occupied the minds of their friends and colleagues above all else.

Wing Commander Allen, officer in command of the RAF contingent operating there with UN forces, was in constant contact with Army leaders and UN civilian representatives who, in turn, liaised with British diplomats pressurising the president of this stricken country. He was said to be deeply upset and angry over the tragedy, and was investigating it personally. (Oh yeah? said 646 Squadron caustically.)

A crew from A Flight had arrived to man the repaired Chinook and relief missions were continuing, but the attitudes of those undertaking them were hardening. Their initial sympathy for the people of the country vanished beneath images of four men's bodies lying deep in jungle to be eaten away by venomous creatures, with nothing to mark their last resting place. Some thanks for what they had been engaged in!

Dirk was watching the usual spectacular sunset that same evening, trying to forget the decision to end the search and instead grow enthusiastic about his plans to ski with Dave Ashmore in the Highlands at Christmas, when he saw Felix Allen crossing the rough campsite now growing firmer underfoot after several weeks of searing sunshine. Something about the man's grim expression suggested that he had more than routine matters to discuss. Dirk's spirits sank rapidly.

'The sunsets are about the only good thing in this benighted place,' he growled as he arrived, sweating heavily. 'I've been given some info, for what it's worth. Make what you can of it. Sounds like a load of bollocks to me, but they're going along with it in case it's genuine.'

'Concerning Rip and his crew?'

'Maybe. Listen, and ask questions when I've finished. Here goes. The people at the distribution centre Rip's aircraft was heading for have come across an envelope addressed to the British Consul. They have no idea who put it there, or even how long it's been lying around, but they suspected it might have something to do with the missing men and passed it to an Infantry officer liaising with them. He contacted Sir

Peter, who instructed him to open it and relay the contents. The message was in block capitals, and began: "I have your pilots. Give me two million American dollars and you can have them back."'

Dirk opened his mouth but the senior man's frown silenced him. 'The whole thing smacks of opportunism by a bunch of amateurs. The name at the bottom was Winston Churchill. Yeah, my reaction entirely,' he said as Dirk registered disbelief. 'But listen to this. News is now emerging of a gang suspected of stealing boxes of medical supplies and, in some cases, high protein foods. Military questioning of those who have received aid has revealed that not everything loaded on the trucks at the centre reached its destination. In each case it was medicines, water purifying tablets, baby food and sterile utensils that vanished en route. It's become apparent that this has been going on for a while. No one thought to check until now.

'The theory is that our man Winston is the organiser – an Artful Dodger with a gang of born thieves mingling with the guys on the trucks. The tyre tracks beside the Chinook suggest that they came upon it by chance and found a plum had dropped in their laps.'

Dirk could hold back no longer. 'They'd have to kill Rip and the others to take it, surely.'

Felix Allen sighed heavily. 'They probably did, then tossed the bodies out later, but this ransom note has to be investigated even though it smacks of a corny plot from TV. Sir Peter is invited to have an announcement made on local radio that a British gentleman is planning to donate two million dollars towards a new irrigation scheme. When that's done, he'll be told where he must go to buy back his countrymen. The Consul personally, mark you.'

'It's a hoax by a madman!' cried Dirk.

'I agree, but madmen are clever . . . and dangerous. Take Idi Amin, Saddam Hussein, Milosovich. Who we're dealing with here is not in the same league, but he nevertheless has the whip hand. He knows we daren't risk ignoring him. At the specified hour of nine tonight Sir Peter's Aide will make the announcement, adding the proviso that the "British gentleman" is waiting for evidence that the irrigation scheme is "alive and well" before giving such a large sum. Then we await developments.'

'If any!'

'If any.'

The sun had now vanished and the noisy African night was all around them. The heat seemed even more oppressive when the encircling rainforest could be heard but not seen.

Dirk shivered. 'If they are still alive out there somewhere I wouldn't care to be in their shoes, poor devils.'

'No . . . but if they are we'll get them back the first chance we're offered, have no doubts about that.'

Randal was once more making pacts with the Almighty. *If you get us out of this I'll never ask for another thing. If you give us a chance to escape I'll never blaspheme again.* He eventually owned that he had already been given more than enough leeway on blessings, and spoke for just the other three in the hope that it might hold greater celestial sway. His friends were probably doing the same.

They had been in this hellish predicament for five days and were still stunned. Lying on the earthen floor on that fifth night Randal knew this reality was worse than any nightmare he had ever had. Was he doomed to die by some bizarre coincidence? He had happened to be passing when a ship's anchor dropped from a motorway bridge. The Grim Reaper had been foiled that time. Now he happened to be forced from the sky when a gang of armed thugs was nearby. Was there some divine plan behind it all? If so, why make three others suffer?

They had chains around their hands and feet. They had

all been beaten during their captivity. They were existing on daily bowls of sour-tasting porridge and a jerrycan of tepid brown water between them each morning. They were filthy and covered in bites. Sandy was growing feverish, Jimmy was desperately worried about his wife and five children, one of Chris's eyes was so swollen it had closed over, and Randal himself had an open wound in the back of his head. They all had diarrhoea. They were going nowhere.

Their only hope was rescue. They knew all the stops would be pulled out, but they also knew that even if their whereabouts were somehow discovered any operation had to be meticulously planned to minimise casualties. That took time, and Randal was not sure how much of it they would be given. They were in the hands of young, volatile, trigger-happy Africans who relished their unexpected power. Whoever believed racism was exclusive to whites had their heads in the clouds. These black hooligans took delight in tormenting and humiliating their captives at every opportunity, Yet they had no secrets to reveal; they were not 'the enemy'. It made no sense.

Painfully easing himself into another position, Randal's weary brain assessed their predicament once more. As their leader he was responsible for the safety of his crew. When he had come round from the initial surprise attack, he had been lying in the back of a truck jolting noisily along a narrow track hemmed in by overhanging branches. Chris and the two sergeants were sitting under guard by four grinning men with rifles. Blood ran freely from a wound above Chris's right eye, and Jimmy was doubled over in pain. Only Sandy appeared untouched. He was sitting on his life jacket, which he must have snatched up on leaving the Chinook, and he indicated optically to Randal that he had activated his personal locator. It would be constantly signalling their position to military security beacons worldwide.

Struggling to sit up in the swaying vehicle, Randal had

demanded of their captors why they had been attacked and where they were being taken.

'You the boss here?' one asked.

'That's right. I'm the captain of this crew.'

'You have too much to say, captain,' he replied with a grin, as something heavy crashed against the back of Randal's skull sending him back into oblivion.

He was next aware of being dragged to the ground in a small settlement bathed in a dramatic blood-red glow from the setting sun. There, they were stripped to their underpants and their bare feet were shackled. Sandy had managed to conceal the locator in his underwear during the drive, but a rough manual search revealed it and he was kicked in the crotch. 'Just to make sure all that is real human parts,' he was told.

They had been given a bucket of foul-tasting water that they could only drink by scooping it up in their hands. While they were doing that Randal gleaned from his friends what had occurred at the aircraft. Chris had attempted to reach the radio, but rifles pointed at Jimmy's and Sandy's heads stopped him. Once their hands had been tied Chris had been smacked across the face with a rifle butt. The unexpectedness of the attack had been total. There had been no opportunity for retaliation.

When it grew dark they had been manhandled on to the truck still carrying the stolen medical packs, and driven over a badly potholed road. The two severe blows Randal had suffered induced nausea and giddiness when his head began drumming on the boards, and he soon re-entered a semi-conscious state. Thankfully, the others had been fully aware during that journey. All they needed was a chance to use to advantage what their training had taught them. In five days there had been none.

Randal racked his brains for some enlightenment as he lay awake yet again. Together they had deduced that their captors were involved in a black market in stolen goods, and had probably been siphoning off batches of supplies from the distribution centre throughout the relief effort. They had also agreed that someone must be masterminding the operation. Through slits in the walls of their wooden prison they could see a stout wire fence running around a large colonial-style bungalow just visible through the trees, where dogs roamed at night. The home of the boss, or just an undermanager?

Their guards changed from day to day, all of them mindlessly vindictive and possibly on drugs. Each time they came Randal demanded to speak to their boss, or whoever lived in the bungalow among the trees. He was treated to a pantomime of mimicry then told to shut his mouth.

'Does he know the conditions we're living in here?' he regularly persisted.

The answer was always the same. 'You living like everyone in this country. Now you know what it like.'

'We're over here to improve things, fly supplies to people who need them. Your boss is stopping us from helping his countrymen. Why?'

'You talk too much, Captain. Shut your mouth or we shut it for you.'

They discussed their situation as each day passed and tried to assess it. It seemed clear enough that they were the victims of cruel circumstances that grounded them just where a truck was heading for the distribution centre. It seemed equally clear that whoever controlled the operation found providence had offered him the means of making more money than he had dreamed of. They had no doubt they would be held to ransom, but were fearful of the outcome. They were not members of a rival gang or another tribe, whose lives could be bartered for on basic terms. This man was way out of his depth here. A small-time racketeer could not abduct the crew of a British military aircraft on loan to the United Nations and expect to sell them back in a simple transaction. Thereby lay the danger. If he was pushed too far, or the negotiations dragged on too long, he was liable to take fright and cut his losses. On one thing they were all agreed. They would not be set free if it all went pear-shaped. Life was cheap in Africa!

On the sixth morning Sandy was shaking and burning up with fever. Randal was determined to get help for him and tackled the pair who arrived with food and water.

'This man is very sick. He needs some of the medicine you took from my aircraft.'

One lowered his shorts mockingly. 'You kiss my arse, I get you some.'

Holding on to his temper Randal said, 'I demand to speak to your boss. I'll go to the house if he doesn't care to come to this stinking hut.'

'You shut your mouth.'

'If he's asking money for our return we'll be no use to him dead, and unless my sergeant is given treatment he soon will be. Tell him that. Tell him that if he keeps us in these conditions much longer, we'll *all* be dead of fever. Is that what he wants?'

The second man swung his rifle at the back of Randal's knees and he collapsed, overturning two of the bowls of porridge. The door was slammed and padlocked as the Africans left without another word.

'We'll never get anywhere with goons like that,' muttered Chris, scooping the food back into the dishes.

Randal vented his anger in blasphemies he had vowed never to use again, adding, 'There'll be an outcry if we're handed over in this state.'

Pushing porridge in his mouth with his fingers, Jimmy said, 'You don't really believe anyone'll do a deal with this mob, do you?'

'Of course,' he lied.

'Bollocks! There's an international policy of not giving in to terrorists.'

'These guys aren't terrorists,' offered Chris.

'You could have fooled me.' Jimmy again challenged Randal. 'You're saying you reckon complicated negotiations are going on at this very moment?'

'Christ, how do I know? An approach must have been made to somebody by now. They'll stall long enough to set up a rescue mission. It's just a matter of waiting.'

'No one bloody knows where we are,' Jimmy reminded him heatedly.

'Okay, you take over and get us out of this if you think I'm making a sodding mess of it,' Randal replied equally hotly. 'Maybe *you'd* like to kiss their arses and expect to get antibiotics for Sandy. Go ahead!'

'All I'm saying is we ought to do something.'

'Like what?'

'Do our own deal with them. Make them an offer.'

'Like "Here's my dirty underpants. You can have them if you remove the chains, give me some boots, a map and enough money to get back to my squadron"?' asked Chris caustically. 'Rip's right. The rules in this kind of situation are to avoid unnecessary injury, stay calm and wait to be rescued.'

'Yeah, and give away nothing but name, rank and serial number under torture,' he sneered. 'These guys aren't enemy troops, they're crack-heads after the main chance.'

'Well, we're not bloody it,' said Randal. 'Look at us!'

Jimmy would not quit the argument. He had a large family to support and was desperately afraid they would never see him again. 'We're from the West. The decadent, rich part of the world. They know that. So we promise them money, a house with TV and a swimming pool. That's something they'd go for.'

Chris gave a mirthless laugh. 'You mean we write them

an IOU and they trust us to honour it when they've let us go?'

Jimmy rounded on him. 'D'you trust *them* to hand us over if they ever receive ransom money? We can identify them, for God's sake! And who d'you think will pocket the ransom? Not these simpletons guarding us. They won't even get a cut. That's why we have to make a deal with *them*. The boss man'll finish us off once we've served our purpose.'

'For Christ's sake shut up!' came a faint voice from the corner where Sandy was lying. 'I feel ill enough without listening to Job's comforters rabbiting on and on. If we're all soon going to get the chop, let's have a bit of peace and quiet first.'

They retreated into their private thoughts. Randal's turned to the time Lydia was abducted. The poor little kid had fortunately had no understanding of her danger, but he had been subjected to the terror of not knowing where she was or if she was still alive. He would have done anything to get her safely back, but he had nevertheless put her life in the hands of those who were experienced in such cases. Now he was on the other side of the scenario, and had put his trust and hopes – possibly his life – in the hands of military experts in this field. In terrain such as this they would need some clue to help them, and he privately agreed with Jimmy that their chances were rather less than slim.

He thought about his children. Fiona would have been notified – she was still his legal wife. Unlike Jimmy he had no worries concerning the well-being of Neil and Lydia. Fiona, through the mouthpiece of her father, had refused offers of maintenance from him. The Hollands were as wealthy as the Prices, and gave their grandchildren everything they could want. At the time of the break there was grave doubt about his own chances of making a living that would support two children. It was cruelly ironic that just as he had realised how much they meant to him and how eager he was to be there while they grew, he might never see them again.

Then there was Maggie. The Station Commander would be kept in the picture, and he would inform Perry Newman. Apart from that, the guys out here in Africa would be phoning home to their friends at Hampton, so she would be aware of their disappearance. He wondered about the situation with her twin. Had she given an organ to save him? How did she feel about his suggestion that there was something between her and himself? He had been listed with those for whom she cared, and she had kissed him goodbye at the Longboat. Was that for the first and last time?

He was roused from semi-slumber by the sound of the door being unlocked. The same two guards entered. They told him to get up and follow them. His spirits rose, and he nudged Chris, saying softly, 'Now we're getting somewhere. I'll do what I can for Sandy and try for a better deal for us all.'

Chris merely nodded.

The sun was blinding after the dimness of the hut, but the air smelled wonderfully fresh. He walked slowly, his ankles still fettered, but it was more by choice. The longer he could remain outside the better. He vowed to demand open air periods for the others. It would boost morale, if nothing else.

When they reached a lone tree in the clearing they told him to stop and wait. His eyes had grown more accustomed to the brightness and they focussed on a figure by the wire fence: a tall man wearing heavy dark glasses and dressed in white trousers and shirt. Undoubtedly the boss man. So what he had said about being of no use if they were dead had got through to him!

Then Randal noticed that the two guards had been joined by two more, and they were lined up like a firing squad. His blood turned to ice, and he gasped for air as the truth hit him.

They raised their rifles. The desire to run was overwhelming, but he was rooted to the spot by horror. Dear God, two years ago he had longed to die. Now he knew how very precious life was, and was desperate to hold on to it.

They began firing. He felt the rush of air as bullets flew close to his head and chest, then kicked up dust around his feet. He began to sway. There were violent pains in his chest and stomach where he must have been hit. He was fighting for breath and grunting with fear as he waited for them to finish him off. The deadly volley continued until his legs would no longer support him, and he collapsed. Deafening silence reigned until it was broken by an outburst of laughter.

Doubled over his knees, his senses slowly recognised what had happened. A mock execution! Another way to humiliate. They had been told about demoralising tactics on their escape and evasion courses. What to expect if taken prisoner. This was not a war situation so he had not expected it.

The aftermath of terror brought violent nausea. He began to vomit and continued until he was too spent to retch further. Then he was hauled upright and half-dragged towards a small hut where the man in white waited. On a table beside him was a small tape recorder and a large sheet of paper. Randal saw it all with blurred vision and mental haziness. He felt utterly dehumanised.

The man spoke in good English. 'That was a hint of what will happen to you if your people refuse to pay what I ask. They want proof that you are alive, so you will read out the message on the paper and make it sound good. Do you understand?' When Randal nodded the paper was put in his unsteady hands, and the machine switched on. 'Start now!'

He spoke stiltedly through teeth that were chattering after the prolonged sickness. 'I am the captain of the helicopter

357

crew. We are all alive and being well treated, but unless you pay the ransom we shall be killed. Please don't let us die. It's a small amount to pay for us. Instructions about handing over the money will be with this message. Please do it quickly. If you wait it will be too late and we don't want to die.'

When he reached the end of the mumbled message Randal began to retch again. The machine was turned off. He was seized and led away by two guards who were still highly amused.

The Puma landed near the distribution centre soon after dawn. Felix Allen and Dirk climbed out, then walked over to where an Army captain stood awaiting them.

'I'm Giles Gates. Good of you to come,' he said, shaking hands with them both. 'It was found here in the early hours. As before, no evidence of who delivered it. So many people going in and out.' He led the way to an office inside the stone building where a tape recorder sat on a table. 'If it's genuine, it's a total breakthrough. The speaker sounds drugged, but the voice should be clear enough for you to confirm that it is Squadron Leader Price,' he said to Dirk. 'You may have to run it through several times, because we need you to be certain.'

Having been keyed up since the summons came through, Dirk prayed he would be able to give firm assurance on this. 'Go ahead,' he said to Captain Gates.

The man pushed the button. The speech was slightly hesitant and some of the words sounded fuzzy, but there was no mistaking Randal's voice with its faint northern accent.

Dirk glanced up. 'That's him. I don't believe the bit about being well treated. He's clearly speaking under duress.'

Gates made no comment on that, merely said, 'Thanks, that's all we need. He's a sharp operator. Those few moments at the end that sound like retching mask vital info giving their approximate position and the fact that guards are armed and they, themselves, are fettered. Useful stuff to know.'

'How on earth did you deduce that?' asked Felix Allen.

The Captain was busy retrieving the cassette as he spoke. 'It's Serbo-Croat. Most of us who served in Bosnia picked up a few phrases. I recognised the words "armed" and "guards", so I guessed what he was up to. A linguist at Headquarters did the rest.' He held out his hand. 'Thanks again.'

'That's it?' asked Dirk with a touch of pique.

'For now, yes. I daresay they'll give you a cup of tea before you go back if you walk through to the kitchen. Can't join you. Things to do.'

The Puma crewmen were already enjoying tea and a bun, but neither he nor Felix was expected to reveal the reason for their presence here so conversation was general. Beneath it Dirk felt tremendously excited by this development. To aircrew, navigation by the sun and stars came naturally. They must have known where they were when the locator was confiscated, and would have calculated the direction and distance they travelled from there. Unless they had since been kept in total darkness they would have noted landmarks visible from the air. They had all overflown this large area enough times to be familiar with these, which were relatively few. How they must have longed for the chance to pass on what they knew! Why Randal had chosen Serbo-Croat from his range of European languages Dirk could not guess. Lucky for him it was recognisable beneath the feigned retching. Lucky for Giles Gates the tape ran long enough to record it. How slim a chance!

The mention of shackles was disturbing, but evidence of guns was even more so. In inexperienced or irresponsible hands (which these surely were) anything could happen during a rescue mission, and one was certain to be mounted soon. The captives would know this and be prepared.

Their next of kin would not be told anything until they

were safely out of captivity. The Squadron would be notified of today's development, so Dirk would put in a call to his friend, Perry Newman, tonight. Unfortunately, when the rescue bid was likely to be made would be known only to those planning it.

When Wing Commander Newman called together for an early morning meeting those squadron officers presently at Hampton, Maggie was highly apprehensive. She had been living on the edge of her normally steady nerves for almost a week. Coming so soon after Phil's near-fatal accident, dread of a tragic outcome in Africa was taking its toll. Her developed sixth sense told her nothing; she had had no magic messages about the man who had laughingly coined the phrase. In her low state it was all too easy again to believe Griff's claim that she induced disaster for those around her.

Eight of them assembled to hear Perry Newman relate news of the cassette tape that had revealed the whereabouts of the missing crew.

'I know you've been concerned about your colleagues so I thought you should be given this info, but I want you to keep it under your hats for the sake of their families. I don't want this gossiped about until they're safely out.'

'Any idea when that'll be, Boss?' asked an A Flight navigator.

'You should know better than to ask. We'll be told when it's all over, Andy.'

Jeff was thoughtful. 'They can't be in too bad a state if Rip had enough wits to remember his Serbo-Croat.'

'Mmm, but we've yet to discover how he came to put his crew in a situation requiring a rescue mission in a country where there are no hostiles operating,' Newman replied.

'We know the answer to that,' said Maggie swiftly. 'They were taking part in a humanitarian aid effort and were jumped by a gang of black marketeers when they were forced to land. Nick Lorrimer phoned the facts to Jeff. He assumed Dirk would contact you with them.'

Newman countered that with a scowl and turned to Pete who asked, 'I hope the affair will be taken up by the UN. It's a fair assumption, surely?'

'It'll be kept low key.'

'SAS ops always are,' agreed a navigator who had served with a Special Forces squadron for a while.

'And it's a small incident which would be politically sensitive,' Newman added. 'Until the facts are known blame can't be laid at any door.'

Maggie was livid. 'I don't see how any blame could possibly be laid on an unarmed crew who're abducted and held to ransom.'

'As I said, until the facts are available neither the MoD nor anyone else is fit to make judgement,' he insisted doggedly.

Jeff elbowed Maggie and whispered, 'Drop it!'

The Squadron Commander brought the meeting to an end. 'I'll give you any news as it comes in. Meanwhile, I'm relying on you to be discreet about this.'

They dispersed to the Crew Room, where Maggie turned on Jeff. 'Why didn't you back me?'

'I don't hit my head against immovable objects. Rip's taller, wealthier, better-looking, more popular and more newsworthy than he is. He can also speak enough Serbo-Croat to get them all out of this jam. It'd make any man resentful.'

'You're not.'

He grinned. 'Ah, I'm better at sport than Rip.'

'Anyone's better at it than he is,' she said. 'That's why he invents rules to—' She turned away to gaze from the window.

Jeff's arm rested lightly across her shoulders. 'I've also

had more women than he has. I've never managed to get you crying over me, though, so that's one up to him.'

His nonsense steadied her and she turned to face him. 'When d'you think they'll go for it?'

'Soon as possible. This is an unknown scenario. They won't risk too much delay.' He cocked an eyebrow at her. 'How is it with you and Rip, then?'

'When he gets back here no one on the Station will be left in any doubt.'

'Mmm, bad as that, is it? Lucky I've never fancied you.'

It raised a faint smile. 'You do me so much good, Jeff.'

He looked horrified. 'I must be losing my touch. My intention towards women is to do just the reverse.'

They flew together later that morning on a routine parts delivery, and Maggie was comforted by his company. Her thoughts dwelt on events taking place in a distant continent, however, and the whole while she feared the onset of a magic message that would signify disaster.

Fourteen

Three days had passed since Randal was terrorised into reading out a plea to buy their lives, three interminable days during which hope had slowly died. On each one of the nine they had spent in captivity they had heard helicopters continuing regular deliveries of essential supplies, and they had yearned to send some kind of signal to them.

They had known from day one exactly where they were being held. Men highly trained in navigational skills could invariably calculate their position from even basic evidence. What they had been unable to do was transmit the information. Even so, they had discussed the possibility of any chance to do so. Fearing that men in an area of Africa that had been under various colonial masters might understand French and German when they heard it, Randal had taught the others the few vital phrases in Serbo-Croat. The prospect of these reaching the right ears was nil, until three days ago.

Randal had only a fuzzy recollection of what he had said and done in the aftermath of the mock execution, yet he believed his numbed senses had instinctively seized the slender opportunity to relay their position under the pretence of retching. He had no certainty that the tape had still been running, or that the people receiving it would recognise the hidden message. The lack of any change in their plight suggested that the faint hope had been in vain. They gave up further conjecture on the subject.

On the tenth day things began to happen. Through the cracks in the walls of the hut they saw signs of activity inside the perimeter fence during early afternoon. Soon afterwards they heard several vehicles drive off, and the faint hope revived. Could it be the boss man and his bodyguard off to collect the ransom? Was it the prelude to rescue? They linked these signs with the sound of a Puma circling high above them early that morning. They had been too lethargic to attach any importance to it then, but it now took on a significance that raised their spirits. Yet they dared not read too much into what was happening.

Randal was tense and worried. Sandy was delirious, badly in need of antibiotics, and they were all weak from dysentery, poor food and lack of exercise. Chris's injured eye was still swollen and Randal's own head wound needed stitches. The gash was now infected and suppurating. Their general health was deteriorating.

Just before dusk two guards came with the porridge. They were the youngest of the gang and gave the impression of being high on drugs. Their English was no more than basic, their movements were usually uncoordinated and their eyes seemed unfocussed. They wore perpetual grins and giggled when spoken to, but they carried rifles slung on their shoulders. Dropping the bowls so the contents spilled they stood regarding the filthy prisoners, giggling and whispering together.

One suddenly pointed at Chris. 'You come outside.'

Chris ignored them and began to eat.

The boys unslung their rifles menacingly. 'You *come!*'

Randal got to his feet. 'He's not going anywhere. You brought food. We're going to eat it.'

The pair hesitated, still grinning. Another whispered conversation, then the rifles were aimed at Sandy lying in the corner. 'He come or we shoot.'

Randal stood his ground. 'He's a British officer working

for the United Nations. Your boss left here a while ago. We only deal with him.'

'We boss now,' one shouted, and the other added, 'He come outside. He very pretty boy.'

The atmosphere grew even more tense. Chris was the only blond among them and he was the youngest. The dread of being gang-raped had been with them the whole time in this continent riddled with Aids.

Randal tried to keep control. 'He'll go with you if I come too.'

A rifle barrel came up to rest against his mouth. 'You shut up!'

Chris struggled to his feet. 'Drop it, Rip, or someone'll get hurt. This could be our eleventh hour so it's best to keep them happy.'

Although Randal was disturbed by the unwelcome development he saw the sense in avoiding any risk of this unstable duo running amok with rifles, especially if a rescue was on the cards.

'I guess it's your turn for the fun and games I had three days ago,' he said with feeling, hoping to God that was all it would be. 'Stand perfectly still until they tire of it.'

'Better than having to *lie* perfectly still.' Chris gave a forced smile. 'Something to tell my boy about when he's old enough.'

'We'll save some food for you,' Jimmy said.

'Yeah, do that.' He shuffled from the hut flanked by the grinning guards. The door was locked.

Randal remained where he was. Jimmy ignored the porridge. They were both tense and listening for clues on what was happening, and it was with a bizarre sense of relief when they heard rifle fire and the excited cries of the youths as they revelled in tormenting a helpless man. Randal relived his own trial of nerves and knew Chris would not be able to prevent himself succumbing to fear, as he had. That was the point of the exercise.

Seconds later the firing stopped abruptly to leave a resounding silence. No laughter. No sounds of a man vomiting. Then Randal heard the thud of running feet.

Wing Commander Allen called a briefing at two p.m. for Dirk and his chosen crew, two paramedics and two additional crewmen. The Chinook was one fitted with a winch and the cabin had been made ready to receive casualties. He began by outlining the details of Operation Mousetrap. The 'cheese' – supposed compliance with instructions for payment of the ransom – had tempted the rodent from his hole. Six members of the SAS had earlier been dropped in the jungle to make their way to the target. Their mission only concerned the British military prisoners. Once they had been brought out safely troops of the local militia already in position around the bungalow would go in. The man calling himself Winston Churchill and his employees were civilians to be dealt with by their own people. A Puma was flying in an Army psychiatrist experienced in hostage situations, an Intelligence officer and Sir Peter's Aide, who would debrief the captive crew and deal with the aftermath of the extremely sensitive affair.

'Because there are a few unknowns we're having to make decisions as things happen in this operation,' Felix Allen told them. 'Thanks to Rip Price we do know the guards are armed but not how many there are, so the SAS could give us no firm timescale for their rescue. We also know the prisoners are in chains, which suggests ill-treatment and constant confinement. We have no idea of their physical condition – whether they were wounded during their capture or if they are ill – so we can't assume they're all able to undertake a jungle trek. Chances are they're in pretty bad shape, so the snatch has to be swift and the airlift must be from a point not too far distant.'

Dirk frowned. 'It's solid jungle all around there.'

'Quite, so it's going to take precision flying on your part. The SAS have radioed the exact position of their selected pick-up site. They say there's a winding track unsuitable for vehicles leading to the bungalow from an abandoned settlement. Along it there is a break in the trees. Not large enough to be called a clearing, but they reckon a winchman could operate there.'

'Did they give the height of the trees, sir?' asked the sergeant who would be going down on the line.

Felix Allen told him, then turned his attention back to Dirk. 'The aircraft will have practically to sit on the trees while ten men are brought up. I'm afraid there's no alternative site.' He gave an encouraging smile. 'You've served in a Special Forces Flight, Dirk. We have every confidence in you.'

Dirk remained silent. His two-year stint flying SAS and SBS troops to dangerous rendezvous during exercises, and once or twice for real, had been some time ago. He did not relish a revival of those skills for this operation tonight. His crewmen during those two years had been highly trained to talk pilots down to anything from a moving train to an oil rig. Ray and Brad, his crewmen for this, were good steady men, but they would be hovering low for long minutes over wildly waving treetops at dusk trying to ensure the winch line did not become entangled. They would have to be absolutely on the ball to carry it off successfully.

Felix Allen wound up the briefing. 'The SAS guys will contact us just before they go in, so you'll need to be ready for take-off at a moment's notice. When you near the rendezvous a flashing light will indicate their readiness to be picked up. Once they're aboard, Rip Price and his crew will be in the hands of the paramedics. When you get here they'll be handed over to the team flown in to debrief them. None of you will attempt to question them. Is that clear?'

They dispersed and sat around in the afternoon heat too tense to settle to anything, knowing what lay ahead.

Almost before he was aware of an additional presence in the hut a hand covered Randal's mouth and a voice with a Lancashire accent murmured against his ear, 'Nod if you're able to walk.' As he nodded he heard the click of chain-cutters by his feet. 'Pull on the boots and prepare to leave!'

Through the darkness Randal saw vague indications of movement – Jimmy bending over his feet, Sandy being lifted across the shoulder of a tall figure – and he thrust his own feet into soft rubber boots and fastened them, marvelling at the stealth of their saviours.

The Lancashire voice spoke again in his ear. 'Your mates are picking us up in fifteen minutes. Let's go!'

He grabbed at the shadowy figure moving away, whispering fiercely, 'They took my navigator and . . .'

'We've got him. Move!'

The night was hot and humid, but the air was fresher than that inside the hut. The men moved fast through the dense trees as they would if wearing night vision aids. Randal stumbled along in the middle of the long line, finding it difficult to keep pace with them. His thoughts were chaotic. They had Chris. Had theirs been the shots that sent the two guards running? How had they entered the padlocked hut so silently? What of the man in white who had forced him to record the ransom message? Where were they being taken now? Was this really rescue or just another means of torment?

His mental meandering halted abruptly as he heard the sweetly familiar thwack-thwack of Chinook rotors approaching. Then, and only then, did he know the nightmare was about to end.

*   *   *

'Rendezvous in five minutes. Closing from the left,' said Nick Lorrimer quietly.

Dirk gazed through his night vision goggles at the green and black scene below. It resembled a solid carpet of vegetation. How would they see a light flashing from the forest floor? And if they did how would the winch operator get a man safely down and back even once, much less ten times? He reduced speed and prepared to circle until they received the password signifying that the rescue had been accomplished.

'We've made it dead on time,' he murmured. 'Let's see how good they are.'

Even as he spoke a firm voice radioed the identifying call sign *Winston* from the ground. 'They're very good,' said Nick and acknowledged.

Dirk alerted the men in the cabin. 'Mission completed. Keep your eyes peeled for a flashing light.'

'Message from *Winston*,' said Nick crisply. 'Rendezvous in two minutes. Stand by.'

Those two minutes passed in a listening silence as Dirk continued to circle at a safe height. Then Nick reported the next radio message. 'They say the signal is being flashed but we are slightly east of target.'

They made the correction and almost immediately Ray and the winch operator said simultaneously that they could see the light.

'Okay, let's go for it,' Dirk announced. 'Watch those trees like hawks. We can't allow anything to balls this up. Those guys on the ground are depending on us.'

While Ray and Brad talked Dirk into position above the narrow gap in the forest canopy, the winchman hooked his harness to the line in readiness. From the cockpit it was impossible to see the signal which had to be directly below the winch placed some feet back in the cabin. Once

369

alignment was reported, Dirk's two regular crewmen began talking him down to a height that would allow the line to reach those waiting below – the most exacting and dangerous aspect of the pick-up.

Listening to the familiar voices over the intercom Dirk knew the safety of so many lay in the hands of the sergeants hanging out through their hatches and judging distances with experienced eyes. Obeying their instructions the moment they were given Dirk took the Chinook slowly down until it seemed the wildly waving braches were mere inches beneath his feet.

'Forward five and left.' 'Steady.' 'Nose left ten degrees.' 'Steady.' 'Height is good.'

The confident instructions continued as Dirk prepared to keep twenty tons of aircraft in the hover while ten men were brought up to the cabin. Intermingled with the crewmen's patter were reports from the winch operator, whose commentary on the activity in his part of the operation was vital to the whole crew.

'First man locked on.' 'Winching up now.' 'First man on board.' 'Going down for second man.' 'Second man locked on.' 'Winching up now.'

Those two years spent with the Special Forces Flight now aided Dirk. He kept the huge helicopter in as steady a hover as a superbly trained pilot could maintain. Any remaining hang-ups over the crash that killed Mike were driven away as the pick-up continued smoothly. This was life in the fast lane with a vengeance and he was equal to it. After tonight, no one would doubt he was a man who kept his head in dangerous and tricky situations.

The skills of the two pilots and four crewmen combined to complete the rescue begun by six jungle-trained SAS soldiers, and when the winch operator gave the word that the last man was safely aboard Dirk said with a hint of triumph, 'Well done, guys, and thanks. Let's go home.'

When Ray and Brad had talked him up and Nick had set the course for the Base, he smiled across at his co-pilot. 'Not bad, eh?'

Nick smiled back in relief. 'I don't think even Rip would give us a bollocking after that performance.'

As soon as he was aboard Randal was given a blanket to wrap around his near-naked body, and a glucose drink. The fifteen-minute tramp through a narrow overgrown track had left him frighteningly exhausted; the familiarity of one of the aircraft he flew gave him no sense of comfort. All feeling had drained from him. He sat hunched in a cocoon of numb isolation, barely aware of the six men with faces blackened and partially hidden who gathered in the shadows near the ramp as they got under way.

Jimmy was huddled several feet away, blanket-wrapped and staring into space. Sandy was being attended to on one of the stretchers attached to the opposite side of the cabin. On another lay Chris's shrouded body. The rescue team had arrived just five minutes too late.

A carefully worded statement was released to the world's media, who soon ferreted out the full story behind those careful words. In Britain it made the main headlines in newspapers and on TV. It was the brand of drama relished by news hounds who, despite UN and MoD clampdown on military detail, went to town on the scandal of stolen medical supplies meant to aid victims of disaster. In the way of investigative journalism similar ruthless black market operations in other afflicted areas were discovered and exposed. Charity and aid organisations were dismayed by the amount of pillaging that had been going on, yet individual members privately admitted they knew it was inevitable in poverty-stricken areas. While it was not condoned by them, it was a known fact of life. To withold aid

371

because of it would merely punish the many for the sins of the few.

There was public protest that money and goods donated in good faith had instead been lining the pockets of vicious gangs prepared to rob their own people of life-saving supplies.

The killing of Chris Foley was widely condemned. Interrogations revealed that he had been accidentally shot during a mock execution set up by two youths during the absence of senior members of their organisation. Under the influence of drugs they had experimented with the sensation of total power over others by copying something they had seen done to the captain of the helicopter crew. When they realised they had actually hit the young officer they ran away, fearing they themselves would be killed by their vengeful leader. They were being hunted and would stand trial for murder.

The country's president was said to be devastated by the terrible crime, and by growing evidence that the generosity of his friends in the West was being abused by men of great viciousness and greed. He sent personal messages of condolence to the dead man's next of kin and to the Royal Air Force.

The man calling himself Winston Churchill, along with many in his employ, had been caught in a trap set by the local militia. His numerous associates in the nefarious dealing were being traced and would be brought to justice.

Everyone at Hampton watched TV footage of the arrival of Chris's body in a flag-draped coffin. Waiting at RAF Benson were his parents, sister and grandmother, with Chloe and the child they had recently acknowledged as their true grandson.

His fellow hostages would arrive back in time to attend the funeral at which Martin Ashe and Perry Newman would read the lessons. Dave planned to take a day off from his pilot training course, and Pete was flying back from Bosnia to go with Jill. Rusty was coming down from Scotland. Jeff would drive to Berkshire for the ceremony. All Chris's boozing pals from way back would gather to say goodbye.

Maggie had volunteered to hold the fort on that day. Jeff was the only one to comment, saying quietly, 'Can't face it?' He did not fully understand. No one did. Chris would have uniformed pall-bearers and a volley fired over his grave. He would have tributes paid by his colleagues. He would have his sorrowing family and his squadron pals. He would have the woman he had never stopped loving and the boy who was a part of the man he had been. Maggie felt her presence there would be a travesty.

For six months they had shared tenderness and under-standing; their intimacy had been mutual consolation for something out of reach. His splendid young life had been terminated so cruelly just as what had been out of reach had come within his grasp. She had pressurised him into taking her to the first night of *Zenda*, which had changed their relationship from professional to deeply personal. She alone was responsible for turning easy companionship into caring. There was no place for Maggie Spencer at his funeral.

This was worse than with Mark. Then she had been able to talk about him; had needed to. She had had long, mainly one-sided, conversations with her father and Phil. It had been easy to speak of her feelings; tell others about the things they had shared and enjoyed, what she had loved about the young pilot. She had poured out her heart to ease her grief. Now she was numb and shunned company. Even Jeff's. Her work was all-important and she had told Perry Newman there was no longer any reason why she could not go overseas. She was sleeping badly, eating too little, and had spent last weekend hiking alone over the Purbeck hills. For two days she had carried out basic load-shifting tasks, but she was listed for Northern Ireland tomorrow. It was a generally unpopular duty, but she welcomed the chance to get away.

Her bag was packed; she was programmed for take-off at 9.30. After a meagre dinner she was back in her room watching a gardening programme on TV. It held no interest for her but the presenters were laid-back and their patter undemanding. The views of flowers, lawns and fish ponds were also undemanding and more acceptable than staring blankly at the pages of a paperback, which was the alternative.

The gardeners smiled their goodbyes and were followed by the urgent jingle introducing the news. Another ultimatum in the Irish peace talks. Then there was a long shot of a VC10 landing, followed by a close-up of the cabin door as the newsreader said, 'The three members of the helicopter crew held hostage in the recent scandal over thefts of medical aid for flood-stricken Africans arrived back in Britain late this afternoon.'

Maggie sat up and increased the volume as the camera homed in on Randal emerging from the aircraft, followed by Jimmy and Sandy. All three looked stressed. The newsreader went over to the special correspondent on the spot, Sean Mills, as the cameras swung to where the men's families waited, lingering on the faces of Jimmy's children before glancing over Sandy's parents to rest on a slender young woman in a coat with a huge fur collar, who was holding the hands of her children as they watched the official greeting by a group captain.

Sean Mills reminded viewers of the recent abduction of Squadron Leader Price's daughter, and of the pilot's determination to fly again after his near-fatal accident two years ago. 'A family that has had more than its share of drama,' he added.

Then the cameras filmed the reunions with loved ones. Jimmy's wife and children all tried to hug him at the same time; Sandy's mother clung to him while his father gripped his shoulder. Fiona went into Randal's arms as if she truly belonged there. When they broke apart he scooped his children up in each arm and there was no mistaking his expression of love as he hugged them close.

Next minute Sean Mills was beside them holding out a microphone. 'How does it feel to be back, sir?'

Randal turned to him. 'Exactly the way you might guess it feels.'

The reporter gave a half smile and hurried on to his next question. 'Can you tell us anything about how you and your crew were treated in captivity?'

'One of us was killed. That says more than I could.'

'Yes, indeed. I understand you were yourself subjected to some kind of mock execution.'

'That's right.'

'So you were all under constant threat?'

'It's usual in hostage situations.'

Recognising stonewall tactics the man changed direction. 'What are your immediate plans?'

'I shall spend some time with my family before those of us who were held with Flight Lieutenant Foley attend his funeral on Friday.'

'A sad day for you all, I'm sure. So, a period of well earned leave and then what?'

'I'll rejoin my squadron. We all will.'

Seeking more newsworthy responses, he turned to Fiona. 'Mrs Price, how does it feel . . . Ah, I won't ask that,' he corrected with a glance at Randal. 'Do you have a celebration party planned for tonight?'

She gave her dazzling smile. 'My husband isn't a party animal. His idea of a celebration is a few beers with the lads.'

Mills chuckled. 'I dare say he'll get around to that in a day or so. Meanwhile, it'll be a quiet evening together getting used to having him safely home again?'

'Something like that,' she agreed.

'We have a car waiting,' Randal prompted, still holding his children.

The man read his cue correctly. 'Thank you for taking the time to answer my questions after your long, tiring flight, sir. I'm sure I speak for the whole nation in welcoming you home and in wishing you and your crew the best of luck in the future.'

Randal nodded and there was finally some warmth in his voice. 'Thanks. I'll pass the message on to them.'

Maggie pressed the remote. The set went dead. For some moments she gazed at the blank screen still seeing that instinctive embrace and the happy children in his arms. So that was that! It was clearly where he truly belonged, and he would be safe with them.

She undressed and made a hot drink which she took to bed with the book she determined to try to read. Halfway through chapter one she had to flick back to the start to remind herself who the characters were. Not that she cared; they were unattractive people engaged in over-the-top merchant banking one-upmanship. Yet she had somehow to pass the time until she was tired enough to sleep. The phone rang. She reached out for it. A revised take-off time. Hopefully not so late she would be sitting around for half the day in the Crew Room.

'Flight Lieutenant Spencer.'

'Hi!'

For once she was lost for words.

'Maggie?'

'You're supposed to be having a quiet evening at home.'

'I don't have a home.'

'So where are you?'

'At a plush hotel. The kids are asleep and the PR exercise is over.'

'What?'

'Couldn't have the hero of the moment returning with no one to give him a welcoming hug, could they?'

Trying to get to grips with that she asked, 'Why a plush hotel?'

'I refuse to stay with her parents and she won't curl up under a bush for the night.'

She said the first thing that came into her head. 'Napoleon's livid about all the publicity you're getting, but he and Pam Miles have been seen having intimate meals in Dorchester so perhaps she'll make him more human.'

'That woman's been dying to mother some man. How's Phil?'

'Getting stronger every day.'

'Have you surrendered a kidney?'

'He refused my offer. Said it would ruin my career. As it happens, both Dad and Charles could provide a suitable organ. The doctors are deciding which way to go on that. Just as well. He'll have a future with one of their kidneys, which he wouldn't have with mine.'

There was silence for a moment or two, and the warmth had gone from Randal's voice when he said, 'This is about Chris, isn't it, and that nonsense about being the herald of doom to anyone you care for? I thought I'd knocked that out of your head.'

'You're not God Almighty, you know,' she cried, the recent numbness starting to melt.

'And you're not the Grim Reaper, chum. How soon can we meet?'

'When you get back with the Squadron.'

'Don't fight me, Maggie. I want to see you before that.'

'I leave for Aldergrove after breakfast. Won't be back until late on Thursday.'

'At the funeral, then?'

'No.'

'Why not?'

'Isn't it obvious? He was fine until I twisted his arm to take me to *Zenda*. He actually said that; said I'd twisted his arm,' she revealed, now fighting back tears. 'We had a lot to drink and were both maudlin. It just happened . . . but I should have ended it there and then.'

'You think if you had those bastards would have shot straighter and missed him?' he challenged harshly. 'For Christ's sake, Maggie, you can't shoulder the blame for that tragedy.'

'It's happened too often to people I care about.'

'Yes, it has. You've had a tough time over the last two years. Most women would find that difficult to handle, without doing what you do day in, day out. That emergency in Kosovo, landing on ships in mid-ocean, water-taxiing with one engine out, searching for sick lads in fog on Exmoor, going in under fire to bring out British peacekeepers caught in a running battle.'

'It's my job. I'm an operational pilot.'

'But you're also a human being, Maggie. You've taken a hell of a battering one way and another, and need a shoulder to cry on. Even we macho bastards need that sometimes,' he added gently. 'I cried on yours often enough. I'm offering mine now, and I want to see you as soon as possible. No arguments!'

'Earliest day is Saturday,' she said thickly.

'Right. The Longboat at noon.'

'That's too near Phil's place.'

'We'll have some drinks and eat their first-rate fish and chips, then I have a great many things to say to you. After I've said them we'll walk over to give Fay the good news to pass on to your twin.'

'What good news?'

His voice grew soft. 'Think about it long enough and you'll get a magic message.'